A Second Chance

Anna Ryland

TSL Publications

First published in Great Britain in 2017
By TSL Publications, Rickmansworth

ISBN / 978-1-911070-42-9

To Caroline and Małgosia,

the best friends a girl can have

*A man travels the world in search of what he needs
and returns home to find it.*

George Moore (1852-1933)

Chapter 1

On Saturday afternoon, Victoria Coach Station was buzzing with the nervous energy of travellers arriving from all corners of Europe. One coach after another entered the crowded terminal and they spewed their human contents onto the melting tarmac. The air in the roofed station was heavy with diesel fumes. Tired and disoriented passengers wandered around the coaches trying to retrieve their luggage. Some were saying good bye to their travel companions. Others waved in the direction of the waiting area where their friends and families had gathered to welcome them.

Having collected her luggage, Maja swung a small holdall over her shoulder, adjusted the handle on her suitcase and began walking to the waiting area. Through the glass, like the walls of a large fish tank, a crowd of people was peering at the new arrivals. Several pairs of eyes were following her as she entered the hall. She lowered her gaze and tried not to stare back but she couldn't resist observing from the corner of her eye. These faces came in so many colours and their features were amazingly diverse. These people represented a new and different world to the one she had inhabited so far. In front of her, a group of girls wearing skimpy summer dresses squealed joyfully next to an ample African woman who had matched a long patterned outfit with an elaborately tied turban. An oriental looking couple — a girl wearing white and red Pippi Longstocking pop socks with a short pleated skirt and a boy in a tennis outfit — was having a noisy reunion.

Moving her eyes from face to face, Maja realised that one person she couldn't see was Ewa, who should have been meeting her here. Her school friend had been living and working in London for a year. It was Ewa who had given Maja the idea of coming to England. With her energy and infectious enthusiasm, Ewa made everything appear simple.

As she moved through the sea of bodies, Maja was scanning the crowd milling around her. The faces reddened and sweaty in the July heat. She should easily have been able to recognise Ewa: her long blonde hair and some bright piece which, no doubt, she would be wearing in the middle of summer. Ewa had mentioned an information desk last time they spoke, so Maja started navigating through the crowd to a yellow counter with information boards installed above it. Two assistants were under siege from enquiring travellers. It wasn't a good meeting point. Standing on her toes and craning her neck, Maja looked around several times. In such a crowded place, she might not be able to meet Ewa. What was she going to do if Ewa didn't find her? Then, she heard a cry: 'Maja, Maja!'

She turned around. A grinning tomboy with a short blonde crop dressed in a red and white striped T-shirt was running through the open door of the terminal. Maja stood mesmerised. Ewa looked so different from the girl she had last seen in Grodek. Her short hair and strong eyeliner gave her a punkish appearance, but the stripey top and white cropped trousers were the essence of her.

Ewa threw her arms around Maja and gave her an enthusiastic hug.

'It's so good to see you!'

She smelled of something sweet and large hoops in her ears patted Maja's cheeks. The wide smile was so familiar, yet there was something different about Ewa although she couldn't put her finger on it.

'Maja, stop staring at me and say something.'

'I'm so happy to see you. I wasn't sure we would find each other in this crowd.'

'A woman of little faith! Of course we would have found each other. Somehow. How was your journey?'

'Good. Very interesting. Exhausting though.'

'Crossing Europe for the first time after all. It will be worth it. You'll see. But first let's get out of here. Give me your suitcase.'

Even before Maja could hand it over to her, Ewa grabbed the

handle of Maja's suitcase, deftly twisted it around and started making her way through the crowd, casting a few 'sorry's to the left and right.

When they eventually reached the street, they stopped for a moment. This was the first opportunity for Maja to look around and get a feel for London. She was tired and overwhelmed. The noisy crowd of passers-by made her feel as if she was observing these scenes from a distance, without being part of them. Ewa used this moment to reach for her mobile phone. She dialled a number and started talking quickly, first in English and then in Polish. At the end of the conversation she screwed up her face, making a mocking impression of someone. Then she slipped the phone into her red handbag.

'How is your mum?' she asked.

'As usual, mum is working too hard in the hospital and dad constantly worries about his job.'

'And how are Zosia and Piotr?'

'Completely puzzled why I gave up my job in the library and embarked on this madcap expedition, as Piotr called it.'

Next, Ewa enquired about their school friends and their favourite French teacher. Ewa wasn't the type to spend too much thought on other people's affairs unless they affected her. Then, she cleared her throat and said: 'There has been a small change of plan. Beata, the girl whose place you were to take, isn't going back home. Not yet. That means that we will have to find another job for you. And a room. Finding a bed won't be a problem because you can stay with me for the time being. My room is quite large. There is an inflatable mattress and I have plenty of blankets and pillows.'

Suddenly everything around returned to sharp focus. It was a moment Maja had subconsciously feared. After all, nothing would be as simple as it appeared in Grodek. Her carefully prepared plans were already falling apart. She had worked so hard to convince her parents that this adventure was a wonderful opportunity to try her hand at something new, while at the same time improve her English. All this was based on the assumption that there was a place for her to work and stay in London. She had put a lot of trust in Ewa. She should have known better.

'I don't want to burden you,' she stammered.

Ewa was her usual self: 'Maja don't look at me like that. Cheer up. You will stay with me. Like I said, I will help you find a different job. Everyone starts this way.'

'Ewa, I am very grateful ...'

But Ewa wouldn't have any of it. She had already picked up the handle of Maja's suitcase and commanded: 'Let's get out of here. Standing here and moping won't resolve anything. We need to get home and start sorting things out.'

The word 'home' sounded out of context here, but Maja had no time to reflect on this because Ewa had started moving through the crowd, nimbly manoeuvring the suitcase. In her high wedge sandals, she made long strides with the confidence of a catwalk model.

The journey to Ewa's apartment was like a fast moving film from which Maja hardly remembered a thing. The mass of humanity on the hot underground platform at Victoria Station became blurred in her mind with people in the crowded carriage. Then, after a half hour journey, they were again on a busy street, navigating between people before turning into a quiet street where Ewa lived. Two rows of semi-detached houses lined the street. They all looked the same. The only differentiating features were the small front gardens. Some of them were bursting with a variety of summer flowers and multi-coloured shrubs, while others were used merely as parking spaces, littered with bags and boxes. The property, which they entered through a creaking gate, had an assortment of potted plants standing by the front window.

When Ewa started climbing a narrow external staircase which led to a first-floor apartment, a girl's face appeared in an open window above them. With a red towel wrapped around her head, she sang in Polish as she waived her tanned arms, shaking a garment through the window. Seeing the girls struggling with their luggage up the stairs, she stopped singing.

'Let me help you,' she shouted.

In a moment, the door sprung open with a bang and the red towel appeared in the doorway. The girl stretched her arms towards Maja.

'Good to see you at last. Ewa told us about you. I'm Jola.' She gave Maja a hug smelling of shampoo and bubble bath.

'Good to meet you too.'

'Tired and starving?' Jola enquired.

'Both, to tell you the truth.' For the first time since she left home, Maja felt that someone had paid attention to her needs. She smiled and confessed: 'I could do with a bath. I'm afraid I smell and would put everyone off their food.'

While Maja was washing off the dirt and exhaustion of the past thirty hours in a bathroom cluttered with a multitude of bottles and pots, a distinctive smell of grilled garlic sausage started teasing her senses. The familiarity of it lifted her spirits. Soon, she was sitting around a small table with two other girls in a cramped kitchen, reminiscing with Ewa about the good old days in Grodek. She began to believe that everything would turn out all right in the end.

They finished supper with a cup of tea and a slice of lemon, just like at home. Afterwards, she went to Ewa's room and with one, quick glance around the room, she collapsed on the inflatable mattress on the floor, instantly falling unconscious.

Chapter 2

Kuba, July 1997

This was one of those summer mornings which made you feel happy to be alive. Leaning on the open window of his cab, Kuba breathed in the cool air and watched the first joggers trot through the gates of Kensington Gardens. Its vast lawns, still green and lush, shone with morning dew. The old plane trees looked timeless in their magnificence. Their enormous parasols shaded the park's avenues.

Kensington was his favourite part of London. At this early hour, still free of crowds and traffic, it had the atmosphere of times gone by. Tall Victorian mansions overlooked generously sized private gardens fenced by dense hedges to protect the residents from prying eyes. Their front steps were tiled and decorated with pots and urns that housed manicured topiary and sophisticated flower arrangements. Front doors, shining with fresh paint, were armoured with brass knobs and heavy knockers. This was the London of wealth, stability and good manners. He never heard raised voices in this district. Its atmosphere and architecture made the city's history come alive for people like him who loved English sagas, stories by Arthur Conan Doyle and Agatha Christie.

He didn't mind doing such an early shift. The air was still fresh and he felt as if he was taking a walk in his favourite part of town. There was hardly any traffic and he still had plenty of time before he was due to pick up his passenger. Gazing at the crystal blue sky, he started to whistle. Looking up at the handsome red brick buildings, he began comparing their tall windows, the sumptuous ironwork of their balconies, fanciful archways and turrets which enthusiasts of medieval architecture imported into central London.

He drove through the red lights. The screech of tyres shattered the tranquillity of the morning. His quick reflexes and the good brakes of his old BMW saved the life of a small ball of fluff tearing ahead of its owner. That morning walk would have been its last. The woman gave a loud cry and she was about to vent her anger when Kuba leaned out of the window and began a profuse apology. 'I'm so very, very sorry, lady. It was so stupid of me to look up instead of looking at the road. Is your dog OK?'

The trembling creature hid behind the woman's legs. A very shapely pair of legs. Kuba couldn't resist another look. The woman's tanned thighs were barely covered by khaki shorts.

The woman caught his glance and suppressed a smile. Being ogled by this foreign hunk wasn't an altogether unpleasant thing. She waived her hand dismissively and briskly walked through the zebra crossing.

When the traffic lights changed, Kuba moved on slowly, feeling like a chastened child. That could have cost him his driving licence. Even worse, he could have hurt someone. What an idiot!

Approaching Victoria Station, he saw the crowd of early arrivals spilling out of the terminal. Young people were carrying backpacks of different colours and sizes. He smiled at the sight of a teacher who was waving her yellow umbrella to herd a group of pupils through a crowd like a general leading her troops into battle. This reminded him of the mischief he had gotten up to during his school trips.

He stopped by the newspaper stand where he was supposed to pick up his passenger. The traffic started to thicken and he wondered how long he would be able to remain by the stand before a traffic warden came to move him along. As he looked around, he saw him.

He wore a shabby coat, a woman's blonde wig and dark crimson lipstick. Leaning against the wall, he was eating a hamburger from a polystyrene container with a certain decorum. Totally engrossed in his meal, he seemed oblivious to the surprised glances of passers-by. Kuba swallowed hard. The distant memory of the homeless shelter made him shiver. How many wrong turns must this man have taken before giving up on the world and its opinions?

Someone tapped him on the arm. A tanned and freckled face

appeared in the open window.

'Are you from Century Cabs?'

'Yes I am. Are you Miss Linton?'

'Annie Linton. That's me. My gran made the booking for me.' The girl was in high spirits. Her tan, creased T-shirt and ripped shorts were evidence of a recent care-free existence in some sunny destination.

Kuba jumped out of the car to help her with her luggage. 'Have you enjoyed your holidays?' he asked.

Her grin grew wider. 'It was great. Everything. There was meant to be some work but ...'

She glanced over her shoulder and lowering her voice, asked: 'Would you mind doing me a favour?'

'Sure. What can I do for you?' He tried not to sound surprised.

'See, on the other side of the street ... but please don't look. There are these two girls, wearing red and yellow tops. They were really mean to me at language camp. Could you pretend to be my boyfriend? Just for a moment? Perhaps give me a hug ...'

'Of course.' Without hesitation, Kuba picked the girl up, took her in his arms and swung her around. Then he opened the front door on the passenger side and helped her in.

She was beaming. 'That was great. Thank you very much, you were fantastic. Those two cows are gobsmacked. Please don't look.'

As they were pulling away, Kuba stole a glance at both girls who were indeed staring at them open-mouthed.

'You're excellent boyfriend material,' said Annie appreciatively. Observing him from the corner of her eye, she added: 'I bet you're very popular with the girls.'

He wondered whether she expected him to respond.

'It's none of my business, but I'm sure you have a lovely girlfriend. Men like you usually do.'

'I don't have a girlfriend. My work doesn't leave me much time, so I don't go out much. Women like men who have time for them.'

Annie looked baffled. 'I'm sorry, I shouldn't have asked.'

'That's OK, I don't mind.'

They drove in silence for a while, both wondering what to say next, until they reached the M4 and the imposing shape of the

Ark appeared in front of them.

'I really like this building,' said Annie, glad that she had found a topic to continue their conversation. 'It's a weird shape for an office building. But I like it because it's so different. What do you think?'

'I like it too. It's like a giant ship moored in central London. It resembles the ferry on which I travelled to England.'

'Can I ask where you came from? Central Europe?'

'Good guess. Very central. Poland. I was born in Opole. An old town in south-west Poland.'

'How interesting.'

'The only interesting thing about Opole is the fact that it hosts an annual festival of Polish song. But nobody in England has ever heard of it.'

'Geography has never been my strong suit.' Annie gave him another sideways glance and asked hesitantly: 'Have you come to London to work?'

'That's right. I had no idea what to do with myself after I packed up my job, so I came here three years ago. I always enjoyed driving ... My English wasn't too good so I joined a cab company.'

'Your English is very good now,' Annie said, with conviction.

'You're very kind. I've been working on it. I attend a language college ...'

'Good God! Working and studying — you're dedicated. It's more than I can say about my Spanish. It must be hard to concentrate late at night after working the whole day.'

'I go to school in the morning, and usually work late.'

Annie started observing Kuba surreptitiously. She glanced at his hands on the steering wheel and then moved her eyes up his bare arms. Then she dropped her gaze.

When the car stopped, Annie, deep in thought, looked up at him startled.

'Isn't this your home?' Kuba asked.

'Gosh, we're actually here. It's my gran's house. I'm going to spend the rest of my holidays with her. That's her. She must have been waiting by the window.'

The old lady was coming down the front steps, waving excited-ly to her granddaughter. Annie quickly got out of the cab and

ran up to her. They embraced with great affection. Then the
woman ruffled Annie's hair and said something which made
Annie roar with laughter. Kuba got out and started taking the
girl's luggage out of the boot. Then he took everything up to the
front door. As he was coming back, the lady took his hand and
pressed a few folded notes into it.

'Thank you very much for bringing my granddaughter home
safely. She told me that you took good care of her.'

Kuba smiled and returned to the cab. He wished all the
customers were like her. The old lady made him think of his
grandmother who had a very special place in his life. He was
already pulling out, when he saw Annie running down the
steps. He stopped and her face appeared in the open window.

'I just wanted to thank you, for driving me and ... for what you
did in Victoria. It was great. Thank you. But ... I don't even
know your name ...'

'Kuba. Short for Jacob.'

'Kuba. Thank you so much.'

She waved to him, and continued waving after the car disappeared round the corner.

He drove through the familiar streets of Ealing which he had
crossed many times, both day and night. By now, West London
was already awake. People were strolling with their morning
shopping and pottering around their front gardens. He heard
children laugh and a mother reprimanding them. He saw a dog
in a window ferociously barking at a passing cat. The smell of
freshly brewed coffee, warm toast and grilled bacon wafted
through the windows. This reminded him that he hadn't had
breakfast that morning. A good breakfast was essential to keep
up his spirits. He started reviewing in his mind the contents of
his shelf in the fridge and decided that it was time to pay a visit
to the corner shop.

He had never acquired the discipline of regular shopping and
made up for it by buying everything he needed in one go. He
rarely visited his local Tesco since he could never find what he
needed. Most of the time he left the supermarket irritated,
having wasted too much time with little effect.

Kuba preferred going to Mrs Shah's corner shop where he was

greeted with a smile and offered plenty of advice. The Polish population in his neighbourhood had swollen considerably and Mrs Shah had started stocking Polish produce. Food-wise, the Poles were like Indian people, in Mrs Shah's opinion, and she enjoyed sharing her views with Kuba. They were loyal to their roots and were prepared to pay a premium for authentic stuff. Mrs Shah was willing to go to great lengths to indulge her customers.

However, this morning, Mrs Shah was standing behind the till, wearing a concerned expression. When Kuba entered the store, Mrs Shah nodded at him to approach. As soon as she had finished serving her last customer, she lowered her voice to a conspiratorial whisper.

'The police have just raided some houses in the neighbourhood. Apparently, they arrested some people without papers and they're going to deport them.'

'When did this happen?'

'Last night.' Mrs Shah's kohl-lined eyes became even darker. 'If you're returning from a night shift, you'd better call your people to check that it's safe to return.'

'I wasn't working last night. I left at six this morning for a job. But thank you for the warning.'

Kuba knew that these raids were becoming increasingly frequent. The police searched the places where they expected to find immigrants without valid visas. He was registered with his cab company and was still officially studying English, so in principle he had nothing to fear. However, his situation was becoming less straightforward because his visa had been extended more than once. This thought weakened his appetite for breakfast and enthusiasm for shopping.

Seeing his indecisiveness, Mrs Shah rushed to offer help and advice. Shortly after, he was leaving her store with four bulging carrier bags. As a sign of her friendship, Mrs Shah gave him a thick slice of watermelon.

The fleshy pink wedge in his bag and the prospect of a good breakfast cheered him up. By the time Kuba reached the door of 26 Cuckoohill Road, all he could think about was food.

Chapter 3

Adam, July 1997

On that hot and airless Saturday afternoon in July, Burrow Road, sneaking away from Greenford High Street, looked uglier than ever. In the sticky urban heat, everything appeared tired and wilting. At five o'clock, the sun was still high and it was burning Adam's shoulders through his dirty shirt. The working week was finally over and he was walking home, feeling empty and exhausted. Usually indifferent to his surroundings, he couldn't help noticing the litter scattered on the pavements. Empty bottles had rolled into the gutter and dirty wrappers lay alongside garden walls. He made long strides to avoid stepping into sticky puddles of spilled drink and vomit. With disgust, he crossed to the other side of the street so as not to walk on the pavement which had been fouled by dogs.

He didn't blame the animals for the mess they left behind. Their owners were stupid and selfish, keeping them in this concrete jungle. At home in Kościelisko, his dogs had plenty of space to run around freely. All of them were mongrels yet they were far more intelligent than the funny creatures he saw in London, wearing expensive collars and ridiculous outfits. His dogs knew what was expected of them. Trained to watch over the sheep, they were very skilled at getting the whole flock back home safely. He proudly watched them run across the meadows, their heads bobbing up and down in the long grass, which swayed like a sea.

'Dreaming again?' A hoarse voice brought him back to the filthy street. 'I've been walking behind you and calling you since the corner.'

Adam groaned. Spending a Saturday afternoon in Piotr's company wasn't a welcome prospect. Six months working with him on a building site in Putney was enough. At times, he wondered why the man bothered to go out to work if by the end of the weekend his pockets were empty again.

'Just tired. Glad that the week is over.'

'Is Karol paying badly as usual?'

'Not at all. He pays every Saturday now. In cash.' Adam hadn't expected to be defending his employer.

'So are you a regular at the bank? Sending dosh to the family?'

'When I need to.' Adam was racking his brain for an excuse to leave Piotr. 'I need to buy some food. I will be going this way,' he said, pointing to a corner shop where a colourful display of fruit and vegetables sat under a large awning.

'I didn't know you're into Indian food. What a change from Polish sausage and pickled cucumbers!'

An asshole. Adam wasn't going to remind him about the same cheap paté which Piotr continuously bought for his lunch and spread with a dirty penknife which he used to cut electrical wires and plasterboard. 'The Indian woman here stocks a lot of Polish food. Bread, pickles and sausage. She even has a selection of vodkas — if you're interested.'

'Sounds like my type of shop. I'd better go with you. I don't fancy eating cornflakes the whole weekend.'

As they entered the store, Mrs Shah raised her hand, welcoming her loyal customer. Adam made a friendly nod. He had grown to respect Mrs Shah as the owner of 'his' local store. It took him a while to warm to her, after all she was Indian and a woman. A year ago, he wouldn't have dreamt that he would be buying Polish rye bread, Krakowska sausage, Polish mustard and pickles from a colonial store run by a shopkeeper who couldn't read the labels of the food she was selling. Despite this, her store offered almost everything a Pole, missing his native staples in London, could need.

With disbelief, Piotr gazed up and down Mrs Shah's well stocked shelves. Finally, he turned to Adam and grinned: 'You will be seeing me here more often. This stuff looks better than the food in the Polish deli on Ealing Broadway. And it's definitely cheaper.'

Regretting his earlier encouragement, Adam pretended to

take no notice of Piotr. He picked up his usual groceries, added a pack of Żywiec lager and walked towards the till. Meanwhile, Piotr piled his basket to the brim with packets and jars, put beer on top and finally added two loaves of rye bread to his load. Then he lifted his shopping with some effort and carried it to the till. Adam wondered whether Mrs Shah was now congratulating herself on her decision to become a supplier to the new labour force for London's construction trade.

Seeing Piotr leave the store with a bulging rucksack on his back and plastic carrier bags in both his hands, Adam said: 'Mate, I'm off now. See you soon. Have a good weekend, pal. Or what's left of it.'

'You're not going home yet? We've just met.' Piotr put his shopping down on the pavement and was wiping his sweaty face with his forearm. 'I hoped we could go for a beer together. There is a good pub on the main road, just round the corner.'

'To a pub, with this lot?' Adam swung his bulging bags, hoping to make Piotr see sense.

'Why not? We could park them under a table.'

'You park it. I'm going.'

'Adam, relax. You're becoming an old bore. Let's sit down on that bench.' Adam followed Piotr's index finger pointing to a small patch of green bordered with tired looking rose bushes. A generously sized bench was standing in the middle of it. It was usually occupied by people waiting for a bus.

'Fine, let's give our feet a rest for five minutes.' It was the end of the week, after all, and he felt exhausted. Eight hours of manual labour every day, six days a week left him stiff with tiredness.

The bench groaned under their weight.

'Still so hot,' heaved Piotr. He unbuttoned his shirt and started wiping his sweaty face with the front panel. 'It's the end of the summer but I didn't have time to even think about a holiday.'

'Too much work?'

'Loads. Summer has been good at Mark's. I'm thirsty. Let's toast our meeting.' Piotr reached into the plastic bag under the bench and produced two cans of Żywiec. Adam didn't need more encouragement. They lifted their cans and took the first gulp almost simultaneously. Ice cold and fizzy, the lager couldn't have tasted better. They sat, lost in their thoughts, savouring the drink. For a brief moment, they forgot their aching limbs, the heat and the grime around them.

'I still like Polish beer best,' said Piotr, breaking the silence.

'Yeah. I can't get used to English bread. It doesn't taste like bread at all.'

'I like to use my teeth on my bread, to bite it and chew it. The white bread here fills your mouth like cotton wool. And leaves you feeling hungry.'

This made them think about their empty stomachs and Piotr reached under the bench for two more cans. Adam stopped his hand.

'My turn now.' He broke his pack of *Żywiec* and handed the can to Piotr. 'It tastes bloody good in this heat,' he said, taking his cap off and wiping his forehead with the back of his palm.

'Sure does. I never thought I was a patriot until I came here. Strange things happen to a man when he is far away from home.'

They didn't notice when they emptied their last two cans of lager. The sun was lower now and the heat had ceased to be as oppressive as before. They felt hungry. Piotr tore the cellophane wrapper off his loaf of bread and was about to roll out the metal lid on a can of paté when Adam took a ring of sausage out of his plastic carrier and broke it in half. The smell of smoked meat with garlic hit their senses.

They ate in silence, enjoying every mouthful. The rye bread was fresh and moist and even without butter it tasted delicious. Garlic sausage was the perfect accompaniment to such bread.

All of a sudden, Adam turned back. He thought he heard a cry, but there was nobody around. He was taking another bite of sausage when he heard the sound again. It was like a child's voice. He looked around. He and Piotr were the only people on this patch of greenery and yet the sound seemed so close. Then, there was a third cry and this time it clearly came from under the seat. Adam bent down and looked under the bench. A pair of green eyes, wide and startled, was staring at him. They belonged to a large ginger cat sitting next to his bag of groceries.

'Piotr, we have company,' said Adam, burping loudly. 'He's come to share the sausage.'

Piotr cautiously bent forward to look under the bench.

'An English cat that likes Polish sausage!' he laughed. 'I'm not surprised.' He bit a piece of meat and threw it in the direction of the cat who caught it in mid-air. Then he placed the morsel on the pavement and started eating it with relish.

'He's not a fool. Maybe he wants a piece of Polish bread to go with it?'

'Don't be stupid, Piotr. Cats don't eat bread.'

'How do you know? This English cat may like some bread. It's late. Like us, he probably missed his dinner,' said Piotr, hiccupping.

'We should be going home.' Adam looked at his watch squinting. In the fading light, he couldn't see the time. 'It's almost nine.'

Piotr got up from the bench to stretch his legs. They felt very soft. He would have fallen down, if Adam hadn't propped him up in time.

'Will any of the buses from this stop be good for you?' Adam asked, pointing to the sign at the edge of the road. 'Let's check.'

While Piotr attempted to maintain his balance, Adam helped him put a loaded rucksack on his back. Then, they walked to the bus stop together.

'What about the 92? It goes towards Acton,' suggested Adam, looking at the headboard of the approaching double decker bus.

'It will do. I'll find my way.'

'Here you go.' Adam helped Piotr to mount the high step of the bus.

'It was good to see you, mate!' shouted Piotr before the door closed behind him.

Not sure, thought Adam. Spending Saturday afternoon on a bench wasn't exactly what he had planned. This filthy heat didn't help. He walked back to the seat to pick up his shopping and saw that the cat was still there. He was staring at the contents of the open carrier but didn't put his head inside. He looked up at Adam as if expecting praise for his good behaviour.

'What do you want? You ... *Marchewka* (Carrot).' The cat didn't take offence. He kept looking up at Adam, his eyes wide open, questioning.

'OK, have another piece. But then we're both going home.' The cat accepted the offering and as before, ate the sausage without haste. Then, he licked his pink lips and looked up at Adam expectantly.

'Finished? Was it good? Ready to go now?' With some difficulty, Adam bent down to pick up his bags. Once upright, he straightened up, swung a couple of carriers over his shoulder and started walking in the direction of Cuckoohill Road. After a while, he looked back. Keeping a safe distance, the cat was following him. Adam stopped and the cat also paused.

'Ginger, I'm going home. You should go to yours.' The cat sat down and stared at Adam. He opened and closed his eyes as if to say that he agreed with him. Adam started walking again. After a short while, he looked back and the cat was just a few steps behind him.

'What do you want? Don't you have a home to go to? I can't take you with me. There is a no-pets policy in our house. You understand — no pets.' The cat narrowed his eyes again, confirming that he fully understood the situation. Yet when Adam reached the front door of 26 Cuckoohill Road and searched his pockets for his key, the cat sat in the open gate. Adam unlocked the door and looked inside. The hall was empty and quiet. He crossed it and carefully opened the door to his room. He nodded to the cat. 'Just one night, mate. One night. Be fast before anyone sees you.'

The cat looked at Adam and in one long leap, crossed the doorstep. He softly padded through the hall and into the open door of Adam's room. With one hand on the handle, Adam looked around and softly closed the door behind them.

Chapter 4

Maja, July 1997

'Do you have relevant professional *expérience*?'

'I am a modern languages graduate and I have worked for ...'

'All our staff speak English. I am asking about relevant *expérience*.'

'Waitressing?'

'Of course waitressing. This is a restaurant. A professional *établissement*, Mademoiselle.' A smartly dressed French woman was getting impatient.

She thinks I'm thick, thought Maja. 'I worked as a waitress in a café in Lublin, in Poland.'

'How long did you work there?'

'Every weekend, for almost a year.'

'Weekends only?' Madame wrinkled her nose, clearly unimpressed.

'It was a very smart café. In the centre of the old town. We were very busy on Saturdays. And Sundays.' Maja was racking her brain for arguments to convince the woman that she knew how to serve tables.

'*Bien*. Complete this form and we will contact you if we have a suitable vacancy.' With a jingle of silver bracelets the woman pushed a sheet of paper across a marble table top. 'Don't worry about the other columns — just write your name and telephone number.'

This didn't sound encouraging. Moreover Maja wasn't sure that there was a telephone in Ewa's flat. She would have to give Ewa's mobile number and hope that she would pass on the message if the woman bothered to call her.

In desperation, she had ventured into one of the large and elegant hotels in Kensington. The miles of shining marble floor separating her from the Reception desk frightened her. She felt out of place in this world furnished by leather sofas, large table lamps and enormous modern paintings. She was about to turn on her heel and run away but Ewa, who had offered to help her that afternoon, firmly held her arm and hissed: 'Off you go. To Reception. Don't be a coward.'

The receptionist wasn't surprised in the slightest and said that she would call a personnel manager to enquire. In less than five minutes, a woman dressed in an elegant navy suit holding a clipboard under her arm appeared at Reception.

'Are you enquiring about a front desk vacancy?' she asked. She looked with interest at Maja dressed in a white blouse and a navy skirt, her formal work clothes. She had put them on this morning despite Ewa's sneering remark that she looked like a stewardess.

'No ..., just a waitressing job, in a restaurant.'

'Do you have any relevant experience?' Remembering the lessons from that morning, Maja described her waitressing job, making no reference to the weekend and part-time nature of it.

'OK. Please complete the application form and leave it with the receptionist. We will be in touch if we consider you suitable for one of the restaurant jobs.'

'Do you have vacancies?' Ewa enquired.

'We have four restaurants, the lounge bar, the casino and a room service,' recited the woman. 'You will hear from us if there is a suitable vacancy.' She handed Maja a clipboard with the application form and a pen, and with a click of her high heels on the polished floor, she departed.

Maja looked at Ewa with hope. Ewa didn't share her optimism. 'Get on with it and let's not waste too much time. We may never hear from them again. They get plenty of applicants. Remember, you don't have a formal work permit.'

At the end of the day, Ewa suggested that they try a kebab shop on Gloucester Road. At five o'clock, it was already very busy. Men, young and old, were coming and leaving the shop. The front door was closing behind the last customer when it was pushed open again by the next one. The smell of fried meat, onions and burnt coffee hung in the air. The girls approached an olive skinned man standing by the till and Ewa fired the opening question.

'Waitressing job? Hmm ... Which one of you is interested?' asked the man, moving his eyes from one girl to the other.

'My friend,' said Ewa pointing at Maja.

The disconcertingly handsome man held Maja's gaze for a while. A long while. A smile appeared under a short moustache.

'Is it your first job in London, miss?'

'Yes, I have just started looking. This may not ...' Maja stopped, angry for starting to explain herself. She didn't like the place. She already regretted coming in here.

'I will check whether there is a place for you.' His eyes wandered from her face, down her neck and along the row of buttons on her blouse. Maja felt as if his fingers were following his eyes.

'Have you worked in a restaurant before?'

'Yes, part time, at weekends. Only for about half a year.' She wanted to get out of this place as fast as possible. But the man with dark velvety eyes exclaimed: 'You're Polish!'

She wasn't prepared for such directness. 'Yes, but ...'

'Polish girls are beautiful. *Jak she mash?*' he lisped.

Maja was about to tell him to mind his own business when Ewa hissed in her ear: 'Don't burn your bridges. You need to start somewhere.'

Maja wanted to say that she was not that desperate, when she remembered that she was still occupying a mattress on the floor in Ewa's room. It was only a temporary solution.

'OK, so do you have any vacancies in your restaurant now?' asked Maja, defiantly looking up at the man who was clearly enjoying the situation.

'I will check with the boss tonight and will tell when you come tomorrow.'

If I come ..., thought Maja, but Ewa said, 'Great, we will pop in to check tomorrow.'

'I hope to have good news for you,' said the man, looking only at Maja. 'See you tomorrow.'

'Bye.'

As soon as the door closed behind them, Maja whispered, 'He gives me creeps.'

'Like every Arab, he is attracted to blonde women.'

'I'm not blonde.'

'But you're fair skinned, Eastern European and pretty. That's enough.'

By six in the evening, even Ewa had had enough.

'You should now know how to look for a job in London. Let's start heading home. I'm hungry and my feet are killing me.'

Maja glanced at Ewa's high platform shoes and then at her own flat sandals. If she had been wearing Ewa's shoes she would be walking barefoot by now.

'I'm also very thirsty. Can I buy some food and drink for supper?' asked Maja. 'I want to start contributing.'

'You'll pay your share once you get a job.' Ewa waved off Maja's protests. 'We have plenty of food. Jola brings nice things from the pub. They always cook too much there, especially at the weekends. And she doesn't mind sharing it.'

As they were climbing up the steep staircase leading to their flat, they caught an exotic smell wafting through the open window. Spicy yet sweet, a very different aroma from those to which Maja was accustomed to at home. Suddenly, the front door to the flat was thrown open and Jola appeared in it, frantically waving a kitchen towel.

Seeing the girls, she shouted: 'I have just burnt popadoms. Not my day.'

'But the curry smells good,' said Ewa, entering the flat.

'Yesterday's chicken Korma. Not bad. But I managed to cremate the popadoms.' Jola was opening all the windows in the small kitchen.

'I wouldn't know the difference,' said Maja. 'This will be my first ever curry.'

'OK, then hurry up girls. Rice is already cooked. Then looking at Maja, Jola asked: 'How did it go today?'

'We've been to a few interesting places. Ewa has been a great help.'

'Let's eat first. I'm starving.' Ewa was reaching for glasses. 'Tap-spa or do we have some mineral water?'

'There is still half a bottle in the fridge. I will buy some more after dinner,' said Maja. She watched as Jola placed a few spoons of rice on each plate on which she dished out a bright yellow stew. It had a delicious unfamiliar smell.

They were ravenously hungry and ate with great gusto, forgetting about calories, tight fitting clothes, proteins and carbohydrate ratios.

'Does this curry have coconut in it?' asked Maja.

'Sure does,' confirmed Jola, wiping the remains of the yellow sauce with a chunk of bread.

'I only ate coconut in cakes and biscuits.'

'You're going to learn an awful lot here. It'll seem at times like Grodek is on a different planet,' warned Ewa.

'Girls, I'd have totally forgotten,' exclaimed Jola. 'A Greek girl who comes to do the bookkeeping in our pub mentioned that her uncle is looking for waiting staff for his restaurant in Hackney.'

'Hackney?'

'North east London. Not another planet,' said Ewa.

'Apparently, it is a nice family restaurant. Maria said that they have many Greek weddings during which staff get lots of tips,' Jola continued.

'It sounds good,' said Ewa.

'Sure. It could be just the place I'm looking for,' said Maja, trying to sound upbeat.

Later that night, lying on the floor in Ewa's room and listening to the even breathing of her friend, Maja was thinking about the events of the past couple of days. She chastised herself for not being more enthusiastic. The girls must have had similar experiences and now they were trying to help her.

She knew what was at stake when she handed her notice in at the Grodek library, relinquishing her safe job. It hadn't been a career she had expected when she completed her modern languages degree.

Maja thought about five hundred dollars, stashed at the bottom of her suitcase. It was the result of months of saving from her meagre salary and from her summer job at the fruit farm. It was to cover two months' tuition at the language school and her initial rent until she found some work. Her mother had secretly given her a few hundred *złoty* to buy some clothes for the trip and a new suitcase. The old one looked as if it had made a round the world journey.

If she was to stay in Britain, even for a few months, she had to enrol for an English language course, otherwise she would be deported as an illegal immigrant. To afford the school fees she had to find employment. A job. She would have to shelve her ambitions and swallow her pride and prove that she could be the best waitress her employer could hire. Whatever it takes.

Chapter 5

Maja, July 1997

The landscape of north east London seen from the elevated section of the Victoria line had a lunar appearance. Rows and rows of joined houses, like uneven walkways, stretched for miles. Many buildings had haphazardly assembled extensions at the back which had a life of their own. Tiny gardens, littered with a variety of domestic junk, were substitutes for nature. Some hosted tufts of greenery and potted plants. Occasionally, a lanky tree hoisted itself above the urban clutter. All the gardens were surrounded by walls and fences, sometimes disproportionately high to the little sovereign territories they protected. An Englishman's home is his castle; Maja recalled a saying which she had learnt at school. The little terraced kingdoms, darkened by years of smog and pollution, were the dominions of English privacy and individuality.

The train stopped, the doors slammed open and the name of her destination appeared in the middle of the navy and red underground circle. Maja instantly got up from her seat and stepped out onto the open platform. The station had the same feel as the rows of terraced houses beyond it. Simple, grey and utilitarian, with no thought spared for embellishments that could have made the buildings look less severe. To compensate for this, an explosion of bright graffiti sailed down the walls of the narrow staircase leading to the station office.

She went through the ticket barrier and took out a map from her handbag which Jola had prepared for her. She had to find the stop for the 279 bus which wasn't difficult as the street was narrow and short.

It was only eight in the morning but a small crowd had already gathered at the bus stop. Maja checked the schedule and positioned herself at the end of what looked like a loosely assembled queue. She was one of the few European faces at the stop. Several olive skinned men were patiently waiting for the bus, looking beyond the crowd and trying to appear detached. Among them stood women covered from head to toe in long flowing robes. Many of them wore black although a few had pastel colour capes edged with embroidery and long skirts of the same colour. They were looking at Maja with similar interest. Some were accompanied by beautiful dark-eyed children dressed in Western clothes. They noisily played together calling each other in English, whilst their mothers reprimanded them in their native language.

Keeping one eye on the arriving buses, Maja looked around. On the other side, directly opposite the stop, a line of cabs waited along the pavement. They received their business from a small office with a dirty sign: Carlton Cabs. Bored drivers leaned out of open car windows. Nursing polystyrene cups, they were killing time reading tabloid newspapers. A few men kept awake by playing loud music. Some tunes sounded like distant calls of exotic countries.

Next to the taxi rank, there was a small shop with a pink marquee and black writing: Jasmine Black Beauty. Snuggled to it was Jazz's Gent's Barber which was already open. Its next door neighbour was Silver Dollar Café, full and oozing a strong smell of fried food. A wooden board standing on the pavement had one message: 'Full English breakfast — £2'. Underneath there were two rows of signs in a squiggly alphabet ending with a two pound sign, translating the message into the locally used language.

Next door to the café was a tattoo parlour, still closed, with examples of its services displayed in the glass boxes hanging on both sides of the red door. The last commercial unit on the corner of the street was occupied by a garage selling second hand cars. Like goods on a market stall, each car had a board mounted on the roof with its name and a price. Although the cars didn't look particularly new or luxurious, the yard in which they were parked was guarded by a gate with tall iron bars, crowned with jagged edges.

A double decker bus appeared from behind the corner. The queue regrouped promptly and Maja again found herself at the end of the line. The rules of queuing in White Hart Lane didn't differ from those in Grodek. Everyone managed to get in, and with a loud thump of the doors and sharp jerk, the bus moved forward.

It was packed like a can of sardines but, unexpectedly, a seat by the window became vacant and Maja gladly slipped into it. At last, she was able to look undisturbed at the changing street scene. Soon, they were following a much wider road which crossed a newly built housing estate. Most of the houses here were only two or three storey high. Bright blue window frames and doors gave them the cheerful appearance of a toy estate. In the middle, stood a brand new medical centre with colourful information panels and shining big windows.

The bus again entered a busy street lined with a motley assortment of small shops. In the middle of the urban landscape, she saw a cottage squatting a few metres back from the pavement. A white board with black lettering said: Greek Taverna. Maja stood up and started squeezing herself through the crowd. Soon, she was out on the street walking back towards the urban cottage.

The walls of the building were covered in greenery. Plants, flowers and creepers were cascading down from window boxes, hanging baskets and various attachments at all levels. A flotilla of potted shrubs and palms stood on the pavement in front of the restaurant, separating it from the rest of the street. The house was more like a garden than a building and Maja wasn't surprised to see a man with a large watering can leaning out of the first floor window.

'Looking for someone, miss?' The question came from behind a hedge surrounding the front patio. A head with a thick, black thatch appeared above the topiary.

'No ..., I mean yes. Is this the restaurant of Mr Dimitrios?'

'Sure.' The man flashed a broad grin from under a thick moustache. 'Are you the Polish girl Maria is sending us?'

News travels fast here. She looked at the moustached face of Ali Baba and asked defiantly: 'Can I speak to Mr Dimitrios?'

'He does not come in until eleven. But the manager is here.'

'Can you take me to him?'

'Her.'

'OK, her.'

'Anything for you, miss.' Another broad smile appeared on the olive brown face, shining like a crust of freshly baked bread.

She was led through a cavernous hall, still very cool in spite of the warm weather outside. Their steps echoed loudly on the tiled floor which a young girl was mopping vigorously. A large number of wooden tables filled the room. Most of the chairs rested upside down on the tables and through the forest of legs, Maja could see an abundance of potted plants and ceramic ornaments on the walls.

In a room at the back, a young woman was engrossed in paperwork. Her small frame contrasted with the vastness of the desk on which documents and folders lay in neat piles. Her white crisp blouse and shiny black hair, neatly pulled back, gave her an air of business efficiency.

'Are you Maria's friend?' she asked without any introductions.

'I am a friend of Maria's colleague from the pub.'

'OK, so what's your name?'

'Maja. Maja Zalewska.'

'You're Polish?'

'Yes, I am.'

'We once had a cashier who was Polish and he was very good. What qualifications and experience do you have?'

Maja smoothly delivered the abbreviated version of her CV, highlighting her restaurant experience and downplaying her academic record. The girl listened attentively but didn't question anything. Finally, she asked: 'When can you start?'

Maja hesitated. To say now would mean that she was desperate and had no other offers.

'Perhaps tomorrow.'

'Excellent. Please come tomorrow morning at the same time as today. We need to show you how we work here.'

At last! It was her first offer of employment in London. Maja felt a tinge of disappointment that it was so easy this time. The place looked pleasant but it was at the other end of London, far away from where she was hoping to live. The cost of coming here every morning would be substantial. The past few days had already made a considerable dent in her meagre budget.

'Do you wish to ask me anything?' the manageress enquired.

'Yes, of course. I have many questions. For example, what is my working day going to look like?'

The girl hesitated for a moment. 'Why don't you stay for a couple of hours? One of the boys will show you round and explain a few things.'

Ali Baba's name was Andreas and with a great deal of glee, he accepted the task of introducing Maja to the Greek Taverna. Being shown around the ground and first floor rooms, she learnt a lot about the history of Mr Dimitrios' restaurant and his love of horticulture. The tavern served not only authentic Greek food but was also proud of its ambiance. Everyone was expected to contribute to it and show commitment to the business.

Grinning the whole time, Andreas told her that she would have to learn the menu, of course he would help with pronunciation. There would be an opportunity to sample all the dishes — in time. She should be able to recommend extras. Andreas would tutor her well and she would see her tips grow from week to week. It was best to start straight away, so Andreas took a leather bound menu and asked Maja to sit down at the table on the patio.

'Would you like a drink? Some juice or mineral water?' Before Maja had a chance to make up her mind, Andreas made a decision for her. 'I will prepare us some good coffee. How would you like your coffee? Strong and black?'

'I would prefer coffee with milk.' A distant memory of some black soot served in a tiny cup, called Turkish coffee, still haunted her from a few years back.

Her fears were unfounded. When Andreas placed two tall glasses of caramel coloured liquid topped with milky froth in front of them, the aroma instantly filled the air. He winked at her as an encouragement to taste it. The steamed milk brought out the flavour of freshly brewed coffee, it was strong but milky. There was also a hint of something spicy in it which she couldn't recognize. She wrapped her fingers around the glass and took another sip. Andreas' grin grew even wider across his burly face. He opened the menu on the first page and placed it directly in front of Maja, propping it on an ashtray. Then he positioned his chair slightly behind hers and, protectively leaning over her shoulder, pointed to the starters page. She felt his warm breath on the back of her neck and her shoulders through the thin fabric of her blouse.

'It is important to encourage the customers to take appetizers. We have a good selection of them, such as fresh *tramasalata*, *dolmades* or *keffedes*. They are spicy and the customers will be buying drinks, wine or ouzo and will stay longer. The overall bill will be higher then, as will your tip.'

Maja moved forward a bit, away from Andreas and now her stomach was pressed against the table. His index finger was going down the list and his arm was now almost resting on her back. She tried to position herself sideways but then her knees touched his. She sensed his quickening breath and his hand moved towards her elbow.

'Spicy sardines and *saganaki* are for customers who like stronger food. Connoisseurs of Greek food prefer ...' Andreas' body was now leaning against hers. He smelled of sweat and musky cologne that she found suffocating. She stood up. 'I need to use the bathroom.' She ran through the dark interior of the restaurant. The cleaning girl stopped wiping the tables and silently pointed to the door at the back of the room. Finally safe behind the bathroom door, Maja looked at her reflection in the mirror. Her cheeks were burning and her eyes, holding back angry tears, were like the eyes of a frightened animal.

The door swung open and the young manageress walked in. She stopped in front of the mirror to smooth her hair and caught Maja's gaze.

'Is everything OK?'

'Yeah ..., everything is fine.' She wished she had thrown the coffee in Andreas' face. It would have made her feel better, Maja thought, but she said: 'I felt a bit hot.'

When the woman disappeared into the cubicle, Maja relaxed her hands on the edge of the basin. Then she ran a strong stream of water and started slowly washing her hands. Was this incident an occupational hazard of working in a restaurant? Or was she just unlucky? She took out her lipstick and applied it slowly once, and then again, adding another layer until her lips shone with red warrior paint.

She zipped up her handbag, slung it over her arm and walked out of the bathroom. On the patio, Andreas was gathering up their coffee glasses with the menu folder under his arm. He turned around, hearing her steps. The smile hadn't left his face.

'Andreas, I have to leave now. I must be back by one o'clock.'

'It's a pity, we could have ...'

'If you give me a copy of the menu, I will study it at home. You could help me tomorrow, if I have any questions.'

'Sure. We can talk tomorrow.'

Armed with a copy of the menu, Maja ran towards the 279 bus stop. She thought about Ewa. Her friend had changed a lot since she left Grodek. Had she also learnt lessons she wished to forget?

Maja didn't expect to be so happy to see the blue door of Ewa's flat again. She retrieved the key from behind a loose brick and with relief walked into the tiny kitchen. The familiar smell of yesterday's food and lemon washing up liquid permeated the air. This made her feel at home. And safe again.

When the girls returned late in the evening, a familiar smell greeted them long before they opened the door to the kitchen. The warm scents of a July evening were mingling with the sweet and comforting aroma of a freshly baked cake.

'God, something smells divine!' exclaimed Jola. Maja was sitting at the table writing a letter. In the middle stood a milk jug with a bunch of white and yellow flowers and next to it a golden tart, lightly sprinkled with icing sugar, was cooling down in a lasagne dish.

'Szarlotka! cried Jola. Maja, you want to destroy me!' She was already leaning over the cake, deeply inhaling the smell of the apple tart. 'I am skipping lunch every day to fit into my white jeans, and you annihilate my efforts in one evening.' Ewa was less distraught. 'I forgot what szarlotka looks like, let alone how it smells. You're making me homesick and I'm not sure it's a good thing.'

'I was sitting here bored and wondered what you might fancy when you got back from work. I also bought a bottle of milk, if you wanted a glass with your *szarlotka*.'

In about twenty minutes, half of the lasagne dish was empty.

Licking warm apple puree from her fingers, Jola suddenly asked: 'How did you find Hackney and the Greek Taverna?'

For a second, Maja considered whether she should tell her what happened. 'The journey is quite long, but the restaurant is a very interesting place. In many ways. They ...'

'Maja, I meant to tell you something but you totally distracted me with the cake. God, I will have to stop eating breakfast too, for a week,' said Jola running her thumb along the edge of the dish, wiping the apple puree that escaped from the cake. 'Now, there is another option.'

Maja's heart started beating faster.

'One of the girls who serves in the pub and also helps with the food is going back to Poland. Should I have a word with the boss for you? It's only Park Royal, about half an hour from here. Obviously you can cook. The job involves preparing some salads and sandwiches. The serious stuff is cooked by the chef who comes in during the day. We just reheat it.'

Maja stopped listening. Did this mean that she wouldn't need to go back to Hackney again? And never again fear Andreas' sticky hands?'

'Maja, did you hear what I said? Should I tell the boss that you're interested?'

Chapter 6

Kuba, August 1997

Kuba closed his eyes. Lifting his face to the sun he felt a warm breeze on his cheeks. The wind brought the scent of dry grass and some late summer flowers, the name of which he couldn't remember.

He was six again. Lost but not frightened, he was wading through the long grass of his grandparents' garden. He knew that at the end of it there was a vegetable plot bordered with a row of red currant bushes. He had been there the day before and saw that they were ripe to eat and hung like strings of glass beads among prickly leaves. If he kept going ahead towards the fruit trees, he would get there eventually. He walked for a while in the same direction but he couldn't see the berry bushes or the vegetable bed. Henryk, his older brother, teased him sometimes about the ghost of an old man who lived in the old cherry tree but Kuba had no reason to believe him. His grandmother always told Henryk off for telling fibs.

This time he must have lost his bearings. He couldn't remember the direction to get back to the house. Even at six, Kuba didn't like to make a fuss. Now he was reluctant to raise the alarm by calling for help as this would inevitably result in a ban on wandering off on his own in future. He stopped for a moment, considering what to do next, when he heard a familiar voice calling his name. He raised his head but all he could see was grass around him. In the distance, slender willow twigs were swaying gently in the wind. Now the voice was closer and clearer. He recognized it as his mother's. He thought that she was in Opole, where she worked while he spent the summer with his grandparents in the country. Unexpectedly, he saw her face just above his, dark in a halo of sunshine which shone through her curly hair. She was laughing, pleased that she had managed to surprise him. Kuba squealed with joy. In response, his mother scooped him off the ground and he flew above the grass, high in the air, as she swung him in her arms. Her summer dress twirled around her and its loose sleeves billowed up, making her look like an angel. She smelled of something sweet. This sweetness was also in the fabric of her dress, her hair and her skin.

If he focused hard, he could evoke this scent, even now — twenty-two years later. But he couldn't remember her face. However hard he tried, he wasn't able to recreate his mother's face in his memory. Some years ago, he almost cried when he realized this for the first time. Of course, there were pictures of her in his grandmother's house — as a girl and a young woman on her wedding day, in a rather stiff pose. None of them resembled the person who loved to pick him up, ruffle his hair and laugh with him so hard that they both almost cried. She knew how to delight him in a way that nobody else ever did.

A sudden thump shook the floor of the patio where Kuba was sitting. Through the back door, Basia stormed out of the house. She marched with her dark hair hanging across her scowling face, her fists clenched. She noticed Kuba, with a book on his lap, his legs resting on another chair. Ready for a confrontation, she threw a challenging glance at him but Kuba pretended not to notice it. Basia glared at him from under her thick fringe and decided to seek solace at the far end of the garden. After a while, she came back.

'What a nice morning,' Kuba ventured.

She stopped and stared at him in silence.

'Maybe not so nice after all.' He suppressed a smile. 'Aren't you going out today?'

'Saturdays suck. Always.' She hesitated for a moment.

'Some people would disagree. But you must have good reason to think so.'

'Some people's Saturdays may be good. Not mine.'

'It's worth trying to change this.'

'If it was up to me, I would have done it. A long time ago.' She decided to sit down on a chair next to his. 'You can make your own decisions.'

'Troubles are only mine too. It would be good to share them sometimes. With someone who'd listen.'

'My parents don't listen to me. They only tell me things.'

'What about your friends?'

'Don't have many here. All my good friends are in Poland. And we're not going there until Christmas.'

'What about your school friends?'

'Don't have many friends at school. Me and Julia stick together. We never go to other girls' homes.' She started carving something with her nail into the surface of the wooden table. 'Other girls are busy after school and on Saturday, they play tennis and go to art and dance classes. Have sleepovers. Go to the movies.'

'You could go the cinema with Julia.'

'Dad wouldn't let us go on our own. London is such a dangerous place,' she mimicked her father's expression. 'So different from Poland.' The groove on the table was already half a centimetre deep. 'I would love to go the cinema with friends but there is no way he'd let me.'

'Would my company be acceptable to you? And to Julia?'

Basia lifted her head. She looked at Kuba, judging whether he meant this as a joke. 'Would you do that?'

'It would be fun. But you need to check with your parents first.'

'You don't think they would …'

'All you need to do is ask.'

'Kuba, you're so cool! I thought that all adults think alike.' She was getting up to go back to the house, when she froze on the half turn.

'Kuba. Look. Here, near the fence. Kitty, kitty … Whaa. He is gorgeous.'

A large ginger cat was strolling along the stone path running across the garden. His red fur shone like a copper pan in the sunshine.

'The neighbours must have adopted a cat. I wonder what his name is. Kitty, kitty, come here,' she squealed.

The cat stopped and turned his head in Basia's direction. He lifted his head, squinted his large green eyes and meowed a greeting.

'He is saying hello,' she yelped in delight.

'Cats can be treacherous,' warned Kuba.

'He likes me.' Basia was already kneeling on the path and running her hands down the cat's lustrous coat.

Zofia, who at this moment had come into the garden, halted in surprise. Without lifting her eyes from the cat, Basia said: 'The neighbours got themselves a cat and he came over to make friends with us.'

Astonished with the sudden change in her daughter's mood, Zofia said, 'A lovely cat, but he may scratch.'

'You wouldn't do such a thing, my lovely. Would you? We're friends already. I'll bring him some milk.'

'We can't keep a cat in the house. You know Mrs Patel's rules.'

'We don't need to keep him. He lives next door. But there is nothing wrong with being friendly with the neighbours.'

'Basia, he may not like milk,' suggested Kuba. 'I read some- where that cats in England only drink water and eat pet food. From a can.'

'I'm going to test this,' called Basia, heading for the kitchen.

Zofia looked at Kuba reclining on two garden chairs. 'Her moods change so fast.'

'Aren't all teenagers like this?' Kuba wasn't sure whether he was expected to offer his opinion on the subject.

'My two sons were easier going.'

Basia reappeared holding a cereal bowl filled to the brim with milk. The cat remained seated in the same spot as she'd left him. She carefully put the bowl down in front of him. The cat looked at her and slowly lowered his head into the dish. His small pink tongue started working very fast.

'He likes milk!' The three of them turned round. In the open window of his ground floor room stood Adam, with a plastic razor suspended an inch from his chin.

'He is a cat, Adam.' Basia was first to respond. 'It's the neigh- bours' cat but he came to say hello to us.'

The cat stopped drinking and looked in Adam's direction. He narrowed his eyes and meowed.

'You see how friendly he is.'

Zofia stood looking at her daughter fussing around the cat.

Watching them, Kuba hoped that the cat would visit again.

'If you keep feeding him, he will be back again,' said Zofia not wishing to be seen encouraging her daughter to break the house rules. She looked at Kuba, who was clearly amused with the situation. Even Adam, usually distant and uncommunicative, was showing some interest in the cat.

The loud shrill of the telephone broke the silence. Zofia hurried back to the house.

Kuba looked at his watch and, stretching himself, said: 'Time for me to go. I have an afternoon shift today.' Basia stopped stroking the cat.

'It's a shame you have to work on Saturdays.'

'It's a good day for me. I have plenty of regular customers at the weekend. But we have a deal.' He winked at her. 'I will be back by six.' Then pointing in the direction of the kitchen, he said: 'Go and do your bit now.'

Twenty minutes later, Kuba was closing the front door of 26 Cuckoohill Road. Changed and refreshed, he was walking to the car when his mobile phone rang. He recognized the number of Century Cabs. The heat was rising and he hoped to cool the car down for a few minutes before heading off.

'Hi. What's up?' The new girl on the switchboard was explaining in a high pitched voice that Mr Roberts of Lexicon Avenue had just called asking to be picked up in half an hour. 'Kuba, he asked for you. Can you do it?'

'Sure, I'll be there on time.' He opened all the car's windows and doors and switched the air conditioning on full blast. As he sat for a couple of minutes, forcing the heat out of the car, he smiled. He had been driving Ashley Roberts for over two years and he enjoyed the acquaintance. Ashley was an actor and dancer who performed in various West End productions. The summer season was not kind to the arts and Ashley had recently been down on his luck. However, he must be performing now if Kuba's services were required.

The moment Kuba pulled up at the front steps of a tall Victorian mansion, Ashley appeared at the top of the stairs. Kuba was always amazed how softly he moved. While other customers would walk or run down the steps, Ashley swept down, with his fair hair flying behind him. With the same graceful movement, he opened the back door and swung a large holdall onto the back seat. In a second, his smiling face appeared in Kuba's mirror.

'It's good to see you Mr Roberts. Where are we going today?'

'The Palladium. Good to see you too, Kuba. What a glorious day. Shame to spend it working.'

'Yeah, but weekends are good for business.'

'And for me.'

'Glad to hear it, sir.' said Kuba, turning the car around.

'Kuba, isn't it time you stopped calling me Mr Roberts or sir. You know my first name.'

'Yes, si ... Ashley.'

'So how's business? How are you getting on with your language course?'

'Well, I may take some exams in the autumn and then decide what to do next.'

'Your English is already pretty good. Much better than some of the Latinos dancing in my current production. What would you like to do? I mean in the future. Once you stop cabbing.'

'I enjoyed my job in Poland.'

'What was it?'

'I worked as a physiotherapist. For a while, I specialized in sport injuries.'

'Good God, Kuba. You must go back to that. The moment I saw you, I knew that there was more to you than driving a cab.'

'My English wasn't good enough.'

'It won't hold you back now. You will find plenty of customers among my lot. Ankle sprains, knee injuries, hamstring pulls and plenty more to put right.'

Ashley Roberts was now leaning forward, his animated face grimacing between the front seats.

'You must go back to your profession. You owe it to yourself.'

In twenty minutes they arrived at the stage door of the Palladium. Ashley looked at the meter and took out a couple of notes from his wallet. 'Please keep the change. And find out about those re-training courses.' Then he put his hand on Kuba's arm and asked: 'Do you enjoy musicals? Musical theatre,

I mean ...?'

'Yes ...' the question took Kuba by surprise. 'I have been to a couple of musicals in Poland ... I have seen many posters for musicals in London.'

'I'm sure you did. I am in some of them. And I can easily get you a ticket — if you'd like to come.'

Feeling Ashley's hand on his arm, Kuba hesitated. Then a sudden recollection of the morning in the garden flashed in his mind. Basia would love a surprise.

'It's very kind of you to suggest.'

'My pleasure. I'd love to be of use. You have always been so flexible.' Ashley reached into his bag and took out a small silver holder from which he produced his business card. He took a pen and scribbled a number.

'This is my mobile number on which you can always reach me. Don't hesitate to use it.'

After two and half hours in the dark, the bright lights of the foyer were blinding them. Carried by a crowd of people dazzled by the epic film, they were moving slowly towards the exit. The girls were surprisingly quiet, exchanging singular comments from time to time. He noticed that both Basia and Julia were wearing some make-up which they had probably put on when they visited the bathroom before the film. He didn't remember seeing the glossy lipstick and heavy mascara when he was picking them up for the evening. Both Zofia and Jan appeared rather amused with the idea of Kuba taking the girls to see *Jurassic Park: The Lost World,* and yet they didn't oppose it. Whether it was the reputation of the film or Kuba's good name in Zofia's books, he would never know. Basia, making herself comfortable on the front seat of his car admitted that her parents' reaction was a great surprise.

Now looking at the pensive expression on the girls' faces, Kuba suggested: 'What about some ice-cream to finish off the evening?'

'Are you sure?' Basia's eyes were smiling. Julia was discreetly looking into her purse.

'It's my treat, girls.' Seeing the long queue leading towards the ice-cream counter, Kuba suggested: 'Why don't you sit down on the chairs by the window and I will wave to you when I get to the front?'

'We can wait with you, if you like.' Julia was trying to appear grown up.

'A good idea, but it may last longer than you think. I promise to call you when I will get to the front.'

The girls looked at each other and giggled but they obediently walked away in the direction of the empty seats.

The queue was moving very slowly. Kuba picked up a leaflet reviewing upcoming movies. The evening had whetted his appetite for a big drama. He hadn't seen one for a while. He fancied a war movie next.

Twenty minutes later, he was still queuing. In front of him was a father with three kids who couldn't decide on the selection of flavours they wanted and a tightly entwined couple totally oblivious to their surroundings. Kuba turned around to check what the girls were doing. His heart leapt. He couldn't see them. He looked around and scanned the milling crowd. Amongst passing girls in the summer outfits he couldn't see Basia's red top or Julia's yellow dress. He realised that the chairs where the girls were sitting were hidden behind a group of rowdy boys. He felt hot and out of breath realising what a fool he was. There weren't many young girls on their own in the cinema foyer. As he strode in the direction of the group, he heard a remark about 'cool birds' and a sudden explosion of laughter. He broke through the gathering and saw Basia and Julia sitting together, their shoulders almost touching, in the middle of a row of empty seats. They were surrounded by a group of jeering youths. Basia was anxiously looking up from under her dark fringe while Julia was wearing a strained smile, attempting to treat the situation as a joke. In two steps, Kuba was at their side. He took the girls by the arm and hissed through his teeth: 'We're off now. Sorry it took so long.'

'Is that your boyfriend? Such an old geezer?!' This remark was accompanied by a whistle. It was followed by a roar of laughter. By then, Kuba was dragging the girls behind him. 'Let's get out of here. Quickly.'

'The boyfriend's losing his temper. A Russian? Probably a

mafia boss.' A spotty youth with slicked back hair was the ringleader. 'Ciao Lolitas. Take care.' Kuba felt a sudden urge to put his hands around the youth's throat but resisted thinking that this would only make the scene more entertaining for the rest of the gang.

Only when they found themselves in the street, did Kuba stop. 'Sorry about the ice-cream. It was stupid of me to leave you alone.'

'It was our fault. We shouldn't have responded to their idiotic jokes,' said Julia. 'You're cool Kuba. And the film was great.'

When they reached the car parked in a side street, the girls slipped into the back seat, quiet and subdued. They sat in silence the whole journey home. Looking back in the mirror, he could see their serious faces by the light of the street lamps. The experience had clearly frightened them and he blamed himself for this. He thought about their parents and what their reaction might have been if they had seen the girls besieged by the jeering youths. He was such a fool. An old geezer with two dolly birds. It wasn't even funny.

They were dropping Julia off first. Her mother thanked Kuba profusely for taking care of her daughter. He couldn't look her straight in the eye and just nodded. When the door was about to close Julia's head appeared in the gap.

'Kuba, it was great. Don't worry.' With an apologetic smile, she softly closed the door.

Chapter 7

Maja, August 1997

Every morning, they came to the pub around nine. First to tidy up after the previous evening and then to make fresh salads and a couple of starters for the afternoon. After Friday and Saturday nights there was more cleaning up to do than usual. The King's Head had a couple of large function rooms upstairs and these were frequently hired for private events, including stag and hen parties. Sometimes, unusual items, and not just underwear, were left behind in the most unexpected places. For large events, Jacek, the pub manager, would hire extra help. However, on most days, between the two of them they managed to tidy and clean the premises and prepare some simple food for the bar. Then Jola and Maja had free time until four when the regulars started coming in.

That morning, Jacek surprised Maja by asking her to come to his office before leaving for lunch. Was it going to be a business-as-usual meeting or should she anticipate problems? she wondered as she walked up the creaky stairs. She knocked lightly. No answer. She knocked again and pressed the handle. Surrounded by piles of papers and open folders, Jacek was working at his desk. Energetically tapping the keys of a battered calculator with the end of his pen, he didn't hear her enter the office. For a moment, Maja stood in the doorway, not wishing to interrupt.

'You wanted to see me,' she said. Only then did Jacek lift his head.

'Maja. Thanks for coming. Is everything good with you?'

'Everything is fine. Tidied and ready for the afternoon.'

'And what about yourself?'

This conversation obviously wasn't going to be about work.

'I'm fine. Enjoying the job.'

'That's good. Have you managed to find yourself a room to rent?'

'No, not yet. But at the weekend I'm going to meet some people renting a house in Greenford.'

'Excellent. Do that. But I also have a proposition for you. You don't need to give me an answer now. It's just another option to think about.'

Maja swallowed.

'You know I live about ten minutes from the pub. My wife, young son and new baby just went to Poland to stay with my mother-in-law. In addition to the pub, now I have a house to mind, full of plants to water, a fish tank and a garden to look after. I'm not good at this sort of thing and I will be in trouble when Elżybieta comes back and finds everything withered away.'

Maja stood listening, her thoughts racing ahead of Jacek's words.

'My family won't be back for two months and I wondered whether you would like to consider a room, rent-free, in my house. But with a string attached, as the English say. It would mean helping me look after the house.'

This was better news than she anticipated. If all he needed was help around the house.

'Maja, I have no other motives here. I would be very grateful for your help. Honestly. Of course, if it wouldn't be too much to ask. Please take some time to think about it.'

'OK, I will. I'll give you an answer tomorrow.'

Then before leaving, she turned around. 'Jacek. Thank you. For thinking about me. Really, I am grateful.'

The midday sun was still very strong, although the summer was coming to an end. She felt it burning her back through her T-shirt. Ealing High Street was busy as usual. The pavements were brimming with people attracted by the end of season sales. She checked her watch and started running. She had only five minutes left. Her appointment with the admissions secretary at the West London School of English was at quarter past twelve. She hoped that there would be a class for her level of ability in the early afternoon. This was the only time she was free during the day.

She was now running so fast that she almost missed the entrance to the school. Her first impression of it when she had come here a week ago didn't conform to an image of any school she had seen before. In Poland, schools and colleges were accommodated in buildings of substantial proportions. They had big entrances and wide, usually echoey corridors. Even the old ones with a shabby exterior usually gave the impression of solidity inside.

The entrance to the West London School of English was a single glass door, not dissimilar to the one leading to a sandwich shop on the left and to a small solicitors' office on the right. Behind the door was a narrow white corridor leading to an equally narrow staircase which spiralled upwards to the first floor. Only then was a visitor's mind put at rest that they were in the right place. A spacious reception and waiting area were furnished with a red and gold sofa and a couple of armchairs that probably originated from a more intimate interior. The bright yellow walls were crowded with shelves housing brochures and information sheets in all the colours of the rainbow.

A busy reception desk was manned by one of the teachers. His informal clothing and relaxed manner fitted well with the rest of this educational establishment. He gave Maja a number of forms to complete and an assessment test.

The classrooms of the West London School of English were also very different from those in which she had sat before. The room was filled with plastic chairs with small wooden flaps that could be raised and opened to create work surfaces. Two oriental-looking girls were already sitting in the room. With great concentration, they were completing their forms; curtains of ebony hair obscuring their faces.

She became aware of someone's stare. She lifted her head and her eyes met the gaze of a girl sitting at the opposite wall, also with a pile of papers on her lap. In an instant, her mouth opened in a wide smile, revealing a set of perfect teeth. Maja smiled back and the girl got up from her seat, making the mop of brown curls dance around her face. She thrust her hand out to Maja.

'I'm Sylvia, from Milan. It's my third time in London. Are you also signing up for this college?'

'Yeah ..., just now,' said Maja with one hand pressing down her papers on a tiny table to prevent them cascading down to the floor. 'Nice to meet you. I'm Maja. I ...'

'Don't tell me,' exclaimed the girl. Let me guess ... You're Swedish. No, your accent is softer. Czech?'

'Close. I'm Polish.

'Like *Papa*! John Paul II is amazing in so many ways. Speaks Italian like an Italian, as well as many other languages. My parents went to an audience at the Vatican and told me ...'

'Sylvia, let's finish with these papers and do the test. I'm free until three thirty.'

In fact, everything was over by two, including paperwork and interviews. Maja secured a place in an advanced class, which was held at midday. Sylvia was accepted into a group a level below, but also managed to get herself into a 12pm to 3pm session. She worked in an Italian restaurant run by a friend of her parents and she was free until five.

After an hour talking to Sylvia in a small leafy square just off the high street, Maja felt as though she knew her all her life. She was a tourism graduate and came to London for a few months to improve her English. She managed to convince her parents, who financed the trip, that this was essential for her future career. She was taking her time to decide what she wanted to do, before committing herself to any job.

Sylvia loved London — its social scene with clubs, pubs and discos and the city's cosmopolitan culture. She believed that all these social interactions would benefit her in the long term.

'Where are you staying?' she asked Maja.

'In West Ealing. Temporarily, with a couple of Polish friends.'

'So you can come and go as you please?'

'Yes, but all of us work long hours, so we're busy most of the time.'

This impressed Sylvia who was staying (rent free) in the house of family friends. This cramped her social life — guests were not welcome and she had to be back home by midnight. She was determined to rent her own room as soon as she had earned enough money, which she hoped would be soon.

By seven o'clock, the King's Head was humming like a beehive and the best tables were already taken. The room was slowly filling up with a cloud of cigarette smoke. The smell of beer and spirits was mingling with a rich aroma of percolated coffee. Somewhere in between, there was a freshness of cucumber and the richness of salad mayonnaise. Shortly, all these aromas would be dominated by the deep satisfying smell of warm *bigos* and all its ingredients: rich meat, wild mushrooms and red wine.

From the bar, above the hum of voices and tinkling glasses, rose Alina's low throaty laugh. She was the chief barmaid and the reigning queen of the King's Head. On first name terms with all the regular customers, with a mane of blonde curls and a low cut T-shirt revealing her best assets, she was laughing loudly and listening to her clientele. She spoke English with a strong Polish accent and wouldn't be held back by the rules of grammar.

'Weeliam, great see you again. The usual?'

A short middle aged man with a bald patch and tired office clothes was staring at Alina admiringly. He was pointing to the box of crisp packets.

'Weeliam, we are in lack of venegar crisps tonight. Would you want a packet of Marmeet crisps instead?' William was happy to accept any crisps from Alina and, having secured a stool at the end of the bar, made himself comfortable on it.

Meanwhile, Jola and Maja were busy taking orders for food at the other end of the counter. Although the menu was cosmopolitan, with lasagne, chicken curry and stir fries being firm favourites, the King's Head had many Polish dishes such as *bigos*, *golonka* or *pierogi*, which had become very popular with the regulars. Together with Polish beers, Polish satellite television and Alina's assets, they were known as the pub's unique attractions.

Maja became accustomed to the requests of her English customers to explain 'what this *bigos* dish is all about' and learnt the names of the ingredients of all the Polish dishes in English. From the way a customer was looking at the menu board above her head, she was able to guess what explanation would be required. Yet the portly man who was now skimming the board, while at the same time looking around, didn't appear interested in the food. She had seen him before in the pub, but never on his own and not on a weekday. Eventually, with some hesitation, he approached her.

'Are you Maja?'

'Yes. What can I do for you?'

'Your friend said,' the man nodded in the direction of Alina 'that you're looking for a room to rent.' Calling Alina her friend was a sweeping generalisation, thought Maja. It was also remarkable that Alina always knew everyone's business in the King's Head.

'Yeah, in the long term, I am.'

'We, that's my wife and I, rent a large house in Greenford. With other people, of course. One of the rooms has just become vacant. It's a nice house in a quiet neighbourhood. My wife is responsible to our landlady for managing it. So we don't want just anyone to join us. You know you can get very strange people from an advertisement.'

'Of course.'

'I heard from Jacek, your boss, that you're a nice girl. The sort of girl we would welcome in our house.'

'Mr ...'

'Kowal, Jan Kowal,' the man stretched his hand over the counter to introduce himself. He smiled. He obviously found the whole situation very awkward and was relieved that the introductions were almost over. He had been looking over his shoulder the whole time. Clearly, he wasn't one of the smooth talkers who asked bar girls when their evening off was.

'Mr Kowal, thank you very much for the suggestion but today someone offered me a room, very close to this place and I am going to accept it.'

'It's such a pity.' The man looked very disappointed.

'However, this room is only for two months so if your offer still stands in a couple of months, I would like you to consider me.' Jan Kowal had a very sincere face and Maja hated to let him down. She wasn't sure how Jacek's suggestion was going to work. She shouldn't be burning her bridges.

'Mr Kowal, perhaps you could give me your number so I can contact you, if my situation changes.'

Chapter 8

Maja, October 1997

She was glad that the summer weather was coming to an end and Jacek's garden would require less attention and time. She had other interests and plans now. Not that Jacek wasn't appreciative of her efforts. Seeing how much time she spent tending the garden, he started paying her. One morning, after a late night drinking session with his friends, when the patio and surrounding flower beds were littered with beer cans, she found a note of apology on the kitchen counter. After a couple of days, another card was propped up against the sugar bowl and next to it lay a small parcel tied up with red ribbon. It contained a bottle of Estée Lauder's Sunflowers.

In comparison to the garden, the housework was relatively undemanding. Jacek stressed that he didn't expect her to do more than vacuum and dust the house once a week, and without putting much effort into it. He shut a couple of rooms upstairs and suggested that they forgot about them until a few days before his family came back home. He was out most of the time, working or entertaining his suppliers. Most afternoons and evenings, when she didn't work, Maja had the house to herself. She slept in a small guest room, spending the rest of her free time downstairs in the lounge watching Jacek's massive TV or studying on the table in the dinning room with a splendid view of the garden.

'My parents never took holidays. With the exception of Chinese New Year.'

'So you have never gone away *en famille?*' Sophie was incredulous. Her large family, together with two dogs, pots, pans and bedding, were stuffed every year into an old camper van for a three week holiday by the French seaside.

'No, never. I only went for school trips. And with my aunt, to visit our family in mainland China. But that wasn't much fun.' Jane, who came from Hong Kong, wondered why others found it so surprising.'

They were enjoying their break together, sitting in the leafy square on the benches arranged in a semi-circle. It was the first week of October and the Indian summer made the school corridors seem even more stuffy than usual.

They studied at different levels but started hanging out together once they discovered they shared more than the desire to perfect their English. The blonde, long-legged Lena, who came from Vilnius to work as an *au pair* for a doctor's family in Ealing, had the same penchant for London's night life as the sensuous Sevki who was taking a break from running her family's travel agency in Turkey.

Maja's encounter with Andreas made her mistrustful of Costa, who came from Greece and revealed that he worked as a bouncer in a night club. Built like an American refrigerator and always wearing a brown corduroy jacket, he was a quiet boy and proved to be a very diligent student. He hoped to join his uncle's real estate business in Rhodes and earn his living selling holiday property to English-speaking clients. He rarely volunteered his opinions.

Meanwhile, Stefan's voice was hanging in the air all the time. The Hungarian felt compelled to add his point of view to every conversation. He developed an instant affinity with Maja, informing the group that the Poles and the Hungarians had always been political allies, sharing kings and some remarkable queens.

'My least favourite holidays were spent with my Austrian uncle who lived in Tyrol. He must have been an Austrian boy scout. He made it his mission to instil in me the principles of physical health, in harmony with nature.'

'What do you mean?' asked Sevki. 'My relatives sought harmony with nature on a shaded terrace with a glass of *raki*.'

'We went camping in the mountains, carrying our sleeping bags, pots and pans and a cooking hob. We used to get up at dawn and wash in mountain streams. I still shiver thinking about it. Unsurprisingly, we felt warm for the rest of the day.'

'It couldn't have been very relaxing.'

'It wasn't meant to be relaxing. The whole thing was about endurance and discipline of body and mind.'

Sylvia moved closer to Maja. 'That reminds me, I have to go back to the restaurant this afternoon. I'm really sorry to let you down. I was looking forward to our sightseeing. Victorio has asked me to help with some function they're holding tonight.'

'It's a shame,' said Maja, trying not to sound disappointed. 'But it can't be helped.'

They had been planning to walk along the South Bank, cross the river and then see St Paul's cathedral.

'We'll do something nice next week.'

The school bell rang through open windows. They gathered the remains of their lunch and reluctantly went indoors.

In the bright sunshine of early afternoon, the monumental façade of St Paul's cathedral appeared more magnificent than she had imagined. The images she had seen on postcards and in her English textbook hadn't reflected the grandeur of the building she was now facing. She travelled along Fleet Street on the top deck of a bus when the road suddenly widened, revealing a breathtaking view of the basilica. The two tier elevation, supported by gigantic columns, was grey from city pollution and the walls behind them were almost black. This only made it look more imposing.

The square in front of the cathedral and its wide sweeping stairs were crowded by tourists. They milled around, stopped and stared, craning their necks to seize a view of the whole building. She heard some women squealing with excitement. They pointed to the best spot where they could photograph themselves against the background of the gigantic structure.

Maja thought that it was like a scene from a historical film populated with too many extras which moved aimlessly until the amplified voice of a director called them to action. She wished that she had come early in the morning before the cathedral was swamped with people. She hoped, perhaps naively, to find St Paul's veiled by mist, with flocks of pigeons circling above the heads of old ladies and children who came to feed them, like Paul and Janet Banks in *Mary Poppins.*

She sat at the top of the grand staircase and looked at the scene before her. She thought about the people who walked up these steps, making history and yet carrying with them their human frailties and fears. She imagined the pomp of the great state processions which passed through the monumental central doors of the cathedral and the funeral corteges of great states-men who were honoured with silence by the waiting crowds. She was so insignificant here. Even the people around her didn't notice her existence. She felt invisible and alone. Alone in one of the most busy places in London.

She noticed that the light had changed. An orange glow was setting on the building. The cathedral would be closing shortly. She got up and hurried in through the side door. At first, she couldn't see anything. She breathed in a familiar scent of can-dles and the cool damp air of old buildings. Gradually, her eyes became accustomed to the low light and she gasped. She was standing at the end of the central nave which, flanked by massive pillars like an avenue, led to the central dome. Beyond it stood dark choir stalls and at the end of the breathtaking vista, there was a magnificent altar. Its ornate canopy was supported by four gilded columns. The sheer size of this specta-cle was mesmerising. She never thought that a church could be so enormous.

She felt a hand on her shoulder. She turned around to face a man in a long gown. In a hushed voice, he explained that the cathedral was being closed to visitors and advised her to come earlier next time. She felt like a child whose dream had been broken.

Seeing her disappointment, the verger said: 'OK, you can stand here for a couple more minutes. But no longer.'

'Thank you. Thank you very much.' She was grateful but it was like being offered a drop of water while a bucketful had been removed from reach.

She didn't move but once again lifted her eyes to the cavern-ous ceiling above her. Only then did she notice that, despite its enormous size, the cathedral wasn't dark at all, as the tall windows in the side aisles let a lot of light in. Now she could see the pattern of the ornate mosaics covering the drum of the dome. Large nymphs were gracefully dancing above her head.

Unexpectedly, a crushing thunder split the stillness of the cathedral. She almost jumped. She saw other heads jerking upwards, searching for the source of the sound. The second chord came, then the third and fourth. Deep thunderous notes were rolling down from the old organ suspended on both sides of the choir nave. The notes of Bach's *Toccata* spiralled up, and after a moment, started cascading down like a fast flowing brook, filling the air with the energy of an electric storm. The visitors stood spellbound.

Travelling back home, Maja had in her ears the tones of Bach's music. She couldn't have imagined that there was so much energy in it. Was it that the cathedral was a perfect place to release it?

It was getting dark when she turned into Elm Grove and the street was already very quiet. She was planning to tell Sylvia that they should go together to see the cathedral properly next time. Perhaps even next week, if they had a free afternoon on the same day.

Lost in her thoughts, she didn't notice that there were lights on in all the upstairs bedrooms until she found herself in front of Jacek's house. This was unusual as Jacek should have been in the King's Head, at least until midnight. Her heart stopped. Was it better to call the police straight away or to run to the neighbours and ask for help?

The window of the master bedroom was flung open and some items of clothing were hurled through it. She heard a high pitched woman's voice shouting abuse at someone inside. After a moment, she realised that the screams were in Polish and the muffled male voice in the background was Jacek's.

'I leave you for a couple of months and you get yourself a whore to keep you company.'

'I told you. She only helped me with the house.'

'And kept the bed warm for you!'

Just then, another garment landed on the front lawn.

'Calm down woman. And close the window before neighbours call the police.'

'Too late to start caring what the neighbours think. You allowed this *kurwa* to live in our house all this time. When people told me what was going on, I couldn't believe it.'

There was a thump inside and it was followed by the sound of glass being smashed. Then the window in the small bedroom was opened with great force and a couple of Maja's English textbooks landed at her feet. She stood in the middle of the path, paralysed with shock, clutching her handbag to her stomach. Then several pieces of her clothing flew through the window. She heard the woman's voice: 'She is here. Your slut.'

A moment later, Jacek appeared on the path. His lip was swollen and a red smudge ran from his temple to his chin. His shirt was stained with blood. Taking Maja by her arm, he walked her to the car parked in the street. Then he came back with a cardboard box and started collecting her things from the ground. When he eventually took a seat beside her he said: 'I'm so sorry about all this, Maja. I really am. I will help you get out of here.'

Chapter 9

Adam, November 1997

As autumn set in, the days became shorter and the mornings got colder and darker, making it even more difficult to get up after a hard day. Adam dressed himself in semi-darkness and fed the cat before letting him out through the window. It surprised him that they had been able to continue this charade for so long. No one had discovered that Ginger spent the nights sleeping at the foot of Adam's bed. Perhaps they were lucky because everyone accepted that Adam kept himself to himself.

He went to the kitchen, took his sandwiches out of the fridge and slipped out onto Cuckoohill Road. The chilly air of the early autumn morning enfolded him like a damp coat. Shivering, he forced his cap deeper over his ears and pulled the zip of his anorak all the way up to his chin. Years of working outdoors had left him with bouts of rheumatic pains which flared up when damp weather set in. The joints of his hands were already swollen and some days he had trouble holding a screwdriver. Yet he had always despised self-pity and believed that every profession had its costs. The ointment which he bought in the chemist with Zofia's help would have to do for now.

The streets were still empty but a group of people had already gathered at the bus stop. They were mostly men whose stained combat trousers and thick soled boots betrayed their association with the building trade. Adam was familiar with some of the men, having seen them at the same place every morning. Yet no one felt inclined to talk and after a couple of nods they stood silent, occasionally glancing in the same direction.

'Here it comes!' A couple of Irishmen who spotted the bus took their place at the front of the queue. Everyone followed and in a moment they were all climbing aboard. From time to time, a new passenger threw a 'hi' or *cześć* but no one was willing to make small talk at such an early hour. They sat in silence, looking through the window and nodding off occasionally. This pattern repeated itself every morning and Adam became so familiar with this route that even with his eyes closed, he could say where they were just from the way the bus shook when taking sharp corners.

He thought about that Saturday morning in early March when he saw a small crowd in front of a mini-market in Kościelisko. Hugging themselves against the icy wind blowing from the Tatra mountains they stood silently, studying a notice pinned up on a freshly erected board. Adam, taller than average, stood behind and craning his neck above the hats and scarves, tried to see what had captivated the interest of the locals. Above four paragraphs of black print, there was a much bigger sign that read: Commercial units for sale.

A new commercial pavilion was to be erected in Kościelisko and the developers were selling eight units pre-construction at substantially lower prices.

As he read and re-read these four paragraphs Adam felt a sudden dryness in his throat. An idea which had crossed his mind a few times before now appeared to him with great clarity. That non-existent commercial pavilion could be the opportunity he had been waiting for. A chance to become his own man, no longer Bukowski's browbeaten son-in-law.

With a pencil, he carefully copied the phone number from the board onto a cigarette packet. He was vaguely aware of the unease the offer caused in the crowd.

'They want to con people by offering non-existing properties.'

'The builders may take the money and run away. Who knows?'

'They think we are fools in Kościelisko.'

'Shut up Kostrzewa. If you read the papers, you would know how business is done today.'

'The rules of honest business don't change.'

The spring was still young in the mountains. Despite the smell of thawing earth in the air, the roadside ditches were full of dirty snow. People were bracing themselves against the chilly wind, putting their collars up, yet Adam felt like he'd just had a shot of vodka on an empty stomach. Blood was racing to his head and his cheeks were burning. For a long time, he hadn't experienced such a feeling of excitement.

He still remembered that sense of elation, when he finally made a telephone call to the developer and heard the conditions of sale.

'Thirty percent up front and then ten percent instalments, paid every second month when construction begins.'

It was a lot of money. Even if he emptied their savings account, there would only be enough money for a deposit. He didn't earn enough at Bukowski's farm to meet the bi-monthly payments. Where could he turn to for a loan? Just then he heard Sowa talking in the Ondraszkowa Izba about his brother who went to London to earn money for the modernisation of his farm and he was doing very well. Even Sowa himself was thinking about joining him.

'They need builders and electricians in London.'

'Polish electricians?'

'Of course. When you have the skill, it doesn't matter what language you speak. The guys who managed to cross the border make good money.'

Adam asked Sowa for his brother's number. The same night, when everyone went to bed, he sat at the kitchen table and on a sheet torn from his son's exercise book, made his calculations.

It wasn't easy at first. Even when he finally found a job working for a Polish builder, he quickly realised that, together with the rest of his workmates, he was being exploited by his employer. Black market labourers worked longer and were paid less than both the local and the Irish builders. Yet it was all worthwhile for him. He had already paid three instalments and by next spring, he would be the owner of his own shop premises. He needed to stay for another year to earn enough money to buy some stock for his hardware shop. His plan was slowly taking shape.

Working for Karol was never dull. His boss simultaneously managed a number of building sites and moved his workforce between them. To meet pressing deadlines, his builders, electricians, carpenters and decorators, who at times did each others' jobs, were transferred between Karol's construction sites.

Today, a big group was furiously working in the large basement of a four storey house in Putney, which a month ago, didn't even have a cellar. Its owner, a city banker, was too busy to go to the local gym in the morning, so he hired Karol to alter the foundations and construct a squash court underneath his house. A few months ago, Adam wouldn't have believed that such a thing was possible but now, steel girders were supporting the ground floor. He heard that in a house down the road, another builder was creating a swimming pool in the basement.

The client, who had an alternative residence somewhere else, was supposed to inspect the progress of the work that morning and Karol was anxious to show him that the project was progressing according to schedule. This meant that even the electrician was asked to lay cables in the bare concrete walls so that the cavernous interior could be lit up whilst the banker was inspecting his dream. Of course, everything would be stripped off again and the work would proceed at its usual pace and in proper order, as soon as he was out of sight.

'*Kurwa*, who has poured water on the floor?' Karol roared from the back of the cavernous basement. 'In this weather, it will never dry out before midday.'

'I was planning to polish the plaster on the wall, as you asked,' said Darek, the youngest member of the team.

'But did you have to slosh this stuff on the floor? Mindless ass. The client will be here in an hour.'

'I didn't want to pour it on his lawn.'

'Just shut up. I don't have the energy to argue with you today. Get on with tidying up this bloody mess.'

Two of the youngest 'all-rounders' rushed to help Darek. With old rags they started mopping the concrete floor. Other men went back to their jobs. Adam retrieved a tape from his tool box and began measuring the windowless gap coming onto the garden.

A sudden ring from a phone echoed loudly in the empty basement. Karol quickly reached into the pocket of his leather jacket and pulled out the phone.

'Hello. Yes, Karol speaking ...'

Karol's English was adequate for communicating with his clients but it quickly deteriorated when he was under pressure. This was obviously one of those days when things weren't going as well as expected.

'I'm hearing you. I'm in the underground. Just wait a minute.' Karol rushed out into the garden through the doorless gap in the back wall. He continued talking agitatedly as he walked away from the house, his voice rising into a shriek.

'The boss is having a bad day,' remarked Darek.

'This guy is giving him a hard time. He wants the project to be finished now,' said Wiktor, who had worked for Karol for over three years.

'And if we don't finish it on time?' challenged Darek. 'It's pissing down every other day. It will take ages for the walls to dry.'

'We will be using electric blow-dryers. The client will be paying for it. And if we don't finish the job, Karol won't get the money and we will all be in the shit.' Wiktor knew how business was done in Karol's company.

'We have rent to pay and food to buy, and other stuff.'

'You worry especially about this other stuff,' challenged Paweł.

'It must be worth our while to keep working here,' said Darek.

'You'll have to borrow. But let's not worry about that yet,' Wiktor calmly meet his gaze.

The conversation stopped as soon as they heard Karol's steps approaching the house. As he entered the basement, his face was pale and jaw clenched. His fingers were tightly wrapped around his mobile phone.

'I want everything to be ready by quarter to twelve. And no rubbish left lying around. I will be back in half an hour. Wiktor, you're in charge.'

He turned on his heel and quickly walked out into the garden and then along the side of the house. His boots were pounding hard on the stone path. In a moment, they heard him slamming the door of his car and the engine roaring. There was screech of tyres on the road and he was gone.

'I wonder what that's all about?' Darek was unmoved.

'It won't be long before you'll find out. We'll all find out. It's Friday, isn't it? Get back to your work,' Wiktor commanded.

Friday was pay day so it was easy to judge how Karol's company was faring. Adam thought about the fourth instalment which he would have to pay at the end of the following week. And the monthly rent was due the coming weekend. After a good summer, things were getting more difficult now. The rainy weather delayed progress on many sites and the amount of work they were handling was thinning down. However, he would have to manage somehow, even if this meant eating only sandwiches for the next two weeks and walking home to save on a bus fare.

Their fears were confirmed at the end of the day. The banker wasn't happy that his squash court would not be ready before Christmas. They also learnt from Wiktor that an Indian woman whose house in West Ealing they were extending and redecorating refused to pay a penny more until at least the bedrooms were ready. Karol had 'cash flow problems' and this was going to affect them sooner or later.

At the end of the day, everyone received just fifty pounds to get them through the next seven days and a promise that they would get the rest in the next week's pay packet.

'I hoped to take Susannah out tonight,' muttered Piotr as they waited at the bus stop.

'Is she your latest bird?' Darek was clearly impressed. 'An English one. Well done. But be careful they tend to be high maintenance.'

'Leave it out. She's a nice girl …'

'You should be thinking what you're going to eat next week,' suggested Wiktor.

'I will. Next week. But I am going to enjoy this one. Life is short.'

'Too short indeed,' thought Adam, stepping off the bus in Greenford. He felt he'd wasted too much of it already. He couldn't let his big chance slip away from him. Like other things …

Ding dong. The door chime in Mrs Shah's shop broke his train of thought. Adam searched his pockets for a scrap of paper on which he'd scribbled the list of things he needed to buy. At the end of the day, he was tired and his memory wasn't too good these days. Without a list he would be buying things he didn't need, especially when followed by Mrs Shah's enquiring eyes.

He went straight to the Polish food corner and started putting things from the list into his basket. He poised his hand over the second jar of *flaki*. He thought about the fifty pounds in his wallet. It had to last until the end of the week. Seven days. He pushed the jar of *flaki* back on the shelf. Staples first. Bread, butter, sausage. What about Ginger? Instead of his usual five cans of Whiskas, Adam placed into a basket three of a different brand, which was a whole 20 pence cheaper. After a moment of thought, he replaced the cheap stuff with three cans of Whiskas. The little bugger would have to eat less. But he wouldn't be giving him rubbish. Why should the cat suffer because Karol had dug himself into a hole? He looked at a picture of a grey cat on the tin and put another one into the basket.

Chapter 10

Maja, November 1997

A high pitch hiss was followed by a cloud of steam. Maja drew her hand away from the metal spout.

'It isn't very hot yet, but it will be. Very soon. *Macchina espresso* must get hot before you start making coffee. You can check if it is ready. Here.' Lorenzo placed his bony fingers on the side of the machine. With his second hand, he started polishing the gleaming steel panel with a soft cloth. Maja nodded giving the old Italian her full attention. He was her true ally here. She needed friends more than ever.

The rows of small coffee cups were standing in readiness by the machine. A bag of coffee beans had already been emptied into the grinder. In a moment, together with the first cup, a bewitching aroma of freshly brewed coffee would fill the restaurant, overpowering all smells of food cooked during the previous evening.

'First class Arabica,' Lorenzo was fond of saying, inhaling deeply the rich aroma. '*Signor* Mazzini doesn't serve second rate *caffè* in his restaurants.'

Every morning the staff of Bella Italia showed their appreciation of *Signore's* choice of coffee. Even *Signora* Chiara, the old cashier with a sour expression permanently glued to her face, asked for her *doppio espresso* before installing herself in the wooden cashier station for the entire morning. It was as old fashioned as *Signora* Chiara herself. With her hair tightly pulled back in a bun, a white blouse, a navy cardigan and a long black skirt she looked like a school teacher who took pleasure instilling discipline in her pupils.

Signora Chiara had a soft spot for Lorenzo who like her had seen the first days of the Mazzini business in early 1960s. She

took time to chat with him before the restaurant became busy
and offered him after-dinner mints, usually reserved for the
customers paying their bills.

To the younger staff, many of whom came from the distant
ends of Europe, *Signora* had a patronising attitude. In her
opinion, they needed to be strictly managed and controlled.
Maja was no exception in her eyes, although she came on the
recommendation of the Mazzini's family friend and showed
impressive willingness to learn. On a couple of occasions *Signora* Chiara attempted to talk to Maja about her professional
experience and became frustrated with the girl's reluctance to
say anything about her previous job in London.

In fact, Maja just followed the advice she received from Sylvia.
A day after the scene outside Jacek's house, Maja told Sylvia
what'd happened. During first break at the West Ealing School
of English, grabbing Sylvia's arm, Maja nervously whispered
that she needed to talk to her in private. When they were left
alone for a moment Sylvia couldn't wait any longer.

'Maja, what's going on? You look so serious.'

When Maja was recounting the events of the previous night,
Sylvia sunk down on the bench with her mouth wide open. Her
eyes grew larger with every word Maja uttered.

'Christ. What did you say to this bitch?'

'Nothing. There was no time for conversations. She kept
throwing my things through the window.'

'So you had no chance to explain?'

'Nope. I was glad to escape. She threatened to murder us,
Jacek and me. She looked possessed. But Jacek helped me
yesterday.'

'He owes that to you. If not for him you wouldn't be in such a
shitty situation. Don't feel sorry for him. What about your job?'

'I had to quit. It was my decision. I couldn't work in a place
where everyone would be talking behind my back. Never,' she
said firmly. 'I think I know who acted as a bush telegraph to
Jacek's wife. Not that it makes any difference now.'

'So now you are homeless and jobless. Thanks to your idiot
employer,' summed up Sylvia.

'I am staying with Jola and Ewa. Again. The room at the

house in Cuckoohill Road may still be vacant. Perhaps I could move in there.'

'First you have to find another job.'

'I know. I cannot think about anything else. I feel like I am back where I started. With nothing to lose. Like on my first day in London.'

'It's not true. It's only a small setback.'

'That's the understatement of the year, Sylvia. I know you're trying to cheer me up.'

Sylvia shook her head. 'Don't let this get you down. Let's see what we can do about a job for you. I have an idea ... of sorts ... You'd better check about that room.'

Sylvia called Maja the following evening.

'The good news is that there is a job in a restaurant run by my parents' relatives. They need somebody straight away.'

'Sylvia, you're amazing!'

'The bad news is that like in most Italian places you will be spending almost the entire day there. You'll be starting in the morning and working until late into the night. But, but ... I've managed to negotiate for you a long lunchtime break in which you can fit school.'

'It's so good of you.'

'One more thing. Say nothing about what has happened to you. I said your previous job was temporary and it came to an end.'

'I won't.'

'Remember, the owners are Italian. Italian Catholics. Conservative with traditional family values, etcetera ... In public, at least. You know, don't you? Poles are probably similar.'

Introduced on a family friend's recommendation, Maja was looked upon with curiosity by the restaurant staff. Particularly since she wasn't Italian.

She worked very hard to prove to the Mazzini family that she deserved their trust. Fitting her studies and homework around several hours of restaurant work wasn't easy. She felt exhausted at the end of the day but she was determined not to show it.

In Bella Italia she was learning about the best of Italian

cuisine from people who knew it well and loved it. She listened to them talking about their favourite food and wines and the places where they came from. Sun and soil were vital ingredients for creating these special flavours. They described how basil or oregano, together with some wine, could transform a simple dish into an irresistible treat.

Tying the straps of a starched apron around her waist, Maja surveyed the rows of glasses on the counter waiting to be polished. Feeling chilled to the bone after a walk through the November drizzle, she longed for a long glass of coffee with plenty of steamed milk. Hearing the soft click of the entrance door, she turned around. A young man was standing in the doorway. His jacket was soaked and rain drops were falling off his curly hair. He looked as if he had just emerged from under the shower. He paused for a moment and started shaking the rain off his clothes. Like a puppy, Maja thought. He took his sodden jacket off, unwound his scarf and without hesitation crossed the restaurant aiming for the table in the far corner.

Customers in Bella Italia always waited to be seated. A small brass board usually positioned by the door served as a reminder of this custom. It was still there but the man obviously decided to ignore it. Maja looked around to check who was going to chastise him. *Signora* Chiara hadn't returned from her lunchtime break, while Lorenzo was still chatting downstairs with other men. It was up to her to manage the situation. The man should be seated by the door and informed that they wouldn't start serving dinner until five o'clock.

Before Maja reached his table, the man grinned at her and exclaimed cheerfully: 'A toasted focaccia with tomato and basil and a large coffee. A very hot one would be great.'

'You will need to take a seat by ...' Now she was looking closely at him. His dark eyes were smiling at her and he wasn't at all sorry for barging in without being invited to sit down. Yet, he didn't appear arrogant. Just blissfully ignorant of making a nuisance of himself at the time of day when the restaurant staff were getting ready for the evening shift. She sighed deeply and said: 'Of course. I'll see what I can do for you.'

Taking from the fridge the ingredients for his toasted sandwich, she thought that at least he gave her an excuse to stop and make a large coffee also for herself. Perhaps she would have a *biscotti* with it. The smell of fresh olive bread made her feel hungry.

With the focaccia under the grill, she turned her attention to coffee. She poured fresh milk into a metal jug and started steaming it thoroughly. Having loaded the coffee capsule with a generous helping of finely ground coffee powder, she put two espresso cups under the spout. In a moment, dark trickles of aromatic liquid flowed into the cups. Maja poured them onto the feathery pillow of steamed milk. Then she spooned more of the milky foam on top and sprinkled some chocolate with nutmeg and cinnamon. With satisfaction, she looked at the final product that not only looked professional but also smelled delicious. She reached for a tray to carry one of the glasses to the table.

There was no need for this as the man was now standing by the counter.

'I couldn't wait any longer,' he apologised. 'I'm starving and drenched,' he said touching wet patches on his shirt. 'Goodness, this looks delicious.'

Maja gave him a glance that was meant to be reproachful. She reached for a plate and started arranging lettuce, slices of cucumber and tomato, rings of red onion and olives into a side salad, placing the golden focaccia in the centre.

'Are you new here?' the man asked unexpectedly.

'Not exactly,' she said sharply. She loathed personal questions.

'I haven't seen you before in La Bella Italia.'

'Well, perhaps you don't come here often enough.' Maja was getting angry. She should be polishing the glasses and preparing tables for the evening not fending off morons who came and went whenever it suited them.

'Probably not. You're right.' The man kept his cool but the tone of his voice changed. She instantly regretted that she was unpleasant to him.

Feeling chastised the man put the plate on the tray next to his coffee and carried it to his table. The thought of *Signora* Chiara seeing a customer carrying his own food on the tray to the table filled Maja with horror. Fortunately, she was the only one witnessing it.

Watching him arrange his food on the table, she noticed that he didn't have a napkin and cutlery. She went briskly to her station and took one of the linen napkins, freshly laundered for the evening. Placing it on the table together with a knife and fork she smiled down on him and said: 'Enjoy your meal.'

'I will,' he said flashing her one more of his wide grins.

Smarmy ass, Maja thought as she returned to the bar. She took a long sip of her coffee and feeling the pleasant warmth spreading inside, she reached for a linen tea towel to tackle a long line of glasses. Only in an Italian restaurant, tea towels would be so starched, she mused.

As she carefully placed the second brandy glass on the counter that now shone like a soap bubble, she heard the man's voice behind her.

'I am so sorry to bother you again, but there is no salt or pepper on any of the tables.'

Indeed, all the condiments were collected after lunch for replenishing and now they were standing on the sideboard. She quickly checked the salt and pepper pots, refilled the bottles with olive oil and balsamic vinegar and brought them to the corner table.

'Thank you very much. It's clearing up now. The evening should be nicer,' he said apologetically looking through the window.

'I hope so.' Maja thought about her late night journey home on the bus.

'The weather is kinder in Florence, even in autumn,' the man said pointing to the large picture above his head.

'In Venice, you mean?'

'OK, in Venice. Have you been to Venice?'

'No, not yet. But I know this picture well. It is by Canaletto. He painted many scenes of Venice.'

'Are you interested in art?'

'Yes.'

'Italian art?'

Maja smiled. But not in Italian men, she wished to say. Instead she returned to her glasses. In a moment, Raul appeared and asked her to help him with the tablecloths which had just been delivered from the laundry. The hum of voices from downstairs was getting louder as more staff were returning for the evening shift.

When she came back, the table by the window was empty. Two crisp ten pound notes were lying next to the empty plate. She cleared the table and put the money on the counter in front of Lorenzo who took over polishing of the glasses.

'This is for a toasted focaccia with tomato and basil and a tall latte. The rest is the tip.'

Lorenzo looked at Maja with surprise. 'He paid?'

'Of course, Lorenzo. Why shouldn't he?'

'Do you know who it was?'

Maja hesitated. 'No. Why?'

'It was Nico, the youngest son of *Signor* Mazzini. A nice boy. I hope that he found everything to his satisfaction. I am sure you were nice to him.'

'Hmm, yeah ...,' Maja mumbled. Then neatly folding her polishing cloth, she added: 'He felt very much at home here.'

Chapter 11

Maja, December 1997

With her feet numb from the cold, Maja was running. It was stupid to wear these fancy pumps instead of her winter boots but she wanted to look and feel special today. This morning she put on a pair of jeans and her favourite red sweater. She took her time with her make-up and styled her hair up. A pair of long oriental earrings from Camden market went well with the roll-neck jumper. Sylvia had always commented on how 'interesting' they were. She aimed for that 'interesting' look since she was a college student today, not a waitress.

She liked her new way home. The streets of Greenford were wider and greener than those in Acton where she lived with Ewa and Jola. Her favourite was Huttington Gardens, where she walked every day. Lined with old trees and ever-green hedges, it looked like a park avenue. Even now in December, the trees were majestic, with their bare branches rising to the sky like modern sculptures. Usually, she slowed down to look at them but today she was chilled to the bone and was charging up the hill following the cloud of her own breath.

Suddenly she heard the sound of a car a few metres behind her. She glanced over her shoulder but kept walking. The car was slowing down to match her speed. Walking faster, she instinctively pressed her handbag with her elbow. She was used to walking home late at night and avoided the streets behind the underground station, where men with time on their hands hung around all day. But this was an avenue with expensive houses inhabited by nice people who smiled at her walking their dogs. And it was only half past three in the afternoon.

She saw the car window slide down. With Ewa's warnings ringing in her head, she steered away from the curb.

'It's only me, Maja,' someone shouted. The face of a young man appeared in the open window. He was leaning across the passenger seat trying to get her attention.

'Hi,' she said suddenly feeling out of breath. The man in the car was one of the tenants of 26 Cuckoohill Road. She had met him a couple of times in the kitchen.

'I could give you a lift. It's freezing.'

'It isn't far.'

'I'm going home too.'

'OK. It would be nice.'

'Get in, Maja.' The man pushed the door open.

'Thanks ...' She didn't remember his name but he had made an effort to remember hers. She got into the car and put her gloved hands on her knees to warm them up. In a minute, they were outside their front door.

'Thank you very much for the lift.'

'Do you often walk home at this time?'

'Only on my days off,' said Maja, heading for the front door.

She wished to finish this conversation, but having just opened the door she couldn't slam it shut before the man locked his car.

'You're a very busy girl. Disappearing early in the morning and not coming back until late at night.'

'I have a very full day. Working and studying.'

'You're very focused.'

'Aren't we all?'

'I have met many drifters in this city. Some were from Poland.'

They were now standing in the entrance hall. All Maja wanted was to dash upstairs to her room to change, make herself something to eat and get on with her essay before the evening arrived. Yet, the man wasn't in any hurry.

'I often work late so I could give you a lift from the station.'

'I couldn't possibly ...'

'I drive a cab, so it's no bother. A girl shouldn't be walking alone late at night. Even here.'

'I have managed so far. But thank you.'

'It wouldn't be a problem.' Then he added, 'I don't pick up all the girls on my way home.'

'Should I feel honoured then?'

'Here is my card. You could use the telephone box by the

station. Or you can call me before you get on the train.'

'It's very kind of you.' She couldn't see herself calling him, but perhaps he was just a nice guy. She noticed his name on the card.

'Thank you, Kuba. See you around.' He instantly realised why she hadn't used his name before and smiled.

He was smart as well as good looking, she thought. And cheeky. She smiled back at him and ran upstairs to her room.

After closing the door, she leaned against it. With pleasure, she looked around her room. Her little kingdom. The room was still warm since the morning and she could smell the citrusy scent of the lemon geranium, which Jan gave her the same weekend she moved into 26 Cuckoohill Road. She clearly remembered how happy and relieved she was to hear that the room was still vacant and that the Kowals were willing to rent it to her. After the fiasco with Jacek, this was the first piece of good news she had received that day. Then Sylvia called her about the job in Bella Italia. She had a place to live and a job with which she would be able to pay for her lodgings. Unexpectedly, her life in London made sense again.

The house was spacious, with a large, well equipped kitchen and two bathrooms decorated with a generous amount of smoked glass and brass finishes. At the back, there was a long garden mostly put to lawn. Two rows of neatly pruned rose bushes and a selection of evergreens were planted alongside the fence.

Maja was to live upstairs in the room which was vacated by a woman who suddenly had to go back to Poland. She fell in love with it the moment she entered it behind Zofia Kowal who was explaining the rules of the house as they were walking upstairs. She never forgot her first impression. Even on that gloomy November morning the room appeared sunny and welcoming. It was decorated with yellow wallpaper dotted with the smiling faces of dancing clowns. The cotton curtains and concertina lampshade had the same pattern. On the shelves above the bed there was a collection of books about rabbits, propped up by wooden bookends carved into clowns. A pine wardrobe and an ample chest of drawers with red and yellow handles were probably installed there to house the garments of the room's young occupant. Only the round table by the window and the single bed with a wicker headboard looked like later additions to the original furnishings.

Back in Grodek, she would have regarded such décor as childish and fussy but now it was like a precious memory. The smiling faces of the clowns greeted her in the morning and winked at her as she put her head on the pillow at night.

She kicked off her shoes and slid her feet into slippers. For a moment, she relished their softness and the returning feeling in her toes. Then she took off her jacket and hung it in the wardrobe. On the inside of one of the doors there was a mirror, attached at the level of Maja's chest. She felt comforted every time she read the words etched on the glass: Tomorrow is another day.

Nico started coming to the restaurant in Duke Street at least a couple of times a week. He usually went first downstairs to the manager's office and spent some time there, behind a closed door. Then he made a point of talking to the chefs, the barman and waiters, all of whom knew him well. From their banter and roars of laughter it was apparent that they genuinely liked him. As soon as he came upstairs, he went to *Signora* Chiara's box. Nothing could please the old cashier more. She glowed as she spoke to him and for a couple of hours afterwards she spared restaurant staff her usual scathing comments.

With the same easy manner Nico approached Maja and asked her if she could make him one of these long lattes which saved him from hypothermia the other day. Although he was trying not to appear too familiar with her, his dark eyes were smiling at her. He just stood by the bar, patiently waiting for his drink. Despite the November weather, he was wearing beige flannel trousers. They were matched with a light brown polo neck jumper and an immaculately cut tweed jacket. A large, no doubt expensive, watch was discreetly protruding from beneath the sleeve. With his shiny black hair and olive skin he was an embodiment of the easy Italian elegance. And he looked so damn handsome. This made her feel uncomfortable. She turned her back to him and busied herself with the coffee machine. She was getting angry with herself for being so taken by him. He was a part of a different world. As the restaurant owners' son, he was her boss. She should be polite to him, nothing more and nothing less, otherwise she may lose her job here. She would be a fool if she allowed that to happen again. She turned around and put a glass of steaming coffee in front of him.

'I wish to apologise for a mean comment I made the other afternoon,' she said without looking at him.

'No need for apologies. I was a nuisance. The boys told me that you are one busy lady — working and studying.'

'Yes, sir, but ...'

'No buts, not apologies, no sirs. I am a prodigal son who doesn't pay enough attention to the family business. Sometimes the truth hurts. Do you enjoy working here?'

'Very much so. I've made some good friends.'

'I heard. All the guys here want to be your friends.'

Maja laughed. He read this as an encouragement.

'Can I help you with these glasses? I'm not bad at polishing. My mother loves entertaining and she trained me well. Will you tell me something about yourself? So ... I don't need to rely on gossip.'

Maja lifted her head alerted.

'They say only nice things about you.' Seeing that she grew uneasy, Nico took a polishing cloth from the sideboard and picked the closest glass. With the serviette inside he twisted it around a couple times and lifted it to the light.

'I had another look at that picture in the corner and I have to admit that it is definitely Venice not Florence. I should have known better. I have been to Florence many times. We have a large family. Where is your home?'

'In a small town in south-east Poland, called Grodek.'

'Is the place worth visiting?'

Maja wondered whether he realised that his question was patronising.

'Definitely. It's a very picturesque place with a renaissance castle on the hill and an ancient monastery.'

'It sounds like one of these Italian hilltop towns.'

'It is probably similar. Lorenzo has been telling me about the place he comes from.'

'Do you miss it?'

'Of course, it's my home.'

'Sorry, it was a stupid question. Will you be going home for Christmas?'

'No, probably not.' She wasn't going to tell him that she simply couldn't afford the airfare at Christmas. 'I'm going to be busy here and I have a lot of catching up on my college work. It would also be nice to see how Christmas is celebrated in London.'

'You're right. The Christmas season in London is spectacular. More commercial than religious, as the English are not great church-goers. In Italy, the commerce merges seamlessly with the religion. Is Christmas a big thing in Poland?'

'It is the most important holiday of the year. The time when all families make an effort to be together.' She didn't want to tell him that she had never been away from home for Christmas and that breaking this tradition this year she would upset them all. At the thought of the empty plate that would be waiting for her this year, she felt a pang of pain in her stomach.

Nico kept polishing glasses and was slowly drinking his coffee. Maja took out starched tablecloths in two colours, the white ones for the underlay and the smaller burgundy ones for the top and started preparing her tables for the evening. She went back and forth to the bar to collect wine glasses, feeling Nico's gaze following her as she worked.

'The coffee was excellent. Exactly what I needed to keep me going for the rest of the evening. Thank you, Maja.'

On the way out he shook the hand of Giulio, the duty manger, made a friendly wave to *Signora* Chiara, and with a click of the glass door he disappeared into the thickening darkness of the November evening.

He was back the following week and the week after. He always came in smartly dressed and with a wide smile. He could have been taken for a customer who was coming to the restaurant expecting a pleasant lunch date. He would attend the usual business first and then chat to the restaurant staff. They treated him with deference — he was a Mazzini after all — but it was combined with a good measure of liking. He always appeared interested in their work and lives.

On one occasion she listened to the men gossiping about the Mazzini family. Roberto, the older son was senior Mazzini's favourite. He was forging a career in high finance in the City but was expected to run the family business in the future. Apart from three restaurants, it included a small luxury hotel, a jewellery importing business and a car dealership. Nico was yet to show his worth to his father if he was to take a part in managing the business. Apparently his easy attitude to life was a disappointment to his father who had built the Mazzini business himself, personally serving at the tables in his first restaurant. He blamed Nico's mother for spoiling him.

At the beginning of December, Giulio announced that the girls, meaning Maja and Sophia, who was twice her age, would have a special task the next day. Although there were still three weeks until Christmas, the whole city was already in a festive mood and they were to introduce the Christmas spirit to Bella Italia.

Next morning when Maja opened the door to the restaurant, her senses were hit with an overpowering smell of fresh spruce. It was like walking into a conifer forest after rain. The table next to the door had disappeared and in its place stood an enormous spruce set into a large glazed pot. Still unadorned, it looked magnificent in its raw beauty, its dark needles still glistening with the drops of rain. Next to it on the floor there was a pile of loose spruce twigs and an assortment of cardboard boxes, some of them already opened and spilling their sparkling content.

'È così bello! Magnifico.' Sophia could hardly contain her excitement. With hands on her hips, she was eyeing the tree up and down. Maja looked at the tree and for a brief moment she saw her father bringing a Christmas tree into the house, smelling of sap and broken needles, and the three Zalewski children jumping around him and arguing over who was going to decorate it.

'It's beautiful, Sophia.'

'Every year we have a tree but this one is a real beauty. We have so many lovely things with which to dress her up.' She said pointing to the pile of boxes. 'She is going to look like a prima donna.'

It was the tree's sheer beauty or perhaps its unexpected arrival in the middle of the city that made everyone who worked in the restaurant stop and stare. They came in one by one, shook rain from their coats and stood staring at the magnificent piece of nature. Shortly, the giant spruce was transformed into a Christmas tree as Sophia and Maja decorated it with glass baubles, shimmering stars and snowflakes, and encircled the tree with metres of frosted tinsel. Finally the fairy lights were plugged in and the magic of Christmas came to life. Even *Signora* Chiara left her box to see the transformation. Unaccustomed to displaying emotions, she just patted a ribbon attached to a large silver bubble and with her fingers started spreading the artificial snow on the branches.

Then there was time to prepare the decorations for the walls. Sophia had done this many times before. She deftly twisted and coiled the twigs, sticky from oozing sap, and tided them up with a piece of wire. She showed Maja how to decorate them with ribbons, frosted cones, artificial berries and fruit, still smelling of last year's festivities.

When they started hanging them up, Maja realised that this was more difficult than she imagined. The arrangements were heavy and they had to be well secured with string and wire to wall lamps and iron candelabras. They were slanting to one side, spoiling the effect the women were trying to achieve.

'Maja, move back a few steps again and check how this stupid thing looks this time,' Sophia commanded standing barefoot on the table moved right up against the wall.

'OK, not bad. Move it a little more to the right.'

'What about now?'

'Better. Much better.'

'How does it look from the aisle?'

Maja walked backwards, tilting her head to one side to get the right perspective. When she moved back another couple of steps ... she heard a hiss of pain and felt someone's hands on her shoulders. She turned around. She saw Nico's face next to her own, twisted in pain. She had trod on his toe with her heel.

'I'm so sorry. I didn't see you coming.'

'Of course, you didn't. You didn't want to punish me ...'

'Have I hurt you badly?'

'I don't think I need hospital treatment.'

'I'm really sorry. Can I do anything?'

'Hmm ... Yes, how about coffee for the three of us? Sophia, who looks fed up on that table, me — the victim of the accident, and yourself.'

Shortly afterwards they sat together drinking steaming coffee and eating crumbly pieces of aromatic panetone which had been delivered that morning. They admired the magnificent Christmas tree and talked about the approaching holidays. He is easy to like, thought Maja. When she was clearing the dishes from the table, Nico came to her and asked: 'Since you're staying in London, wouldn't you like to see the Christmas lights? In Oxford Street, Regent Street, Burlington Arcade ...'

'Yeah, I was planning to do something like this.'

'Would you accept me as your guide?'

Maja paused for a moment startled.

'We could go together one evening with a camera and see the Christmas lights in the best places. Have a bite to eat afterwards?'

'Wouldn't you rather take some girl you know ... Your ...'

'No, Maja. There is no one else I would rather be seeing Christmas lights with than with you. Would you be my companion?'

Maja looked at this dashing man, kind and funny, pleading to go out with her, a waitress in his restaurant, and thought that this may not happen again.

'I would love it. Thank you for offering to be my guide.'

Chapter 12

Kuba, December 1997

Kuba was looking at an empty street through his bedroom window. It was only six o'clock in the evening but the world outside had already sunk in a thick winter night.

Having spent eight hours behind the wheel in an overheated car, he was glad to be home. He felt tired and restless. A run in the cold and then a long hot shower should settle his mind for a good night's sleep. He was getting his jogging clothes out of the wardrobe when he heard the familiar jingle of his mobile. He recognised the number of Century Cabs.

'Yes?' He had no intention of hiding his irritation.

'Josh had to take his mother-in-law to the A&E ...' Roxy's voice was rising.

'So ...'

'Kuba, would you come back for a couple of hours? We have so many bookings. There are two of us on the switchboard and we barely have time to answer the calls,' the girl was pleading. 'You could take this time off during the week. I will speak to the boss.'

'OK, I will come ... I will eat something and will be back for eight.' Kuba switched off his mobile and slipped it back into his pocket. No jog after all. He walked back to the window and resumed observing the world outside. There was something very comforting about seeing people's daily routine. He remembered watching the lives of the residents of the house opposite in Opole when he was a small boy. Several families lived in the flats opposite and their tall windows were like the frames of a film revealing their goings-on. At the end of the day, people retired to their homes like toys he put away into his toy-box every night. Everything was in order. With longing he thought about the time when his life had a clear sense of purpose and he enjoyed making plans.

Suddenly he heard the thump of the entrance door below. Door slamming was Basia's prerogative but Basia wouldn't be leaving the house alone at this time of the evening. It sounded as if the door was slammed by the wind. A woman in a padded jacket, walking away from the entrance was taller than Basia. After a few steps she stopped and looked around. At that moment he recognised Maja. That illusive girl who intrigued him since she moved into their house a few weeks ago. Her head was barely protruding from the coils of a thick scarf. She walked a few steps and stopped again. Then she saw what she was looking for because she suddenly started walking fast down the road. A yellow sport car was parked several metres away. A man got out of it and opened the passenger door for her. In a moment the car turned around and roared up the road. Kuba stood staring through the window. A boyfriend with a Ferrari picking her up on a Friday night. She was obviously aiming high. And he offered her a lift in his cab …

Two hours later he was driving westwards along the A40 glad that Friday was finally over. He would have a long lie-in tomorrow morning and perhaps go for a jog. Rested he would think about the issues which unnerved him today. He was always reluctant to consider big decisions, fearing their life-changing consequences. He knew that he should start thinking about the future. Next year he would hit thirty and having no plans would no longer be cool. No big dream eluded him and small things made him happy which was probably a serious character flaw. Was he happy? he recently started asking himself. He couldn't say. By many people's standards probably no; yet he wasn't unhappy. He enjoyed helping and pleasing those for whom he cared. His relationships with women followed this general pattern but none of his girlfriends was allowed to get too close to what he regarded as his inner space.

A sudden sound broke his thoughts. It took him a moment to realise that it was the ring of his mobile phone. Again, it was Century Cabs. For a moment he considered ignoring the call. He felt worn out physically and indifferent to the world's concerns. Then he thought better of it. Perhaps they had decided to alter his rota and he might have the whole weekend free.

'What's up?' he asked. The soft tone of Roxy's voice meant a request for a favour.

'We've got a call from Ashley Roberts asking to pick him up from the West End. It's urgent as he is not feeling well. When he heard that you're still on the road, he asked for you.'

'*Cholera*,' he swore aloud.

'Does that mean you will do it?'

'Yes, I will do it, Roxy. But after this, consider me dead for the next twenty four hours. OK?'

He reached the Palladium faster than he expected. Ashley was waiting for him by the stage door. He wasn't alone. Shocked, Kuba watched as Ashley was being helped by another man to cross the pavement to the cab. The man opened the door and lowered him down on the back seat. Ashley groaned in pain.

'Can I help you, Mr Roberts?'

'Kuba, we agreed that you call me Ashley. Frank has already helped the invalid. Please just drive me home.'

'What's happened?' Kuba couldn't help asking, looking at the pale face in the mirror.

'I think I have pulled my Achilles tendon again.'

'Shouldn't I take you to the hospital?'

'Oh God, no. I can't bear the thought of being stuck in the A&E for hours. Just to be told what I already know. Just get me home. I will call my physio and she will sort me out tomorrow. A few cubes of ice will do for now.'

'As you wish. It won't take long. The traffic is easy tonight.'

Ashley closed his eyes and leaned back against the seat. His face was deathly white. Surrounded by the folds of his dark coat, it looked like a mask. He remained silent for the whole journey. It was very uncharacteristic of Ashley and Kuba kept looking back at him in the mirror to check whether the man hadn't fainted.

Once in Lexicon Avenue, Kuba managed to find a parking space almost opposite the stairs leading to Ashley's house. He had never noticed before that the staircase of the Victorian mansion was steep and tall. Perhaps it appeared higher in the dark.

'Ashley, you're home,' he said softly looking back at his passenger.

The dancer opened his eyes slowly as if waking from a deep sleep. 'Oh, good. I will be fine once I get to bed. Then looking through the window he asked: 'Would you help me to mount this final obstacle?'

'Of course. I didn't expect you ...'

'A good *pas de deux* would get us half-way up. But I have no energy left today.'

The situation was more difficult than Kuba expected. Even with his arm around Kuba's shoulder, Ashley wasn't able to walk up the stairs on his good leg. He cried in pain, as he put his injured limb on the ground.

'Is there anyone in your house who could help me carry you upstairs?'

'Carry me? Good God, what a grand entrance I'll be making! I'll be in the local paper tomorrow,' he chuckled. 'There's a bunch of students living in the basement flat. A nice crowd, though a tad boisterous at times. Go down these steps on the left and press their bell. Hard. You will have to do that a few times if you hear the music.'

Having left Ashley resting on a low wall, Kuba did as instructed. After a couple of minutes he emerged from the basement followed by a youth in a dark T-shirt with a fuzzy Scorpions' logo on the front.

'Oh, Josh, it's so good of you to show charity to the stage cripple,' exclaimed Ashley.

'No probs, Ash. How do you wish to be transported to your penthouse?'

Josh didn't look like someone devoted to personal fitness but he proved to be surprisingly strong. Once they formed a seat with hands and arms on which Ashley could sit, they were able to hoist him relatively easily off the ground and carry him up the stairs.

They paused in front of a large mahogany door while Ashley searched his pockets for the key. Once they were inside Ashley's apartment, he pointed to the light switch which Josh pressed with his shoulder. Instantly the vast stage of Ashley's living room was revealed. With high ceiling and three tall windows draped in heavy curtains the room looked like a period stage set. A couple of low sofas in the same shade of gold as the curtains were a depository of cushions in various colours and sizes. The elegance and perfect harmony of the apartment surprised Kuba. Weren't artists supposed to live in bohemian chaos? Many times observing Ashley's long hair and flowing garments, as he swept in and out of his cab, Kuba imagined him living in some messy studio with pieces of eclectic art around him.

Still suspended between Josh and Kuba, Ashley commanded: 'Straight ahead.' They crossed the vast expanse of beige carpet and deposited him on one of the sofas. Then Kuba helped Ashley to lay his injured limb on a low glass table, and placed a cushion underneath his leg.

Lifting his face towards Josh, Ashley said: 'That was an act of real kindness, pal. Once I'm in working order again, there will be a few rounds on me in The Swan.'

'No problem, Ash. Get yourself mended. If you need me again, you know our number.'

When Josh departed Ashley looked at Kuba pleadingly. 'Could you make me a cup of tea before you go? I would ask for something much stronger but I have been popping pills since I hopped off the stage.'

'Of course. Would you mind if I made a cup for myself too?'

'Oh God, Kuba. I am a selfish beast when I am not well. Please make a pot of tea. There is also a tin of biscuits in the kitchen. Or perhaps you would prefer a sandwich?'

Ashley's kitchen was as impressive as his living room. Never before had Kuba seen such a perfect marriage of old fashioned furniture with the latest kitchen appliances. Everything was spotless, tidily arranged and perfectly coordinated. The shining chrome kettle matched the toaster which sported the same design and finish as the coffee machine. Mugs were in the cupboard above the kettle and teaspoons in the top drawer below it. He was certain that Ashley could find everything there without switching on the light.

When Kuba put two mugs of tea on the glass table in front of Ashley he noticed that the dancer was still very pale.

'Can I have a look at your leg?' he suggested. 'I used to deal with injuries, in Poland.'

'Of course, you did. But I will call Karen in a moment and

she'll be here before nine tomorrow. If I need a doc she will take me to the surgery.'

Kuba gently removed a loafer from Ashley's left foot. Even before he pulled off his sock he could see than Ashley's ankle was very swollen. The slightest pressure made him wince in pain.

'OK, OK. I will start from a cold compress and I suggest that we support your ankle to reduce the pain at night. Then you'll place your leg on the pillow while sleeping.'

'I have some bandages in the bathroom.'

'I would need something to tie your leg to … Perhaps a ruler?'

'No chance. I finished with maths before A-levels.'

'A wooden spoon perhaps.'

'That's better. They will be in the kitchen, in a stone jar.'

Crossing the hallway Kuba noticed an old fashion shoehorn hanging on the dresser. Returning to the living room he saw that Ashley had managed to slip his coat off and, with an array of cushions, made himself comfortable.

'Can I use this?' Kuba asked waving the shoehorn.

'What a good idea! My old aunt gave me this heirloom. She couldn't have predicted that it would save my life.'

'It's just the right thing.'

Looking around restlessly, Ashley asked: 'Kuba, before you turn me into an Egyptian mummy, can you do one more thing for me? Please switch off the main light. It's so strong and it gives me a headache. These lamps by the sofa will do nicely instead. And please sit down and drink your tea. It has been a long day.'

Feeling exhausted, Kuba didn't protest. He took his mug and sat next to Ashley on the sofa. They sipped their tea in companionable silence. The large room, now lit only by a couple of lamps suddenly lost its dimensions, becoming cosy, almost intimate. The dimmed lights and the comfortable furniture created a relaxing atmosphere. Two speakers stood on both sides of a large bookcase, which in addition to books, housed some pieces of modern sculpture and glass. The screen of a large TV was reflecting the light. Ashley must love his pad, Kuba thought.

'Ashley, I better prepare you for the night, before you fall asleep,' said Kuba breaking the silence. The dancer was dozing off and he opened his eyes startled.

'Of course. Do as you must. I promise to cooperate.'

Kuba began from preparing a cold compress. With amusement, Ashley watched as Kuba proceeded to tie a bandage around the shoehorn. When it was well padded, he fixed it to Ashley's left ankle. The contraption was surprisingly comfortable and during this process Ashley winced in pain only once. Finally, Kuba asked him to stand up and checked whether he was able to move around the apartment.

'Will you be OK until tomorrow morning?'

'Kuba you're wonderful. I may even get some sleep,' said Ashley sitting down again. 'You're wasting your talents.'

'Ashley ...' Kuba waved his hand as if defending himself from an obtrusive fly.

'No, I won't shut up. Have you done anything to validate your qualifications?'

'Not yet, but ...'

'I have an idea. I will speak to Karen tomorrow. She is a New Zealander and I think she had to do so something with her diploma when she came here.'

'I wouldn't like to bother you ...'

'It's not bother. You helped me many times. I want to do something for you. Unless, of course, you will tell me that your lifetime ambition is to be a London cabbie.' He patted a seat next to him. 'Kuba, please sit down. I'm straining my neck trying to talk to you when you're towering above me.'

He took another sip of his tea and said: 'You're a super guy. You need to give justice to your skills. Will you talk to Karen when she calls you tomorrow?'

Kuba hesitated. He hated the idea of a pep talk from some patronising woman.

'Will you?' Ashley insisted.

'OK, I promise.'

'Good man!' Ashley slapped Kuba's thigh with surprising strength and flashed him his usual radiant smile.

After a minute of silence Kuba said: 'You know, Ashley, this is the second time today I have been reminded that I have got stuck in a rut.'

'People obviously care about you.'

'Well, perhaps ...'

Ashley put a hand on Kuba's shoulder. 'You can always count on me.' They sat like this for a moment. Kuba felt the warmth of Ashley's palm through his shirt.

'I'm very grateful. Thank you. I need to go now,' he said getting up.

'Kuba, thank you. With your help I will survive the night. And tomorrow things will sort themselves out.' Then he added reflectively: 'I may have reached a turning point in my career.'

Running down the front steps of Ashley's house, Kuba thought: 'I may have reached a turning point too.'

Chapter 13

Adam, December 1997

Hardened by years of working outdoors, Adam knew that he could always rely on his robust health. This made him feel indestructible. Yet, one Monday morning life dealt him a nasty surprise. He woke up with an excruciating pain in his abdomen. It felt as though pieces of broken glass had lodged themselves in the lining of his stomach and lacerated it every time he moved. The severity of the pain frightened Adam who had never experienced anything like this before.

He managed to stagger to the kitchen hoping to find something to alleviate the pain. Wrapped up in her pink dressing gown, Zofia Kowal was sitting at the table with a mug of coffee. The sound of a Polish broadcast was seeping from a small transistor radio.

'Adam, are you ill?' she exclaimed seeing his ashen face.

'It's in my stomach. I need something to stop the pain.'

'What pain? Have you eaten or drunk something which disagreed with you?' Several times Zofia had witnessed Adam's unsteady returns home but this wasn't the time to remind him about it.

'No, *pani Zofio*, I haven't touched a drink for over two months.'

'Perhaps it's just bad heartburn ... Have you eaten spicy food? Pickles?'

'No, I cooked some chicken on Sunday.'

'Is it very bad? I mean the pain.'

Adam hated to feel sorry for himself but felt forced to admit: 'It's sharp.'

'Where it is?'

'At the bottom of my stomach,' he said placing his palm on his abdomen as if trying to prevent another stab of pain.

'It could be an ulcer,' suggested Zofia. 'Have you ever had such pains before?'

Some years ago when the relations between Adam and Bukowski were particularly hostile, and Adam felt a great need to visit Ondraszkowa Izba more often than usual, he experienced a bout of stomach pains. At that time Hanka went to the old Pietraszkowa *babka* who was more trusted by the people in Kościelisko than the local doctor. The old woman gave Hanka some seeds to brew. Adam drank the oily goo in the evening. It was disgusting but it worked. He never thought about this incident again, until now.

'You need to see the doctor. It could be something serious,' stated Zofia with authority.

'I need to go to work now,' he said screwing his face as another bout of pain assaulted him. Zofia knew Adam well enough to believe that this stubborn ox of a man would drag himself to work regardless of his wretched condition.

She went to the cooker and warmed some milk. She poured it into the cup, spooned something into it and offered it to Adam.

'Just drink it now. It may help.' Then she remembered something. 'I may have something for you.' She hurried up to her bedroom. A few minutes later, she returned with a half-empty bottle of pills.

'They worked for Jan when he had stomach trouble, they may work for you. At least until the doctor sees you.'

Adam had no time for doctors. There weren't available when he could see them. On Saturday afternoon or Sunday, doctors, like everybody else, took time off to rest. He didn't even know where the local surgery was. He had hoped that he would never need to find out.

So he took the pills Zofia gave him and hoped that they would help him to get through the day. The medicine worked surprisingly fast and he was able to forget about the pain during the morning.

In the afternoon, the pain returned. For the rest of the day, Adam was barely able to move. He would have to see the doctor after all. The thought of having to find a local surgery and to explain what was wrong with him gave him another bout of pain. He resigned himself to confiding his problem to Wiktor.

Having spent three years in London, he should know how these matters work here. Yet, Wiktor wasn't much help. Only once had he been in contact with the medical world in England and it was with a dentist. In fact, he wasn't sure that he had dealt with the English health system since the dentist was Indian and his assistant was a Greek.

This wasn't helpful. Meanwhile, the pain was getting worse and he had to stop working. He sat down on the floor in the corner of a vast loft apartment on which they were working and drew up his knees close to his chest. Seeing him so changed, Wiktor came up to him.

'You need to get yourself to the doctor, mate. Fast. Speak to people in your house. They will know where the local medic is. Take a day off and sort yourself out.'

'I will talk to Karol,' conceded Adam. He also decided to ask Zofia for help. Zofia Kowal was a decent woman but he was reluctant to involve her in his affairs. There were things in his life which didn't fit into the rules of 26 Cuckoohill Road and Mrs Patel appointed Zofia as a rule keeper.

'You can always use a Chinese doctor if the English medicines don't work,' Wiktor said sagely.

'Chinese doctor?'

'Haven't you heard about Chinese medicine? Herbs, acupuncture and stuff like this?'

'Yeah. Vaguely. In Kościelisko there was a *babka* who used herbs to cure people.'

'Chinese stuff is even better. It tastes like poison but it works. My Marta had stomach problems last year. She took these herbs and swears that they cured her.'

Following Marta's instructions, he was now walking down Uxbridge Road looking for the Chinese clinic. He shortly located no less than three places with Chinese lettering in the window. The closest one to the station had frosted panels in the windows which made it impossible to see what was inside. Two others had some sort of shop on the front with signs and anatomical drawings of a human body, suggesting that there were therapy rooms at the back. This was a very different type of medicine than that practised by the doctors he visited before. He would have to go in and ask. If he could ask.

He returned to the last place — the supermarket with a Chinese clinic at the back. He stood outside considering what to do next. His hesitation caught the attention of a Chinese shop assistant. Her weather beaten face wasn't friendly and she started questioning him aggressively. He stood impassively looking at the old woman whose voice soared to a high pitch. His lack of response seemed to aggravate her further. She began waving her arms and making hostile gestures. Adam decided that it was time to retreat.

An hour later when he was getting ready for bed Adam heard a faint knock on his door. He never had any visitors. Anxiously looking around, he scooped Ginger off his bed, opened the window and sent him for an evening stroll.

There was another knock, this time more energetic. Adam turned the key in the lock and asked, 'Who is it?'

'It's me, Maja. From upstairs.'

'Please come in.' He pushed the door open.

'Sorry for coming so late,' she began hesitantly. 'Zofia has told me that you need to make an appointment with a Chinese doctor in Ealing Common.'

He was astonished with Zofia's efficiency. 'Yes ..., I do.'

'I pass through Ealing Common everyday. I would be happy to do this for you if you could tell me where this Chinese clinic is.'

Unable to contain his embarrassment, Adam explained to Maja what had happened a couple of hours before.

'No problem. I will try to find it,' she said. 'What day would be best for you?'

'Saturday afternoon. Any Saturday afternoon.'

He was sure that he appeared pathetic to this girl. 'I'm sorry to bother you.'

'It's no bother at all.'

He suddenly realised that he should have opened the door wider to appear more friendly, but he hated people prying into his life. He could see that the girl was curiously looking beyond his shoulder into the room. He just said: 'Thank you.'

'Good night then.' And she was gone.

He closed the door slowly and turned the key in the lock.

Things might still turn OK after all. He had to show Zofia that he appreciated her help, he thought. And get something for the girl as a thank you. The events of the day had left him exhausted and he longed for his bed. His fingers began moving down the buttons of his shirt. Half way down he stopped. His eyes rested on a half-empty bowl of cat food standing on a window sill. Ginger's shinning eyes were staring at him through the glass.

When he finally collapsed into his bed exhausted he couldn't sleep. In his mind he went again and again over the events of the day and he felt defeated. The sense of failure which he had managed to suppress during the last eight months was again hanging over him.

His father-in-law had always considered him a disappointment. From the moment fifteen years ago when Hanka told her father that she was pregnant with Adam and she was going to marry him with or without her father's blessing, Bukowski began despising him. Yet, he agreed to the marriage, believing that the status of an unmarried mother in the deeply religious *góral* community would harm his daughter more than a useless husband.

At the time Adam was working as an apprentice to the local carpenter. Apart from his good looks he had nothing to offer Hanka. Bukowski paid for a large wedding, which lasted three days and had all the trimmings of a traditional *góral* feast. He also gave the young couple a house. It was built for his eldest son who went to America and showed no intention of returning to run his father's farm.

Since the farm was large and managing it required considerable effort and skill, an extra pair of hands was always welcome. Adam became experienced with calving and lambing, extending and mending farm buildings, and repairing the ageing machinery which the mountain soil ground down with vengeance. However hard he worked, the old man never acknowledged his skills or his contribution to the family business. Having never forgiven him for 'trapping' his daughter, Bukowski made him feel indebted to him.

The Bukowski family was one of the oldest and most influential in Kościelisko. Every new parish priest and new *wojt* within

days of taking over their posts paid a visit to the Bukowski farm
on Gubałówka, which enjoyed unsurpassed views of the Tatra
Mountains. There, on a large wooden veranda, blackened by
years of exposure to rain and wind, over dishes of steaming stew
and glasses of home made vodka, the matters of local politics,
religion and investment were discussed in confidence. None of
the local officials, no matter how corrupt or honest they were,
would introduce any changes to the local *status quo* before
consulting with old Bukowski.

Over the years, Adam's resentment grew. Meanwhile, old
Bukowski lavished his attention and money on Adam's and
Hanka's children. Particularly Jędrek, who bore an uncanny
resemblance to his grandfather, was the old man's favourite.
Adam's Sunday visits to Ondraszkowa Izba, the most popular
tavern in Kościelisko, became regular and increasingly longer.
He wouldn't be a *góral* if he couldn't handle hard liquor but as
he got older his strong head was becoming less reliable. The
bracing mountain air usually helped him to sober up by the
time he reached home, four and half kilometres away, mostly
uphill.

During one of the climbs up Gubalowka hill, when Adam's
legs felt particularly heavy and his head unusually cloudy, he
stopped by the large boulder laying on the bend of the road. It
had been there for as long as he could remember. The stone,
polished by rain and wind, provided almost no support for his
tired legs so he slid down its side and sat on the ground shel-
tered from the wind. He leaned his head against the ancient
stone and gazed at the breathtaking panorama of the Tatras
mountains. Their jagged edges appeared both beautiful and
menacing against the bright blue sky. He grew up with this
sight and knew every peak and every ridge from memory. As a
child, he heard countless tales about these summits and people
who braved them and never returned to their villages. These
mountains were in his blood and nothing made him more alive
than a gust of cold wind coming down from those peaks.

A black Mercedes pulled up a few metres further. Dressed in
his Sunday best, old Bukowski stepped out of the car. He took
one look at Adam and opened the rear passenger door. For a
moment he stood above Adam, with pity and disgust looking

down on his son-in-law. Then with one movement of his powerful arm he lifted Adam by the collar of his jacket. He picked him
up, dragged him a couple of metres and threw him onto the back
seat of his car. Slamming the door he hissed: 'Bringing shame
on the family. On Sunday!' Then he spat on the road and
returned to the driver's seat.

Chapter 14

Maja, December 1997

Could she survive in London if she couldn't speak English? Maja wondered as she hurried across Ealing Common towards Uxbridge Road. It was the middle of December and as soon as the sun disappeared behind the horizon, the temperature dropped by a few degrees. The freezing wind was blowing through her quilted jacket. Maja shivered. It wasn't a night to be homeless.

She was standing on Uxbridge Road in front of a shop with frosted windows. A line of black oriental lettering ran on the side of each glass panel. It didn't look like a Chinese clinic but Maja didn't know what to expect. She pushed the door open and went in. A narrow corridor led into a room filled with tables covered with white tablecloths. Before Maja could retreat, an oriental girl with a doll-like face approached her.

'A table for one?'

'Oh, no! Thank you, no. I've made a mistake. I wasn't looking for a restaurant.'

Good God, how daft she was. Back in the street she noticed that on the door underneath the oriental signs, there was a line in English: Mura, Japanese restaurant.

She imagined Adam staring at the frosted windows trying to figure out whether this place offered solutions to his health problems.

She began walking again, carefully scanning shop windows on both sides of the street. The Chinese clinic couldn't be far. Indeed, several metres further she saw a shop window with Chinese writing and charts of the human body attached to the glass. With a great deal of hope she pushed the door open. The first glance inside made her realise how wrong she was. It was a shop with oriental foods. Bags of rice were piled on low tables, crates of exotic vegetables stood on top of each other. Cans with strange looking content were arranged like Lego bricks. In the corner, behind a wooden counter there was a wall of shelves with jars containing dried leaves and seeds. 'Chinese herbs' stated a gold and green sign.

Another miss. Maja turned around and was about to leave the shop when she suddenly had a thought. She walked up to an old Chinese woman in a white lab coat standing behind the herb counter.

'Is there is a Chinese clinic nearby?'

The woman picked up one of the leaflets on the counter and handed it to Maja. 'There are many Chinese medicine places in West London. They are all in this brochure.'

'Is there one on this street?' The woman looked at her carefully. 'What kind of medicine do you need?'

'Well, herbs, acupuncture ... that sort of thing.' Maja waved her hand in the direction of the wall of jars.

'You must see a doctor before you start taking Chinese herbs.'

'I know. But where can I find one?'

'The brochure will tell you. See the addresses inside.'

'So there is no Chinese doctor on this street?'

'Doctor? No. There is some treatment place further down the road but not a clinic.'

This was perhaps a matter of definition, Maja thought. She took the leaflet and thanked the woman. As she walked towards the door, she could feel the woman's gaze on her back.

The cold air hit her face when she opened the door. Third time lucky she thought to herself. In her mind, she pictured Adam in the same place trying to negotiate his way into the world of Chinese medicine in London. Ridiculous and sad. Perhaps an immigrant's destiny always borders on the ridiculous and pathetic? She pulled her hat down deeper and strode towards the end of the street. Almost at the end of the rank of shops there was ... another Chinese supermarket. In the window, there was a poster advertising Chinese treatments. It was curling at the edges and its black print had turned to sepia.

A young Chinese man with a happy face greeted her politely.

'I am looking for a Chinese doctor.'

'There are therapy rooms at the back. A woman there does

massage and some acupuncture. Would you like to see her?'

Maja nodded and fixed him with her brightest smile. The man opened the back door of the shop and, letting Maja in first, said: 'This way.'

The concrete floor of a damp backyard was covered with crates of rotting fruit and vegetables. Even on a cold day, the stench was oppressive. An open metal staircase was rising from the middle of the yard. Placing one hand on the peeling handrail, the young man pointed to the floor above. 'The rooms are on the first floor.'

Maja thanked him and with a heavy heart starting mounting the metal steps which clanked loudly with her every move. On the first floor landing there was only one door painted in bright red. There was no bell so Maja opened it and found herself in a corridor which served as a waiting area.

As she stood staring at the posters on the wall trying to determine what to expect of this place, a round Chinese lady in a short-sleeved white coat appeared in front of her. She brought with her a scent of menthol and eucalyptus.

'Do you have an appointment?' she asked in a business-like manner.

'No, I just came.'

'No problem.' The woman reached for one of the forms which were neatly stacked on the coffee table. 'Have a look at our treatments. You need to complete the last page. I have a patient now. I will be back in fifteen minutes.' She disappeared as unexpectedly as she had arrived. Oriental charms attached to the door frame kept dancing long after she was gone.

Maja was left standing with a form in her hand. She looked through four pages of small print listing different kinds of massage and limb manipulation. It was fascinating but none of this appeared to have any relevance to Adam's problems. She folded the form neatly and slipped it into her handbag. Closing the door behind her softly, she walked out. She wished to get away unnoticed but with every step the iron staircase groaned mercilessly. The noise resonated loudly in the concrete back-yard. It sounded like jeering at her failed mission.

The following Saturday they were sitting together in the waiting area of a Chinese clinic in Greenford, both uncertain whether this was the real thing this time. The walls were covered with drawings of the human body and home-made posters advertising the services of the clinic: Chinese medicine, acupuncture and beauty. On the opposite wall there was a poster with the words: Alcohol, Smoking, Addictions. One next to it stated: Weight loss 3-5kg, Bloating, Constipation, Stress. A notice above their heads said: Impotence, Sex Drive. Was Chinese medicine able to regulate all human desires and cure all ills? she wondered.

'Adam Bugaj!' The voice sounded like a school register. As Adam got up, a small, efficient looking woman in a white doctor's coat nodded at him to follow her into the consultation room. Maja also rose. 'I'll be helping with translation,' she explained.

'Are you Mr Bugaj's wife?'

'No, just his friend. I came to help.'

'I will examine Mr Bugaj first. You have to wait here,' the doctor said firmly. Adam shrugged and with an anxious expression followed the doctor to the surgery. Maja watched the door close behind them, wondering how they would communicate.

She looked at people in the waiting room. A large woman with the golden complexion of a southern European was knitting. She was pulling the yarn from a bag situated between her feet.

'Are you a regular patient here?' ventured Maja, trying to keep the tone of her voice friendly but not too inquisitive.

'Oh, yes. This is my second round of treatment. I still cannot believe what good these herbs have done for me.'

'Sorry for asking, but what medical condition are you treating here?'

'That's OK. I had very bad pain in my joints. Couldn't get up in the mornings. My daughter's husband told me to try Chinese medicine and it worked like a miracle on me. Praying to saint Servatus helped too.'

'So what's the doctor giving you?' prodded Maja.

'Different herbs to drink, then some acupuncture and herbs again. At first, they made me feel *orrible*. I was thinking they were going to ...'

The door of the surgery swung open. The Chinese doctor

motioned at Maja and commanded: 'You can come in now.'

Adam was buttoning his shirt when Maja entered the room. She sat on the chair next to him.

'I've examined your friend and have a good idea what his problem is but I need to ask him a few questions. Please translate his answers to me.'

'Of course,' said Maja eagerly.

'Did he experience such stomach pains before?'

Maja translated Adam's account of his earlier gastric troubles.

'How many years ago was it?'

'Over ten.'

'Is he allergic to anything?'

'No, he's never had any allergies,' confirmed Maja after Adam.

'I didn't think he had,' said the doctor glancing at Adam. 'Does he drink? Alcohol, I mean?'

There was a moment of silence. Adam took a sip of water from a plastic cup standing beside him. He understood the question and asked Maja to translate his answer.

'No, he says. He hasn't touched alcohol for at least two months.'

'And before? In Poland?'

Not meeting Adam's eyes, Maja asked him the question.

Adam shifted in his seat and looked up at the doctor. 'Maja, please tell her I used to drink back at home. Sometimes a lot.'

It seemed that the doctor knew the answer before Maja translated it. She was compiling a long column of words on a piece of paper. For a moment she stopped, looked at Adam, and added a couple more items to the list.

'This is your prescription, Mr Bugaj. You should start from a herbal mixture — to be drunk twice a day. I also recommend that you take a series of acupuncture sessions after two weeks of the herbal treatment. It will help to detoxify your system. Acupuncture sessions should be taken at least once a week, for six or twelve weeks. The clinic is open until 8pm.'

'What is the cost of the treatment?' Maja interrupted the fast flow of doctor's recommendations.

'The series of six acupuncture sessions costs £120 and the series of twelve is £220. The supply of herbs for six weeks is £60.'

Maja translated the doctor's words anxiously looking at Adam. His face became totally still and he fixed his eyes on the opposite wall. Watching them the doctor suggested: 'Perhaps you would like to discuss the treatment with your friend in the waiting room. When you have made up your mind, please knock on my door.'

They went out and like conspirators huddled together in the corner of the waiting area. Maja remained silent. Adam's face reflected the effort of trying to come to terms with a serious dilemma. He took out a piece of paper from his pocket and wrote down some figures on it. After a moment he crossed them out. He lifted his eyes and looked at Maja. Then he went back to his calculations.

Unexpectedly he asked: 'Maja, how much do you pay for your school?'

'Two hundred and eighty pounds per term,' she answered automatically.

'Is this a large proportion of your earnings?'

'About a half. When I started working, it was more.'

'You don't have much left once you've paid for your room and food.'

'That's true. But I don't mind. Paying for the college is an investment.'

Adam stuffed his calculations in the breast pocket of his jacket and muttered: 'I've also been investing, but now I need to invest more. For the future.'

Chapter 15

Maja changed three times before she found the right outfit for the evening. She began with a navy and white dress which she had bought on sale a couple of weeks before, thinking that she would need something smart for a big occasion. Yet she felt overdressed in it. The second option was a clingy dress from Sylvia. A silver thread woven into the fabric accentuated every curve of her body and she felt almost naked in it. The third option was a velvet skirt from Principles which she found in a charity shop. It cost four pounds as it was size 10 shrunk to size 8. She matched it with a navy chiffon blouse, with large white polka dots. It had generously cut sleeves that billowed gracefully when she moved. A belt with a diamante buckle, a gift from Sylvia who had a fabulous collection of accessories, gave the outfit the finishing touch she was looking for.

She wrapped herself in her quilted jacket thinking that it would be nice to have a long coat for such an occasion. It would cover an evening outfit and taking it off would be like unveiling a surprise. Well, she didn't have one, so her jacket would have to do, she concluded and went downstairs.

She told Nico to meet her at the bottom of the street to avoid more questions and speculation at 26 Cuckoohill Road. Basia had already commented on Maja's boyfriend's cool car, warning her mother that when she became eighteen she was going to get a rich boyfriend and move out. Maja felt sorry for Zofia and was tempted to explain that there was more to Nico than an expensive car, but she feared being drawn into a conversation about him. She didn't want to talk to anyone about Nico because she didn't yet know how she felt about him. Perhaps this evening would help her see things more clearly.

They were now standing at the bar of the Her Majesty's Theatre in the first interval, sipping champagne which Nico ordered to celebrate their evening together. And there was plenty to celebrate, she thought. He had taken her to see the *Phantom of the Opera* and she was bowled over with the famous musical. From the first thunderous chord which split the old theatre, she sat on the edge of her seat mesmerised with the production. The stirring music, the powerful voices, the lavish sets and costumes combined to create the magic. She had never seen anything like it before. Nico was right. She would always remember that night. Even now standing next to Nico, who looked very dashing in his navy blazer, she was still trembling with emotion.

Trying to make himself heard in the noisy bar, Nico moved closer to her and asked: 'Are you enjoying the *Phantom*, Maja?' She smiled and holding his gaze, she said: 'I love it, Nico. Everything. Thank you.'

Then something happened that Maja would never forget. Nico took her by the elbow and gently pulled her towards him. Burying his lips in her hair he said: 'I love seeing you happy. You look more beautiful than ever.' She didn't answer but just rested her head against his shoulder. The intimacy of this gesture surprised them both. They stood like this for a moment in the middle of a crowded bar with people milling around them, shouting and laughing above their heads.

Then at the same time they stepped apart, startled with what had happened. Nico reached for Maja's glass and handing over to her, said: 'To us.'

They stood in silence looking at each other. Then the bell rang and the crowd slowly started leaving the bar. It was time to go back to their seats.

When the last chord of music died down and the theatre sunk into darkness, there was a moment of total silence. People held their breath spellbound with the power of the music and the magic of the performance. Maja sat still, squeezing Nico's hand, unaware of what she was doing. Then the lights flooded the stage and thunderous applause shook the auditorium. Maja looked around as if she had just woken up from a dream. People around her were clapping madly and when the actors reappeared on stage, the crowd got to their feet and applauded them standing up. It felt as if a thousand volts of electricity were charging the air.

Nico leaned towards Maja trying to tell her something but she couldn't hear a word above the frantic clapping. So he shrugged and gave her a massive grin. She smiled back at him and thought that this was a moment of perfect happiness.

Eventually the applause died down and they were able to talk. Looking at Maja, at her shining eyes and gleaming cheeks Nico said: 'You look radiant.'

'It was a magical performance. You're my fairy godmother who took me to the ball.'

'Perhaps a godfather?'

They laughed and chatted about the musical as they were making their way out of the stalls. Suddenly Nico looked at his watch. 'It's already quarter past ten. I had enough change to feed the metre until half past ten. Do you mind collecting our coats? I will hurry up to the car before the ticket runs out and will pick you up from the front of the theatre.'

'Of course, Nico.'

Slipping the cloakroom disks into her hand, he leaned towards her and whispered: 'The magic coach will be waiting at the entrance for my princess.' He winked at her and ran downstairs.

The queue to the cloakroom was moving slowly but Maja didn't notice this, absorbed in the memories of the past three hours. With her fingers she was caressing the glossy cover of the theatre programme which she planned to study late into the night.

At last it was her turn. She put a few coins into a 'Thank you' box and slipped on her jacket. She folded Nico's coat and hung it over her arm. Despite its bulk, it was light and soft. As she walked down the winding staircase, decorated with white and black photographs of famous actors and posters of past performances, she snuggled Nico's coat to her face. It smelled of tobacco and musky cologne. She recalled smelling this scent on him one day but now it was much stronger and closer, almost intimate. She noticed that there was a beige checked scarf tucked into one of the sleeves, which now was hanging down to the ground. She pulled it out and folded on the top thinking how well it matched the black coat. Nico inherited his sense of style with his Italian genes.

She went outside and stood under the grand portico of the theatre entrance wondering from which direction Nico would be coming. After ten minutes she started walking from one end of the entrance to the other to keep herself warm as the night grew increasingly chilly. Pacing up and down the pavement with Nico's coat on her arm she caught a few curious glances of the people also waiting at the entrance. She ignored them but, as she stood by the curb looking around, a black cab pulled up. Leaning out the window, the driver shouted to her: 'Waiting for transport, Miss?'

Startled, she just walked away. Anxiety slowly started creeping in. She wondered what was keeping Nico for so long. Perhaps he exceeded the credit on the meter and had been stopped by a traffic warden. Maybe his car was clamped and he was trying to reclaim it. She vaguely remembered where they left the car and decided to find it.

While the Haymarket still pulsated with night life and traffic, the side streets behind it were surprisingly quiet. Maja could hear the tapping of her heels on the pavement in the empty street. She walked for about five minutes when she recognised a small bistro situated on the corner of the street which they passed on their way to the theatre. It was still open although the staff were now folding the menu boards and taking in wooden boxes with ornamental topiary. At the end of the street Maja stopped for a moment trying to decide which way to go next. Suddenly she saw the lights of an approaching car. Thinking that this was Nico she started waving. As the car approached she could see that it wasn't yellow so she dropped her hand. Disappointed she walked fast to the next junction. The street was so silent that she could hear her quickening breath and pounding heart. Left. She ran to the next corner. She was about to turn right when she heard a screech of tyres and saw a fast moving car emerging from the street on the right and speeding into the street ahead.

At the same time she heard a man's hoarse voice just behind her. 'Miss, don't go there. Not now.'

The warning came from a man in shabby clothes who suddenly appeared behind her. He pulled her towards him and they fell together down the basement steps of the house behind them. She tried to scream but the man clamped his smelly hand over her mouth. His rasping voice whispered a warning: 'Be quiet. I won't hurt you. They have just shot somebody there. They will kill us too if they see us.'

She heard a car speeding in the street above them. The man was dirty and smelled revolting but Maja was too terrified to move. After a couple of minutes when the street became silent, the man released his grip on Maja and said: 'Let's get the hell out of here.' With great difficulty Maja walked up the steps leading to the street. She had hurt her leg during the fall and her whole body was shaking violently.

She looked at the man in a shabby coat standing beside her. He pulled his woolly hat deeper over his ears and said. 'Run home miss, and forget that you have been here. These gangs don't leave witnesses alive.'

'But my friend's car is in that street. I have to see if ...' She pulled her sleeve from the man's grasp and ran towards the corner of the street. She raised herself on her toes. For a moment, she couldn't see anything through her tears. Then she lifted a hand to her mouth and a cry died on her lips. In the light of a street lamp, she could see Nico's yellow Ferrari parked in between other cars. On the bonnet lay the body of a man face down with his arms outstretched above his head. A black trickle of blood ran from his head down the middle of the bonnet.

Chapter 16

Kuba, January 1998

It took him exactly twenty minutes to drive from Greenford to central London. He didn't take his foot off the gas pedal from the moment he jumped into the car, after receiving Maja's call, until eleven when he found her in the doorway of a corner bistro in the West End.

When he heard his mobile phone ring a short while after he had fallen into the bed, he considered ignoring it. He had just spent ten gruelling hours on the road. Such moments made him realise how much he wished to quit this line of work. When the ringing didn't stop, he thought that this could be someone else other than Century Cabs. He fumbled for his phone in the dark and when he accidentally sent it flying to the floor, he saw the caller's number. It was a landline from central London. He lunged forward, almost falling off the bed. A female voice speaking in Polish was barely understandable. For a moment he thought that something had happened to his family and a stranger was calling to tell him about this.

'Kuba, please come here. Help me. Please ...'

'Who is this? Maja? What's happened?'

A pleading voice offered an incomprehensive explanation.

'What? Where ...? Where are you now?'

From the few words she managed to utter between spasmatic sobbing, he understood the seriousness of the situation.

'Maja, calm down. I'm coming. Please walk to the nearest street corner and read for me the name of the street.' He waited for a moment. 'Stafford Street. Very good.' He scribbled the name on an old cinema ticket.

'Is there a restaurant or somewhere where you can go in and wait for me? You're near a bar? Good, I will find you. Don't stand in the street alone. No ..., just stay there. I'm coming.'

'Jesus,' he said aloud after snapping his phone shut, with one leg already in his jeans. She is in real shit. A dangerous one. How had she got herself into such a mess? A girl like her? He snatched his jacket from the door hook and ran downstairs.

Doing ninety miles an hour down the A40 towards central London, Kuba was trying not to think about speed cameras and the tickets he was earning. He felt adrenaline rising in his blood and tiredness ebbing away. It was going to be one hell of a day.

The moment he woke up that Saturday morning Kuba remembered that he would have to confront some unresolved issues that day which he would rather leave alone. At least for a while until he made his mind up about what he wanted to do. However Ashley had started the ball rolling, as he promised he would, so now he had to step in and deal with what was coming his way. At ten he was meeting Ashley's physio, Karen. She was to help him to find out how he could get his diploma validated in the UK to be able to practise one day. On the phone she suggested that he might also need to take some refresher courses. They would look together through some college brochures.

'Everything depends on what area you wish to specialise. Eventually.'

'I need to think about this.'

They agreed to meet in a coffee shop on Ealing High Street. He arrived half an hour earlier to give himself time to think. He wasn't sure he was ready for a radical change to his rather predicable existence in London. He didn't have answers to two fundamental questions: what he really wanted to do next and where he wished to settle down. Resolving this had a strong feeling of permanency and he disliked permanent solutions. OK, cabbing was just a temporary fix while he was making up his mind. Some time ago he played with the idea of going to the States. Apparently employment opportunities there were much better than in England. Did he want to come back to physiotherapy? He enjoyed it all right, but perhaps he was better suited to a different career?

With the corner of his eye he caught a glimpse of an attractive girl entering the café. She had shining chestnut-coloured hair pulled back in a ponytail and was wearing a leather jacket, jeans and very white trainers. She paused by the door looking around the place. The moment she caught Kuba's glance, she waved enthusiastically in his direction.

A casual observer would have thought that they were a pair of old friends, reflected Kuba and felt compelled to wave back. When she reached the table, she slid a large holdall off her arm and dumped it on one of the empty chairs. Offering her hand she exclaimed: 'Karen, Karen Lipman.'

'Kuba Baranski.'

'Nice to meet you at last! I can recognise a fellow physio the moment I see one.'

Kuba intended to say that he hadn't made his mind up about the whole thing, but before he had an opportunity to interrupt her, Karen reached for her bag and took out a wad of papers.

'Tea or coffee?'

'I called a couple of colleges to send me their brochures so you can see what entry qualifications they require ...'

'Karen, would you like tea or coffee?'

Interrupted she frowned and repeated: 'Tea or coffee? Of course! Skinny latte. Thank you. With one sugar. I need to keep my energy levels up,' she added apologetically.

Kuba got up and walked to the coffee bar glad to escape Karen's outpouring and earning himself more time to think. She obviously took her role as his advisor very seriously. Perhaps she felt it was her mission to help him better himself. Kuba wondered what motivated her.

When he came back with their drinks, he noticed that she had already opened a couple of brochures and highlighted some sections.

As soon as he placed the cups on the table, Karen asked: 'Are you ready? We can start form this.' She passed one of the brochures across the table.

Kuba smiled a resigned smile. There was no way to stall the efforts of this woman.

'These are standard entry qualifications for anyone considering a physiotherapy course in higher education. BTEC National Diploma in Health Studies, HND International Baccalaureate, Advanced GNVQ etc ... or an appropriate foundation course.

Your Polish diploma should allow you to skip these. What diploma do you have?'

'I have a degree in physiotherapy from the Academy of Physical Education in Katowice. Then I practiced for four years.'

'Goodness! You have a solid background and a lot of experience. You may have to do a refresher course but they may let you to skip some stages. I'm happy to call the Health Professionals Council to check how your training and work fit into the British system.'

'How did you go about fitting into the system?'

'I qualified in Auckland, but our system is very similar. So my example won't be much help for you. But the guys in the HPC should be able to advise us.'

Kuba was uncomfortable building a debt of gratitude to a woman who was a complete stranger to him only a week ago. He felt uneasy about accepting more help but he couldn't quite find the words to tell her this.

'Karen, I don't want to burden you with my problems. I am sure you're very busy yourself ...'

'Not at all,' she protested. 'Many people helped me when I was starting here. It's my turn now. Besides, Ashley is not only my patient but also a good friend. You're his friend too.'

Kuba hesitated. For a split second he considered whether she had read into his friendship with Ashley more than he wished. He looked at Karen over his coffee. She was very attractive and there was a strange seriousness in those large brown eyes. Her strong mouth suggested determination. She could be a formidable ally and probably a steadfast friend too.

'Kuba, are you happy for me to investigate this on your behalf?' Karen's raised voice brought him back to the coffee shop. He wasn't sure what she had said but didn't doubt her sincerity. He wished to say 'Do I have any choice?' but confirmed instead: 'Yes, I'm very grateful for your help.'

'I will make a few calls and give you a ring before Friday.' This meant that next weekend he would have to make more decisions.

He was thinking about this when he received a call from Century Cabs. A hurried run to Heathrow was the first of many jobs he did that day. However, the call from Maja pushed everything else into the routine category.

It didn't take him long to find the street where Maja was waiting for him. Frequently picking up customers from the West End, he was familiar with the warren of back streets and the complicated one-way system which trapped unsuspecting drivers like a spider's web.

Anxiously looking around, Maja was standing in the doorway of a bistro with a piece of clothing on her arm. When he approached her, he saw how frightened she was. He took her gently by the arm and led her into the car.

'Kuba, thank you,' she managed to whisper. He pulled her to himself and hugging her, he said softly, like to a child: 'Maja, it'll be OK. You're safe now.'

She didn't pull away from him, comforted by his closeness. Suddenly she asked: 'Can we go there — to see. I need to see it.'

With his arm protectively around her, Kuba asked: 'Are you sure you want to do this? Will it be safe?' Looking down, he realised that the garment she was holding was a man's coat.

'I want to check whether there is something I can do,' she said firmly.

'OK, Maja. I will drive you there. Show me the way.'

He helped her to the car. When she sat down next to him she was clutching the coat to her chest. Her face was like a plaster mask.

They drove for a couple of minutes when pointing to the street ahead, Maja exclaimed: 'It's there. The street on the left.'

Kuba parked swiftly, jumped out of the car and walked around to help her get out.

'We'd better leave it here,' he suggested, taking the coat from her and placing it on the back seat. 'Let's go.' He led her firmly but gently, instinctively knowing that he would be making decisions that night.

Before they turned the corner they saw blue flashing lights bouncing off the walls of the Victorian mansions. A policeman was cordoning off the street with yellow tape. An ambulance was standing in the middle of the street and several uniformed policemen and paramedics were rushing around between the cars.

'Maja, they are in control now,' Kuba said putting his arm around the girl and nodding in the direction of the commotion. 'There is nothing we can do. It'd be better if you're left out of this. For your own safety.'

Maja was standing still, staring blankly at the scene in front of them.

'I ... I was too late.'

'You saved your life by being late. We must go.' He made her turn around and they walked back to the car. When she sat down he could see that she was trembling feverishly. He reached for the back seat, took the coat and wrapped it around her legs.

'You need to have a rest now. Tomorrow we will think about what to do next.'

Chapter 17

Kuba, January 1998

It felt like a normal Sunday. At eight o'clock in the morning the house appeared to be still asleep, with not a single sound breaking the silence. Yet, today the silence wasn't comforting Kuba as usual. The curtains were drawn in the lounge and in the hall the pile of unopened mail and advertising junk was as large as ever.

Kuba went into the kitchen and softly closed the door. He filled the kettle and reached for a packet of his favourite dark roast coffee. He needed time by himself to think through the events of the previous night. Sighing heavily, he pushed the plunger down through the black velvety liquid. A bewitching aroma was filling the empty kitchen.

Upstairs, Maja slept, sedated with pills which he'd bought for her in a 24 hour pharmacy. With a single stroke of bad luck Maja had got herself involved in a tragedy. She always impressed him with her confidence and focus. And this single-minded girl, with poise and style, overnight became a hysterically sobbing wreck. She narrowly missed being murdered together with her boyfriend, but would she ever feel safe again? It pained him to see her so frightened and her confidence shattered to pieces. In his profession he had seen enough fear and suffering but this never made him completely prepared for another example of human misery.

Kuba heard a clip clop of Zofia's slippers on the stairs. Should he tell her what had happened last night? Zofia was a woman with a big heart and plenty of common sense and she may be able to help. Yet, Maja's problems were her business and she should be able to decide with whom she wanted to share them.

'*Dzien dobry*, Kuba. Up so early on Sunday?'

'Good morning, *pani Zofio*. I have just made some coffee.

Would you like a cup?'

'I would love one. You've had such a busy week. You should have a good lie in on Sunday.' Zofia rarely missed a beat regarding the goings on at 26 Cuckoohill Road.

'I'm fine. I may go for a jog in a moment.'

Every Sunday after preparing a substantial breakfast, Zofia took her family to a mass at eleven thirty at the Polish church in Ealing. Kuba knew that the Kowals took the third commandment very seriously. Yet these Sunday visits to the church not only had a religious significance. English people played cricket or golf in their clubs at the weekend. Many times he watched the camaraderie of men in white outfits in the park and felt that this was so much more than playing the sport. To the Poles in England the church gave a similar sense of belonging. On Sunday, the church in Windsor Road was filled to the brim during each of its six Sunday services. On numerous occasions, Kuba caught curious glances of passers-by looking at the crowd of people flowing out of the church door.

After the service, the Kowals went to the Windsor Road café with their friends. Afterwards, if the weather was pleasant, they took a stroll in the local park. They were usually back in the early afternoon. With Adam most likely keeping his own company until lunchtime, the house would be empty until the Kowals returned. This meant that he could talk to Maja, if she was able and willing to discuss her problems with him.

'I'd better go for that run,' Kuba said, hoping that the cool morning air would clear his head.

He had no time to start worrying about how to approach Maja. The moment he stepped out of the shower after a long jog, the doorbell rang. He quickly dried his hair and wrapping the towel around his waist run downstairs. A woman of about seventy, dressed in a grey flannel suit, was standing on the doorstep. A pair of dark eyes was anxiously examining him.

'Can I speak to Miss Maja Zalewska?' she asked in a barely audible voice.

Kuba became instantly alert. Different thoughts were racing through his mind. What if the murderers of Nico were already looking for Maja?

'She ..., she is still sleeping.'

'Is it a bad moment?' the old lady whispered looking at his sparse attire.

'No, no. She is just tired.'

'I can come back later.'

Kuba looked carefully at the woman. She was dressed in old fashioned but good quality clothes. Her regular features suggested that she might have been very attractive in her youth and there was no malice in her face.

'Would you like to leave a message for Maja?' asked Kuba testing her intentions.

'Yes, please tell her that Lorenzo's sister wishes to see her. My brother works with her in Bella Italia and I have a message from him.'

At this point, Kuba decided that Maja should speak to the woman herself. As soon as possible.

'Please come in. I will go and wake Maja up.'

Leading the woman to the lounge, Kuba enquired: 'Can I make you a drink? It may take a few minutes.'

'Just a glass of water. Thank you.'

When Kuba returned with the drink the woman had already sunk into one of Mrs Patel's tanker-like armchairs, with her hands folded on her lap. She didn't have an appearance of the mafia accomplice, he concluded.

Ten minutes later Maja came down wrapped in her blue dressing gown looking pale and strained. With a weak smile she offered her hand to the old woman.

'Thank you very much for coming, Mrs ...'

'Elena Agnesi.'

'Mrs Agnesi, I heard that you have a message for me.'

'Lorenzo and senior Mazzini are very worried about you after this terrible accident last night. There was some mistake. A tragic one. Poor, poor Nico. He was such a lovely boy. He must have been taken for someone else.'

'I was delayed at the theatre and came too late ...'

'Mr Mazzini guessed this. Mercifully, you were spared.'

'I am so sorry, I couldn't help him ...'

'Maja, I will get you a coffee,' said Kuba leaving for the

kitchen. He sensed that Maja was barely holding herself together. He also felt that the women wished to be left alone.

He took his time brewing a fresh pot of coffee and arranging a
few biscuits he found in his cupboard on a plate. When he came
back to the room, Maja was sitting on a chair next to Lorenzo's
sister, who was patting her hand. Maja's eyes and nose were red
and she was nervously plucking a tissue in her hands. The old
woman's eyes were also moist. He felt like an intruder so he
pulled the coffee table towards the women, placed cups and
plates on it and promptly left the room.

He sat in his bedroom for a while watching a news channel but
soon realised that he hadn't understood a word of what was said
and decided to go for a walk. Passing the hallway, he was
surprised that he couldn't hear a sound form the lounge. He
knocked on the door. There was a weak 'please, come in.'

'Maja, I just wanted to let you know that I am going out but I
will be back in half an hour.'

Maja looked up at him for a moment but he got the impression
she didn't comprehend what he said. Then she wiped her eyes
and said: 'Kuba, I haven't even introduced you to Mrs Agnesi.'
Then turning to the woman she said: 'This is my Polish friend
Kuba Baranski. He helped me last night. When ... when I saw
Nico. He brought me home.'

Now the eyes of both women were on Kuba. Maja's eyes
appeared to search for reassurance, while the old woman was
looking at him with some mistrust. He felt that Mrs Agnesi was
assessing his intentions.

'You have a lot to discuss together. I'll be back soon.' He pulled
one of his Century Cabs cards and placing it next to Maja's cup
said: 'Call me if you need to speak to me.'

He walked up and down the small green at the end of their road.
He even made a call to Henryk in Opole, but since he called his
brother only a few days before, they didn't have much to say to
each other and neither of them was in the mood for small talk.

When he came back and knocked at the lounge door there was
no answer. Alarmed he swung the door open. Lorenzo's sister
was gone. Maja was sitting alone with her face in her hands.
Kuba wasn't sure whether she was crying or just wished to be

left alone. He touched her shoulder.

'Maja, are you OK?'

Without removing her hands from her face she shook her head.

'I will make you some breakfast. It's almost midday.'

Another shake. Kuba swallowed hard and kneeling in front of her he touched her hands.

'Maja, I want to help you.' After a moment of silence there was a sob and she lowered her hands. Tears and words flooded out like a torrent.

'No one can help me now. No one. Mrs Agnesi told me that *Signor* Mazzini will send me money but I shouldn't go back to the restaurant. It isn't safe. Lorenzo suggested going back to Poland.'

'Maybe that's not a bad idea.'

'No! Kuba, no!' she cried vehemently. What am I going to tell my parents? My brother and sister? My friends? That I failed at everything and I am running away. I was working and studying ...' She was now crying hysterically. 'I met this lovely man ... And I managed to lose everything.'

He saw on her face something he had never expected to see. Desperation. Sheer despondency. He wished to take her in his arms and sooth her like a child but felt that she may misread his intentions.

'None of this was your fault. Maja, remember how lucky you were. You survived. It's terrible what has happened to your friend, but it had nothing to do with you. Perhaps nothing to do with him too. Let's hope the police will get to the heart of this.'

'He was so kind to me ...' Another heart-breaking sob.

'Maja, you are a very special girl. Any decent man would see this.'

Suddenly, Maja lifted her head and stared at him. 'Nico said ...' and then she stopped.

'Maja, I am going to buy some food for us. I'm starving. You could change in the meantime. Then we can go for a walk.' He watched her for a while, hoping that Maja would respond to this coaxing, but she just sat there staring ahead of her.

'We are dealing with a patient's denial,' he heard the words of warning in his head. 'A piecemeal approach would be advisable

here.' He got up and walking towards the door in an authoritative voice issued a warning: 'I'm going out to the shops.'

An hour later when Kuba returned from Sainsbury's and started taking his shopping out of the boot, he suddenly noticed that
Cuckoohill Road had become very animated since the morning.
People walked and drove up and down the street. The doors
were being open and shut and metal gates clanked. He could
hear some children playing in the garden. Everything appeared
so normal.

He wondered whether he would find Maja sitting alone in the
lounge. He had no right to boss her around, he reminded himself. But he also knew she shouldn't be left alone in her present
state of mind. He knocked at the door to the lounge. There was
no answer. He hit the door open and saw that the room was
empty. He dumped the shopping in the entrance hall and ran
upstairs two steps at a time. Half way up, he heard the hum of
water in the shower. He sighed heavily and relaxed. It was a
good sign. He went to the kitchen and started unpacking the
groceries. He lined up a couple of cartons of chicken soup (his
grandmother always made chicken soup whenever someone in
the family was ill) and two containers of lasagne. He assessed
them critically for their comforting properties. That should do,
he thought.

For a while, Kuba stood outside Maja's door listening for clues.
There were none so he energetically knocked.

'Please come in.' Still in her dressing gown, but visibly refreshed, Maja was standing by the window looking out at the
garden. She crossed her arms in front of her, hugging herself.

'Lunch is on the table.' No response. 'Please don't tell me
you're not hungry,' Kuba said with a tinge of irritation in his
voice.

She suddenly turned around. Her face was still ghostly white
but she appeared to control her emotions. 'Kuba, I am not
hungry. But I will go down and eat with you because you have
prepared this food for me. I have been behaving like an ungrate-
ful cow.'

'You're upset.'

'I feel like I lost the ground under my feet but it's not an excuse to be rude to you. After everything you've done for me.'

They ate in silence but there was no awkwardness between them. The events of the previous twenty four hours bound them together in an expected way.

When they finished, Kuba suggested. 'What about a walk now? It'll do us good.'

'Us?' Maja put her mug down on the table and fixed her eyes on Kuba. 'You're one of the kindest men I've met. We were strangers two days ago. But you helped me as if I was your sister. And you keep looking after me ...'

'Well ...' Kuba didn't know what to say. Why did he get involved in her life? Why did he care what would happen to her? 'Perhaps it was meant to be that way,' he said philosophically.

Maja spent the next four days in her room. The traumatic experience of Saturday night made her physically ill. She was also grieving for Nico, Kuba concluded. She looked very pale and spent most of the time in bed. He considered calling the doctor, but when he suggested this to Maja, she told him that she just needed to be left alone. 'It's not only my body which needs mending. I also need time to think.'

Kuba kept his distance but dropping into the house in between the jobs he was able to observe what was going on in Maja's life.

By the middle of the week she was ready to see her friends. First a chirpy dark-haired girl spent an afternoon in Maja's room. Then a couple of Polish girls came bearing gifts of food and a large pot of scarlet azalea. Then the weather suddenly improved and the sounds and smells of nature tempted Maja to venture out doors. On Friday afternoon, Kuba saw her returning to the house with bags of groceries. She walked slowly but didn't have the absent look of previous days. However, she wasn't her old self. There was a shadow on her face which had never been there before.

At half past eleven Kuba settled himself in bed with a book. He felt tired and he doubted that he would be able to get to the end of the page. Suddenly there was a knock on the door. A feeble, hesitant knock.

'Please come in.'

A door opened slowly and Maja's face appeared in the crack. 'I didn't know you're already in bed. I'll come tomorrow.'

'If you're not offended by the sight of my old pyjamas, please come in.'

'You must be very tired ...'

'Yes, I am but I'm happy to talk to you.' He indicated a chair standing at the foot of the bed on which he shed his clothes every night. 'Just toss them on the floor.'

Maja lifted his shirt and trousers and laid them on the back of the chair. Then she sat at the edge of the seat.

'I just wanted to tell you that I took a decision.'

'OK ...?'

'I decided that I'll stay in London.'

'Yes ...'

'I won't run back to Poland. I will find another job and continue with the college. I feel scared but if I returned to Poland, it would be as if I gave into bullying. I will never do that again.' Her cheeks were burning and her voice quivered but she continued. 'In the letter which *Signore* Mazzini sent me with the cheque he said they had destroyed all my records and apart from Lorenzo no one knows where I live. But he told me never to come back to the restaurant and not to contact anyone from Bella Italia.'

'Good advice. You have to be very careful now.'

'I know. But I when I come back from work it's usually late ... I have to find a way.'

Kuba looked directly into her eyes. 'You have done the hardest bit deciding what you want to do. The rest is just a matter of reorganising your life. I'm sure you can do that and there'll be other people who would help you.'

Chapter 18

The house was quiet again. Everyone was either out enjoying themselves on Saturday night or still working. It was already dark outside and sitting in the warm kitchen over a bowl of hot food felt like being at home again. With a piece of bread, Adam wiped clean the bowl which had been brimming with warm *flaki* five minutes earlier. Their spicy aftertaste still lingered on his tongue. It was just what he needed on a cold evening. He took a sip of black and very sweet tea which he always found very fortifying. By now it was lukewarm and its surface was covered by an opalescent film. He had never noticed things like that before. Back in Kościelisko, food preparation was Hanka's prerogative. He ate whatever she put on the table. In London, he learnt that feeding himself required foresight and planning.

Thinly spreading paté on a slice of bread, he wondered how long it was going to last. He lifted a round tin and looked at a picture of a boar head on the label. The animal was baring massive fangs as if giving credence to the claim that the spread contained boar meat. It made Adam smile. Judging by the popularity of this cheap spread, boar would have become extinct in Poland a long time ago. Yet the stacks of the boar paté filled the shelves of any shop in London that sold Polish food. The spread was preferable to the watery jam which remained on his shopping list since his financial troubles began.

Karol wasn't a reliable payer and all his team grumbled about this. Only a few of his men had enough confidence in their skills to leave him. Adam knew that there was a great demand for carpenters in London but he needed to speak English to sell his skills. Thousands of foreign labourers worked here using just a few basic English phrases. He was no different. He wouldn't need English when he went back home and he had no time or money to waste learning a language which would be of no use to him.

'Adam, you're day dreaming.' Zofia was standing in the doorway in her going out clothes. With an amused expression, she watched Adam talking to himself while staring at a picture of a pig on a tin. Adam flinched, as if he had been caught with his hand in a church collection box.

'I thought that everyone was out.'

'They are out. We were half way to Slough when Jan realised that he forgot the present for his friend.' She turned around to go upstairs when suddenly she stopped.

'I forgot to tell you ... Mrs Patel is planning to change her kitchen cupboards and was looking for a carpenter.'

Adam fixed his eyes on Zofia's face. Did she know about his problems? He couldn't stand to be pitied.

'Should I tell her that you would be interested?'

Would he be interested? 'Yes, of course. Thank you. When does she need this work done?'

'Quite soon. I think she knows what she wants but needs your skills.'

At this moment, the car hooted in the street.

'It's Jan. I had better get going. Tomorrow, I will tell Mrs Patel that you're happy to help her.' For a brief moment, Zofia hesitated. 'Adam, before you agree to anything, set a price for the job. Remember, it's business, not charity.'

Before Adam could open his mouth, Zofia left. Only her floral scent still lingered in the kitchen, proof that he hadn't dreamt this God-sent opportunity.

He sat in the kitchen with his eyes fixed on the window behind which lay a cold London night. Hundreds of kilometres away was his home and his family. It was only a year ago when he bought a ticket for a coach bound for London. Yet, so much had happened since then, that it seemed as if he had made that journey several years ago.

He wasn't an excitable man but the opportunity to earn extra money cheered him up so much that he decided to make himself another sandwich. He also decided to buy a pack of *Żywiec* tomorrow to celebrate.

A sudden thought paralysed him. How would he communicate with Mrs Patel? He needed to find out what she wanted, before he could set a price on the job, as Zofia had suggested. Admitting to Zofia that he wouldn't be able to take the job because he couldn't speak English was humiliating. Suddenly the warm kitchen felt stifling hot. He saw his scarlet face reflected in the window pane. He looked as if he had just returned from Ondraszkowa Izba on Sunday afternoon. This brought back the memories of Bukowski, his scorn and his own sense of helplessness which, he thought, he had left behind in Kościelisko. He slammed down the mug of cold tea with such force that he spilled half the contents onto the table.

Classic Kitchens' showroom had an aura of professionalism and efficiency. At the sales office, located next to the entrance, the walls were covered with a vast display of finishes, handles and kitchen accessories which suggested to Adam that this place was much better organised than similar outlets which he had visited before. The clientele wandering around the showroom, neatly divided into kitchen units, also looked more affluent than the average punter in MF5 or Wicks. He was glad he made an effort to put on his leather jacket and a fresh shirt. He followed Zofia and Mrs Patel who twittered animatedly, pointing to various furniture arrangements stopping to touch wood finishes and worktops as they passed from one kitchen set-up to another. Adam walked behind the women like a dejected husband, not able to take part in their conversation. But he comforted himself that this wasn't unusual as most men tailed behind their female companions with resigned expressions.

Zofia explained to him that Mrs Patel was keen to give her new kitchen an English country look but wished to combine it with the latest in kitchen appliances. She was expecting her family from India in a few weeks' time. Her relatives loved cooking and they would be spending a lot of time in the kitchen. News travelled fast in her home country and the 'family telegraph' had amazing powers to build or destroy reputations.

'Adam, what's your opinion on this finish?' Zofia decided that

Adam should show more interest in Heena Patel's project.

Adam hurried into the kitchen arrangement in which both women had already opened every cupboard door. Glancing at the design of the top and base units he ran his hand along the front panel of the hanging cupboard.

'*Pani* Zofio, please tell Mrs Patel that it is a nice design but it is in pine. It isn't very durable and may warp in a frequently used kitchen. Oak or ash would be better.' Zofia promptly translated Adam's advice. Mrs Patel listened attentively and nodded her head in agreement. Then she walked to the service counter at which a small queue had already formed. She waited for a moment but shortly became impatient with the slow pace of its progress. Seeing a showroom assistant crossing the floor, she rushed in his direction. Putting a hand on his shoulder, she asked for help.

In a moment, the three of them were trailing behind the young man who led them from one kitchen arrangement to another. All were finished in oak. In each one, the women found something worth their attention. Some designs were very modern with simple, clean lines and plenty of glass, others wouldn't look out of place in the mountain chalets of Zakopane.

Suddenly, Mrs Patel halted her quest. She threw her arms in the air and exclaimed something to Zofia. In response, Zofia waved at Adam to approach.

'What's your opinion on this? Mrs Patel loves the style of this kitchen.' Adam looked around the set up. The design was that of a traditional country kitchen, finished in light oak. Everything from doors to handles had a feel of solidity. Even the glass in the doors of a display cabinet was unusually thick.

'This kitchen is definitely going to last.' He ran his thumb along the grooves on the cabinet doors. 'The oak is dense and well dried. Very good quality. The handles are well matched to this style. They're steel so they won't wear out or rust.'

Zofia promptly translated Adam's comment. A large triumphant smile spread across Mrs Patel's weathered face. She said something to Zofia and to the shop assistant.

'She says that this is precisely what she was looking for.' Afterwards, she made another remark to the shop assistant. Adam noticed that the young man surreptitiously started watching him. This compelled Adam to undertake a close investigation of the drawer closing mechanism. He also opened the base unit and examined the fittings, assessing how easy it would be to assemble them. Nodding in the direction of Mrs Patel, he confirmed; 'Good, very good.'

This sealed Mrs Patel's trust in her contractor. She beamed at him.

'Mrs Patel says she is sure that you will build her dream kitchen,' translated Zofia, suppressing a smile.

Next there was a lengthy consultation on the type of worktops that would match the selected kitchen design. Assisted by Zofia, Mrs Patel touched and caressed various types of stone and man-made materials, running backwards and forward with the samples to see 'how they worked' with the dream kitchen. Adam wasn't surprised to see that black granite with sparkling quartz specks won out. He was expected to nod in approval and as he did this, he secretly hoped that Mrs Patel would leave the worktop installation to the specialists.

Finally, order placement and delivery arrangements were discussed. '*Pani Zofio*, please explain, that I have to first measure Mrs Patel's kitchen and discuss with her the layout of the cabinets before we can order anything.'

Mrs Patel accepted this but a shadow of impatience crossed her face. She wished for work to begin as soon as possible so she went to the counter to enquire about the times and terms of delivery. The information she received clearly didn't please her as she came back and recounted something to Zofia in an irritated tone of voice.

'We can register our order now, Adam. She will call later with the details.' Mrs Patel nodded to Adam to approach the service counter. Zofia followed to help with translation. She listened attentively to the clerk but when she turned back to Adam, he instantly knew that there was a problem.

'This is a trade account outlet so you have to operate as a company to place an order here. I don't think Heena Patel knew this.'

Adam felt his throat tightening and his palms starting to sweat. He wouldn't be doing Mrs Patel's kitchen after all. The whole thing appeared too good to be true. He watched the counter clerk continue explaining something to Zofia. Digging his hands deep into his pockets, he stood behind her back, staring ahead through the window at the bleak landscape of the industrial estate.

Suddenly, he realised he was turning over a piece of paper in his fingers. He pulled it out and his heart stopped. He held a receipt for material he had once collected for Karol. The details of Karol's company were at the top of the page. The full address and contact telephone number. He hesitated for a second. Then touching Zofia's arm, he showed it to her. 'Will this do?' Zofia scanned it quickly, looked at Adam and put the paper on the counter in front of the clerk.

The man flattened the receipt with his palm and examined it for a moment. He opened a book and began writing the details down.

'You're in business,' Zofia whispered. Adam took a large handkerchief from his trousers pocket and wiped his forehead.

Chapter 19

Maja, April 1998

She never forgot her first impression of the pianist. To the staff of the Metropole Hotel she was known as *Mademoiselle* Fournier. Standing by the bar in the first floor lounge and waiting for a cocktail for one of her customers, Maja saw a petite woman dressed head to toe in black lace gliding across the marble floor like a swan. The train of her dress swished behind her and she moved so lightly, it appeared that her feet weren't touching the floor. She held her head high on a long neck. Her dark hair was piled on top of her head and her deep-set eyes shone from under thick eyebrows. With no sideways glace, she crossed the floor. The scent of her perfume lingered in the air long after the first notes of the grand piano began filling the lobby.

'She is wasting herself here,' said Jack, following Maja's gaze. This comment stayed with her for a long time. He wedged a slice of orange on the brim of a shallow glass and pierced it with a cocktail umbrella. Then, with a wink he pushed it across the counter towards Maja. His white shirt, black waistcoat and slicked-back hair gave him an air of sophistication and danger. This was a new world in which she would need to move carefully, she thought.

'Thanks Jack. You're an artist.'

'I could fix you something nicer if you come after your shift.' This was precisely what staff weren't permitted to do. Maja just gave him a fleeting smile and placed the glass on the tray.

The Metropole Hotel was recently refurbished and all the public areas, from the enormous entrance lobby to its smallest bar, were decorated to impress. When Maja walked into the lobby of the hotel with Ewa ten months earlier, she was intimidated by its grandeur. She thought that this temple of luxury was out of her league and people working there were a chosen race with unique skills. When she returned there after Nico's death, the feelings of desperation and anger helped her to deal with the expression of indifferent superiority on the face of the personnel officer. With a nod, she acknowledged Maja's wish to join the ranks of the Metropole's staff and proffered an application form to complete. Two days later, a call from the hotel's HR department came through. There was a vacancy in one of the hotel's restaurants and Maja's experience matched the requirements of the post.

'Are you still looking for a job?'

'Oh, yes!'

'When can you start?'

Her academic qualifications may not count for much but at least her waitressing skills were in demand, Maja thought bitterly. Relieved and delighted, she stood with a receiver in her hand and felt tears rolling down her face. She could hardly send this news to her parents, who had made so many sacrifices to educate their children.

The Metropole Hotel, with its four restaurants, 400 guest rooms and a banqueting and conference business, was governed by numerous rules which layers of managers were trained to implement. Maja, together with a team of waiting staff from the Garden Restaurant were managed by two supervisors. In their early twenties, the fresh graduates from a catering college took their duties very seriously and bossed the staff with the zeal of young puppies taken off the leash.

'You could be polishing the cutlery as you are standing by your stations. I can see the stains from the dishwasher,' Nigel was haranguing two middle aged Philippine waitresses. His spotty complexion was almost as bright as his red hair. The women looked at him indulgently.

'Yes, Nigel.' As soon as Nigel disappeared from earshot Bernie added: 'And we will wash the floor and iron the linen while we're at it.' She smiled protectively at Maja. Looking around, she added: 'It's dead quiet. Maja, love. Why don't you go to the staff-room and make a pot tea for all of us? A nice strong one. If a customer is seated in your area, I will attend to them.'

Maja hesitated for moment. There was still over an hour to her break and she feared that if he noticed her absence, Nigel would sit someone in her area hoping to get her in trouble.

'He is a nasty piece of work,' Bernie said. She saw him once grassing on someone to Mr Cassidy, the restaurant manager. Unlike the supervisors, he was a very amiable man. 'That comes from being Irish,' insisted Bernie.

Most of the time, the Garden Restaurant was very busy but the pressure mounted much faster during breakfast when all the guests wanted to be served at the same time. Maja was glad to be given the choice of working on the afternoon and evening shift as most of the women preferred to work during the day. Her journey home proved easier than she had thought. Kuba insisted that she called him if she had to walk home from the underground after a late shift. For the staff working after midnight, the Metropole provided its own cabs.

The early afternoons were much easier to handle, with customers leisurely enjoying their tea and light meals. It was a good time for people watching and the world came to the Metropole Hotel in various guises. In Grodek, she had learnt about different countries and cultures from books, newspapers and television. Here, this information was within arm's reach. It was fascinating and bizarre at times. Bernie and Doris would just shrug their shoulders when confronted with things out of the ordinary. 'People are queer. In this city, there are many strange things.' These strange things would not alter their perception of the world, they were too level headed for that.

'You're young and easily impressed,' they would say to Maja when she commented about something that fascinated or surprised her. 'But that's OK, everyone grows out of it.'

The previous evening, a doctor's family from Syria told her about the mountains in the north of the country which were white in April from the blossom of flowering almond trees. Never before had she heard about the towns and temples carved out of rock, hidden for hundreds of years by the desert sands. She moved among the guests, who sipped their afternoon tea, and dreamed about the places she would visit one day.

The soft tones of classical music created an atmosphere of a

country picnic. Through the floor-to-ceiling window, green reflections of the swaying tree tops danced on the walls. Two
enormous bouquets of lilies stood in glass vases by the entrance,
filling the room with their heady fragrance. It blended with the
aroma of strong tea and freshly laundered table linen.

All of a sudden, a commotion at the entrance shattered the
serene atmosphere of the afternoon. Everyone in the restaurant
raised their heads and looked at the door. A group of Japanese
tourists formed a bee line outside the entrance. Their leader,
standing at the front, was waving his arms, explaining something. The people stood silently, nodding in agreement. Several
hands were raised and questions followed. The guide attempted
to answer and the chorus of questions escalated to such a degree
that he had to wave his arms again to signal for silence, like an
orchestra conductor closing a musical sequence. He turned to
Nigel, who nervously hovered by the entrance, trying to take
control of the situation. After a brief consultation, Nigel gave a
sign for the group to follow him.

Serving thirty people at once wasn't a task anyone welcomed,
so all the waitresses stood in anticipation. The speculation
ended quickly as Nigel walked past the German hospitality
students and led the group straight into Maja's station.

'You're the lucky one,' Catherina hissed.

'Don't worry, love. We're not busy,' reassured Bernie.

'The tables have to be joined together,' commanded Nigel,
showing everyone who was in charge.

Bernie gave Maja a sign to start collecting flower vases holding a single rose before the tables were moved as the vases
would have tumbled down flooding the tablecloths. Maja also
wanted to take off the crockery but Nigel was already shunting
the tables. Any resulting mess would be hers to deal with. The
women quickly rearranged the china and started distributing
the menu folders.

'We no need this,' cried the group leader.

Maja stopped with her hand in mid-air. Nigel, who was standing nearby, opened and closed his mouth. When he recovered,
he quickly approached the leader for an explanation.

'The guide will be making a selection,' he said to Maja. Then
lowering his voice, he offered an explanation: 'Not many people

in the group understand English. And we don't have a menu in Japanese. Although we should have the Japanese version,' he stressed.

Maja whispered the message to her support team and the women started collecting the menus, leaving just one copy in front of the group's guide. He opened the book and started studying it with a great deal of attention. The rest of the group just waited, sending him anxious glances from time to time. After a while the man closed the folder, got up and walked to the middle of the table. There he made an announcement, which was followed by some nodding and a few questions. Then the man waved his hand to Maja, commanding her to approach. He opened the page with desserts and pointed to a Viennese cheesecake. 'We will have this. With tea. English tea. The one for the afternoon.'

'Everyone will have the cheesecake?'

'Yes, we will all have it. Twenty six cheesecakes.'

'Of course. But perhaps someone would like to try a different dessert.'

'No, we all have the same,' said the guide firmly.

Maja looked up. Twenty six pairs of eyes were fixed on her.

'No problem. Twenty six portions of cheesecake and English tea.'

Maja thought better than to mention that there is a choice of Assam, Dajeerling, Earl Grey, Jasmine ...

'Any problems, Maja?' Nigel sprung to attention, seeing hesitation on her face.

'No problem. I am going to ask in the kitchen whether there is enough cheesecake to serve the whole group.'

'Do as he says.'

Fortunately, fresh pastry had been delivered this afternoon. The chef took the whole supply of cheesecake out of the fridge and cut it for the Japanese guests.

With the help of other waitresses, Maja laid the group's long table with plates of cake, cups, saucers and silver jugs of tea. In addition to milk, she asked the kitchen for lemon slices. She had noticed before that some Japanese customers took tea with lemon. A few appreciative nods and smiles confirmed her decision.

For a while, there was a silence at the long table interrupted only by the clinking of cutlery and china. Then as she was collecting the teapots for refilling she noticed that one of the Japanese women hadn't touched her desert and was hesitantly looking around.

'Can I help you?' Maja ventured hoping that the woman would understand her?'

'Yes … *Avez vous quelque chose sans sucre?*' the woman asked in French.

'*Bien sûr, Madame.*' Maja was relieved that they could communicate without resorting to the guide's help.

'*Nous avons des petits sandwiches, des tartines, et une sélection des fromages.*'

'*Je suis diabetique,*' explained the Japanese woman apologetically. '*Je prefere les petits sandwiches, s'il vous plaît.*'

'*Au fromage, au jambon, au sardines?*'

'*Au fromage, serait parfait.*'

'*D'accord. Je les vends …*'

As Maja hurried out of the room, she caught Nigel's surprised expression.

Maja urged the cook to prepare the order promptly as the group was half-way through their snack. Carlos, the young Spanish sous-chef, was in a good mood and the sandwiches were ready in five minutes and artistically garnished. Maja gave him the widest of her smiles to which he responded with a wink.

The Japanese lady beamed seeing the plate and couldn't stop thanking her.

'You made her day,' whispered Bernie, helping Maja at the table.

'I'm glad I could.'

'It's a shame she is Japanese.'

'Why?'

'The Japanese are not the best tippers,' stated Bernie sagely.

'It doesn't matter.'

'Oh, it does when we split the kitty at the end of the day.'

The woman surprised them. When afternoon tea was over and the Japanese guests started leaving, the woman came up to Maja and pressed a five pound note into her hand. Then she said something to the group's guide who relayed the message to Nigel.

'A decent Japanese after all,' remarked Bernie, when Maja put the note into their tips kitty.

None of them noticed Mr Cassidy, who had come into the restaurant a few minutes earlier. He stepped aside to give way to the leaving Japanese group.

Chapter 20

Maja, April 1998

Maja picked up a chicken salad from the bar and took out a small flag with the name Fournier which was hoisted on a cherry tomato. Then she walked to the bread basket and selected one white and one granary roll. They were still warm and their aroma made her instantly hungry. She added a wine glass to the tray and gave it one last glance over. Then she hurried back to the restaurant through the revolving door. She learnt to kick it with sufficient force so it opened wide enough for her to pass with a tray without bouncing back too soon. She learnt how essential this skill was.

On her third day at the Garden Restaurant, she was carrying a tray full of wine glasses and with her elbow she pushed the door open. The spring mechanism yielded reluctantly just a couple of inches and then with full force bounced back sending the tray flying against the wall. She stood frozen to the spot waiting for the reaction of the kitchen staff. Surprisingly, the mighty crash of thirty glasses cascading down to the floor didn't attract too much attention. Ivan, the Ukrainian who operated the dishwashing machine, brought her a pan and brush. Helping her to sweep up the debris, he said quietly: 'Don't worry, Maja. The hotel has a budget for breakages. I've seen the chefs smash plates against the wall when customers changed their orders.'

At five thirty, Maja approached the corner table where Yvette Fournier was waiting for her early dinner. She was staring straight ahead, deep in her thoughts. She wore a bottle green taffeta jacket with a long skirt of the same colour. The jacket was cropped just above her tiny waist. As always, the pianist's lustrous hair was swept into a tight chignon at the back of her head.

Maja placed the plate on the table as softly as she could. Yet the sudden movement of Maja's arm startled the pianist and she flinched.

'Oh. Thank you,' she said curtly.

'Will you be drinking water and wine, as usual?'

'Of course.'

'Would you like a glass of house wine or should I bring you something from the bar?'

'House wine will do.'

Maja turned around to walk away when the woman suddenly asked: '*Peut être* I could have a glass of red wine today?'

'*Bien sûr, mademoiselle.*'

Yvette lifted her eyes in surprise. 'Do you speak French?'

'Yes.'

'Are you one of the trainees?'

'No, I work here full time.'

'Waitressing?' she asked surprised. Then she quickly corrected herself. 'We all need to earn money.'

Maja looked at the small elegant hands clasping a glass of water.

'You're not English ...'

'I'm Polish.'

'I love Polish music,' she exclaimed. 'Chopin, Padarewski, Szymanowski. I played Polish music in Cracow. Many, many years ago.'

For the first time, Maja saw the pianist smile. She smiled back.

'Chopin, in fact, was half French. And he died in Paris,' she said trying to maintain the unexpected connection.

'So many famous people came to Paris and died there. That's for you our *joie de vivre.*' They both laughed. From the corner of her eye Maja noticed that Nigel had already seated new customers in her section and was glaring at her across the room.

'I'd better get you that glass of wine,' said Maja indicating with her eyes that she couldn't give her undivided attention.

She was taking an order from a young American couple who wished to have a light meal before going to the theatre, when she felt a hand on her shoulder.

'Mr Cassidy wishes to speak to you,' said Nigel in an officious tone.

'Should I see him now?' she asked searching his face for clues as to why she was being summoned by their boss.

'Leave this order with Brenda. I've asked her to deal with it,' Nigel said coldly. 'Do you know where his office is?'

'No.'

'Fourth floor. Room 404. Use the service lift.'

'Of course.' She turned around and headed for the door. Playing the events of the last few days in her mind, she searched for an explanation as to why Mr Cassidy would wish to see her. The accident with the glasses should have been long forgotten. So what's wrong? She needed this job; the income and security it gave her. It also fitted so well with her college. Had anyone complained about her?

'Come in,' a distant voice called when Maja knocked on the door of the restaurant manager's office. Maja entered hesitantly. Behind a thickly padded door there was a carpeted office that looked more like a corridor than a room. At the far end John Cassidy was seated behind a large desk. On his right hand side, there was a bookcase full of manuals and folders and above it in gold-edged frames, hung certificates and diplomas with various seals and crests.

'Thank you for coming, Maja. I apologise for calling you so unexpectedly here. There is never a good time for a chat in this business. Please sit down,' he said pointing to the chair on the other side of the desk.

'How is the work going?'

'Very well, thank you.'

'I watched you last week and have no doubts that you're very good at your job. In fact, you're overqualified for what you do.'

Maja's heart sunk. 'I am happy with what I do.'

'I know you are. But you could be using your skills better.'

'But ...'

'What I had in mind,' he said pausing. 'If you agree to it, of course, is a change. I asked the personnel department to send me a copy of your application. You stated that you speak French and German in addition to English. This is far beyond what we require in your current job. In fact, we wouldn't be able to afford waiting staff with such qualifications.'

'I don't expect higher pay,' Maja exclaimed in desperation.

'I know you don't but we should recognise your potential. We need people with language skills at the Metropole.'

Maja blinked. This was what it was all about. They needed her somewhere else. Straightening her fingers, she smoothed her skirt.

'I saw how hard you work and how personable you are with the customers,' Mr Cassidy continued. These are great assets in the restaurant. I'd love to keep you there. But you have much greater potential. As your manager, I have to recognise this. Are you planning to stay in Britain?'

'Yes. I'd like to.' Maja recognised that this wasn't the time or place to elaborate that she needed to reapply for a visa extension, which could, of course, be rejected.

'Then you may consider joining one of our training schemes. The Metropole is a large hotel chain which offers many opportunities to progress within the organisation. Of course, this is if you like the idea of a career in the hospitality industry.'

Maja was staring at the face of John Cassidy. Instead of sacking her, he was offering her a promotion. More than a promotion. An opportunity for a proper career.

'Am I moving too fast?' he asked puzzled with Maja's lack of response.

'No, Mr Cassidy. I have never considered a career in the hotel industry. In my home town this wasn't an option. I still didn't know what qualifications or skills would be required to have a professional career in a place like the Metropole. But I would like to try. Very much.'

'I expected you to say this, Maja.'

Maja just smiled relieved.

'I haven't walked from Limerick straight into this office. I know how it is to start from the bottom. There's nothing wrong with it.'

Maja looked at John Cassidy and for the first time she saw a different man. He wasn't only a restaurant manager in an immaculate black suit, with a calm voice and a composed manner.

'You're well educated, hard working and have a personable nature,' he continued. 'This is good baggage to travel with up the career ladder. I suggest that you pick up from the personnel department information about the available training. This should be your long-term plan. However, in the meantime I suggest that you apply for the vacancy at the Customer Relations desk.'

She hesitated to admit that she had no idea what the Customer Relations desk did and how she could possibly be a suitable candidate. 'Will I be trained for the role? If I get it, I mean.'

'Of course. They will give you a proper induction. They need people speaking more than one language. They deal with customers from all over the world. Let me know when you complete the form. I will write you a reference.'

Following John Cassidy's advice, she applied for a post at the Customer Relations desk and was called for an interview. In the offices of the personnel department the same young manager, who three months earlier showed no interest in her academic skills, questioned her at length about her education, language skills and previous work experience. Maja noticed that the woman was completing a score sheet as she interviewed her, making numerous ticks as Maja answered her questions. She also asked for a copy of her university diploma. Two days later she was offered a post at the Customer Relations desk.

It was Nigel who delivered her a white envelope embossed with the hotel's gold crest.

'Jumping ship already?' he asked knowingly, curling his upper lip in a scornful smile. Maja wondered what Mr Cassidy had told his supervisor.

'I had an opportunity and took it.'

'With patrons in the right places, some people have more opportunities than others.'

For a split second, she thought about challenging him, but decided that this would be a waste of time. It wouldn't change Nigel's opinion about her. Not that she cared what he thought about her any longer.

Bernie and Doris were pleased for her when she told them her news.

'Good for you, girl. I always knew that you're cut out for better things than waiting at the tables.'

'I am only going down to the lobby. We'll be still seeing each other in the canteen.'

'You are not a hoity-toity type so you may stay friends with us but things might change. Anyway, enjoy your new job but watch your back. When people move faster than others, they make enemies.'

On her last day, she received a large Good Luck card signed by everyone, including Nigel. Afterwards, in the canteen, the waiting staff had with their tea a spicy cake which Bernie had baked to mark Maja's departure from the restaurant.

There was one more surprise before they all went home. Just before midnight already standing in their coats, Bernie and Doris presented her with a small box tied with a red bow. Inside there was a silver compact. On the mother-of-pearl background, a four-leaf clover in pale green ceramic was set in.

'It's so beautiful,' exclaimed Maja, deeply moved. 'Thank you. I am sure it was expensive.'

'It's for good luck in your new job, and for the future,' said Doris, clearly pleased with Maja's reaction.

'Bernie, Doris ...' Moved by their friendship and generosity, Maja put her arms around both women. 'I will treasure it and always think about you when I use it.'

There were tears in all three pairs of eyes. The women hugged and kissed as if they were never to see each other again.

Two weeks later at 8am, after leaving in the locker her coat and an emergency kit which included two pairs of spare tights, Maja went into the bathroom. She took her jacket off and let her hair fall to her shoulders. The morning drizzle made the loose strands of her hair curl. Now they stood like a halo around her face and neck. She took out a large paddle brush and ran it through her hair several times until it shone as if waxed. Then she pulled it back in a long ponytail which she twisted tightly and pinned up at the back of her head. ('No loose hair on the front desk'). She looked in the mirror and spotting an offending sheen on the tip of her nose promptly quashed it with a puff from her beautiful compact. It was her good luck charm. With her finger tips she caressed its pearly finish, thinking about the day ahead. Finally, she straightened her blouse and put on her jacket. The dark navy suit, which was now going to be her uniform, looked good on her. She turned sideways and looked at her back in the mirror checking for stray hairs and fluff. Everything was in order.

Then she thought about Nico. He would have been proud of her now. The realisation that she would never be able to share anything with him brought a sudden pang of pain. She felt tears prickling her eyes. She slung the strap of her handbag over her arm and hit the door with her palm trying to stop the grief rising inside her. Not here, not now. She ran out of the bathroom.

'Is this our new star coming?' The comment came from a large man behind the Customer Relations desk which was positioned almost in the middle of the vast lobby.

'James, just shut up,' hissed a girl standing next to him. She had a rosy complexion and a head of unruly dark curls escaping from under a thick hairband. She gave Maja a welcoming smile.

'Don't forget where you are, you two,' reprimanded a man standing at the end of the polished counter, lowering his voice. As he lifted his eyes from the file he was studying, he noticed Maja standing at the other side. 'Miss Zalewska?'

Maja nodded and smiled.

'Welcome to Customer Relations. You're early,' he added appreciatively. 'Alan Riley,' he introduced himself. 'This is Amy Cohen. You will be working together.' Then, pointing to the stout man in a green uniform, he said: 'This is James Henderson. He works at the Concierge but gives us a hand when we're are busy.'

Amy's eyes, as dark as her hair, were smirking as she looked at Maja.

'Thank God, we have another girl on the team,' she whispered, as she took Maja to the back of the station to show her where she could stow her handbag.

'Is it so bad here?' Maja whispered back.

'Not really. Though James can be a real pig and Alan totally lacks a sense of humour.

Chapter 21

Kuba, April 1998

'Kuba, wish me luck!' cried Basia, bursting through the kitchen
door. She stopped abruptly. She had expected to find Kuba in
the kitchen at this time of the morning but what she saw left
her open-mouthed. 'Her' Kuba, who caused such a stir among
the female population of Roxmead High when he picked her up
at the school gate, was behaving like a schoolboy. From a book
propped against the biscuit tin, he was copying something into
a notebook lying between a plate of half-eaten toast and a mug
of black coffee.

'I'm sorry I didn't know you were ... working.'

'Studying. Just like you.'

Basia hesitated, not sure whether she should probe further.
Perhaps it was his secret. 'What are you studying?'

Kuba smiled, seeing her astonishment. 'I'm revising. The stuff
I learnt some time ago. Now I'm doing it in English.'

'Surely not maths?'

'Oh, no,' he laughed. 'I revise maths only with you. And I
really enjoy it. Is your test today?'

'Yeah ... I'm bit scared. It would be much worse if you hadn't
been helping me.'

'Stay cool. You have a good head for maths. All you needed
was some revision.'

'You're just saying that.'

'Not at all.'

She suddenly glanced at the kitchen clock on the wall.

'I must run. I'll let you know tonight how my test went. Will
you tell me about your classes?'

'Solemn promise,' said Kuba, raising his hand in salute.

She grinned and flew out of the kitchen. In a second, the front
door slammed and the window panes rattled. Today, there was

more energy than anger in that thump, thought Kuba. He lifted his breakfast plate and slid the half-eaten toast into the bin. He poured his already cold coffee into the sink and decided to make himself a fresh cup.

As he waited for the kettle to boil, he looked out at the garden. It was already mid-April and the signs of spring were everywhere. Jan's roses, which during the previous summer had fragrant cabbage-like blooms, started timidly unfurling their first leaves. The clump of daffodils by the patio looked like a splash of yellow paint on the grass. The cherry tree in the neighbours' garden stretched its candy floss arms over the fence. The air smelled of change.

He reflected on the events of the spring. He still couldn't believe that by September he would be a student of the London Metropolitan University. A part-time student but at graduate level. He surprised himself how much he enjoyed the thought that he would be studying again, although in his first year he would be mostly revising the material he had covered years ago. But he would be studying in English and this would be a challenge which he relished.

Little did he know, meeting her for first time in January, that when Karen put her mind to something, like helping him 'realise his potential', there was no stopping her. Bursting with energy and ideas, she rolled forward like a panzer tank crushing obstacles in her way. Kuba suspected that Ashley was encouraging her, and perhaps aiding her efforts. Although Kuba's application was too late for the next academic year and the classes were already full, when Karen logged an appeal on his behalf, a place was found for him.

It turned out that Kuba's help on the night of Ashley's accident and his unorthodox use of a shoe tree had saved Ashley's tendon from a long-term injury. Now, Kuba not only regularly drove Ashley to work but was questioned at length about his studies.

'Once you're able to practise, you will have a queue of lame birds like me. Almost everyday someone injures themselves. You could call yourself the West End Rescue.'

The prospect of being a higher education student gave him

advantages he never considered before. He now had a solid reason to apply for a visa extension and a good chance of getting it. He did this in late March, and to his great surprise, received a 12-month visa instead of the usual six-month one. He felt as if his status in England had been elevated a few notches. Undertaking professional training was making him more desirable in the country where so far he felt only a guest and not always a welcome one.

A sudden thought dawned on him that he should use this newly acquired status to visit his family without a fear of not being allowed in upon return. A quick mental calculation made him realise that he hadn't seen them for almost four years.

Every time Kuba spoke to his father, he sensed a growing sadness in his voice. He also imagined his father becoming increasingly lonely since his retirement two years ago. Although he lost his wife almost twenty years before, Jerzy Baranski never remarried. He divided his time between bringing up his two sons and his work as an engineer at Opole's large railway works. When his sons grew up, he spent more time at work and four years ago he took up lecturing evening classes in the local technical college. Since his retirement, the college was his only escape from the empty flat and painful memories. Not that his father ever complained or discussed his feelings with anyone. Often with annoyance, Kuba thought about his father's ability to resign himself to whatever life dealt him.

With a heavy heart, Kuba listened to his father's account of the evenings spent in the company of his students' papers. When asked whether he ever saw his old work colleagues, he excused himself with lack of time.

'I want to get my students interested in engineering so I prepare plenty of project work for them. But then, of course, this has to be checked and assessed. You understand, don't you?'

Kuba stopped asking his father how he spent his weekends to spare him embarrassment and himself a sense of guilt. He knew that Sunday after Sunday his father went to his mother for lunch, on arrival handing over a bag of groceries and a few little luxuries like a packet of good coffee. With his throat clenched, Kuba imagined the couple of old people sitting at granny's round table under the antique glass lamp and eating a three

course meal in almost total silence. Kuba's grandmother was a
happy person at heart and very popular in her neighbourhood.
However, she accepted that her son was a very private man,
unwilling and unable to talk about his emotions.

They often discussed Kuba's father in their weekly conversations. Almost as soon as Kuba arrived in London, he began
calling his grandmother once a week, sharing with her his
reflections and observations. They continued this tradition for
four years. He knew how much these calls meant to her and in
his mind he often pictured her sitting in her capacious armchair
in anticipation of his telephone call. She understood his uneasy,
temporary situation in Britain and never asked when she would
be able to see him again. Kuba knew that his grandmother
knew him better than anyone and allowed him to be himself.

When the LOT plane cut through the last layer of clouds giving
a clear view of the land below, Kuba felt his throat tightening.
The familiar patchwork of fields stretched all the way to the
horizon. Grey and monotonous in early spring it would be like a
richly woven carpet in summer. And yet even in its present
bleakness, it appeared beautiful to him.

After the floor-to-ceiling glass, steel and stone of the Heathrow terminal, Katowice Airport seemed even smaller and more
provincial than he remembered it. A couple of concrete blocks
and a few planes scattered around them looked more like an
industrial estate than an international gateway receiving
flights from major European cities like London, Paris or Frank-
furt.

The immigration procedure was exactly the same as he remembered it. A distant and severe looking officer measured him
up suspiciously when Kuba placed his passport on the counter.
Without a shadow of emotion, he proceeded to verify Kuba's
identity, taking his time to check his visa and look through the
passport. There was a distinct sense of power behind the office
and both Polish citizens and foreign guests were made to experience it. Then, without raising his eyes from the computer
screen, the officer passed Kuba's passport back and said: 'Next.'

A large crowd gathered to greet the arriving passengers. In the sea of animated faces, waving hands and swaying bouquets of flowers, Kuba searched for familiar features. From time to time, the ranks were broken and someone lurched forward to embrace a new arrival. Then a whole family spilled over into the path of the emerging travellers and proceed to kiss, squeeze and cheer a young couple. He scanned the crowd again, this time from left to right. His eyes lingered longer on the faces of older men, trying to imagine how four years could have changed his father. Surely, they hadn't forgotten ... Then suddenly, on the far right, he saw them. His father in his woollen winter coat and a matching hat looked very formal. He must have dressed like this when he used to greet visiting dignitaries, during his old factory days, thought Kuba. Next to him, leaning forward on a metal barrier, stood Henryk. A small boy at his feet holding a balloon stick in his clenched fist was surely his nephew, Konrad. He was still in his buggy the last time Kuba had seen him.

They didn't notice him, so for a brief moment, he could observe them.

His father stood upright as ever but his face under the brim of his hat appeared gaunter. In contrast, Henryk's face and figure had filled up and his cheeks, like the face of his son, were reddened by the cold air. Propping his bulging suitcase against his thigh, Kuba waved. They saw him at last. Everyone smiled, energetically waived at him and stepped forward to help him with his luggage. Kuba's father gave him a firm embrace and Kuba saw that his eyes shone with emotion. Even through the coat, Kuba felt that his father had lost weight. Henryk gave him a couple of bear hugs, one noisy kiss and a slap on the back. After a lot of coaxing from his father, Konrad reluctantly granted his uncle a peck on the cheek when Kuba kneeled on the floor to scoop the little stranger in his arms.

'Konrad, give the balloon to Kuba. You have brought it for him,' reminded Henryk.

Seeing how hard it was for Konrad to part with the gift, Kuba suggested: 'Konrad, why don't you look after my balloon until we get home?' Then turning to Henryk and his father, he asked: 'Is Maria well? How is granny?'

'Both are well. They are waiting for you at granny's, who is fussing over dinner for her favourite grandson.'

Some things would never change, mused Kuba.

Sitting around a large table, Kuba's family was doing their best to make the return of their prodigal son a special occasion. Dinner was served on granny's best china and a starched table-cloth. With the lace edging reaching the floor, the table looked like an altar, thought Kuba. Over plates of steaming *rosół*, the heavenly aroma of which filled the room, many compliments were exchanged and questions asked.

Kuba sat next to his grandmother, who was wearing her family heirloom topaz broach and beaming with happiness. She already told Kuba three times that he looked well. She kept touching his arm at every opportunity as if making sure that he was really there.

Everyone wanted to know about Kuba's life in London and how different it was from their life in Opole. Was the house in which he lived very modern? Was the food nice?

'Have you met the Queen?' asked Konrad, directing his serious gaze at his uncle.

'Not yet. She doesn't take taxis. She has her own cars driven by chauffeurs.'

'You could be her chauffeur ...'

'Sure, I could.'

'Then, would you bring her here? To Opole?'

'If she wanted. I could.'

'She could stay with us. Mum and granny could cook for her. All this ...' He made a sweeping gesture above the food laden table. 'Would she like our *rosół*?'

'I'm sure even the Queen would love granny's *rosół*.'

'So why, uncle Kuba, are you living in England if even the Queen would eat better here?' At five, his nephew was a good listener to his parents' conversations, thought Kuba.

'I work in London. I will also be studying soon.'

'Why? You already went to school. Like daddy, in Poland.'

'I'll be learning new things.'

'So what are you going to do with these new qualifications?' asked Henryk. 'Are you going to stay in London?'

Kuba saw this question coming. Granny and dad would ask him this tomorrow, in private, but Henryk always enjoyed confrontations.

'Now I'm using my time better. Working and studying. Perhaps in a couple of years, I will be able to work as a physio in London.'

'You could do this in Opole.'

'Yes, but with more skills, I will have more choice.'

'Good physios are needed here. You have plenty of experience.'

'Kuba will do what he considers best for him.' Kuba's father interrupted. 'There is nothing wrong with broadening one's qualifications. People keep learning their whole life.'

'Everyone has to grow up at some point. We all have responsibilities. How will he be able to look after you when you get old and frail?'

Kuba flashed Henryk a warning glance but his father stood his ground.

'I don't intend to slide into decrepitude anytime soon. Your grandmother feeds me like a king. And teaching keeps me busy.'

'Perhaps you could all come and visit me in London,' suggested Kuba to defuse the situation.

'What a good idea!' laughed his grandmother. 'I didn't expect to travel beyond Opole at my age. But I'll come if you invite me.'

'Maybe we will all come and then we could visit the Queen,' suggested Konrad.

'But before we do this, we will have a second course. Kuba, please collect the plates and take them to the kitchen,' commanded his grandmother, taking control of the conversation. 'Let's check the duck,' she added, looking at Maria. 'Jerzy, before you open another bottle of this wine from the shop, please check the cabinet by the window. A bottle of my red currant wine should be there. You could decant it before the dessert,' she suggested to her son.

Looking at his grandmother with affection as she walked briskly into the kitchen, Kuba reminded himself what a formidable woman she was. With the passing of time he began to understand why she disguised her sharp mind under a kindly manner.

Chapter 22

Kuba, April 1998

Later on that evening, when Henryk's family had returned home and Kuba's father excused himself with his college work, Kuba was at last alone with his grandmother.

'Don't you think we deserve a drink now?' she asked, wiping her hands on a tea towel. They had just finished drying a vast assortment of bowls, plates, side dishes, cups and glasses — proof how much food had been cooked and consumed to welcome him.

'Definitely. But why don't you put your feet up while I stow away all this stuff,' proposed Kuba. Although his grandmother appeared to be bursting with energy the whole evening, Kuba noticed that she sat down a couple of times while tidying up the table.

'I'll rest for a moment. But perhaps you could also put the kettle on.'

'Consider it done, general.' He saluted, grinning at her. He picked up an old fashioned metal kettle, filled it up and switched on the gas. Noticing how heavy it was, he made a mental note to buy her an electric kettle.

At last they were sitting down, his grandmother in her favourite high backed armchair and Kuba on the sofa next to her.

'It's so good to have you back, Kuba,' she said patting his hand. 'I often wondered if we were ever going to sit together again.'

'*Babciu*! I know I shouldn't have left it so long to come back. But you see, until now my situation was different. I wasn't able to travel to Poland so easily.'

'I know, I know,' she said soothingly and placed her warm hand on his knee. 'Tell me more about London. Do you really like living there?'

Unable to decide where to begin, he started from telling her about his studies and the house on Cuckoohill Road. There was a lot more but he wanted her to know about the good things. His grandmother was a perceptive woman and would read between the lines, anyway. He told her about Ashley's accident and the way he was able to help him.

'How clever of you. I always knew that you have the most common sense in this family. Just like your grandfather Franek who could cook soup out of nettles and used newspapers to line our winter coats during the war.'

Kuba knew from his father that despite all the marvellous inventions with which granny credited her husband, they survived the war because of her steely determination and ingenuity.

'The survival instinct runs in our family, granny,' he said smiling at her.

'Perhaps another one of those?' He pointed to their mugs. They almost finished sipping their tea which she laced heavily with her famous raspberry liqueur.

'Oh goodness no. We will have a headache tomorrow. At my age it takes much longer to recover. I don't do this too often,' she said apologetically and she gave Kuba a mischievous grin. 'But should I make you one?'

'No, granny. I will be tempted to linger here longer. I have to go soon. Dad won't go to bed until I get home.'

She just smiled and said nothing but Kuba sensed her hesitation. 'What is it granny?'

'I wouldn't like to pry into your life. I know that when you're ready, you'll tell me.'

'Yes ...'

'I wondered whether you met a nice girl in London. One who means something to you.'

He looked at her with affection. '*Babciu*. Not really. Nothing to report. Karen is just a friend. To Basia I am like an older brother. The girls I had met before I have already forgotten. But I don't live like a hermit. I go out and meet people. I have fun sometimes.'

'A nice girl would add a sparkle to your life. She will make you look to the future. If ...' she hesitated. 'If you ever decide to stay in London.'

He realised his grandmother knew him better than he knew himself.

'A good woman inspires a man to go beyond himself,' she added.

After a moment of hesitation, Kuba said: 'There is a girl in my house who could inspire me, as you put it. But she is just a friend. I helped her when she was in trouble but I doubt that she would be interested in me.'

'You could give her time to get to know you better ...'

Kuba laughed. A happy laugh with which he managed to light up the face of his granny. She obviously thought that he could be a gift to every woman he chose. He took her hands in his own, veiny and marked but always soft and smelling of lemon hand cream. He lifted them to his lips and kissed tenderly.

The wailing guitar chords and the voice of Sting bemoaning the fate of Roxanne hit him the moment he opened the glass door of the club. The music was coming from the corridor which led off the brightly decorated lobby. Located in a narrow cobbled street, a few metres off the main square of Opole's old town, the club drew a trendy crowd and had ambitions to impress. The spacious lobby, which also served as a bar area, was decorated in glass mosaic patterns swirling from the domed ceiling down the walls to the floor. The uplighters embedded in the floor dazzled with different colours. The glass shelves with rows of unusually shaped bottles were illuminated with similar flamboyance. It wasn't a place for reticent types, decided Kuba.

'Have you come to see Rafal?' a female voice enquired as he stood in the middle of the room taking all this in. He turned around in the direction of the voice. Between tall glasses standing on the counter, he saw a head of a girl with a ponytail. She gave him a coy smile and an explanation.

'Rafal mentioned that you would be coming to see him. You're Kuba, his school friend?'

He nodded. The girl threw the polishing cloth over her arm and emerging from behind the bar said: 'Please follow me.'

They entered a dark passage which led in the direction of the thumping music. He was glad that the girl was guiding him as the only sources of light in the corridor were dim lamps in the walls. He followed the sound of her shoes that clip-clopped on the stone floor. Suddenly the corridor opened up into a cavernous space that appeared limitless in the dark. Only the dance floor was faintly outlined by red lights. At the far end, on the elevated DJ station, Rafal was busy at work. With his head encased in a pair of large headphones, he was looking down at an assembly of mixers, keyboards and turntables, moving his hands among leavers and buttons. He was absorbed in his work and Kuba wondered how long they would have to wait before Rafal noticed them. The girl was obviously used to this because she crossed the floor, stepped up on the platform and pressed one of the buttons. The music stopped and Rafal looked up. The expression of surprise changed instantly when he saw Kuba. He pushed the headphones back and rushed to greet him.

'So good to see you mate.' He held Kuba tightly and visibly moved kept slapping him on the back. Finally, when their arms disentangled, they gawped at each other, uncertain what to do next.

'After all this time ... Kuba. How many years was it? Five, six?'

'Over four. Too many.' Reluctant to make excuses to his friend, Kuba changed the subject. 'You have an impressive place here. Very trendy.'

'Just doing a job. But the location is excellent and business is good too.'

'I can see that. You must be busy ...'

'At night, we attract a good crowd. Every weekend is a sell-out. We have regulars who are serious about music so we started differentiating the themes. Tomorrow will be classic rock. Of course, in addition to the usual dancing mush,' he said, waving his hand in the direction of the floor.

'It must be fun to have a job you love.'

'It is. But it is a hard slog too. Long hours, late nights. Day time reduced to sleep. But it is fun. You must come tomorrow night, Kuba. Spend some time here and then we will go to my place. I want to show you my pad.'

'I'd love to see it,' said Kuba eagerly but a note of anxiety entered his thoughts. Rafal was his only true friend, but he wished to avoid comparisons. At least for the time being. He remembered Rafal telling him that he bought a loft apartment which he planned to redecorate.

'I would love to hear about your life in London. You mentioned that things were on the up for you.'

'At least they seem that way.'

'Good. Very good. We have a lot of ground to cover then.'

They chatted for a while until Kuba noticed that Rafal glanced at his watch.

'You'd better get back to this,' he said pointing to the maze of keys, knobs and twinkling lamps.

'I'm sorry. I still have to prepare a few things for this evening. Until tomorrow then.' Rafal placed the headphones back on his head, grinned widely and put his thumbs up in Kuba's direction.

'I will be checking on you tomorrow night,' shouted Kuba.

Walking through the infernal corridor, Kuba thought how easy it was to be Rafal's friend. He was smart but modest. Always generous with his time. He was probably the only person Kuba knew who was completely devoid of envy. Perhaps this was the reason why, even at school, he had been so popular.

It was well after midnight when Rafal decided to give his customers a bit of light relief after three hours of classic rock. They listened and sang to Led Zeppelin, Iron Maiden and ACDC. Now they welcomed a change. Not that they didn't approve of what he selected for them. They clapped and cheered and waved their arms to him when he played the familiar hits. Sitting at the small table next to the DJ's stand, reserved for the club's management and staff, Kuba observed not only Rafal's technical skills but also his ability to manage the emotions of the crowd.

'I have been asked to indulge you tonight in something lighter than Metallica. A group of ladies asked for karaoke. I ...' A loud cheering erupted from the middle of the floor. 'Can we humour them tonight?' More clapping followed, reinforced by some whistling.

'To make it fair for everyone, we will have some Polish and some foreign hits,' continued Rafal, this time looking at Kuba.

'Oh God no,' thought Kuba shaking his head. But Rafal only winked at him and continued explaining the arrangements.

What followed was the usual mix of fun and embarrassment. A group of volunteers, some with reasonable voices and some with a desire to show off, reproduced or reinvented popular tunes. Their friends rewarded their efforts with exaggerated applause. Kuba waited for the show to end so that Rafal could close for the night. He looked forward to spending the rest of the time alone with Rafal.

A dusky voice drooling about the perfect moment interrupted his thoughts. After a minute, he recognised Edyta Górniak's famous hit. The woman sang the English version. She wasn't bad. He craned his neck to catch a glimpse of the singer. With a waist length mane of onyx black hair, sparkling top and a pair of black slacks, she was a striking sight. With raised hands above her head, she swayed her body to the rhythm of the music. Kuba wondered who she was and noticed that Rafal gave her a thumbs up. Then he turned to Kuba, signalling that the show would soon be over. The girl followed his gaze and now she was staring at Kuba as she sung undulating her body to the tune. She closed her eyes and tossed her hair back. It cascaded down her shoulders like a black liquid running off her bare arms. Now the whole of her, from her fingers above her head, through her hips and legs, swayed softly as if she was a piece of fabric undulated by a breeze. It was a mesmerising performance. She kept her eyes closed but Kuba knew that she was now singing and dancing only for him.

'I would keep away from her if I was you,' he heard Rafal's voice behind him. Already free of his headphones, Rafal was packing up his business for the night.

'Why, Rafal?'

'She mixes with the wrong crowd.'

'What do you mean?'

'Drugs, smuggling, dodgy dealing.'

'It's a shame that such a pretty woman has such bad judgement.'

'One of her ex-boyfriends disappeared a year ago. No one's heard about him since. People have been saying different things.'

'She doesn't appear to be mourning him,' said Kuba looking at the raven hair beauty holding the attention of the crowd.

'She is not that type.'

The music stopped and the girl gave a bow to loud applause. She waved to her fans but instead of joining her friends, she approached Rafal's station.

'Can you introduce me to your friend?' she asked with a kittenish smile. Taken aback, Rafal hesitated. He looked at her for a moment and then reluctantly walked with her to the table where Kuba was sitting.

'My friend Kuba. Kuba, this is Judyta Marzec.'

Surprised, Kuba got up slowly. Judyta offered her hand and shook Kuba's enthusiastically. Looking straight into his eyes, she said: 'I haven't seen you around. Are you new to Opole?'

'Kuba came to visit his family. It's a brief visit. We are now off,' said Rafal curtly.

'Is it a closed meeting?'

'I am afraid it is. Boys only night.' Rafal flashed her a wide grin and taking Kuba by the arm, nudged him in the direction of the exit.

'Good night, Judyta. You were fantastic tonight. Top marks,' he shouted over his shoulder.

'Good God, you must be very proud of this place,' exclaimed Kuba standing in the middle of Rafal's apartment. It was located on the top floor of a tall townhouse at the edge of Opole's old town. The night sky seen through the windows in the ceiling was velvety black. In the distance, the lights of the town were twinkling weakly.

'Over the last two years, I put every free minute and last *złoty* into renovating it,' said Rafal. 'When I first looked at it, it was a loft, used for drying clothes. It was piled with junk dumped here by the people who live below. "With lots of potential" said the guy who sold it to me. And with all the planning restrictions you could imagine.'

'You've done a great job mate,' Kuba said surveying the vast expanse of the polished wooden floor divided by bookshelves. An ottoman bed screened by shelves, a couple of low sofas and cushions scatted around a round glass coffee table constituted the furnishing of the studio. Its open plan design perfectly complemented its unique architecture. White sloping walls were spanned by a dark beam running the whole length of the apartment. Kuba imagined sunlight streaming through six velux windows during the day. A perfect refuge for a man who needs his own space.

'This must have taken a lot of thought and planning.'

'I got some help from a mate of mine who is an architect,' admitted Rafal.

'All the same. Excellent job! Cheers.' Kuba lifted the can of beer which Rafal had handed him.

'Cheers, Kuba! To us.' Placing the can on the kitchen counter he said: 'I missed you pal.'

'So did I. I didn't know how much until I saw you again. Things have moved on here since I left.'

'For better or worse?'

'With you, only for the better. I was very impressed, watching you commanding the scene in the club. You not only know your music.'

Rafal didn't respond straight away. He walked to the corner of the apartment which served as a kitchen and started taking out glasses and crockery from the cupboards. Filling the bowls with crisps and nuts, he reflected: 'When you eventually get into a job which fits you like an old pair of jeans, you work on it. At some point, it stops being a chore.'

'I know what you mean. It is like you suddenly found a compass.'

It wasn't long before they were reclining on the carpet around Rafal's glass coffee table, propped up by enormous cushions. With their drinks just at arm's length, they were catching up on the past four years. They jumped from subject to subject, amazed and exhilarated by the renewed intimacy and friendship.

Ten years had passed since they sat on the wall surrounding the school grounds on the last day of the final term. They shared an illicit cigarette and talked about the future that, like an open field, stretched before them. Rafal was going to Kraków where his excellent exam results had won him a place on the engineering course at the prestigious Jagiellonski University. Kuba was to stay initially in Opole and begin the physiotherapy course at the local college while continuing to help at the tennis club, an arrangement that allowed him to practise for free.

Rafal, a star member of the school 'Big Bang' band was looking forward to joining the student's music scene in Krakow. It
launched the careers of many respected names in contemporary
music. In fact, this excited him more than the engineering
course. Another reason why Rafal couldn't wait to move to
Krakow was the fact that Marta was also going there. Ambitious and hard working Marta, who was the only girl in form 4A
to remain unmoved by Rafal's overtures (and lyrics written and
performed by Big Bang), secured a place at the Jagiellonski
Medical School. Having outperformed 24 other candidates, she
was planning to prove to the world that she was going to become
someone they would have to reckon with. The world, in particu-
lar, included those mocking her mild-mannered father who
worked as the school caretaker.

Rafal's crush on Marta remained an unrequited passion,
which none of his subsequent liaisons managed to extinguish.
Even now, a decade later, Rafal gave Kuba a detailed update on
Marta's life and her meteoric rise in Opole's teaching hospital.
Rafal's current girlfriend didn't get too many mentions, although Kuba saw her framed picture on the bookcase. His work
in the club, of which he was one of the owners, put heavy
demands on his personal life and the time he could put into a
relationship. From the tone of his voice, Kuba inferred that this
didn't concern his friend too much. In return, Kuba confessed
that his current life also didn't leave him much time for a
serious relationship.

Chapter 23

Kuba, April 1998

They forgot about the time, recalling memories of their school transgressions. Suddenly, Rafal asked: 'Kuba, are you hungry? It's ... three in the morning but I could murder a pizza.'

'A hot pepperoni? With extra cheese? Definitely!'

'Just the thing I had in mind.' Rafal rolled over onto his side and reached for the phone. He spoke quickly, laughing at the joke of the person taking the order. 'You know me well. All the usual trimmings. And a large bottle of Coke.' Then placing the receiver with a thump he triumphantly grinned at Kuba. 'Done. Twenty minutes. Fancy another beer?'

'That would be great.'

They were lying on the floor with two cans of *Tyskie* when the intercom bell rang. Its chirpy sound appeared incongruous in the middle of the night. Rafal got up with some effort and a bit unsteady on his feet, walked towards the door.

'Come in,' he shouted into the intercom. Then he had second thoughts. 'I'd better go down. There're four floors to climb after all.' However, before he could say this to the person delivering the pizza, they heard a cheerful: 'Coming up,' and the line went silent.

'Rafal, don't bother. They don't have too many orders at this time of the night. He will get a tip,' advised Kuba and he reached for his jacket lying on the back of the sofa.

He was still fumbling for his wallet when there was a ding dong at the door. Rafal went to open it. He switched on the light in the small entrance hall and grappled with the bolt. There was a groan of badly oiled hinges followed by a silence.

'What are you doing here?!'

Kuba sat up. He couldn't see what was happening in the small hallway but Rafal's exclamation startled him.

'What a warm welcome!' a female voice exclaimed. Next there was a burst of laughter and a reprimand: 'What a display of gratitude for climbing eight flights of stairs with your supper!'

'Thank you. Your sacrifice touched my heart. How did you intercept my order?'

'I was in La Florentina when it came in and thought we could continue our conversation.'

'What a genius!'

'I brought you something to help you digest the pizza,' said the woman. Kuba heard the clinking of the bottles.

'You shouldn't have bothered.'

'Really?' The voice was now clear. Kuba could swear he had heard it before.

'Will you keep me standing in the doorway?'

'Come in.' said Rafal with resignation.

The voice was familiar because it belonged to the dark haired beauty who had given such an impassioned performance on the dance floor of Rafal's club only a couple of hours before. Wrapped in a short fur jacket, she was now standing in the doorway positively beaming at Kuba.

'Hi stranger!' Her voice, bold and melodic, shattered the comforting atmosphere of Rafal's apartment.

'Hi,' said Kuba raising himself up from the carpet. 'I didn't think many people would still be awake.'

'I don't go to bed early.'

'That's obvious, Judyta,' said Rafal sarcastically. He placed the pizza carton on the kitchen counter and started taking out plates from the wall unit. If she wasn't here, we would be eating straight from the box, thought Kuba.

'Where do you keep wine glasses, Rafal?' asked Judyta, taking out two bottles from a plastic carrier bag. They clinked hard on the granite worktop.

'Red or white?' she turned to Kuba lifting the bottles in his direction.

'Red.'

'Good choice. Goes nicely with a pepperoni pizza,' She gave him a satisfied smile and proceeded to pour two glasses of red wine.

'What about you, Rafal?'
'A glass of white will do.'

They perched on the high stools by Rafal's kitchen counter and shared the pizza, which was very hot even by Kuba's standards. They tried to soothe their taste buds with more wine. Kuba soon switched to water as he sensed an onset of a headache — the result of another late night. Mixing beer with wine always had a bad effect on him. Soon they moved to the sofas, taking their drinks with them. Judyta took off her long boots and reclined like an odalisque on the deep pile carpet. Focusing her attention solely on Kuba, she asked him question after question about his life in London.

Not in the least bit discouraged by his laconic answers, she proceeded to tell him her life story. The most enjoyable aspect of owning a hair and beauty salon in a prestigious location were the social contacts it facilitated. It helped her to keep her hand on the pulse of the town and spot opportunities when they were forthcoming. She wasn't specific as to what opportunities she had in mind, and Kuba didn't bother to follow this line of conversation. He was only too aware that Judyta had already outstayed Rafal's hospitality.

Yet she was clearly enjoying herself and didn't seem to notice her host's growing irritation. Throwing her head back and tossing her luxurious mane, she laughed throatily, flashing Kuba her dazzling smile. She was extraordinarily beautiful and she knew it. He watched her as she slowly slipped sliver bangles off her arms, one by one, and piled them in an empty ashtray on the coffee table. She wasn't looking at Kuba now, but the meaning of this gesture wasn't lost on him.

Suddenly, Kuba remembered her saying that she had left her car near Rafal's house. Looking at the empty bottles of wine and cans of beer, he made a mental calculation of his own alcohol consumption. He decided to take a risk and free his friend from the unwanted company.

'Let's call it a night,' he said looking at Rafal. 'You need to get some rest, mate.' Then, turning to Judyta, he said: 'Shouldn't you be catching up on your beauty sleep? I could take you home.'

They drove for about ten minutes when suddenly Judyta commanded: 'Kuba, stop here.'

He looked at her, surprised. 'Are you OK? Do you need some fresh air?'

He feared she was going to be sick. They stopped in a road that cut across a park. He slowly pulled up close to a deserted bench and switched off his lights. There was no one around. Only the chilly wind was whipping the bare branches of young trees and sickly looking bushes.

Judyta's face was very pale and her heavily made up eyes appeared enormous in the darkness.

'Would you like me to help you out?'

'No, just move my seat back.'

Kuba leaned across her and pulled the handle on the other side of her seat. It slid back with a jerk.

'Is that better?'

'Much better ...' Before he could utter another word, she put her lips on his and started devouring him passionately, cradling the back of his head in the palm of her hand.

At first Kuba gasped, taken by surprise, but Judyta was an accomplished lover and soon he was melting in her embrace. He felt her searching hand on his chest and soon she was unzipping his leather jacket and tearing open his shirt, its buttons popping off one by one.

'This is what I wanted to do the whole evening,' she purred. 'It was such a long night.'

He suddenly felt her hair fly across his face as she threw it back. She swung her jacket onto the back seat. Then she reached across his body and pulled back the leaver of his seat. It jerked back like the start of a rollercoaster ride.

She was now sitting astride him. She reached behind her back. In a second her naked breasts were pressing against his chest. Her flesh was hot and already perspiring. She thrust her tongue deep inside his mouth. Her fingers were now manipulating his zip fly and it wasn't long before any semblance of control was abandoned. His heart was pounding and his temples were exploding with pulsating blood. He felt her hot moist flesh engulf him and heard her begging cry. Her wanting matched his and they gave into the ecstasy that astonished them both.

Chapter 24

Maja, May 1998

The windows of the House of Fraser store in Kensington High Street were polished to perfection. The low afternoon sun reflected from the sheet of glass was blinding Maja and Amy who, shading their eyes, were looking at the floaty summer dress. Its luxuriously thin fabric draped a mannequin in the window.

'You would look divine in that frock,' said Amy looking at Maja. 'A straw hat with a large brim and a sash in that pale pink would transform you into a nymph,' she pointed her finger at the display, narrowing her eyes. 'You would have men falling for you like flies.'

Maja laughed and shook her head. 'These patterns and colours are designed for you. With your dark hair and olive skin you would look stunning. Like some exotic gypsy.'

'A squatty, short legged pixie more like,' Amy said with a tragic expression. I'm too short for such a long dress. But, you would look like a summer dream.'

'Rubbish, Amy. Dreaming, that's all we can do. Look at the price tag. Three hundred and ninety nine pounds.'

'The shoes are cheaper. One hundred and ninety nine.'

'Well, we won't be buying them. They are not meant for us. Not good enough,' said Maja and they laughed. 'I think we will be wasting our time going into the store. Instead we could …'

'… Have an iced coffee. Frappuccino perhaps, and a piece of cheesecake?' suggested Amy.

'What about the diet which you began on Monday?'

'Maja. Don't be a spoil sport. I will have a cake and no dinner.'

'OK, I have done my duty as your friend.'

Still laughing, they turned the corner and walked into a side street at the end of which there was a bistro facing a small square. Usually it was quiet in the afternoon. However, today it was teaming with people enjoying the May sunshine. The large front windows were opened up in the Parisian style and tables spilled out onto the pavement. For a moment, they stood looking at the animated crowd.

'Maja, go and grab that table in the corner before someone sits there,' commanded Amy. 'I will go to the bar and order us some sustenance.'

Amy entered the bistro while Maja started manoeuvring between the chairs towards an empty table in the corner. She had to turn sideways and pull her stomach in to squeeze through. It wasn't surprising that no one had been able to get so far. She battled through, saying sorry a dozen times. Eventually she reached her destination and with a sigh of relief, she flopped down on one of the empty seats. As soon as she sat down, with horror she noticed a light linen jacket lying crumpled on the ground between the chairs. She rushed to retrieve it before the owner noticed what'd happened. Yet the moment she reached for the jacket a man at the next table turned around. Catching a glimpse of Maja diving down behind his seat, he craned his neck to better see what was going on. Maja lifted the jacket, shook it, and carefully placed it on the back of the seat. Just then, she noticed a patch of dirt on one of the sleeves. She started brushing it off but a long smudge of grime appeared on the light fabric. She was mortified. Lifting her eyes, she met the gaze of the jacket's owner.

'I'm so sorry. I've ruined your jacket. I'll pay to get it dry cleaned.'

Surprisingly, the man appeared amused with the situation.

'No problem whatsoever. The jacket is not ruined, only dirty. It was due for a clean anyway.'

'I could hardly squeeze between the seats,' she explained.

'It's very crowded here. It could have happened to anyone.'

'Yeah ... You won't be able to use it today.'

'He won't freeze. Besides he has other things to wear. Don't worry please,' said the man's companion. He was looking at Maja with interest. 'What about a drink to settle the issue?'

Maja hesitated.

'A cocktail or a soft drink?'

'Thank you but my friend is at the bar ordering drinks for us. We were ...' she stopped seeing Amy emerging from the bistro and waving at her. Between them there were half a dozen tables occupied back to back with customers. Maja envisaged Amy trying to squeeze through the crowd and attracting amused glanced. Knowing how sensitive her friend was about her weight, Maja got up and gestured to her to stay where she was.

'We've changed our mind,' she said briskly. 'Thank you for the offer and understanding. It's very kind.'

She noticed an expression of disappointment on the men's faces and smiled apologetically. She got up and started moving towards Amy. When she emerged from the crowd, she sighed with relief.

'Amy let's have drinks at the bar. That last table is empty because it's inaccessible. I just ruined a man's jacket knocking it down on the pavement.'

'Has he threatened to sue you?'

'No. He suggested a drink as a peace offering.'

'One of those good looking guys at the next table?'

'Yeah ... The one in the shades.'

'Well ... What did you say?'

'That my friend has already ordered me a drink.'

'That was cruel.'

'C'mon Amy, let's go in. By standing and gawping at them we will give them the wrong idea.'

'And what would this be?'

But Maja was already inside striding towards two empty stools at the end of the bar. Amy reluctantly followed. As they were making themselves comfortable on their high stools, their drinks and cakes arrived.

Amy took a long sip of her frappuccino, pleased to see that it was generously topped with whipped cream. She dug her spoon into the creamy flesh of a Viennese cheesecake, and putting its aromatic content into her mouth, made appreciative noises.

'Maja, I envy your ability to walk away so easily from things you deep down want and like. You're so damn sensible about it.'

Maja looked up surprised at her friend and smiled. 'I guess it's because I don't expect to get them. Elegant shops in Grodek were only there to look at. My mum avoided looking at expensive things so she didn't have to admit that they were out of her reach.'

She squeezed a slice of lemon with a teaspoon against the side of her glass and the tea suddenly turned amber. She took a sip of it, inhaling its zesty scent. 'There are better things than money,' she added.

'Such as?'

'Seeing places, films, theatre ... Our parents took us to the cinema — almost every week and gave me money to go for school theatre trips.'

'My family also believes in education all right. But even more in financial security. I guess it comes from being Jewish and having to move from one end of Europe to another. My father keeps telling me that I should know on which side my bread is buttered.'

Maja looked at her curiously.

'I wish I knew on which side my bread is buttered,' sighed Amy. 'But I have no intention of devoting my life to making money.'

'Many people do.'

'I already disappointed my parents by not going to train at my uncle's law firm. When I opted for a hotel school, they were warning me what an insecure career it was.' For a moment, Amy gave her full attention to the dessert in front of her. She finished her coffee, scraped the remainder of her cheesecake off the plate and licked her lips. Wiping her mouth with a tissue, she asked: 'Have your parents told you whom you should marry?'

'No. But my aunt kept telling me that unless I started looking for a husband, I would become an old maid.'

'Fat chance of that Maja. You trample on some bloke's jacket and he offers you a drink. I flirt with them and all they do is to put their sticky hands on my ass. What's the secret?'

'Be mean to them. It obviously works.'

They laughed. But Amy was in a reflective mood and asked: 'Have you ever been with a man whom you really, really liked but couldn't have?'

It wasn't territory Maja was willing to enter on this sunny May afternoon.

Amy wasn't put off by her silence and said: 'For almost two

years I was dating my driving instructor and managed to keep it secret from my family. Amazing really.'

'What was the problem?'

'He was a Scot. Divorced with a child.'

'So ...'

'My father would go ballistic if he knew that. I am not supposed to marry outside the faith. Another Cohen would be a perfect match.'

'I see ... So what happened to the Scot?'

'Became fed up playing the hiding game with me. He also felt guilty taking money from my father when he knew that I was perfectly ready to take a driving test.'

'And ...'

'I passed it. First time. I couldn't believe it. My father was so delighted that he suggested that I take my driving instructor for a meal as a thank you.'

'That was very nice of him.'

'That was the last time I saw Ian.'

'Couldn't you try to convince your father that he meant a lot to you?'

'Things like that are not negotiable with my father. Besides Ian said that he couldn't face becoming a hate figure in my family. He already had his share of marital grief.'

'And you ...'

'I obviously didn't deserve him if I couldn't stand up to my family.'

'Amy ...' Maja patted her friend's hand affectionately.

'I will learn to stand up to them. One day.'

Then Maja caught a glance of a portly man sitting at the other end of the bar. His large hands were cradling a minute espresso cup. His eyes were focused on his coffee but she was certain he was listening to their chat. Their private conversation. Angrily she twisted her stool so now all he could see was her back. She leaned forward to Amy, lowered her voice and said, 'So you were saying that you will stand up ...'

One morning looking across the lobby, Maja noticed a new face at Reception. A young woman dressed in a black suit and crisp white shirt was briskly moving around. It was just before eight and the Reception desk was still quiet so the girl took her time to talk to each receptionist in turn. Her dark hair was smoothly swept back and the uniform contrasted sharply with her pale complexion.

'Jess is back from holidays,' remarked James following Maja's gaze. 'The girls were able to breathe easier for a week while the old dragon was away. Now she is putting them through their paces again.'

Leafing through her 'to do' lists, Maja was observing the head receptionist from the corner of her eye. A paragon of profession-alism and efficiency, she thought.

When a solitary customer appeared at the counter she was first to greet him. With a wide smile, she started a conversation, no doubt enquiring whether he was satisfied with his room, the food and the service. In a moment she nodded at James to call a taxi for the customer. Next, she was marching through the lobby to reposition the brass stand displaying information about the functions taking place in the hotel that day.

Watching her disappear and re-emerge from the back office countless times during the day, Maja had no doubt that Jessica was in control of every aspect of the Reception's work. In the afternoon, she took the lift upstairs and didn't return until four o'clock.

'Jess is getting a briefing from the bosses,' commented James with a crooked smile.

'Do we report to her in any way?' enquired Maja anxiously, sensing that Jessica Dryer had a lot of influence at the hotel.

'Theoretically no. We are accountable to Mr Clifford, front office manager who answers to Mr Brown. In practice, Jess pokes her nose in the business of all the front of house depart-ments so she can show the boss how well informed she is.'

'She is very efficient.'

'Driven,' corrected James. 'She has her sights set much higher than the Reception desk. Like almost everyone in this business, she lives to work.'

'She is very attractive.'

'Apparently, Hitler was attractive too.'

Maja laughed but quickly suppressed her smile. Jessica was coming out of the lift. Holding her head high she walked across the lobby with the confidence of a supreme commander. With her jacket fully buttoned up and a pad under arm, she was the very image of professionalism. After a brief spell at the Reception counter she directed her steps towards Customer Relations.

'Here she comes. Keep tight,' muttered James.

Ignoring James altogether, Jessica approached Maja. Extending her arm over the counter she said: 'Jessica Dryer. Welcome aboard Maja. Robert Clifford told me that you joined us last week. From the Garden Restaurant?'

Maja's smile stiffened on her lips.

'Yes, I was offered a position here together with training.'

'Is your background in the hospitality industry?'

For a second Maja, considered the purpose of the question.

'No, but I have the right skills.'

'And what's your training?'

'I am a language graduate. I was advised that foreign language skills were needed in Customer Relations.'

'The hotel industry requires a very specific set of skills. But languages are always useful while serving the customers.'

It wasn't going well, thought Maja. She didn't want Jessica to be her enemy. She held a lot of influence in the hotel and it would be foolish to antagonise her in any way.

When Jessica departed, Maja sat at a small table at the back of the station to start her daily report but her thoughts circled around Jessica. Seeing her unsettled, James came up to her and putting his hand on her shoulder said soothingly: 'You were forewarned.'

Maja sighed deeply and opened her file.

'Don't let her upset you. You're well educated and pretty and the old dragon doesn't like competition. But don't worry, there are plenty of nice people in this hotel.'

Since starting on the Customer Relations desk, Maja began attending a bi-weekly hospitality course where a broad range of skills were taught — from computing, accounting and customer care to human resource management. She already knew some of these subjects but because the courses were hotel-specific she found them interesting and relevant to her work. What a pleas-

ure it was to study again! She was constantly learning new
skills in the hotel but it was only when she opened her new
textbooks and inhaled the smell of fresh print that she felt that
forgotten excitement of embarking on a new adventure with
limitless possibilities.

'Of course, we will be able to help you, madam.' A stout middle-
aged woman standing in front of her looked as if she just had
completed a long distance run. Large red blotches appeared on
her face and she was perspiring heavily.

'Can I take your full name, Mrs —?'

'Kühn. Adela with an 'a' not an 'e' at the end. Miss Kühn.'

'Thank you, Miss Kühn.'

Having put Miss Kühn's name into the hotel system, Maja
learnt instantly that she came from Munich and it was her third
stay at the hotel.

'And your friend's name is Hanneck, isn't it?'

'Elsa Hanneck. Double 'n',' stressed Miss Kühn. 'She should
be arriving here today but she telephoned me this morning to
say that she slipped and broke her ankle. So she won't be
coming to London or Scotland with me.'

'Very unfortunate, indeed.' Maja looked up at Miss Kühn's
troubled face and gave her a reassuring smile. She also glanced
anxiously in the direction of the sofas where a diminutive
Japanese lady was studying a list of London colleges which
Maja had printed for her.

Today Amy called in sick and George, who replaced Alan, was
called upstairs for a meeting. Maja and James were manning
the ship on their own trying to keep the number of people
waiting at the desk to a minimum. A queue at the Customer
Relations desk wasn't acceptable at the Metropole. 'The
Metropole is not a Citizen Advice Bureau and customers who
need assistance cannot be kept waiting,' she had heard during
the induction.

From time to time she looked in the direction of Reception.
She didn't want Jessica to notice a growing queue of guests
waiting for their attention. She was anxiously scanning the
gathering at Reception for the familiar pale face when she saw
him. The man whose jacket she had knocked to the ground only

two days before. He must have been a guest of the Metropole because he was now leaning on the counter and writing something down. Presumably settling the bill. She wished Miss Kühn was taller and she could hide behind her. She stooped as if getting a better look at the computer screen.

'I can see your reservations with Scotland Travel and I will give them a ring to check whether we could cancel your friend's reservation. Would you be happy to go alone?'

'Yes, since I am already here. But we were to share a room. Will I have to pay the full cost of it?'

'Let's see what we can do. This company is usually very accommodating. We put a lot of business through them.'

Her unfortunate acquaintance now turned around, threw a mac over his shoulder and picked up his briefcase. He was walking towards the revolving door when he spotted Maja. Maja lowered her gaze at Miss Kühn's anxious face, praying that the man wouldn't stop. But he turned around and was now heading directly towards the Customer Relations desk. Oh God, she didn't want to go back to that incident again and have to apologise in front of her customers. Seeing how busy she was, the man joined the queue. He took a newspaper out of his briefcase and was leafing through it patiently waiting for his turn. Maja noticed how well and relaxed he looked this morning. The shadow of a smile lingered on his lips as he listened to Maja's efforts to solve Miss Kühn's problems. He was much better looking than she remembered from their first encounter.

Eventually it was his turn, and with Miss Kühn still waiting for the resolution of her enquiry and the Japanese woman studying her list, for a moment, he had Maja to himself. He leaned towards Maja and whispered confidentially: 'If I knew you worked here, I would have asked you to dry clean my jacket. That would have given me a legitimate excuse to see you again.'

'I thought you had absolved me from the crime.'

'Not as much as to let you get away without accepting a drink.'

'Socialising with the hotel guests is not acceptable.'

'Do you leave this building at the end of the day, Ms Zalewska?' he asked, looking at her name badge.

'I also study. In the evenings.'

'Every day?'

Just then, an elderly couple positioned themselves next to her acquaintance, hopefully smiling at Maja.

'I stay in the Metropole a few times a year and my company has an account with the hotel,' he said unexpectedly: 'I have been asked to enquire whether we could use your meeting rooms at a special rate.'

She wondered whether he made this up on the spur of the moment but replied with full seriousness: 'I would have to verify this with our corporate service department but I am sure that they will be able to prepare a special offer for a regular client.'

'What about this afternoon after work. I won't be leaving London until tomorrow morning. Can you spare me an hour in the afternoon?'

Maja hesitated weighing up the suggestion.

'There is a French café just round the corner in Gloucester Place,' he said.

'I know.'

'Settled then?'

At that moment to her horror Maja saw Jessica emerge from behind the man. She wondered how much she had overheard of their conversation. Seeing the change in Maja's expression the man turned around and found himself face to face with the head receptionist, her brass badge gleaming like a jewel.

He turned again to Maja. 'Miss Zalewska, when you receive the answer from your corporate business department, please call me on this number.'

Out of his wallet, he took out a business card. He turned the card over and started writing something on it.

'Maja, are you managing?' Jessica asked impatiently, not used to being ignored. 'The queue is forming.'

'We are fine Jessica. Everything is under control.'

Turning to the guest Jessica asked: 'Is there anything I could help you with?' Maja saw that Jessica's grin was brighter than the standard professional one.

'Not at all. Miss Zalewska is dealing with my enquiry. But thank you for asking.' He was polite but curt. The flirtatious glint in his eyes wasn't there anymore. He waited until Jessica walked away and passed the card to Maja.

'On the back is my mobile number and the name of the place

where I'll be waiting for you. That is of course, if you haven't
received a better offer by then.'

Maja looked down at the card. Luke Hastings, Account Director at Ashton & Rogers advertising agency.

'Mr Hastings, that coffee will be on me,' she said firmly. 'It'll
be my apology for the ruined jacket.'

Chapter 25

Maja, May 1998

Maja arrived at the French bistro ten minutes late. It was just round the corner from the Metropole but appearing eager to this attractive and confident man would have been a big mistake. In fact, she regretted agreeing to this meeting at all. The memories of Nico were still too painful for her. She also instinctively knew that hers and Nico's story wasn't over yet. And what was this man trying to achieve anyway? If this was his way of picking up girls, she should have shown him that she wasn't that type of girl.

'I thought you wouldn't come,' he greeted her. He stood up and moved the chair for her.

'I won't deny I was considering doing that.'

'I'm glad you decided to brave the danger of meeting me again.' He flashed her a wide grin and she noticed that his eyes were cornflower blue. Seeing that she was trying to free herself of her work jacket, he got up to help her out of it.

'Thank you,' she gave him a grateful smile.

'So what made you change your mind?'

She hesitated for a second but decided against flattering him.

'A feeling of guilt, to be honest.'

He made a disappointed expression. 'That is not an answer a man inviting a girl out likes to hear, but I appreciate your honesty.'

'Keeping things clear is best, don't you think?'

'Of course,' he confirmed but the corners of his eyes creased into something resembling a smirk. 'You don't wish to be beholden to anyone, do you?'

'I learnt to stand on my own two feet. Any kind of dependence only complicates things.'

Luke looked at her carefully. Then with a straight face he

asked: 'Would it interfere with your independence if I order two pieces of lemon cheesecake for us? I tested it before. However, coming from Eastern Europe you may have high expectations of cheesecake. Am I right?'

'Where in Eastern Europe have you sampled cheesecake?'

'Prague, Moscow ...'

'You're obviously well travelled.'

'It was work related. But I haven't been to Poland so Polish cheesecake is an unknown territory for me. As much as ...' He bit his tongue.

'As Polish girls?'

'Polish things in general.'

Maja noticed that he again suppressed a smile.

'I am happy to test that cheesecake. Just for the record: Polish cheesecakes are based on the Viennese ones. Creamy but zesty,' she said authoritatively. He was flirting with her but it amused her. She was happy to play this game but on her own terms. Propping her chin on one hand, she looked directly into his eyes and said: 'Mr Hastings, I'd love to hear more about your travels. I am always interested to hear Westerners' impressions of Eastern Europe.'

'Please call me Luke. May I call you Maja?'

She never forgot that moment. It was such a simple question but the way he asked it startled her. He said it with hesitation, softly, as if caressing her name with his voice. She never said yes and didn't say no. She just looked at him and couldn't understand what had happened. Until that moment they were barely acquainted. Now she felt as she knew him already.

Getting ready to meet Luke Maja promised herself not to spend more time in his company than was necessary to make an apology. And yet they sat for two hours talking and with fascination looking into each other lives.

Suddenly Maja looked at her watch. It was already six thirty. In thirty minutes her classes would begin.

'I really need to go now. Otherwise, I will be late.'

For a second, Luke looked as if he hadn't understood what she had said. Then his expression relaxed. 'Of course, you said you study in the evening. I ... I forgot.'

She shook her head. 'You didn't believe me.'

'It crossed my mind that you may have been excusing yourself. Where are you going?'

'Marble Arch.'

'Why don't we get a taxi together? I will drop you first and then go and see a friend whom I planned to visit this evening.'

The taxi ride wasn't long enough to finish their conversation so while helping her out of the cab, Luke asked: 'Would you consider having another coffee with me again? I will be back in London in two weeks' time?' He looked at her hopefully.

'Yes ... I would be happy to do so,' she said lightly. 'You mentioned you took lots of pictures while travelling.'

She surprised him by planting a kiss on his cheek. Then she waved him good-bye, turned around and dashed towards the redbrick building. If she looked back, she would have seen Luke following her with his eyes until she disappeared behind a corner. With one hand suspended in the air, he was bidding her good bye.

She didn't have to wait even a week to speak to him again. The Corporate Business department agreed to let Ashton & Rogers use their conference facilities at a special rate, so she had to call him to give him this information.

The letter was already in the post but she wanted to personally deliver the news. She considered calling the main office line and asking to be put through to him. But if he was out, she would have to leave a lengthy message about something which he may have made up on a spur of the moment. She turned his card over and called his mobile number. She adopted a formal tone of voice, asking whether she could speak to Mr Hastings. There was a second of silence and then a delighted laugh.

'Maja, you have managed to surprise me again. Are you well?'

In a professional manner, she informed him about the positive response to his request.

'I had almost forgotten about that, but I am very pleased that the hotel gave us the green light. I'll be able to see you more often.'

There was a silence at the other end.

He instantly realised that this was meant as a business call made from her office. 'Miss Zalewska, I am extremely grateful for your help and assistance. I will communicate the news to my boss. May I call you later to express my gratitude? Perhaps you could give me a number on which I could call you later.'

With her eyes firmly fixed on the papers in front of her, Maja muttered into the receiver the telephone number of 26 Cuckoohill Road and her mobile number. Only last week she had become the proud owner of a mobile phone, and Luke was the second person, after Amy, who received her number.

'Excellent. Once again, thank you very much for your help. I'll be in touch.' Luke was clearly in high spirits. She put the receiver down and for a moment kept her hand on it, imagining his face at the other end of the line.

She was putting her dirty dinner plates into the sink when Basia burst from the sitting room shouting: 'Maja, there is a call for you.' Well, he kept his word, she thought.

'I will take it on the landing,' she shouted back firmly closing the kitchen door. She hurried upstairs and picked up the ringing phone with one hand while carefully treading the long lead into her room with the other. Leaning against the door to close it, she lifted the receiver.

'Hello?'

'Maja, *kochanie*, how are you? I cannot catch you in the evening, you're working or studying ...'

'*Mamo*, is everything OK? I would have called you at the weekend, as usual.'

'Sure, it is. The house is quiet at this end, with everybody out, so I thought I'd give you a ring to have a chat.'

Instantly Maja had a strange feeling of foreboding. Calls abroad were expensive and her family rarely called her 'for a chat' outside the clearly agreed time.

'Are you well, mum?'

'Yes, a bit tired but well.'

'What about dad? Zosia and Piotrek?'

'They are fine too.'

'And dad?'

'He is well, overdoing things at work, perhaps more than

usual.'

'Why mum?'

'You see, they will be laying off people in his plant.'

'Oh, mum! What are you going to do if that happens?'

'Maja, don't worry, we will be OK. I still have my job and with his experience he could pick up something part-time. It's just ...'

'What, mum?'

'Since he found out about the possibility of redundancy, he is not himself. He became very bitter, depressed. He keeps saying he put 25 years of his life into this factory and now they are trying to replace him like an old piece of equipment. You know him. He bottles everything inside him and this worries me more than anything else.'

'What can I do to help, mum?' Maja asked with desperation in her voice.

'Nothing at the moment. You have a good job and this takes some weight off my heart. You're happy with what you're doing now? Are you?'

'Yes, of course, mum. I work in a very smart hotel and I'm studying to improve my qualifications.'

'That's good, darling.' There was a pause on the line and then her mother said hastily: 'Maja, I can hear your dad at the door so I need to go. Don't tell him we spoke but try to cheer him up when you call at the weekend. Will you?'

'Of course, mum. I love you.'

With a heavy heart Maja put down the receiver. By now she was sitting on the floor cradling the phone on her lap and replaying the conversation in her head. She wondered whether things at home were worse than she was made to believe and her mother gave her an edited version of the truth. How long had her fathers' troubles been going on for? How selfish and wrapped up in her life in London she was not to notice anything. It was so much easier to believe that everything at home was the way she had left it eighteen months ago.

She almost jumped when the mobile suddenly rang in her pocket. Instinctively, she picked it up expecting a continuation of bad news.

'Yes?'

'Maja, it's me, Luke. Are you OK? You sound as if I woke you up. It's only eight o'clock,' he chided her.

'I ... I was thinking ... I just received a telephone call from my mum,' It was bad timing. She didn't want to draw him into her personal troubles. She closed her eyes thinking how to excuse herself.

'Is everything OK at home?' his voice took a different tone.

'Yes, it's all fine ...'

'You don't sound very convincing.'

'Oh, God no. I have just learnt that my father could be made redundant. Quite soon. And he is not copying with it well ...' She felt she couldn't keep the bad news to herself. 'And I am here not able to help them ... I didn't suspect a thing.'

'Maja, you couldn't. You live at the other end of Europe now. They didn't want to upset you, that's all. Don't blame yourself because your presence in Poland would not have made a bit of difference. You can call them, even visit them but that's all. You could take a few days off and see them.'

'I have been in the new job for only two months.'

'When is your next day off?'

'Next Wednesday,' Maja said automatically.

'That's perfect. I have a meeting in London on Thursday. I will drive down on Wednesday morning and we will take a day off. Together.'

'Luke ...' she didn't have time to gather her thoughts.

'Don't say anything. That's settled. I will whisk you out of London if the weather is nice. If not, we will anchor ourselves in one of the galleries and have a leisurely lunch.'

She was touched with his thoughtfulness. Yet, she felt that their acquaintance was progressing faster than she felt comfortable with.

'Luke, you don't give up?'

'Do you?'

'Perhaps not.'

'So we are likely to understand each other well.'

Chapter 26

Maja, June 1998

Maja woke up to a breathtakingly beautiful morning. Opening the window she took a gulp of garden-scented air. The sky was blue and cloudless and the breeze that touched her face was cool — a reminder that this was only the beginning of June. It was a day for wearing a dress, light and flirty, like the wispy creation which she admired with Amy in the window of the House of Fraser. Such garments were made for summer picnics.

She opened her clown-patterned wardrobe and dived in. Her clothes collection was rather limited and she was able to make up her mind quickly. Soon, a red dress with white polka dots and a short cotton cardigan were spread out on the bed. The only shoes in her possession that would match this outfit were a pair of white sandals. They had small heels which would not be entirely suitable for a picnic, but they would have to do.

Once a dry and sunny spell was forecast for the week, Luke asked her to get ready for an outing to the country.

'Where are we going?'

'It's a surprise. But I won't be dragging you through the fields. No need for wellies and waterproofs.'

'What should I prepare?'

'Nothing, just yourself. Should I meet you at your place?'

'No,' she said firmly. 'Do you mind meeting me at the corner of Cuckoohill Road and Orchard Grove? This … would be best.' The memories of Nico picking her up at the front door were still too fresh in her mind. She wished to keep her friendship with Luke off the radar of 26 Cuckoohill Road.

As soon as they left the outskirts of London, Maja began watching the changing landscape with rapt attention. For several minutes they hardly exchanged a word. Seeing her fascination, Luke drove off the motorway and took an A road to give her an opportunity to see more.

'I didn't realise that the English countryside is so beautiful,' she said dreamily.

'In spring and early summer, England is always at its loveliest.' He glanced at her red and white outfit. 'Especially when the sun is shining. I am sure you have noticed this.'

'I don't really know England outside London ...'

'For many overseas visitors London is England. They may catch a glance of the countryside travelling to Bath or Stratford-upon-Avon, or through the windows of an express train to Edinburgh.'

Maja couldn't bring herself to admit that her furthest venture outside London was to Windsor.

'Well, you have some catching up to do.'

'I know,' she sighed heavily. 'For months I was concerned with more prosaic things ... Where are we at the moment?'

'We are driving through Surrey, about to cross into Sussex. We will stop at a nice viewing point soon. On a clear day one can see the Sussex Downs from there.'

'Are we going south?'

'South east. I hope you will like our destination. Once you hear about its history, you'll understand why I chose it,' he said with a smile.

'I already love the trip.' She folded her hands on her lap and fixed her eyes on the hills on the horizon.

'I didn't know that such places still exist,' exclaimed Maja, looking with amazement at the fairytale setting of Leeds Castle. They left the car in the car park and were now crossing the vast lawn towards the edge of the water to get a better view of the medieval castle perched on the island.

'It's so beautiful.'

'It has always been a special place.'

Maja was feasting her eyes on the silver grey ramparts and towers surrounded by the inky water of the lake framed by the lush greenery of the rolling meadows.

'It's so perfect. Like a postcard.'

'A lot of effort went into renovating it.'

'Most of Poland's ancient castles are in ruins. Burnt and trampled by armies marching from north to south and west to east,' she said quietly.

'I didn't know that Poland had such a painful history.'

'Poland's location in the centre of Europe made her a buffer zone between the East and West and was responsible for her many misfortunes. What's the history of this beautiful place?'

'Let's go inside. All will be revealed,' said Luke with a smile.

The lawns surrounding the lake were speckled with daisies and clover, whose sweet scent permeated the air. The grass was like a thick carpet and the heels of Maja's sandals sunk deeply into the turf. She took her shoes off and felt its soothing coolness under her feet. It brought back the memories of her childhood. She longed to run across the grass as she had done many times along the banks of the Chodelka with Zosia and Piotr. She felt like tossing her shoes into the air, doing the same with her cardigan and spinning around from the physical pleasure of being alive on such a perfect day.

She was walking a few steps ahead of Luke who was searching for a good spot for their picnic. Her red and white skirt billowed behind her in the breeze which eased long strands of her hair from the knot at the nape.

With every minute she looked more like a gypsy. Following her with an amused expression, Luke watched as she hopped and skipped. Was she the same person who in a buttoned-up suit advised customers in the hotel? Amazed by this transformation, he kept walking behind her, afraid to break the spell.

Suddenly Maja turned around and asked: 'Is this the right place? Are we far enough from everybody else?'

'Of course. Why?'

'Don't you like plenty of space around you?'

'Maja, not every Englishman needs a castle with a moat around him,' he said placing the basket on the ground. Then he unfolded the blanket and looking around at groups of people who had already occupied the lawn, said wistfully: 'It would be nice to have this place to ourselves for the afternoon.'

As they made themselves comfortable on the blanket, Luke

started emptying the contents of their picnic basket. On a check tablecloth, he placed plates, cutlery, tumblers and wine glasses. Then he opened a couple of containers with salads and chicken legs and unwrapped a plate with sandwiches.

'Good God, it's enough to feed an army. You're very experienced at this sort of thing,' said Maja appreciatively. 'How many times have you done this before?'

'A few.'

'I can see that.'

'A picnic is a part of English culture, almost as much as cricket and warm beer. We picnic in all weathers.' He handed her a wine glass and out of a tube-like cooler, produced a bottle of white wine. 'Cheers.'

'Cheers.' She took a sip of her wine and savouring its cool crispness she said: 'Delicious. It's a feast. But I find it hard to believe that you've prepared all this food.' She waved her hand over the meal splendidly spread out on the tablecloth.

'I couldn't take credit for this. Even if I did, you wouldn't believe me.' He grinned widely. 'It's my mother's making. She has always prepared top-quality picnic food.'

'And your mum didn't mind doing this and you taking these dishes and the basket.'

'It's hardly a family heirloom. She was curious about you.' He bit into a chicken leg and looked up at her examining her reaction.

'And what did you say?' Maja asked with uneasiness in her voice.

'That the girl whom I'm taking for a trip came from Poland.'

'And your mum thought that being a poor Eastern European immigrant she needs fattening up ...'

'Not exactly. But my mother knew that you must be a special person if I asked her for help.'

'Do you always treat your female friends so nicely?' she said before she could stop herself.

'That is an unfair question, Maja.' It was obvious that he was hurt by her words. She checked herself and looked at him carefully. This charming man sitting opposite her made such a generous effort to amuse and please her and she had managed to offend him. He didn't deserve this. She felt angry with herself. 'Luke, please forget what I said. It was mean of me.' She got up and moved to his side of the blanket.

'It has been a wonderful day. The best one since I came to England. I love everything. Thank you.' Then she grinned. 'From now on I'll only be nice to you.' She put her arm through his and placed her head on his shoulder. Without looking at him, she knew that he was smiling.

Chapter 27

Adam, August 1998

A feeling of happiness, almost elation, made him walk faster. The trail was now sharply climbing up but he felt young and fit. The pulsating blood made the whole experience only more arousing. He used every muscle in his body and this gave him a sense of power. He remembered that after the steep climb there would be a large clearing, jutting like a stone shelf above the valley below. On a clear day one could see amazing views of the Ridge from there.

Everything was exactly as he knew it. The clearing was now overgrown with a meadow. Crossing it, he found himself in waist-high grass, thickly woven with wild flowers and herbs. As he waded through it, he inhaled their bitter sweet scent. It went straight to his head like a shot of vodka. The far end of the clearing was like an open balcony with only soft mosses covering the edge. A sheer drop of hundreds of metres awaited those who dared to lean over it. Every autumn the *halny* wind uprooted any vegetation that managed to establish itself in the meagre soil of the verge. That's why the view from the *polana* was so breathtaking, allowing one's gaze to fly over the canyon to the granite walls of the Ridge at the other side. Their jagged edges rose up hundreds of metres towards the blue sky. For most of the year, they were dusted with snow which filled the gullies. They remained in permanent, menacing shadow that attracted all kinds of predators.

That view was the reward for a three hour climb. It got mountain lovers out of their beds before dawn so that they could catch the unforgettable sight before the clouds heading from the north veiled the mountains again. With alarm, he noticed a low hanging cloud slowly moving in from the north. When one of these lodged themselves between the peaks or in the gullies they were not easily blown away by ordinary winds. Indeed the cloud was now slowly sliding into the valley, filling it in entirely. It was only a matter of minutes before the mountains completely disappeared from view. All of a sudden, the world around him shrunk to a few metres of grass turf on which he was standing. The light faded and heavy mist slid over the clearing like a thick feather duvet.

The void and the calm surrounding him were suddenly broken by a piercing noise. It seemed to come from the mist directly in front of him and he couldn't identify its source. For a moment, the noise subsided but then a minute later it began again, at a higher pitch. It was a while before his consciousness returned and he was able to identify it as the alarm on his watch. Adam opened one eye and grabbed it to quash the offending noise. Then his alarm clock started ringing. He hit the button with his palm and placed it carefully on his pillow. He would allow himself another ten minutes to snooze before crawling upstairs for a shower.

Sunday mornings were the hardest. After five and a half days spent working for Karol, he devoted Saturday afternoon and Sunday to 'his own business'. He had continued this punishing schedule for the last six months and there were days when he felt like he wouldn't be able to drag himself out of bed in the morning. Even his body's iron constitution demanded some compensation. Time to rest was a commodity he was short of.

Despite this he was a contented man. He completed Mrs Patel's job in late February, giving the delighted woman her dream kitchen. In fact, he exceeded her expectations by customising the cupboards so that she could fit all her pots, pans and cooking utensils of various shapes and sizes. In one of the awkward corners, he built special shelving for her spices. She was so pleased with it that she purchased identical containers for all of them so she could proudly display her collection.

For his efforts, Mrs Patel not only surprised him with a hefty bonus but also recommended him to her friends. Now he was fitting his third kitchen. This time he was working for Mrs Patel's niece, Nisha, a young doctor whose tastes couldn't be more different from her aunt's. He enjoyed the challenge of a super modern design with all its unusual closing and opening mechanisms, a variety of downlighters and uplighters and the integrated appliances which were to fit seamlessly into the whole.

At last, fate smiled on him. With the current volume of 'private' work, he had grounds to believe that by next Christmas he would have more money than he needed to open his hardware store in Kościelisko.

His six month visa had expired a long time ago and he didn't dare apply for an extension since he had no legal grounds to request it. If he came into contact with the authorities and was asked to present his passport, he would be deported on the first coach bound for Poland.

He opened his eyes and saw that it was now quarter past seven. If he closed them again, he would fall asleep. He threw off the covers and sat up. At this moment he remembered that he had to call Darek, to wake the silly bugger up. God knows what he had been up to last night. Saturday evenings were dangerous territory for him. He didn't care how Darek entertained himself after work but if he wasn't able to get up on time, it would delay the work they planned to do today.

Darek was one of Karol's 'finds'. He picked him from among the men who hung around the 'wailing wall' by the POSK Institute in Hammersmith, where newly arrived 'tourists' advertised their services. Usually reluctant to speak to the desperados coming off the coach straight from Poland, Karol changed his approach. He urgently needed another pair of hands to complete a job which was delayed by a series of problems. Luckily for Karol, Darek proved to be not only keen but also experienced in decorating and tiling. He also worked hard. He had a girlfriend in Poland to whom he was planning to get engaged in autumn.

Despite his twenty five years Darek wasn't a fool. He suspected that behind Adam's reluctance to take any overtime at Karol's were private jobs. Desperate for extra cash, one Friday afternoon, he asked Adam whether he knew where he could find weekend work.

'I am too knackered at the weekend for extra work,' said Adam avoiding Darek's gaze. He started packing his tool bag with a great deal of concentration. He felt a twinge of sympathy when he looked at Darek's young face, but he had no intention of confiding in any of his workmates.

'If you need a *fucha,* you need to ask the guys you live with. There are also various jobs in the free newspapers which you can get at POSK.'

This didn't fool Darek. He was sure that his assumptions about Adam were right. 'Damn, mean *góral,*' he muttered to himself.

One Monday morning during a rare moment of idleness, while they were waiting for supplies, Darek approached Adam. The older man sat alone on a wooden crate cleaning his tools. Taking them out one by one from this toolbox and dabbing them with a cloth soaked in oil he appeared oblivious to the chit chat going on behind his back.

'Good weekend?' he asked tentatively.

'The usual. Had a chance to sleep longer,' answered Adam without looking up.

'I couldn't sleep at all.'

'What's the matter with you?' This time Adam glanced up at Darek surprised by the anxiety in his voice. There were deep shadows under his eyes.

'I got news from Lila. We'll have to skip the engagement party and start planning the wedding.'

'What's the rush?'

'I'm going to be a father.'

'Waa ... that's big news. Are you sure that it's your kid?' Having uttered these words, Adam suddenly remembered his brother asking him the same question some 15 years ago. He recalled the image of Hanka's worried face and Bukowski's wrath when he found out that Adam had gotten his daughter in trouble.

'It's mine. Lila is a good girl. We just got carried away when we saw each other last.' Then lowering his voice he asked: 'Adam, could you help me? Extra work at the weekends would make a big difference to me. To us. We have to start saving for the future. You know I'm not idle. I can turn my hand to most things really.'

Adam hesitated. Could Darek keep a secret? He was already on his third kitchen project and there was plenty of work to do if he was to finish it on time. He had already met his fourth client. Plastering and tiling took ages. He could do with another pair of hands.

'Adam, you can trust me. You won't regret it, I promise.'

Darek, true to his promise, proved to be an asset to Adam. Working side by side, they were able to progress much faster than when Adam laboured alone. Adam also surprised himself asking Darek for a second opinion. Particularly when the finishes were an issue, Darek, who was twenty years younger, had a more modern taste.

The only thing that Darek really struggled with was getting up in the morning, particularly on Sunday. He lived in a very busy house rented by a Polish family from an English landlord. The turnover of tenants was rapid and various human interactions were carried on late into the night. Even for Darek, who usually slept like a stone, the going-ons were too loud and too frequent. He suspected that other tenants, mostly single men, who arrived in London for a bit of moonlighting on the capital's construction scene, disappeared as soon as they found an alternative place where they could lay their heads.

This didn't seem to worry the Markiewicz family who appeared to have an inexhaustible supply of tenants. They were equally unfazed about the constant bustle in the house, accepting this as part and parcel of the tenants' financial contribution to their livelihood. Carl, their golden retriever, seemed equally resigned to having to share his limited space with a black cat with mean habits and a large tank of fish whose silent presence ceased to fascinate him a long time ago.

Looking into Carl's pleading eyes, Darek thought that resigning yourself to things beyond your control was a good survival tactic. That's how he returned to the Markiewicz household evening after evening hoping that the things may change.

Keeping the phone some distance away from his ear, Adam let it ring several times. Suddenly he heard Darek's muffled voice.

'OK, OK, I am up. You'll get the whole house up in a minute.'

'As long as I drag you off your bed ... Hurry up. We have a lot to do today.'

Twenty minutes later, he was at the bus stop — one of three people already heading for work on this day of rest. Adam didn't wish to admit to himself that he had become sentimental since he came to London. Increasingly often he longed for a proper Sunday, with a satisfying meal on the table and Hanka and the children pottering around him. He sometimes wondered what Hanka's reaction would be if she knew that he hadn't been to church for five months. Would old Bukowski consider him a total loser?

His faith wasn't affected by the fact that he had stopped taking part in Sunday mass. Going to church on Sunday gave any man a modicum of respectability in the eyes of the Kościelisko community. It was also a sign of belonging.

Adam hoped that God, in his greater wisdom, understood that he had no intention of offending him and the holy Catholic Church by working on Sunday. In fact, he sensed that the Almighty supported his efforts by blessing him with opportunities he hadn't even dreamt about. Perhaps this was the divine's approval of the fact that he had given up drinking. Adam promised himself to make a generous donation to Our Lady of Kościelisko once he returned home, having accomplished his plan.

Seeing an approaching bus, he reached into his pocket for his travel pass. With his finger tips he felt a bundle of thin sheets. They were the receipts from Classic Kitchen for Nisha. Damn. He was such a fool, keeping them in the jacket which he wore to work at Karol's.

Only a few days ago, Karol came up to him thrusting the catalogue of Classic Kitchens at him.

'I don't know why that blasted place keeps sending me this crap all of a sudden. I haven't dealt with them for months.'

'We bought quite a few things from them before.' Adam tried to keep his voice steady as he swallowed hard. 'We run up high bills with them.'

'Perhaps. But since they are offering me 15% off fittings and handles, you may as well check whether we can find anything for Mr Bardolini's house there. Isn't he planning to have some cupboards in that extension?'

'Yes, he is, boss. I look into that.' He put the Classic Kitchen's catalogue under his arm and not daring to look at Karol, hurried to the room upstairs where he was setting in a couple of expensive door frames.

He was treading on thin ice. Karol wouldn't tolerate any interference in his business and forgiveness wasn't in his nature. At the mere thought of what might happen, Adam felt a tightness in his chest. He reached into his pocket for a handkerchief stinking of kerosene and mopped the sweat from his brow. There was no room for mistakes here. He had to keep his weekend work a secret at all costs. Then he thought about Darek and realised that by letting another person in on his secret, he had already breached his defences. He squeezed the receipts in a ball and kept scrunching them until his fingers hurt.

That Sunday night Adam fell into a deep dreamless sleep almost as soon as his head touched the pillow. He didn't hear the knocking on his door. Only when the rapping became more energetic, did his consciousness surface again.

'Yes, yes ...' he mumbled. Feeling the warmth of Ginger on his feet he hesitated.

'Adam, there is a man at the door asking for you,' he recognised Maja's voice.

'For me?'

'Yes.' Her voice trailed away for a moment. 'His name is ... Darek.'

Angry to be woken up and so unexpectedly disturbed, Adam got up and threw the covers back, almost forgetting about the cat. He reached for his flannel shirt and opened the door just a fraction.

Behind Maja, who looked like the Madonna, in her blue night gown and with a veil of long hair covering her shoulders, stood Darek. His face was ghostly white and he was clutching a rucksack to his chest. Adam had never seen him so frightened.

Dreading the news that Darek had come to share with him, he took the boy by the arm and pulled him inside. Then he remembered about Maja. Poking his head out, he whispered to her.

'Thank you. I am sorry that he disturbed you. I will see him out in a moment.'

Closing the door carefully he pointed to the only chair in the room, now covered by a pile of clothes.

'Sit down and tell me what's happened,' he told Darek, who didn't need encouragement. The information, together with frustration, poured out of him. He didn't know that despite the crowd of tenants, the Markiewicz family was in serious financial trouble and everything had come to a head on Sunday. They had plenty of unpaid bills, road fines and owed money to various people. On Sunday morning, the bailiffs came to the house and gave them an hour to get out of bed before the furniture was to be taken away. The car was already clamped on the street. According to the neighbours, the Markiewicz's showed unusual ingenuity and organisational skills and, with the help of an acquaintance, they cleared out of the house within an hour. It was not only deserted but also totally empty of possessions when Darek returned from work. He scooped his clothes from the cupboard in his room into the rucksack and left through the back door. Jumping over the garden fence into a patch of nettles while wearing shorts, he added physical pain to his moral anguish.

All in all, he lost the roof over his head together with a hundred pound deposit.

'I had nowhere else to go. Will you put me up for the night?'

Adam looked at his wretched state and, reaching for one of the blankets folded on the top of the wardrobe, said firmly: 'Just one night. Otherwise we both will be in the street tomorrow.' Then pointing to the floor, asked: 'Will the bottom bunk do?' He opened the cupboard to look for an old jacket for a pillow.

When he turned around Darek was still sitting motionlessly on the chair holding the rucksack on his lap. He looked desolate and frightened but there was a strange expression on his face. Adam followed his gaze. Just above the corner of his duvet, with his green eyes wide open, Ginger was staring back at him.

Chapter 28

Kuba, August 1998

'It's none of my business and I have no intention of interfering. I just cannot stand watching you being manipulated.' Karen spooned instant coffee into two mugs and vigorously stirred it.

Kuba looked at Karen and smiled. 'One sugar in mine, please.'

She gave him an indignant look. 'I remember.'

They were standing in the tiny kitchenette of Alan & Taylor where Karen was a staff member. The premises of the physiotherapy practice were surprisingly small. Beside a sunny reception area, where an abundance of lovingly tended plants created the atmosphere of a conservatory, it consisted of only three consultation rooms. It was because most of the work undertaken by Alan & Taylor staff was carried out on the clients' premises. Staff interactions were taking place either in the bathroom or in the kitchen. The kitchen was a generous name for the recess in the wall that housed a sink, a fridge, a kettle and an assortment of mugs.

'I appreciate your concern,' he said softly. 'I will be for ever grateful for your help. But I am a big boy and can look after myself.'

'Really?' Karen's contacts with the opposite sex left her with the belief that most men saw what they wished to see, particularly in relation to women. Stella Reybourn, however brilliant with her serve and strategies on the court, was quite transparent in her intentions towards Kuba.

From the first morning when Karen and Kuba walked into the club to discuss the rehabilitation programme for Jack Smith, a fast rising tennis star, Stella beckoned at Karen, pointing to her shoulder.

'Are you OK, Stella?'

'So, so. The pain in my right shoulder has returned. I may

need some more manipulation and massage that worked wonders before.' As she said this, Stella pulled out an elastic band that held her hair up and a mass of auburn curls cascaded down her shoulders. She straightened her back so her ample chest further strained her lycra top. 'What's your opinion?' She addressed the question to Kuba, standing a step behind Karen.

'I don't really have one. I don't know your case and your medical history.'

'I could brief you quickly and you would be able to give me a second opinion.'

Karen gave her an outraged look. 'Kuba is on a summer placement with Alan & Taylor. He has structured training.'

This didn't put Stella off. Running her fingers through her hair she said sweetly: 'Treating sport injury will only broaden his experience.'

'I have handled several sport injury cases. But now, I have to stick to what Alan & Taylor has planned for me,' he said firmly.

'Well done Kuba,' said Karen as they walked away, leaving Stella gasping with indignation.

'Well done for what?'

'Escaping Stella. She thinks she is a superstar and cries for attention at every opportunity.'

'Someone, somewhere made her believe she can do that.'

Kuba knew better than to upset Karen. She was a friend but also his professional sponsor. She prepared a plan for Kuba's summer training, making sure that he got the best experience possible. And the placement was progressing extremely well. He was getting a variety of responsibilities which helped him to demonstrate his skills and also experience — which Kuba suspected Karen wished to prove to her colleagues. She asked him to assist her with her regular clients and in front of them she treated him like a fellow professional not a trainee student. She frequently asked for his opinion. Kuba wondered sometimes whether she did this in the same way as a teacher tests their pupils' confidence or whether she genuinely believed that he could make a valuable contribution. As a result, Karen's patients treated him as one of Alan & Taylor's therapists and put themselves into his hands with confidence.

Slowly lifting Mrs Jones' foot, Kuba was looking at her with interest. She wanted to learn on 'dry land' the exercises which she should be performing during her weekly sessions in the swimming pool.

'You could raise your leg even higher if you can. But please don't move your hips forward,' he was coaxing her. Were her minty green track suit and stripy green and yellow socks an expression of confidence or defiance?

Standing next to the wall with one hand resting on the back of the chair, Mrs Jones moved her bemused gaze from her foot to the face of the foreign hunk who was kneeling before her. With his blond hair, blue eyes and muscular body, he could have walked straight off the set of one of those Australian daytime soaps. She hoped that her feet didn't smell. But his smiling face next to her foot reassured her that this wasn't the case. Listening to his patient instructions she was inclined to believe that he enjoyed helping her. He hadn't looked at his watch even once since she came in.

'Should we repeat the same movement with your right leg?' suggested Kuba.

Taking the nod as a sign of agreement, Kuba rearranged the chair and waited patiently as Mrs Jones turned around and repositioned herself to be able to lift her right leg. They repeated the exercise a few more times until Kuba could see that she was comfortable doing it.

When the session was over, and Mrs Jones, having slipped on her shoes, was buttoning up her jacket, she looked appreciatively at Kuba.

'Righty ho. At my next visit, I will let you know how I get on in the pool.'

'It will be easier there. The water will support you.'

'I would rather be supported by you,' she smiled mischievously. 'But I know, I know. Dr Goldwater told me that these exercises will do me and my poor spine the world of good.' Then, sensing that she owed him some explanation, she said: 'I have done too much standing in my life and I started stooping. As with old bad habits, I have just got used to it.'

'Don't we all do that?' asked Kuba, suddenly realising how

true her words were.

The summer placement with Alan & Taylor reminded him of things he used to be good at and the work he enjoyed. Perhaps forgetting this made things easier for a while. He tidied Mrs Jones' records and put them into her folder. He smiled thinking about her. She was of the same generation as his grandmother and she had a similar attitude to life: just getting on with it, without fuss and complaining about its unfairness.

'So the wonder boy has been working on his own again.' Kuba recognised the voice of Mike, another trainee whom Alan & Taylor took on for the summer. He softly closed the surgery door behind him and paused on the landing. He loathed eavesdropping but this concerned him and felt compelled to hear more.

'Obviously someone thinks he is better than the rest of us.'

'Sure. Someone is prepared to take a risk ...'

He had to watch his step here. He didn't realise that Karen's protection had already made him enemies. Perhaps he shouldn't have accepted her offer of a placement with Alan & Taylor ... Then he instantly rejected this thought. He would have been a fool to refuse such an opportunity. They are talking behind his back, so what? Human nature demonstrated itself in exactly the same way in London as in Opole.

Suddenly, his thoughts turned to Maja. She appeared so single minded about forging her new career in the hotel. Most evenings she came back late from college and when she appeared downstairs, she never stayed long to chat. Even during the weekend she was rarely around. Yet despite the long hours she put into her work and studies, she looked remarkably well and full of energy. Even he who paid no attention to women's clothes couldn't help noticing that she looked increasingly sophisticated.

There was Judyta, of course, but Judyta was a completely different story. She tried hard to secure herself a more permanent place in his life than he wished. After their initial passionate encounter in Opole, she managed to get his mobile number and called him regularly. She clearly knew how to keep a man interested. In addition to frequent texts, letters and cards, both humorous and romantic, she started sending him gifts. Some were most surprising, such as the pair of knickers which she wore on that memorable night. Other like aftershave, belts or T-shirts were to keep her in his thoughts, he assumed.

Last week she announced that she was coming to London 'on business'. There was a hair and beauty show at the London Olympia, with new products and styles and she 'simply couldn't miss it'.

'Will you find time for me?' she purred into the receiver; her husky voice already a promise of things to come.

'Yeah ...' he faltered. He intended to work on both Saturday and Sunday since his placement with Alan & Taylor kept him busy for most of the week. 'I'll have to work, at least during the day. But I will keep the evening free. And the best part of Sunday.'

'That's fantastic, Kuba. I don't know London so you'll show me the best bits.'

'I'll try.'

'We'll have fun. I cannot wait.'

Kuba agreed to pick Judyta up from the hotel in Earl's Court where she was staying. As he waited in the cramped lobby, he was glancing through the leaflets of London attractions tightly packed into a display stand on a reception desk. The hotel catered for budget travellers. For lower rates, it offered everything in a meaner measure, space being the main commodity. Its thick synthetic carpet and gaudy wallpaper stank of cigarettes and fried bacon. The customers, young and old, were constantly coming and going, creating a crowd in the small lobby.

'Qué belleza!' exclaimed one of the young men with Latin looks waiting at the reception desk.

Kuba swung around to check what had attracted their attention. On the landing, with one hand on the rail paused Judyta, looking even more ravishing that the last time he saw her. The moment their eyes met, she waved to him enthusiastically and started walking down as fast as her high heeled sandals allowed. She wore a pair of white jeans and a white lace top. Her long neck was framed by a mass of black hair, kept away from her face by a pair of sunglasses. As soon as she reached the lobby, she ran across it and threw herself into Kuba's arms.

Over Judyta's head, Kuba saw the astonished faces of the Span-
iards.

Throughout the day, he caught glances of men looking at
Judyta as she walked beside him, clinging to his arm and
hanging on his every word, as he played the role of London
guide to her. She tilted her head back, tossing her hair and
laughed loudly at his humorous remarks, looking at him admiringly. Kuba saw that men not only gawped at Judyta but also
glanced at him to establish how he had managed to attract such
a woman. He caught himself grinning from ear to ear as he
imagined their thoughts and almost laughed out loud at the
silliness of it all. But he took Judyta by her elbow and pulled her
closer to him whispering into her ear an observation about an
odd couple walking in front of them. She laughed her throaty,
sexy laugh and snuggled even closer to him. This felt good. He
wished that one of those city gents that nonchalantly reclined
at the back of his cab could see him now.

Judyta loved everything about London. The city was so full of
life, so chic and fascinating. There were so many nationalities
there, which dressed and expressed themselves in their own
unique way. She could never be bored living in such a place.
Even the 'old bits' such as Buckingham Palace, Big Ben and the
Tower of London were interesting. She asked Kuba to take a
photograph of her on Oxford Street and then pose with her with
Big Ben in the background. She was planning to put it up in the
salon in her gallery of favourite photographs. Kuba wondered
how many boyfriends were already featured there.

She even took off her gold high heel sandals to feel the grass
in Hyde Park, which was so much greener and thicker than in
Poland, she said. She read an article in a women's magazine
about the special qualities of English grass and now standing
barefoot, up to her ankles, in it she was going to test. The lawn
was freshly mowed so it looked and felt like a thick carpet.
There was no breeze and the warm air of late summer was
heavy with the scent of dry grass. In her white clothes, Judyta
looked like an exotic flower on this green canvas. She dumped
her handbag on the lawn and motioned to Kuba to do the same
with the carrier bags containing souvenirs and guidebooks. She
tapped his arm playfully and cried: 'Chase me,' and started

running away from him. Shrieking with laughter, she circled the trunks of old maples and ran around the shrubs. She was fast and nimble and it took Kuba a while to catch up with her.

When he finally scooped her up off the ground, she squealed in delight. She put her arms around his neck and, pressing herself closely to him, kissed him passionately. Kuba felt every nerve in his body tingling and it took him a while to regain control. When they eventually drew apart, still panting Judyta said: 'I haven't had so much fun on the grass since I was a little girl.'

'Neither have I,' admitted Kuba, gazing at her parted lips and heaving chest. Then he added: 'Playing cowboys and Indians wasn't the same thing.'

At nine o'clock, he was walking her back to the hotel after a meal in a Mexican restaurant (she liked 'all things spicy'). When they reached the Reception, he handed over her carrier bags, wished her good night and a safe flight which was scheduled for early next morning. She smiled, shrugged her shoulders and said: 'I cannot carry all this upstairs. Will you help me?'

As he trailed behind her, up the narrow carpeted staircase smelling of disinfectant and stale cigarettes, he wondered how soon he would be able to extricate himself from Judyta's company. He was booked for a night shift which began at 10pm. He didn't wish to offend her but he would have to make a swift exit. Her company was like test driving a powerful car — intoxicating — but the possibility of an accident was just round the corner. That afternoon he came to realize that Judyta was a highly intelligent woman, constantly hungry for new experiences. She was perfect company for any man. She knew how to flatter him to get what she wanted. Yet he sensed that she could be ruthless with those who crossed her.

Dumping her bags next to the double bed, covered with outfits which she must have been trying in the morning, she said: 'Thank you for a great day. It was fun being with you.'

'My pleasure. I enjoyed it too.' He patted her arm and said softly: 'I have to go now. My shift starts at ten.'

'It's only just after nine,' she exclaimed, her arched eyebrows meeting in the middle. 'The night is so young.'

'I couldn't ...'

'Oh, yes you could …' She closed his mouth with a passionate kiss. Her breath was hot and tasted of Spanish wine. The smoke of the restaurant grill still lingered in her hair and it mingled with the musky scent of her perfume. She gently pushed him down onto the bed so his face was now at the same level as hers. With one lift of her arms, she slipped off her lacy top and her bra at the same time. Her hair cascaded down his face but as he closed his eyes he felt her breasts under his lips. Her porcelain smooth skin felt amazingly cool on such a hot evening.

He didn't remember her helping him out of his clothes. But suddenly, they were both naked on the bed. They wanted each other with an equal passion. He exploded almost on entering her and felt her body contracting in a spasm of pleasure. Her nails dug into his buttocks as she moaned and begged him for more.

Ten minutes later, already wrapped up in a satin gown, she was helping him pick his clothes off the floor.

'I don't like rushing. But you said you were in hurry tonight,' she said with an amused expression giving him his belt back.

Chapter 29

Maja, August 1998

The notes of *Rhapsody in Blue* were floating through the open door of the lounge. There was longing and excitement in the music. It blended with the tinkling of glass and china, a sign that Luke was busy setting the table for dinner.

Stirring Bolognese sauce in the kitchen, Maja was listening to the notes that rose and fell, altering the tone and the pace of the music, and thought that it was like her life in Britain. Surprising and exhilarating, frightening at times and completely unpredictable. Tonight Luke was going to prove to her that he could cook. He said that he could make a Bolognese with a difference. Inhaling the aromas rising from the bubbling stew, she was inclined to believe him. Through the scent of marjoram and oregano and the acid notes of red wine, an earthly smell of wild mushrooms was coming through.

The aroma of cooking food, the warmth of the small kitchen and the wine she was sipping started to relax her. Her hectic day in the hotel seemed like a distant past. She smiled to herself as she licked the rich sauce from her lips. Luke picked her up from the station that evening and gave her a quick tour of Bath in preparation for the sightseeing which he'd planned for the following day. She expected more surprises. He always made their time together memorable. But, this didn't stop her questioning what she was doing in his apartment that Friday night.

When Maja confided in Amy that she had regularly started seeing Luke, her friend warned her to go steady.

'You know so little about him and what he does at home. He may have a girlfriend and fancy some company during lonely evenings in London.'

'He told me that since he stopped seeing his last girlfriend, there was no one special in his life.'

'All men say this. What about casual dates? And nights?'

'Amy, I have no intention of interrogating him about his past love life.'

'Let's assume it is in the past.'

'I enjoy his company, he enjoys mine. We have a good time together and have become good friends.'

'Friends?'

'Yes, he is interested in history, knows an awful lot about art, and not only modern art, on account of his job. He is a great photographer. His pictures say so much about the way he sees things.'

'That's fantastic. You won't get bored with each other quickly. But most men, in my experience, are after one thing.'

'Luke hasn't even attempted to kiss me.'

'That surprises me. Perhaps he bats for the other side.'

'I don't know what sports he plays.'

'No, silly, I meant he could be gay.'

'Don't think so.'

'But don't go too far before you check him out. If he asks you to go to Bristol …'

'Bath.'

'Anyway. Just say no.'

'Of course, I will say no. I don't know him well enough.'

This was what she should have done when Luke suggested that he would show her Bath. He painted the picture of a sightseeing weekend. Famous historical sights during the day and then an evening out. He was describing the plans with such enthusiasm, suggesting all the places which might interest her, that she couldn't decline his invitation.

Now she was standing in his kitchen, helping him with the cooking and wondering what was likely to happen next. She was touched by the attention he was showing her and his hospitality. But was this the way he treated all his girlfriends? Was she special? Perhaps she was reading too much into his good manners. He hadn't suggested that they could see his family or friends who presumably also lived in Bath or nearby. If he did, would it mean that he regarded her as a more permanent fixture in his life? This thought left her with a feeling of unease.

She felt his hands on her shoulders. Placing his chin next to her neck Luke deeply inhaled the aroma of the stew. Then he nuzzled his face into her hair.

'I am not sure what smells better, the dinner or your hair.'

'My hair must smell of dinner by now. Garlic and wine.'

'A bit, perhaps, but it predominantly smells of you. Your shampoo and your perfume.'

His next gesture startled her. 'Forgive me,' he whispered and took out a large grip that held up her hair. Her freshly washed hair spilled down her nape and shoulders. She wasn't prepared for this invasion and turned around to protest. Yet when she met his apologising gaze, she said nothing. She allowed his hands to encircle her waist. Now there was hardly any space between them and she felt the warmth of his body through his shirt. With the citrusy notes of his aftershave, she breathed in the musky smell of him.

They held each other's gaze for a moment and taking her face in his hands, Luke started kissing her. First, he touched her lips very gently as if checking their taste. Then he was more daring. Their noses didn't touch but their mouths made a perfect fit. It was a very long kiss.

When their lips finally parted, Luke whispered: 'I wanted to do this for a long time.'

'Did you?'

'I wasn't sure that you had any feelings for me.'

'I wasn't sure of this either.'

Their next kiss was more passionate. It was a revelation for both of them. When Luke placed his lips on Maja's she almost melted in his embrace and held him tightly. She felt as if he was opening some secret door inside of her and she didn't know what lay behind it.

When they finally drew apart, Luke said: 'It was magical. You're a great kisser, Maja.'

'Am I?' she asked with genuine surprise. 'I guess I don't practise enough,' she said smiling.

He wrapped his arms around her and they kissed again until Maja caught the smell of burning.

'The food!' she cried, breaking away from him. She turned

around and frantically started stirring the sauce. A thick crust
had already formed at the bottom of the pan.

'I lost concentration and burnt the dinner.'

'It was worth it,' he said smiling. He reached for another pot
and started transferring the remainder of the sauce.

When they put their dishes into Luke's small dishwasher (Maja
wondered why anyone living alone needed one), they sat on the
carpet and leaned against the sofa sipping the rest of their wine.
The music had stopped a long time ago and the evening silence
made the atmosphere more intimate. Luke's apartment was a
blend of tradition and modernity. The high ceiling and tall
windows were left unadorned. A modern painting was reflected
in a large mirror with a heavy gilded frame hanging on the
opposite wall. An abstract wooden sculpture standing on one
side of a TV cabinet was balanced with a regency-style candela-
brum on the other.

With only a candle burning on the table, darkness filled the
empty spaces, making the room appear smaller and cosier.

'Do you enjoy your work?' Maja asked.

'The creative side is still a challenge that keeps me in the job.
Yet having to constantly pitch for new accounts, I feel like a
prostitute always on the look out for new clients.'

'Why did you go into advertising?' she asked, glancing over the
rim of her glass at Luke's somehow dishevelled appearance. His
blond hair was falling across his forehead and his shirt, unbuttoned at the top, was revealing his chest. He appeared younger
than in his work clothes and more attractive.

'I was good at English and easily produced witty one-liners. I
liked the arts at school and I have developed an eye for design.'

'A good fit for your line of work.'

'I went for a management training scheme at M&S after
university and after a while I was approached by an agency that
was pitching for one of their projects.'

'How long ago was it?'

'Over a decade. I became a copywriter and I enjoyed that. I
always liked playing with words, discovering their power.' He
took a sip of wine and looked at Maja listening attentively.
'When I progressed to account management and started chasing

business, the fun fizzled out of my job.'

'Why didn't you move on to something else?'

'After many years in advertising, I felt I knew it so well. It was like baggage which I couldn't bring myself to abandon.'

'What about the glamorous side of advertising?'

'One gets used to this and takes it for granted. There is never enough time to really enjoy it — the travel, hotels, dining out, socialising. It is exciting at the beginning but it gets tiresome.'

Maja thought about her library job in Grodek. The most glamorous moment was a Christmas outing to a newly opened bistro.

She noticed Luke was trying to suppress a big yawn. 'The wine has knocked me off my feet. I am sorry ...' He looked at Maja apologetically.

'Not at all. I am struggling to keep my eyes open and will be glad to go to bed. It had been a long day.'

'You don't mind?'

'Of course not. I am looking forward to seeing Bath tomorrow.'

'We will have fun, I promise.'

'I know we will.'

Maja set down her glass on the coffee table and rising to her feet she planted a kiss on Luke's cheek. 'Good night.'

Placing a hand on her arm he pulled her towards him. 'I need more than that to send me off to sleep,' he said and kissed her on the mouth.

When their lips parted, Maja smiled. 'Good night, Luke.'

'Are you always so sensible, Maja?' He was looking deep into her eyes with a half pleading, half seducing gaze.

'Most of the time.'

The next day was everything Luke had promised and more. Sightseeing the Roman Baths, the Abbey, the Regency architecture of the Crescent and exploring the old town and its shops full of curiosities with Luke as a personal guide was both fascinating and fun.

Now they stood outside the Scotch House window displaying a rich array of kilts and tartans. Against a panorama of the Highlands stood male and female dummies displaying traditional Scottish attire.

Wrinkling her nose and tilting her head to one side, Maja asked: 'I always wondered about this. Men in skirts. Why do they wear them?'

'I am happy to try one for you. Should I?'

'Yes.' She smiled mischievously.

'Mind you, the sight of my knobbly knees and hairy legs may be your most lasting memory of your trip to Bath.'

'I don't think so.'

'In that case, I am going to try it on. I'm ready to challenge the cultural prejudices of the Europeans.' He took Maja by the arm and led her into the shop. Astonished and amused they saw a man trying the kilt. She abandoned the tease not wishing to offend. Seeing a shop assistant approaching them, she turned her attention to a rainbow display of cashmere scarves. She caressed them with her fingertips.

'I didn't know that wool could be so soft.'

This was just what Luke was waiting for. He picked a selection of scarves and started winding them around Maja's neck.

'I thought that this rich blue with yellow would suit you best, but no, red, red with a little bit of green goes best with your skin and your eyes.'

'Luke …'

'Shush … Let's try the effect of the yellow one. No, no it drowns your colour. The red is best.' He walked her towards the window. 'Definitely.'

Before Maja could protest more vigorously, a shop assistant was already lining the red scarf with petal thin tissue and folding it into a smart bag.

When they found themselves back in the street, Maja stopped Luke and looked at him reproachfully. 'I don't feel comfortable accepting presents from you. Particularly expensive presents. This weekend is already a treat.'

'Why?'

'I wouldn't be able to reciprocate your generosity,' she said bluntly.

'A contradiction in terms. It wouldn't be generosity if I expected it to be repaid.'

'I don't accept presents from men.'

'Why?' he continued to tease her.

'On principle.'

'Would you make an exception from that principle for me?'

'Why?'

'Because it would be rude if I took this scarf back to the shop now.'

'Perhaps you can wear it. Or give it ...'

At that moment Luke took the bag from her hand, ripped the fancy ribbon and tied the scarf around his neck. 'I may as well start wearing it now ...' With a red scarf, worn over his short sleeved shirt he looked like a clown.

They roared with laughter. Luke scooped her up and lifted her in the air. 'My silly, precious girl. You're very special.' Looking down at him, Maja wondered for a second whether with all this fooling, Luke was trying to blot from her memory the incident from the morning.

After a full English breakfast, which on Luke's insistence included mushrooms, tomatoes and beans, Maja could hardly breathe. She needed some exercise straight away and suggested she tidied the kitchen up while Luke took his turn in the bathroom. She wasn't going to use the dishwasher though. It didn't take her long to find an apron hanging on the back of the door. She placed the dishes into the sink, poured some hot water into the frying pan and went to the CD player. From a stack of disks on the window sill, she selected a couple of classics matching her mood. Outside, there was a glorious summer morning. Not a cloud marred the vivid blue sky. A smell of grass and pine resin wafted through the open window. How long was it since she had been for a holiday? The prospect of two free days made her dizzy with excitement. As the first notes of Vivaldi's Spring concerto filled the kitchen, she started daydreaming. Lifting a handful of soap suds on her palm, she blew the bubbles through the window. She watched them float up, carried by a breeze and dissolve into the azure sky.

Suddenly, she heard the bell. She went to the door just to realise that it was the intercom buzzer. Without hesitation, she pressed the button and shouted: 'Please come in.' Only then, she looked in the direction of the bathroom. From the humming of the water and whistling, she guessed that Luke would not be ready to receive his guest.

After a couple of minutes there was a ring at the door. When she opened it, the first thing she saw was the wide brim of an indigo blue hat. A couple of rosy cheeks protruded from underneath. The round person wearing the hat matched it with a floating outfit and an assortment of bold jewellery. There was surprise in the dark eyes looking at Maja from under the brim.

'Isn't Luke in?'

'Yes he is. He is in the bathroom but he won't be long. Please come in.'

As the woman marched in, a powerful dose of floral scent entered the hall.

'I'm in a rush. Too many rounds this morning to wait. I have some papers for Elizabeth. Luke's mother. It's urgent stuff.' She spoke fast, trying to catch her breath after the climb to the second floor. She huffed and puffed as she moved and this reminded Maja of the Polish children's poem about a locomotive.

Taking a file out of her carpet bag that may have belonged to Mary Poppins, the woman said: 'He promised to post this to his mother with the other correspondence. Here they are.'

Maja took the papers and placed them on the table in the hall. 'I will show it to him as soon as he comes out of the bathroom.'

'Please don't forget.' She snapped her bag shut and was already walking towards the door when she suddenly turned around.

'What's your name, darling?'

'Maja.'

'Maja, please make sure that he sees these papers straight away.'

At this moment, the bathroom door opened and Luke appeared in a cloud of steam. He was wrapped in a white bath robe and his towel dried hair had a wild appearance. He smelled strongly of shampoo and soap.

'Rosemary!' He rushed forward to hug the ample figure in the hall. 'Haven't seen you for ages.'

'You're never around those days when I come to see your mother. Now that she disappeared over the Atlantic.'

'Only for three weeks, Rosie.'

Maja promptly retreated to the kitchen, feeling that her presence was no longer required.

'Make sure that she gets these committee papers. We need her views on this project. As soon as possible. She can give me a ring.'

'Of course.'

'I gave the envelope to your cleaner. Here it is — she put it on the table.'

There was a pause in the conversation. Then Luke rushed to clarify things.

'Maja is my friend.'

'Well, ... sincere apologies. Her unusual accent misled me. There are so many girls from Europe who work in the town. They help around the house ...'

Maja opened the tap and let a stream of water hit the dishes at the bottom of the sink. Then she started scrubbing them vigorously, rinsing and putting them on the rack. The clatter of the crockery and swishing water drowned the rest of the conversation in the hall.

Sweeping back a strand of Maja's hair so he could kiss her neck, Luke asked: 'What are you thinking about, my angel?' Since she didn't answer he took her hand, interlaced his fingers with hers and started kissing them one by one. Then he whispered again: 'Penny for your thoughts.'

She just looked at him and said nothing.

'Are you OK?'

She moved closer to him and placing her head in the hollow of his shoulder, said: 'Everything is just perfect. Too perfect.'

Luke gave her a quizzical look but seeing that dreamy gaze in her eyes, he settled for caressing her cheek.

The day was breaking behind the heavy white curtains of Luke's bedroom. Through the narrow gap in the fabric, Maja saw the deep velvet of the night get paler until it became light grey. Then the flecks of orange started dancing on the ceiling. The furnishings of the room were slowly acquiring their shapes and their colours were changing from monochrome. Outside, the call of the first bird was joined by the second, third and fourth voice, all competing for dominance on the morning stage.

They hadn't stopped making love since the previous evening, when Luke began kissing her while helping her out of her jacket. They had just returned from the outdoor concert in Victoria Park. The jacket slipped off her shoulders and was still lying on the floor in the corridor. Luke carried Maja to the lounge where they forgot about the world around. Already seduced by the music under the stars, she melted in his arms and surprised herself with the willingness with which she returned his kisses. His warm lips and his caressing palms were unblocking some deeply buried emotions. Reliving these moments afterwards she wasn't sure that the woman who responded to Luke with such desire was her.

Kneeling at her feet and moving his lips down her stomach, he whispered looking up at her: 'Has anyone told you how beautiful you are? So perfect? So sensuous?'

She looked at him surprised and said nothing. What could she say? That it was all new to her? That it was the first time in her life that someone made her feel beautiful. And so desired. That she yearned for his love because he wanted her with such a passion? This made her bold. She could tell him to love her again, brazenly guiding his hands and lips to pleasure her in a way no one had ever done before. He let her experience tenderness she never knew existed. But wasn't this dangerous? Perhaps foolishly she again allowed herself to be vulnerable.

Much later when they were resting in each other arms, she asked a question which had haunted her almost from the day he invited her for a coffee in the French bistro.

'What do you like about me, Luke?'

He looked at her surprised, and taking her hand to kiss it again, said: 'Everything. The whole package.'

She looked at him. 'Be serious.'

'Your eyes, which can be piercing at times and so dreamy a moment later. Your perfect little mouth, determined and so passionate. I love looking at your profile and the way you tuck your hair behind your ears. Your gorgeous body which I have discovered tonight. Next question?' Then he smiled mischievously. 'Oh, I almost forgot your mind.'

'Am I to take this as a compliment?'

'Of course.' He pulled her closer to him. 'Seriously, I found you so irresistibly attractive and interesting in many ways. So different from other women.' She ruffled his hair to hide her embarrassment.

When she felt his even breathing, she mused: Am I interesting? Different? Exotic? She was flattered by his attention but she couldn't understand what attracted Luke to her. With his charm, his looks, his professional prospects he could have a girlfriend who was more beautiful, more interesting and sophisticated than her. She may be naïve but not so stupid to believe that she was a match for him. Would she be able to sustain his interest when they got to know each other better? How long would her 'exotic' appeal continue to fascinate him? And then what? A voice in her head had warned her: she had become involved with him much too soon.

'You're a fast worker, Maja,' exclaimed Amy after hearing Maja's edited account of the weekend. They were sitting in the same French café where Maja had met Luke three months before. 'But if you feel he is the man for you, then go for it. Just don't fall in love with him straight away.'

It's probably too late for that, thought Maja but she said: 'I should know better than this. I have a knack of making a mess of relationships.'

Amy placed her wine glass on the table and carefully looked at her friend.

'If you knew why I quit my previous job ...'

'You didn't have an affair with the boss?'

'Oh, no. Much worse,' Maja sighed heavily. 'I developed an attraction to the boss' son who was murdered on the night we went out.'

'Good God, Maja. How did it happen? Can you talk about it?'

Recounting the events of the night of Nico's murder to Amy, Maja realised how fresh and painful these memories were in her mind. She could still smell the revolting stench of the tramp's clothing. Was he her saviour? 'I haven't spoken about this to anyone, except my friend who helped me on the night of the accident. I have been urged by Nico's family to keep quiet and never to contact them again, for my own safety.'

'Have you contacted the police?'

'No, but I saw the police at the scene of the murder. From a distance ... The Mazzini family didn't mention my presence on the night because if the mafia was involved, it wouldn't be safe for me.'

'You didn't consider going away somewhere safe ... like Poland?

'I did. But running back to Poland would not solve any of my problems. It would only complicate things at home.'

'Someone could be looking for you here ...'

'*Signor* Mazzini said that they destroyed all my details and told staff that I had left because of an illness in the family.'

'This doesn't mean that someone wouldn't be following you. You could be in danger, Maja.' Amy leaned forward and took Maja's hand. 'You need to be careful.'

'It's already been months since that night and I managed. Now and then I do look over my shoulder to check whether someone is following me. A couple of times I saw people looking at me but don't people gawp at others all the time? I don't want to get paranoid. I need to get on with my life, But I'll never forget Nico.'

'Wouldn't you like to know what happened that night?'

'Yes I would. I felt very guilty for not being with him then. I thought I could have helped him somehow ... Nico wasn't even my boyfriend. Just a very dear friend. I couldn't interfere in his private business and family affairs.'

'The Mazzinis must have had shady connections.'

'Perhaps. Nico mentioned that the family came from the south of Italy. But I don't believe that he was involved in any dirty business. He was such a genuine guy ...' Maja fell silent for a moment, remembering Nico's smiling eyes and his child-like grin. She had learnt to trust him. 'I should contact Lorenzo to find out whether anyone has been arrested for Nico's murder. It's the least I can do.'

Chapter 30

Adam, October 1998

They should have finished working over an hour ago. It was already quarter past eight and they were still in Nisha Patel's kitchen making final adjustments to the wall cabinets. The journey home would take at least another half an hour. The rest of the world was enjoying the last hours of Sunday. Through the open patio door they heard animated voices from the neighbouring garden where a BBQ party had been going strong since the early afternoon. The aroma of the sizzling food was tantalizing their senses for the past four hours. They ate their sandwiches at one o'clock and they were now ravenously hungry and dog tired. Adam felt as if his empty stomach had glued itself to his spine and the hunger pains were making him ill. The aromatic tea and a couple of vegetable samosas that Nisha Patel had offered them at midday were long forgotten.

They had worked since nine thirty in the morning hoping to complete the job tonight as they planned to start another project next week. However, there were faults with the fittings, and getting things right took them more time than they expected.

Adam was glad he had Darek to help him. The boy proved true to his word and didn't complain once about the long hours they put in every weekend. He was a quick learner and showed a number of surprising talents. He had an eye for colour and design. He suggested to Nisha Patel that dark blue tiles would create an interesting contrast with the brown wooden worktops on which she was so keen. She loved the combination and Darek instantly grew in her eyes.

Darek wanted to create a good start for Lila, himself and their baby. The fast approaching date of the baby's arrival was like a ticking time bomb which he followed with growing anxiety. His

six month visa was due to expire shortly and he had no grounds
to ask for an extension. So he intended to use his remaining
time with maximum efficiency. His face became gaunter and
the shadows under his eyes were a permanent feature. Despite
this, most of the time he was in an upbeat mood, happy to take
on any work that came their way. Darek was a great help
providing that Adam was able to drag him out of bed every
weekend, which wasn't easy since the boy now had his own
lodgings.

Early one morning, while he was still camping on Adam's floor,
Zofia met Darek on the stairs as he was creeping up to the
bathroom. She asked him whether he needed help with finding
accommodation. This wasn't a moment to start making up a
story so he admitted to Zofia that he would be grateful for her
assistance. The solution was found unexpectedly quickly since
Mrs Patel recently confessed to Zofia that her house felt very
empty. Her youngest daughter had recently got married and
left the family home. After the departure of her Indian relatives, who had stayed with her for a couple of months, she felt
lonelier than ever in her large house. She was willing to consider a well mannered lodger who would observe her house rules.
She and Mr Patel needed peace and quiet, so bringing home
guests, especially female companions, was a definite 'no'. Since
the only thing Darek brought home were his tired bones, together with a friendly manner and an eager smile, he managed to
win over his landlady very quickly.

The night when he met her in the kitchen waving the plunger
over a blocked sink was the moment when she first appreciated
the presence of a Polish handyman in her home. Mr Patel,
whose talents were confined to spreadsheets and trial balances,
never interfered with home maintenance. With the help of a
plunger and a piece of wire, Darek made the sink instantly
useable, promising to finish the job the next day. The bottle of
muriatic acid did the trick.

Suitably impressed with his DIY prowess, Mrs Patel told him
she wished he spent more time at home. She meant, of course,
that he should rest more and take better care of himself. Seeing
that he hardly ever ate a cooked meal she started leaving

generous portions of 'left overs' for him every evening. It gave her a lot of satisfaction, she admitted to Zofia, to see Darek empty his plate every evening and wholeheartedly praise her cooking. Mr Patel took her culinary talents for granted.

'The end cornice is still not right, boss. It isn't touching the wall,' said Derek. With his hands on his hips, he was standing in the middle of Nisha Patel's brand new kitchen. The fault, which he had just spotted, could have meant two things: either the wall cabinets weren't hung evenly or the cornice was warped. Either way, they would have to come back next week to sort it out.

'*Kurwa mać*,' Adam swore in frustration, confirming Darek's fears. He was standing on a ladder running his hands over the top of the cabinets trying to determine where they had gone wrong. His forehand glistened with perspiration and his flannel shirt was glued to his back. They both stank of sweat and wood adhesives. Their eyes were red-rimmed and their faces and forearms were covered with sawdust.

What happened next seemed to occur in slow motion. Darek saw Adam lift his hands to his temples and at that moment, he started keeling over backwards. Darek instinctively lurched forward to catch him but Adam's falling body toppled him to the floor. They tumbled down, pulling with them a metal kitchen stool which fell with an almighty crash on the tiled floor.

The next thing he remembered was seeing Nisha Patel's worried face leaning over them.

'I'm OK,' he tried to reassure her. 'But something happened to Adam.'

The young doctor was kneeling next to Adam with her full medical armoury around her. Wearing a pair of jeans and a pale blue T-shirt and with glossy hair tumbling around her shoulders, she looked girly and vulnerable. Yet when she took a stethoscope out from her medical bag and started examining Adam, while at the same time ordering Darek to bring her various things, she was in total control of the situation.

'Your friend fainted,' she explained. 'There could be a concussion so I'll take him to A&E.'

'Aje ...???'

'Accident and Emergency. I'd like to have a look at you too, Darek.'

'Me? Why?'

'Both of you had a nasty fall.'

'I wasn't standing on the ladder.'

Nisha Patel wasn't in the habit of arguing with her patients so she ignored Darek's plea and turned her full attention to Adam.

'Do you hear me Adam?' she gently shook Adam by his shoulders and pinched his cheek. 'That's better,' she said, seeing that Adam had opened his eyes and took a sip from a tumbler which she was holding to his lips. She felt the back of his head. When she moved her hand down to his shoulder, he hissed in pain. Next, she checked his arms, his lower back and his legs. It appeared that his lower body was unharmed by the fall.

'Darek, please grab the cushions from the sofa and help me support Adam with them,' she commanded. 'I will make a pot of strong tea for us all and I will drive us to the hospital.'

'To the hospital?' repeated Adam, opening his eyes, his voice rising in panic.

'Yes, you need an x-ray of your shoulder. And perhaps of your head too.'

'We must go to work tomorrow,' pleaded Darek.

'We will see about that.'

'Karol will sack us if we do not turn up tomorrow.' Darek thought that Dr Patel clearly had no idea of the nature of their employment.

'If necessary, you will call your boss to explain that you're not able to come in. I will write you a note.'

'A note?' asked Darek, instantly realizing that he sounded like a village idiot.

'Every employer has to respect a doctor's note. So don't worry and let's get going. Sunday night is not best time to be visiting A&E.'

The Accident & Emergency waiting room was unusually empty. The large room smelled strongly of clinical disinfectant and its functional furniture was designed with no thought for comfort. The plastic chairs, occupied by a handful of people who looked alternatively anxious and bored, were hard and cold to touch. The strip lights were so bright that both men kept wincing. Darek thought that this must be how bats feel when they were forced to fly into the light. Adam was still unsteady on his feet. The light probed his brain like a knife blade and he kept touching his head. In a corner of the room, there was a play area for children separated by a colourful picket fence from the rest of the room. Plastic toys lay scattered around a blue slide.

Darek kept glancing at the play area and Adam could read the boy's mind. He thought about Jędrek and Ewa and realized that he didn't know how his children spent their free time, once they had finished their homework and domestic chores. He made a mental note to ask Hanka about that the next time he would call home. Perhaps he could ask Zofia to help him choose Christmas presents for his children. He remembered seeing somewhere these gigantic chocolate bars and imagined Jędrek's face when he took it out from his Christmas parcel.

Suddenly their names were called out. They simultaneously got up and followed Dr Patel. A pretty nurse in a blue uniform led them to a cubicle, not much larger than a horse box, where they were asked to sit down and complete a form clipped to a board. They glanced at it and looked at each other with horror. They were expected to give answers to a long list of questions that trailed down the whole length of the page. Beyond the first couple lay unknown and potentially dangerous territory. What were they to say when asked how the accident happened? That they not only worked illegally during the week but also moonlighted at weekends? Straight from the hospital, they would be taken to a police station and shipped back home. Darek saw Adam shooting furtive glances at the door as if checking for an escape route.

Nisha Patel didn't need any more clues. She took the clipboard from Adam and moving closer to him started completing it. She asked Adam to write down his surname and home address on a piece of paper which she took out of her handbag. Then she attempted to piece together his medical history, by pointing to various parts of his body and making illustrative sounds and movements. The chart of a human body which hung just outside the cubicle proved invaluable. She handled Darek's form in exactly the same manner. She remained cheerful throughout the whole process but from time to time she glanced at Adam whose face appeared very pale in the bluish light.

When they had almost finished, the young nurse came back and regarded them with a curious gaze. She must have heard their conversations and drawn her own conclusions. She collected the forms and checked them in a brisk and efficient manner, directing her questions to Dr Patel. Looking at her fresh face and unperturbed smile, Darek wondered whether she ever got emotionally involved in the misfortunes of her patients.

An hour later they were again sitting on the back seat of Dr Patel's Golf. They were so exhausted that they almost forgot how hungry they were two hours before. Between them on the seat, lay brown paper envelopes with their x-rays, the evidence that after a thorough examination, they were found generally unscathed by the accident. Adam's shoulder was bruised but his collar bone had not been fractured. The doctor who examined him also discovered bruises and some tissue scarring on his lower back and told him to report to a GP surgery if he felt pain in his kidneys. This didn't satisfy Dr Patel. She wanted to see Adam in her surgery the next morning. She scribbled a note which she handed to Darek and instructed him to give it to their boss the following day.

By now, there were hardly any cars on the road and the pavements were also empty. The deserted streets of London's suburbs on Sunday evening always puzzled Darek. It was as if everyone went to bed at 8pm. If he wasn't dog tired every Sunday night, he would be out enjoying himself, not cutting short his weekend.

It was too warm in the car for comfort but he was glad they were not waiting at the bus stop on that cold and windy night. On the empty Greenford High Street, even the red lights of the kebab shop on the corner were extinguished. Gusts of wind lifted torn newspapers off the ground and tossed them down a few metres further. Empty cans rolled along the pavements and rattled, buffeted by the wind.

Holding his rucksack on his knees, Darek stared through the window, wondering what he was going to say when he faced

Karol tomorrow. Dr Patel insisted on seeing Adam in the morning in her surgery. To his repeated plea 'I am OK tomorrow,' she just waved her hand as if chasing away an intrusive fly. Darek noticed her large kohl-lined eyes studying them in the rear-view mirror. She left them under no illusions as to who was taking decisions here.

He looked at his dirty fingernails and palms with broken skin and rough with calluses. He remembered when he noticed how damaged Adam's hands were when he started working with him. Now his hands looked exactly like Adam's and he was some twenty years younger. He wasn't precious about his appearance but this observation rattled him. He was aging fast. He looked and felt a decade older than his twenty five years. Did he have other options? Certainly not now. He was lucky that Adam took him on. His dreams would have to wait until it was the right time to think bigger. Feeling completely exhausted, he put his head down on the rucksack and closed his eyes. As long as he was able to rest for a few hours, he would handle whatever life would throw at him next.

Chapter 31

Adam, November 1998

'Call Adam and tell him to get his ass here. Fast,' Karol barked as he paced the pavement outside the house in Worple Way. It was drizzling and his leather jacket was zipped all the way to his chin. Wet strands of his fringe were dripping water on his face and nose. There was a match in the corner of his mouth on which he was biting nervously.

'I'm sorry boss, but ...'

'I don't care whether his bus has broken down this morning. Tell him to get into a cab. Ted Johnson has found some fault with his banisters and he is waiting for us this morning with instructions on how to get them right.'

'Yes, he will be.'

'He is to be here now. Do you understand? Johnson has already been hollering to me over the phone that he has to leave for the office soon. Adam on his own won't understand what the man wants.'

'Perhaps I could go with you boss,' Darek suggested. Karol's face was already crimson which was a dangerous sign.

'You?' yelled Karol incredulously. 'You're not the one who did these fucking banisters and you are not a carpenter. Where is Adam?'

'At the doctor's, boss,' Darek spat the words, instantly relieved that the news about Adam was out.

'At the doctor???' wailed Karol. 'What he is doing at the doctor's on Monday morning?'

'He fell down on Sunday.'

'Is he drinking?'

'No boss, he fell off the ladder. He was helping ... my land-lady.' Darek slowly reached to his pocket and took out a carefully folded piece of paper. 'This is a note from the doctor.'

Karol looked at him puzzled. This wasn't one of the usual tricks with which his men presented him from time to time. With some caution he took the paper from Darek, opened it and scanned it quickly. He hesitated for a moment. Then he folded the sheet and stuffed it in the breast pocket of his leader jacket for further examination later.

'This shit is not going to help us with Johnson. He may refuse to pay for the job if he is not happy with it.'

'Boss, let me go with you. I will see what's needed to be done. And I will help Adam to finish the job.'

'Since when have you become such good friends?'

'We work together. I stayed with him for a while.'

'So you can tell him that he let me down today. When I urgently needed him.'

'I will do that. Can I go?'

Seeing that everyone else has already dispersed to do their jobs, Karol commanded: 'OK, get into the car before Johnson gets totally pissed off with us. Let's get there fast.'

He pointed the automatic key towards his Range Rover mounted on the pavement and the car blipped and flashed in response. They jumped in and Karol turned the car in a single sweep.

At the first traffic lights, Karol leaned forward and took a packet of cigarettes from the glove compartment. He asked Darek to pass him a lighter and once an orange glow appeared at the end, he inhaled deeply. Darek heard from other guys that no one was allowed to smoke in Karol's car since his missus hated when the car stunk of cigarettes. Now he had too much on his mind to pay attention to house rules. Darek sensed that it was going to be one of those mornings when few things go according to plan.

Ted Johnson greeted them with an expression that would sour even pasteurised milk. Looking at his watch, he opened a heavily varnished black door.

'Hello,' he hissed through clenched teeth. He let them into the hall and raised his arm to point to a magnificent staircase that graciously curved upwards to the half floor landing, where it turned right and led to an open gallery.

Darek gasped. Adam didn't say a word about this job. He mentioned that he was refurbishing some banisters but never boasted about the palatial scale of this project.

Karol silently followed Ted Johnson up the staircase. It was fitted with beige carpet so thick that their steps were muffled as though they were walking through snow. When they reached the first floor gallery Ted, who was very tall, knelt down to show something to Karol. A moment later, both men were on their knees closely scrutinizing the balustrade. Darek could see their animated faces appearing in the gaps between the banisters and thought that this was what children living in this house must have been doing when they wanted to spy on adults gathered downstairs in the hallway. Suddenly he heard his name being called and saw Karol beckoning at him to come up.

For a moment, he hesitated at the foot of the staircase fearing that his work boots would soil the carpet. Taking them off would be embarrassing so he returned to the entrance door and brushed his soles several times against a large doormat. As he walked up he could not resist touching the polished handrail imagining what fun it must be to slide down it.

When he reached the landing, both men were again crouching examining a different part of the balustrade. Karol ordered Darek to do the same and after apologizing to Ted Johnson, switched to Polish to explain the problem. Some of the banisters had to be replaced and Adam managed to source the right type of oak for replacements which were made to measure in a timber workshop. Once he had polished them, he selected the wrong type of varnish and the new banisters were clearly distinguishable by their offending sheen. Darek saw that Ted Johnson was looking at him with suspicion. He didn't blame him. This piece of furnishing was obviously precious. Karol also noticed Ted's alarmed looked and rushed in with lengthy explanations.

Darek understood that he only had to assist Adam as the man wasn't able to come today. It would be Adam, Karol's most experienced carpenter, who would be completing the job.

The moment they were back in Karol's car, he reached for the cigarette packet. 'Have you seen how much money is at stake there?' he asked inhaling deeply.

'I have boss. The man is very rich and demanding.'

'Adam should have been there with us,' said Karol tossing the empty packet onto the dashboard. 'He was looking at you as if I brought him a monkey.'

They drove for a moment in silence, each man lost in his own thoughts, when Karol suddenly asked: 'Could you see the difference between the old and new banisters? Without getting to your knees?' he jeered. They were stuck in the traffic and Karol's car was slowly nosing forward.

'No boss. Who will be kneeling down to see the difference?'

'He will. And he could give us hell if we don't do what he wants. What time is Adam going to appear today?'

'By lunchtime,' Darek wasn't sure that Adam would make it to work today at all, but this wasn't the time to give Karol more bad news. 'Definitely lunchtime.' Darek made a mental note to call Adam the moment he was alone.

'By lunchtime!' snorted Karol. 'Now, when we are drowning in work he takes time off to see the doctor.'

After a moment of silence, Karol asked: 'Is he OK?'

'He will be fine. We should be able to get back to Johnson's job this afternoon.'

'Don't you have something else to do?'

'I do but if we start sanding those banisters together we will finish sooner. If necessary, we could stay longer.'

'That's good. Could you come in on Saturday?' asked Karol as he searched his pockets.

Darek swallowed hard. He knew that this question would come up sooner or later. Suddenly, inspiration struck. 'We are helping our landlady to redecorate her kitchen as she is not charging me much. Perhaps we could come for a half day on Saturday and sort her kitchen out in the afternoon. She is desperate to start using it.'

As the car moved slowly through the thick traffic of Western Avenue, Karol took out a piece of paper from his jacket and placed it on the driving wheel. He studied it for a moment and pocketed it again.

Although Darek had his gaze fixed on the line of cars before them he felt Karol's penetrating gaze on him.

'OK, do what you need to do this Saturday,' said Karol in a

conciliatory tone. But next Saturday I may ask you to come in. Do you understand?'

'Sure boss,' confirmed Darek, trying to sound enthusiastic.

'That's good because I will have another job to attend to on Saturday.'

Although it was only quarter past nine, the car park of Classic Kitchens was already half full. It was a cold and misty morning and the Indian autumn which they had recently enjoyed was a distant memory. Karol parked in the second row from the front door, behind a blue van. He was able to see the entrance to the showroom in his side mirror but his Range Rover was obscured by the van. He anticipated a long wait so he brought with him a copy of *Which? Car* which he would never have been able to study in peace at home. He felt that it was the right time to buy Monika a new car. His young girlfriend had proved her loyalty to him. It would be two years, this month, since he'd managed to persuade her to move in with him, and she'd done a good job of looking after him. Of course, he took care of her too and made sure that she had everything she needed.

The sound of approaching steps on the gravel path broke his train of thought. It was unusual as most of the customers of Classic Kitchens were builders who arrived in their vans. He waited until the person climbed the short flight of steps leading to the front door and appeared in his line of vision. He almost whistled. Luck was on his side this morning. With one hand on the iron handrail, Adam was walking up the concrete steps. With a rucksack on his back, he moved slowly and more cautiously than usual. Obviously, he wasn't himself after that recent fall.

A wide self-congratulatory grin spread across Karol's face. He touched his pocket in which lay a note from Classic Kitchens telling him that he had been overcharged on his last transaction. The kitchen cupboard handles he purchased were from old stock and cost less than he was asked to pay. Mr Arthouse, the office manager, was offering him a refund on his next purchase. Karol was very busy and stressed, yet he knew perfectly well that he hadn't done any kitchens during the last few months.

Chapter 32

Maja, November 1998

Maja walked out into the November sunshine. She squinted and shaded her eyes against rays so sharp that they made her eyes instantly water. A cloud of breath floated before her as she walked along Cuckoohill Road. It was a crystal clear morning and the world appeared like a black and white photograph in sharp focus. The chestnut trees lining the street stood bare, stretching their gnarled arms to the blue sky. There was a dusting of frost on the grass and the last of the autumn flowers stood blackened and fossilized in the front gardens.

Some days it felt as if she only worked and studied, studied and worked, with eating and sleeping squeezed in between. In the evenings she fell asleep as soon as she touched the pillow. Despite this she was happy. Perhaps happier than she had been for years. Luke, loving, funny and wonderfully generous, had a firm place in her life. She frequently acted as the duty manager at the Customer Relations desk and came the top of her class in the half-term tests. At last, she felt that she was making tangible progress in her professional life and she could proudly report home that the previous eighteen months hadn't been a waste of time.

Yesterday, John Cassidy asked her to come to his office. This strangely long room with a padded door and thick carpet no longer intimidated her. She could see that he was relaxed here away from the hassles of the restaurant. He smiled broadly as she walked in and she sensed that he may have good news for her.

'Are you busy as usual?' he asked, pointing to the chair on the other side of the desk.

'Most of the time. We have many Christmas shoppers and

people are coming to see West End shows at this time of the
year.'

'That's good … Are you still enjoying your work?'

'Very much so.'

'You probably don't have time for a personal life.'

Maja hesitated for a moment. She had learnt to keep her
private life private.

'Enough to see people I care about.'

He just smiled. Maja knew that John Cassidy didn't always
verbalise his thoughts. After a moment, he said: 'I have always
considered you a very capable girl. I can see that you are
working very hard and I would like you to consider another
opportunity.'

Maja held her breath.

'I have just learnt that there will shortly be a vacancy in
Corporate Events as a result of a maternity leave. It's a very
busy department and although the vacancy is initially for six
months it is likely to be extended to a year. It could also become
a permanent post.'

She smoothed her skirt and looked up at John Cassidy. 'Do
you think I have enough experience for this job?'

'Definitely. I think you have already proved that you are an
asset to this company. I'll be happy to write you a recommendation but I am sure that James Clifford, your boss, will give you
a good reference. Although he may not be pleased to let you go.'

Maja walked into the staff canteen and made herself a cup of
coffee. As the aromatic liquid slowly filled the mug, she thought
about the reaction of her colleagues when they learnt that she
was moving, only six months after she started at the Customer
Relations desk. She didn't want them to think that she was
moving because she didn't enjoy working with them or that she
considered herself better than those who had worked in the
same post for much longer. There would be those who would
accuse her of opportunistic careerism. In fact, nothing was
further from the truth. Being able to put her mind and heart
into her job had always been the most important thing for her.
Having to try harder was just part of being an immigrant.

She scanned the half-empty room and headed for a quiet

corner surrounded on two sides by a latticed fence.

In her handbag, there was her mother's letter which she was itching to read. She called home every weekend but she became aware that her parents always kept these conversations upbeat and exchanged mostly good news. Her mother's letters written as she sat alone in the kitchen late at night with a glass of tea that had gone cold, were a better reflection of what was going on in the Zalewski household.

Maja reached for a knife and opened the envelope. Four sheets of wafer thin air mail paper slid down on the formica table. The letter was much longer than her mother's regular correspondence. She smoothed the sheets and anxiously scanned the familiar handwriting. After the usual update on what had recently happened at home, grandparents and neighbours, half-way down the second page she noticed an ominous sentence. 'Everyone was led to believe that after the buy out, the company would take on more projects and would expand its workforce ... Yet at the meeting with the new management they learnt that the company will be expanding its activities but all office-based functions will be modernised with the use of new computer systems. The same will apply to planning and quality control. As a result they will be cutting the number of staff, not expanding.'

She guessed the rest. The news which her father had feared for the previous twelve months had just been confirmed. She felt her throat tightening. She shut her eyes to stop the tears welling in her eyes. Poor, poor dad. What is he going to do now? His job was his entire life. As long as she could remember, her father's work took precedence over everything else. He began his professional life in Poltrans as a young engineer and climbed up the career ladder to become a senior inspector. What will happen now that the focus of his life was taken away from him? She instinctively knew that it was her mother who was the emotionally stronger party in their marriage although she always gave her father all the credit for what they achieved together. What will happen to them now? Will her mother manage to support the family just on her nursing job?

She knew that she should be right beside them telling them that everything was going to be OK. They would cut non-essen-

tials and they would manage. But she wasn't with them, neither
to console them nor to offer them help. There were many times
in the past when she felt guilty about leaving her family behind,
with all their worries and problems. When she struggled in
London and kept the truth to herself, the burden of guilt appeared lighter. But when everything went well, in her mind, she
always sought their approval. She wished to make them proud
of her. She wanted them to believe that she was making the
right choices.

Now when the wellbeing of her family was crumbling, she felt
that her place was with them in Grodek. In London, she was a
nobody. Everything she loved belonged to that far flung little
town in eastern Poland. All the good things and times she
experienced in England were merely like a holiday which was
bound to end sooner or later.

'Maja, what's wrong?' cried Luke. She was standing in the
doorway of the apartment in Wetherby Place used by Luke's
company as a London base for its senior staff. She was chilled
to the bone and her red rimmed eyes appeared enormous in her
ghostly white face. He stepped forward and put his arms around
her. Looking at her carefully, he tipped her chin up to kiss her
mouth. Her lips felt cold and dry. He led her indoors and helped
her out of her quilted jacket.

'Come into the kitchen,' he commanded. 'I will make you a hot
drink.' He wore a green checked shirt with sleeves rolled up to
the elbows. There was a dark brown smudge on his chin, a sign
that dinner was underway. An aroma of grilled sausages wafted
into the hallway.

She forced a smile and said: 'Everything should be fine. I may
move to Corporate Events. I also received top marks in my
group for our last project.'

'But not everything is well ...' he shook his head. 'OK girl. A
glass of wine or would you rather have a cup of tea?' He put his
arms around her and held her close.

The whole day, she had longed for someone to do just that.
Afraid that she would burst into tears, she stood silent and just
kept looking at him.

'Is it going to be tea after all?' She nodded.

'There may even be some lemon in the fridge. Will bangers and mash do for tonight? They are comfort food after all.'

Without a word, Maja hid her face in the fabric of his brushed cotton shirt. In a moment, it was damp as her tears spilled on his beating heart. He let her cry, silently holding her in his arms.

Only when she appeared calmer, did he say: 'Let's eat first, then you will tell me what upset you, baby.'

Much later that evening when she lay close to him, sedated by food, wine and his affection, Maja was able to tell him what had happened at home.

'I doubt that your mother and father would feel better if they found out that you gave up a promising job opportunity just to share their problems. Perhaps you could help them financially. I would like to help out too.'

'No, Luke.'

'Why not?'

'This is my responsibility. And besides ...'

'They would not approve of my role in your life?'

'No, I think they would like you but ...'

'What sort of but is it?'

'Oh Luke. They don't know you exist,' she blurted out.

There was a long silence.

'You've never mentioned me to your family?' he asked incredulously.

'No, I wanted to do it when the time was right. I hoped to go to Poland to see them early in the New Year. But if I was lucky enough to get this job, that would be out of question. The beginning of the year is a very busy period for this department.'

'Why were you so reluctant to mention me? Are you ashamed of our relationship?'

'Of course not, Luke. It's just me.'

He waited for her explanation.

'I haven't had much luck with boyfriends. Ever. I have made a mess of things before. My parents have a lot on their mind and I didn't want to worry them.'

Luke rolled away from her. In the faint light of the street lamp she could see that he was lying on his back with his arm under his head, a sign that he needed to think. It was clear that she had hurt him. Surprised him too. Now he was wondering whether she was the person he thought her to be.

'Luke ...'

'I have some news for you too. Seeing how upset you were tonight I didn't think this was the right time to tell you ...'

Alerted by a sudden premonition, she raised herself on her elbow and reached for the lamp switch. A sudden burst of light made them both squint.

'Shortly after Christmas I have to go to the States. The company is reorganising the New York office and they asked for my help. They want to start attracting a different type of business than before so we need to change our approach.'

'Are you telling me that it's over between us?' she managed to whisper.

'No Maja, not at all.' Through the sheets, he felt that she was trembling. 'Oh silly girl. Come to me.' Her reached forward and scooped her into his arms.

'Of course, not. I will be away for a month or two. And although you may be reluctant to admit my existence to your family, my mother is dying to meet you. And I promised her I would bring you to Bath before Christmas.'

'Your mother?'

'Yes.'

'I'm not sure I ...'

'Shush ...' He closed her mouth with a kiss. Reaching over her head to switch the lamp off he said: 'Enough news bulletins for tonight. I had different plans for the evening.'

The November wind sweeping over the Round Pond was sharp like a razor. Despite the blinding sunshine, the air was chilly and even the ducks weren't displaying much enthusiasm for the treats that Kensington Gardens' regulars brought them that morning.

Huddled in her padded jacket, Maja was about to circle the pond for the second time when she recognised him. Protected by a grey wool coat and matching hat, Lorenzo appeared smaller and thinner than she remembered him. Out of a paper bag, his gloved hand produced pieces of diced bread crust which he scattered among the ducks that gathered at his feet.

She was certain that he had also seen her but he continued feeding the birds right up to the moment when she stood next to him. She smiled at him through tears. 'It's so good to see you Lorenzo. Thank you for meeting me.'

Without a word, he offered her the bag. Maja took some crumbs and scattered them in front of her. The wind blew them onto the heads and wings of the ducks. When the bag was empty, they walked away from the pond. Like casual acquaintances, they strolled along a plane tree-lined avenue that was completely empty on that freezing morning.

'I am so happy to see you Maja.' Lorenzo studied her face for a moment. 'You look lovelier than ever, *cara.*'

She laughed. 'With my red nose and streaming eyes?' She put her hand on the sleeve of his coat.

Patting it, he said: 'It only makes you more charming. It never surprised me that Nico was so smitten with you.'

Pressing her cheek to the prickly wool of his coat, Maja asked: 'Was there any news from the investigation? Are the police any closer to finding Nico's murderers?'

'No, love. *Signor* Mazzini told us that there weren't any breakthroughs.'

'There was nothing in the papers.'

'No ... We all think that Nico's death was a tragic mistake. Apart from the restaurant, he wasn't involved in any other family business. But, no doubt, it was a dirty job. The mafia's dirty job. Their arms are very long.'

Maja shivered. 'So Nico died in vain and no one is going to bring the murderers to justice?'

'The family may deal with the matter in their own way, but I doubt that is going to be reported in the papers.'

'I found it hard to deal with,' she said with anger.

Lorenzo looked at Maja gravely. 'You must put the past behind you, Maja. And never go back to Bella Italia or try to contact anyone there. It's enough that you risked seeing me. I heard that there were people asking after you when you left.'

'Nico's death left me devastated with grief but I recovered. Yet, I am still so angry at the pointlessness of this all and I feel like I don't care if someone follows me or not. I am not going to start hiding now.'

'Maja, I am going back home soon.'

'To Italy? To your Panicale?'

'Yes, for good. My sister is coming with me ... But I want to know that you're safe ... and happy. So take good care of yourself and don't take any risks. You have no idea of the potential dangers. Promise me this.'

She swallowed hard, touched by his concern. 'I won't do anything stupid. I promise, Lorenzo. I will be thinking about the two of you enjoying your retirement in your family house surrounded by cypress trees. I will imagine the sights and smells of Umbria, as you had described them to me. I'm sure you will be happy.'

'I need rest and peace of mind at last ... and I don't think I would find it here.'

'Of course, I understand. I also long for familiar faces, sights, smells.'

'I know you do, *cara*. People who leave their countries behind always miss these things.'

'Coming back to what you said. I'd never seen or felt that anyone had been following me, so they probably decided that I wasn't worth the effort,' she said smiling, and tenderly looked into his pale grey eyes.

Chapter 33

Maja, December 1998

Luke stopped the car at the end of the gravel path and switched off the engine. A moment later, a blue door opened and a tall woman stepped out and started walking towards them, waving energetically with both hands. Her smiling face was framed by a cloud of chestnut hair billowing in the wind. The moment Maja stepped out of the car she received an expansive hug.

'I am so happy to meet you at last, Maja,' the woman sung with an East Coast lilt. Maja forgot that Luke's mother was an American.

'I made Luke promise me that he would bring you down here. He told me how busy you are, so I am glad that you took time out to visit me.' Watching Maja gather her things from the back seat, she added: 'You're lovelier than I imagined.'

Maja blushed embarrassed by the compliment.

'Old boy, give your mother a hug,' she commanded, turning to Luke who promptly enveloped her in his arms.

'We live in the same town but we see each other once a month. If that. He is so busy. Always going somewhere — to London, up North ...'

'Mum, you're hardly at home yourself ...' protested Luke.

'Well, OK, I like seeing people. With family abroad, there is always an excuse to go away. But I don't believe that Luke has time to miss me.' She affectionately tousled his hair and wiped a smudge of lipstick from his cheek.

Luke's mother was almost as tall as him. She was more solidly built but there was a striking resemblance between them.

'Ladies, I haven't introduced you yet,' said Luke, trying to get control of the situation.

'Mum, this is Maja Zalewska, my lady friend and muse,' he said, winking at Maja.

'Maja, this is Elizabeth, my mum and the chief commanding officer of the Hastings household. By the way, no one calls my mother Liz or Lizzy. Be warned.'

'I will remember that' said Maja. She couldn't imagine calling this regal woman Lizzy.

Seeing Maja's unease, Elizabeth explained: 'My mother came from a very traditional Presbyterian family in which nobody used diminutives. One wasn't baptised Jeremiah to be called Jerry, she used to say.' She picked up one of Maja's bags. 'Honey, come inside, you will be chilled to the bone if we stay out chatting. Luke, please, take Maja's suitcase to the guest bedroom. I hope you won't mind sleeping in your old bedroom. All your books and model airplanes are still there,' she added, smirking conspiratorially at Maja.

'Before I show you around, I need to check on the bird in the oven,' she said taking Maja into a large front room. 'Please make yourself comfortable. I will be back in a minute.' She hurried in the direction of a mouth-watering aroma of roasting food.

Maja was glad to be left alone. She was longing to have a look around without appearing nosey. She had promised Amy to give her an account of the visit. Her friend believed that houses said volumes about their owners.

The lounge had a high ceiling and the tall windows were elegantly draped in heavy bronze curtains. A stone fireplace was the focal point of the room. A large mirror hanging above it reflected a vase of white chrysanthemums that stood on the mantelpiece. Directly opposite, there was a low table flanked by two plump sofas and a couple of armchairs — an arrangement suggesting that this was a place for relaxed conversations. The opposite wall was taken by floor-to-ceiling bookcases tightly packed with volumes, some of which were very elaborately bound. Maja wondered who was the book lover and collector in Luke's family. There was a number of sideboards and smaller tables scattered around the room bearing a variety of photographs, lamps and ornaments. She noticed a couple of seasonal arrangements made of holly, mistletoe and spruce. Their resinous smell lingered in the air and, together with the aromas of the cooking food, gave the room a festive atmosphere.

Then she noticed it. In the corner, at the opposite end of the room from the fireplace, stood a magnificent three-metre high spruce. Like a bashful maiden that paused in the doorway of a ballroom, the tree stood in the shadow, out of the reach of sun beams streaming through the tall windows. It was decorated with a profusion of silver and gold baubles and bows, with angel hair cascading from the tip to the floor. She imagined that when darkness fell outside and the tree was lit up, the glow from the lights and their reflections would illuminate the whole room, creating a magical atmosphere. She wondered whether Zosia and Piotr had already decorated their Christmas tree. It was the second Christmas she would be spending away from them. She thought about the empty plate that would be left for her at the Christmas Eve supper and only Zosia helping mum in the kitchen.

'Are you OK, honey?' asked Elizabeth, appearing in the door-way with an oven glove on one hand.

'I am fine. I was admiring your beautiful tree.'

'I am glad that you like it. I hadn't had a proper size Christmas tree for a few years. When Luke and Alice left home it no longer made sense. But this year both of you came and Alice is expecting a baby, so it feels like a real Christmas again.'

Maja wondered how long Elizabeth had been on her own. She remembered Luke saying that his parents were very close.

'Can I help you in the kitchen?' she suggested instead.

'I'm almost done. We will have a light lunch now but everything is also ready for the dinner. Once the turkey is out of the oven I will make the gravy. But your dress is much too nice for the kitchen.'

'I do help at home.'

'Why don't you make coffee for us all? Unless you prefer a glass of wine,' suggested Elizabeth.

Nothing prepared Maja for the sight of the Christmas dinner table that night. The large dining room was lit by four candles in the silver candlesticks standing in the middle of a table covered by a snow-white tablecloth. There was a linen napkin in a silver ring and a piece of holly on each plate. Next to it lay a tube covered in gold paper and tied with a ribbon. In the candlelight, the silverware gleamed and crystal glasses sparkled, making the whole scene appear like a feast from a fairy tale.

With amusement, Elizabeth watched Luke showing Maja how to pull crackers and helped her put a paper crown on her head. It was too large and kept slipping down, almost to the bridge of her nose.

'This proves that royal insignia are not for me,' laughed Maja pushing it back once again.

'To the contrary, it proves that you are a real princess and a paper hat just won't do for you. But ...' said Luke and disappeared in the kitchen. When he came back he had two strips of cellotape stuck to his fingers. With one of them he tightened her crown at the back. He used the second one to attach a silver star from the cracker to the front of the crown.

'What about this?' he asked admiring his handiwork.

'This reminds me of my outfit at a kindergarten party. I even have a picture of it.'

'We should take some pictures tonight,' exclaimed Elizabeth. 'Maja may like to send them home. I would also like a reminder of this evening.'

Elizabeth's Christmas pudding, golden, aromatic and moist, bore no resemblance to the hard cake Maja had tasted a year before. When there was time to eat it, Luke generously baptised it with brandy and lit it up. Enchanted, she watched blue flames dancing on the dark mould.

Gazing at Elizabeth looking regal in her emerald green dress and Luke smiling at her across the table, Maja thought about the efforts they had made to welcome her. This was a different world from the one she inhabited at the Cuckoohill Road. It was a thousand miles away from the greasy kebab shop in Earl's Court and the beer stained tables of the King's Head. She felt different about herself sitting here together with these kind and generous people who welcomed her to their home and their world.

'Be careful, Maja,' warned Elizabeth, passing a plate with a

piece of glistening dark cake. 'In my family, the pudding contained a surprise. Before steaming it, my mother always put
silver coins in — for good luck. Your good fortune the following
year was judged by the number of coins found in your piece of
pudding.'

'My brother and sister would have loved this idea.'

'I had only two pieces of luck this year,' said Luke spearing the
last crumbs of the pudding with his fork and making a disappointed face. 'Can I have another helping to improve my chances?'

'No,' said Elizabeth laughing. 'That won't count. But look at
Maja. She found four coins.'

'Five,' corrected Maja, lifting a sticky disk from the remains of
her pudding.

'That's the beginners' luck,' said Luke. 'I think that's confirmation that you will get that job in Corporate Events. Should
we have another drink?'

'What about coffee?' suggested Elizabeth, looking at Maja. 'Or
tea if you prefer. But let's take the tray to the sitting room.
Luke, you're on tea and coffee duty today. We will retire to the
lounge,' she said, smiling at Maja.

Many times afterwards Maja would recall the sight of Elizabeth's sitting room prepared for Christmas. Closing her eyes,
she could feel the warm glow of the fire on her face and the
resinous scent of the spruce, mingled with the aroma of warm
brandy, cinnamon and cloves. She would see in her mind's eye
the soft light of table lamps and the dancing flames in the
fireplace that made the room appear so warm and intimate. She
would feel the soft carpet under her feet as she stood admiring
the Christmas tree, now alight and resplendent in silver and
gold decorations.

'This is my favourite moment,' said Elizabeth, making herself
comfortable on one of the large sofas by the fireplace. She
tucked her legs up and, patting the cushion beside her, invited
Maja to sit down. 'I have enjoyed cooking special meals for the
family but being able to sit down and chat together, without
interruptions, was the moment I always waited for.'

Observing Elizabeth curled up like a girl on the sofa, Maja thought that she looked so young. Her openness, energy and easy manner belied the grey strands that ran through her chestnut hair. She didn't remember her mother being so relaxed and thought that if her mother smiled more, and she had a beautiful smile, she would look younger.

'Do you have large family gatherings at Christmas, Maja?' asked Elizabeth, interrupting her thoughts.

'Not really. Our family is scattered around Poland, so there are often just five of us and granny for Christmas. For New Year's Eve we sometimes go to my mum's family in Krakow or uncle Henryk, dad's brother, comes from Germany. But then there are usually too many people for relaxed conversations. We are all working hard preparing food and then we're busy tidying up.'

'George, my husband was a very busy man, working and travelling all the time. He would even spend evenings in the study, preparing articles and presentations. He worked for an economic agency dealing with developing countries. We always had to compete for his time, so I introduced these sit down sessions so we could talk together as a family and catch up on what was going on in our lives. I have moved these two sofas closer,' she waved her hand, 'to bring us together and talk. Do you think that is strange?'

'Not at all,' said Maja, surprised by the question. 'Many families rarely find time to talk. Or perhaps they find it difficult to be open with each other about things that really matter.'

'Some of my friends here thought that I was very American in my approach. Perhaps I am,' she added, musing. 'Do you find England and English people very different to your own folks?'

'I did and I still do, but I've accepted that I'm a guest here and have to adopt an English way of life. I may think differently about certain issues but this hasn't stopped me from making good friends here.'

Elizabeth smiled. 'How did you and Luke meet?'

'One of my summer jackets played an instrumental role,' interrupted Luke walking into the room with a tray laden with cups, saucers, a tea pot and a cafetierre. 'It's a shame I have laundered it because it could have served as a memento for future generations,' he added, grinning at Maja.

When Elizabeth was pouring the drinks, Luke recounted their first meeting. He described his astonishment when he saw Maja behind the Customer Relations desk in the Metropole.

'Well, it sounds as if you were destined to find each other,' said Elizabeth with a smile, passing a cup to Maja.

'You said exactly the same thing about your meeting with dad,' said Luke archly.

'Perhaps I like to believe in destiny.'

Next morning, Maja was woken up by a gentle knock on the door. She was surprised to see Elizabeth in her dressing gown holding two mugs of coffee.

'I hope you don't mind me waking you up.'

Maja quickly glanced at her watch lying on the bedside table.

'Oh, no. It's already nine. I rarely have the luxury of sleeping so late.' She ran her fingers through her hair, hoping she didn't look very dishevelled. She propped herself up against the pillows and pulled her legs up so that Elizabeth could sit on the bed beside her. She sensed that she wanted to talk to her.

Elizabeth just smiled and passed her a mug of coffee. Freshly made, it smelled divine. With her voluminous hair flowing down her shoulders and in her white gown wrapped around her, she looked like a medieval queen.

'I have just sent Luke to the corner shop for some milk and thought I would come up and have a chat with you. I hope you don't mind?'

'Of course not.'

'Yesterday, when you went to bed, Luke told me that he would be going to the States shortly after the New Year. I hoped to see the two of you more often.'

'It was a surprise to me too,' admitted Maja. 'Hopefully it is going to be only for a couple of months. At most.'

'I hope so too. It would be a terrible shame if anything went wrong again.'

A shiver went down Maja's spine. The bed, so soft and warm, suddenly didn't feel cosy anymore. 'What do you mean, Elizabeth?'

'The moment I saw you, I knew you were the right girl for

Luke. He told me a lot about you and the things you share.'

'I also felt he was very special. We grew close ...' she heard herself admitting.

'Has he ever told you he suffered from depression in the past?'

'Depression? Luke?' Maja cried out shocked. 'He always appeared so upbeat.'

'I'm sorry to break this to you. It's much too soon. But I thought that if you really cared about him, you should know.' She paused giving Maja time to absorb the news. 'You may be able to help him.'

Maja was staring at Elizabeth unsure whether she understood her words. Was Luke a different person than she believed?

Elizabeth put her mug on the bedside table and moved closer to Maja. Lowering her voice, she explained. 'I am telling you that because if you decide to continue seeing him, and I dearly hope you will, you would be able to see, even from afar, the danger signs approaching.'

'Such as?'

'Mood swings, restlessness ...'

'But why do you think it will return?'

'For the last few months he has been very happy. I think you should take a lot of credit for this. He hasn't complained about his job once.'

'Has he done so before?'

'Many times he wished to quit the agency. But he must be on top form now — hence the assignment to New York.'

'Do you think this trip could trigger the condition?'

'He told me last night that he wouldn't go if he had a choice.'

'Doesn't he?'

'No, if he wishes to stay with them. At least for the time being. I am afraid that being away, under a lot of pressure, he may face his old demons again. He is not likely to confide in anyone about this.'

Suddenly, they heard the thump of the front door. Elizabeth whispered: 'Please keep this a secret between us, at least until the moment comes that he needs help.'

Astonished with what she had just heard Maja just kept staring at Elizabeth. Then she put her coffee down and taking Elizabeth's hand in her own, she whispered: 'I promise.'

Chapter 34

Kuba, December 1998

Kuba swallowed hard. He felt as if a tennis ball had become lodged in his throat. When he finally spoke it was someone else's voice coming out of his mouth.

'So you think you could be pregnant?'

'I am pregnant. I did the second test this morning. Isn't this wonderful? We will have a baby!'

Judyta squealed with delight at the other end of the line. 'I always wanted to have a baby but our baby will be just perfect. Beautiful and brainy. Don't you think?'

He transferred his mobile phone from one sweaty palm to another. This news hit him so hard that he couldn't think. His brain felt paralysed as if someone had just trashed him with a club. His mouth was dry and no sound came out of it.

'Are you still there?' Judyta's voice came back. This time there was a tinge of irritation in it.

He had to say something. Something ... 'I am very happy, naturally. A bit surprised but pleased for you ... for us. How far along are you?'

'Four months.'

Good God! Soon it would be too late to do anything. 'That's great. How do you feel?' He slumped down on the only chair in the room. A couple of hours ago, he had placed on it a pile of freshly ironed T-shirts.

'Fabulous. I don't have any morning sickness. Perhaps that's why I hadn't realized what was going on. The girls at the salon tell me that it must be a boy. That's great, don't you think?'

'Of course ...'

'Don't all men wish to have sons?'

Not now, he thought. Not now. He hoped to find love one day and babies would naturally follow. How he got himself into this?

At last when things started falling into place for him and he began to feel at home in Britain, he had smashed everything up with his stupidity.

'Kuba, your line seems to fade.'

'Yeah, it's a bad line. I ... I'll call you later. Take care of yourself.'

'Of course I will.' There was a little pause and then Judyta asked: 'You're not angry with me that I sprung this news on you?'

'No, of course not. You had to tell me.'

'I knew that you would understand, Kuba. I love you for that.'

Kuba sat motionless in the dark. The room was so quiet that he heard the blood pulsating in his temples.

'I can't hear you, Kuba. I had better finish now. Will you call me tomorrow? So we can talk. Properly. And plan.'

'Yes, Judyta, I will call.'

'What's happened, Kuba? I can't hear you. Wait and I will get out for a moment. Be brief, I start in ten minutes.'

Against the thumping noise of the background music, Kuba heard the shuffling and tapping of steps on a stone floor. He imagined Rafal walking through the dark corridor towards the entrance lobby of his club. Suddenly, there was an onslaught of voices and clinking glasses. Then there was the creak of a door.

'Are you still there, Kuba? Tell me what's happened.'

In a detached voice, that he barely recognized as his own, Kuba recounted the news he had received from Judyta.

'I cannot believe this! You're a bloody idiot! Total cretin. Imbecile!' Rafal bellowed, hardly pausing for breath. 'Why did you get involved with her? I warned you. Couldn't you see what kind of woman she is? A *kurwa* who sleeps with anyone who comes along. A pretty slut. Among her boyfriends were all the fat cats of the Opole mafia.'

'Rafal, I made a mistake.'

'A mistake?' roared Rafal incredulously. 'That's the understatement of the century. You've fucked your life up.' His friend's anger hit him as if he lashed out at him with his bare fists.

'I know.'

'What do you know? You don't know anything. This kid may

not be yours at all.' Kuba could hear Rafal pacing up and down the cobbled street outside the club. For a brief moment, he stopped for breath.

'I wonder what she wants from you. Women like her use men. Manipulate them.'

'I should have seen this coming.'

'You should have thought with your head. Not with your dick.'

'It's too late for that.'

'I will do what I can to find out what she has recently been doing. And whose company she was keeping. That may help you. But you may have to make her to do some tests when the kid is born.'

'Rafal, you have always been my best friend ...'

'I still am, but you're in deep shit mate. And at this moment, I cannot see how you're going to get out of it.'

'I need to think what to do. But I can't think now.'

The second Rafal hung up, Kuba threw his mobile in the direction of his bed. It hit the wall and slid down to the floor behind the bedding. He made no effort to retrieve it. He wanted to create as much distance as possible between himself and the message he had just received. Just as he smugly believed that he started steering his life in the right direction, this little piece of news from Opole derailed all his efforts in one fell swoop.

He walked towards the wardrobe and after a short search he pulled out a sweatshirt and a pair of jogging pants. The rest of his clothes fell on the floor but he didn't stop to tidy them. He pulled the clothes on so fast that he almost tore the leg off. He ran downstairs, crossed the hall and bolted out through the front door as if someone was chasing him.

The night was dark and freezing but he didn't notice that. It was good to be in the open where he could breathe again. He ran, ran and ran. Only when his lungs started to hurt from taking too much razor-sharp air in, did he slow down and consider where to go next. The park gates were already shut so he decided to follow the road that went up the hill and circled the park. The sheer physical effort of running up a steep incline was exhausting but it was also calming his nerves. Punishing exercises always worked like a sedative for him. By the time he had circled the park he felt like he was able to think again. Judyta may be lying, as Rafal suggested. There were probably other men before she met him in London and after she returned to Opole. She should know who the father of her baby was. A DNA test would be able to confirm this. But before they go down that route he needed to talk to her. He would meet her and try to suss out whether she was playing a game. A trip to Poland seemed inevitable. Not an easy thing to do without alarming his family. He racked his brains for possible explanations for his sudden visit. He would also have to get an authorized absence at the college and catch up on the lectures he would miss. Suddenly, an excuse came to his mind. That would do. At least for now. He relaxed his jaw, did twenty press-ups and decided to do another round of the park.

He was still reviewing his story and testing it in his mind for potential inconsistencies when his suitcase emerged on the conveyor belt at Katowice airport. He strode towards it, hoisted it up and tossed it on the tiled floor with such force that the metal studs at the base groaned. He would need a lot of nerve to tackle this problem and would have to control his emotions if he was to establish the truth. Judyta had plenty of experience with handling men and twisting them around her little finger. She was so sweet with him, making it clear how much she fancied him. She also told him that he was a cut above all the men she had ever been involved with. Yet he should have kept his head screwed on and treated her like a pleasant diversion, as an experienced man would have done. He would have nothing to regret now. He proved himself to be a young fool (at twenty nine, youth was not an excuse) and he would be paying a high price for his stupidity. Before he established how costly his mistake was, he would have to make sure that he wouldn't hurt the people who loved and trusted him.

He observed a young family preparing themselves to meet their grandparents. Suppressing a smile, he watched the mother instructing her brood on what they should say. How different his state of mind was when he had landed in Katowice only a few months before.

This time, he instantly noticed his father's now familiar silhouette. With his hat and old-fashioned coat, he appeared more formal than the rest of the crowd waiting for the arriving passengers. He lifted his gloved hand and waved the moment he saw his son. It choked Kuba to see what a solitary figure he was in the crowd. He rushed to embrace him. He couldn't help noticing how little of the former imposing figure was left under the wool coat. The smell of his familiar cologne was as strong as ever and the scent of moth balls was a sign that his coat didn't get much of an airing these days. This reminded him of the distant past when his father, with his suitcase already at his feet, leaned down to kiss him before departing for one of his business trips. He would then kiss Henio, the name Henryk abandoned on his sixteenth birthday, and wrap his arm around his mother's waist as she stood on her tiptoes to receive his kiss.

'We didn't expect to see you again so soon after your last visit. I am afraid granny will think that you'll be popping in every couple of months.'

'I will definitely come more often than before,' Kuba said firmly. 'But this time I decided that it would be easier if I go personally to my old college and ask for copies of all the necessary papers relevant to my current course. Rather than starting a lengthy correspondence, with all the potential mistakes.'

'You could have asked me. I would have been happy to help you,' said Kuba's father reproachfully.

'I know, dad. But I'd rather go there myself. I don't remember all the modules we've done. I may find out something useful.'

'It's a shame that this didn't come up before. You could have sorted these issues the first time you came and saved money.'

'I got a very good deal on Ryanair. Flying in the middle of the week makes a big difference. In fact, I didn't expect the fare to be so cheap.'

'I thought that everything only goes up.'

'It's a budget airline. So you get what you pay for. No luxuries, only the most basic service.'

'We are delighted to see you again. You look really well. Granny is waiting with her *rosòl* for you.'

Kuba glanced at his watch. 'By the time we get to Opole, it'll will be well past ten. Isn't too late to visit her?'

'I tried to tell her. But she insisted that after such a long journey you need a hot meal. Guess who won the argument?'

It was half past midnight when Kuba slowly sank into the freshly laundered bedclothes in his old room and heard the chime of the wall clock in the hall. Years ago this was the last sound he remembered before falling asleep. Now, it felt as if he had never left home. He was a boy again and he had just returned from some adrenaline-charged summer adventure to the safety of his bedroom. For the time being he could be himself again.

He couldn't stop thinking that he was a fraud. He had told a whopping great lie to his doting grandmother and concerned father, both of whom kept repeating how proud they were of him. He could hardly look them straight in the eye. And yet their presence and affection relaxed him and started to restore his peace of mind. It felt so good to be cared for, to be loved unconditionally. He fell into a deep dreamless sleep, the sort experienced only in a place of safety, and for a few hours forgot about everything.

Chapter 35

Kuba, December 1998

Kuba was relieved to be given a table by the window. He took it as a sign of good luck. He wanted to observe Judyta before she noticed him. Every time they met, she managed to surprise him and take control of the situation. He believed that if he could catch a glimpse of her unguarded, this would help him judge whether she was playing a game with him.

It was one of those winter days when mornings look much the same as late afternoons and people are reluctant to venture outside for fear of dampening their shoes and spirits.

He arrived half an hour early in Dino's to gather his thoughts and consider the options open to him. That morning, when he weighed up the potential implications of becoming a father to Judyta's baby, he broke out in a cold sweat. It was like playing a poker game for very high stakes. No, it was worse, as he didn't even know his cards. For a brief moment, he thought about leaving the whole mess behind and catching the first plane back to London. The old Kuba may have done exactly that, but the new man in him warned him that this would be the coward's way out and it wouldn't achieve anything.

He ordered a large *Żywiec*. After a few sips, he felt calmer and started looking around.

Dino's had a bright décor, combining modern interior design with the traditional elements of an Italian trattoria, such as red and white check tablecloths and displays of Italian wines. The aroma of food cooked with garlic and basil was wafting from the open kitchen. The staff, dressed in white shirts and black trousers, hovered in the background. There were just enough of them to take care of the customers without making them feel like they were under constant surveillance. A young waitress came back to him to ask whether he would like to order some food.

'A bit later. When my companion joins me.'

So, he would not call Judyta his girlfriend, yet he was already inextricably bound to her. He started observing the waitress. She was pretty, graceful and intelligent, perhaps a student supplementing her grant. No doubt, there were plenty of men who wished to call her their girlfriend. She was now talking to a young man in an oversized jumper and collar-length lanky hair. The dishwater-shade jumper must have survived too many hot washes. He was staring at the waitress in dog-like admiration. Love takes different forms, thought Kuba.

Just then, he noticed Judyta through the window. She parked her silver BMW just outside the restaurant. She was wearing a white fur jacket which he had seen before, and a pair of large shades. The day was rather overcast yet she obviously knew that the sunglasses suited her. She reapplied her lipstick in the driver's mirror and ran her fingers through her hair. Then she pressed her lips together and with another glance in the mirror she opened the door. A leg in a high heeled boot appeared on the pavement. It was followed by the second leg and then the rest of Judyta emerged, looking like a catwalk model. She slammed the door, pressed the automatic lock and strutted towards the restaurant swaying her hips. Walking just twenty metres between the car and the entrance, she managed to turn a couple of heads. It's not surprising she was used to eating men for breakfast, thought Kuba. What an adversary to have!

A moment later when she paused in the restaurant's entrance, the sunglasses were already perched on top of her head and her jacket was unbuttoned. She was holding a pair of gloves in one hand, while an expensive-looking handbag was resting in the crook of her arm. This sight reminded Kuba of leather goods advertisements in glossy magazines.

The moment she saw Kuba, she enthusiastically waved to him with her gloves. She ran towards him and put her arms around his neck even before he had got to his feet. Kuba felt that the eyes of all the customers in Dino's were on him.

'Kuba, it's so good of you to come. I know how awfully busy you are ...' Judyta prattled on as he helped her to take her jacket off and moved out the chair for her. She was wearing a pink fluffy jumper which made her look sweet and feminine. He had never seen her in a loose fitting garment before. Her eyes shone and her cheeks were flushed by the cold air.

'You look beautiful,' Kuba heard himself saying.

'I feel well.' She smiled. 'Very well. After all pregnancy is called a blessed condition. But you look even more handsome than the last time I saw you.' She affectionately patted his chest with her manicured hand. The deep magenta nails made a scratching sound against the wool of his jumper which almost made him flinch.

'Do you have time to exercise?' she asked coquettishly.

'Hardly. Some days, I run in the evening. When I have some energy left.'

'Oh God, I have plenty of energy now but I am hungry all the time. And I want to be in bed by eight.'

It was a good moment to change the subject. Indicating to the waitress that they needed menus, Kuba asked: 'What do you fancy?'

'One of their scrumptious pastas and a big dessert afterwards.'

Kuba wasn't hungry at all. Thinking how he would introduce the reason for his visit to Opole, he chased a piece of veal around a spacious plate and watched Judyta eating. With great gusto, she applied herself to a bowl of tomato soup, which was followed by a portion of spinach cannelloni ('spinach has plenty of iron and is good for the baby') and a large green salad ('half my daily portion of vitamins and minerals'). He couldn't tell what a meringue with a mountain of whipped cream and half a dozen raspberries was meant to supplement but decided that broaching the subject of the baby's paternity during the meal would give them both indigestion.

He politely listened to Judyta's account of her health check-ups, diet and plans for accommodating the pregnancy into her work schedule. From the corner of his eye, he watched the lovesick student and his attempts to keep the attention of the waitress. The girl clearly wasn't interested but he wasn't accepting this. She was getting annoyed, having to go back to his table time and again. After a plate of spaghetti, he was now drinking a second glass of tea. Feeling sorry for him, Kuba followed his pitiful attempts to amuse her with a paper napkin trick. When the boy ordered his third glass of tea, the waitress brought him the bill showing that her patience had run out. The student reached for his trouser pocket. Unable to locate his wallet, he searched the pockets of his jacket. Obviously it wasn't there so he began searching again. This time he found his bank card. With relief he put it on the bill, took a small red carnation from the vase on the table and placed it on the saucer next to his card. The girl picked it up with a smirk and briskly went to the counter.

'So do you think I should begin exercising now to stop putting on too much weight? The girls at the salon tell me ...'

'You should find a pre-natal exercise class to keep fit and take plenty of rest.'

'Kuba, I knew you would give me the best advice.'

The girl was back with the card indicating that something was wrong with it. She no longer restrained her annoyance with the boy. She slammed the saucer on the table and walked away with an expression of indignation. The student was mortified. His pasty face suddenly went crimson, his large ears were burning like red peppers. He had not only been rejected but also managed to humiliate himself in front of the woman he loved.

'Please excuse me for a moment,' Kuba apologized to Judyta who was now describing the design of the latest car seats for babies. He walked to the boy and placing his hand on his shoulder, leaned in to whisper something to him. The student's face lit up for a second and then he started shaking his head in protest. Kuba leaned down again and told him something. Then he strode straight to the waitress who was watching the scene from behind the counter. He said something to the girl whose expression softened.

'What was that all about?' questioned Judyta, looking at him reproachfully when he returned to the table.

Evading her gaze, he stirred his coffee and said: 'I knew this guy's brother so I left a message with him. Can I tempt you with a walk when you finish your tea?'

Judyta hesitated for a second. Then she leaned across the table and taking Kuba's hand into hers she smiled. 'On your arm I can confront all the snow in this town even in these shoes,' she said, pointing to her heels.

They left Dino's arm in arm, a golden couple, all smiles, the envy of every man and woman who saw them. Cruising around the old town square, they met Judyta's friends and clients whom she greeted with a radiant smile. When they stopped to chat, she introduced Kuba as her boyfriend. Thankfully, he wasn't presented as the father of her child, he thought. Embarrassed by this parade, Kuba suggested a walk in the park, which was only ten minutes away. He was anxious to find an opportunity for a serious conversation.

'There is a lot of snow in the back streets. I am not sure I'll be able to walk through it,' she purred sweetly.

'I'll carry you!'

'Will you?' she asked coquettishly, clearly loving the idea.

'What about this?!' Kuba scooped her off the pavement and strode across the road carrying her in his arms, carefully negotiating the puddles and piles of melting snow. He almost collided with a tugboat of a man with a shaven head walking from the opposite direction.

Judyta giggled and, putting her arm around Kuba's neck, snuggled closer to him. When they reached the other side of the road he lowered her down with great care and offered her his arm.

'Thank you, my prince,' she said nodding gracefully. 'I always knew that I would be safe in your hands.'

'Be careful where you step. A stroll in the fresh air will do you good.'

'Yes, sir.'

They walked almost the whole length of the park before Kuba found a quiet spot which was unlikely to be invaded by Judyta's acquaintances. When he saw a large fallen tree, he took her by the hand and led her to it so that she could lean comfortably against the trunk.

'I want to talk to you,' he said facing her.

'Well ... Why else would you be dragging me into the most deserted spot in the town?'

She wasn't a fool.

'The news about your pregnancy came as a big surprise to me.' He was weighing his words carefully.

'Didn't you know that sex may lead to babies?'

'Judyta, I am serious.'

'So am I.'

'How do you know that this is my baby?'

'You were the only man I have been with when the baby was conceived.' Seeing his questioning gaze, she added: 'Of course, I haven't been celibate before but I haven't slept with anyone else since my trip to London.'

'OK, but ...'

'Besides, I would not be so happy carrying someone else's baby but yours. And I believe our son will be very special.'

'But how would I know you're telling me the truth?' he finally spat out.

'You have to trust me.'

Kuba gasped. He instantly imagined Rafal's reaction when he repeated Judyta's words to him.

'Of course, you could demand a paternity test when the baby is born,' she said calmly.

'But until then ...'

'Nothing. You have to take my word.'

What did he expect her to say? Should he tell her that their relationship was all about sex, mind blowing sex, in fact, but not about trust? The life-long commitment of a child definitely wasn't included in it. She would accuse him of taking advantage of her, and she would be right. He left her leaning against the tree and started pacing up and down making an ankle-deep rut in the wet snow.

'So this is why you came?' she shouted angrily. 'To find a way to extricate yourself from the relationship with me and our baby?'

Kuba stopped. This conversation was deteriorating fast. He wasn't going to find out anything but would only earn her hostility.

'No, Judyta. I don't intend to renege on my responsibilities. I only wish I had some say in this situation.'

'Kuba, for God's sake, stop walking like a robot and come here,' she said in a softer tone. 'I had no intention of trapping you. I still don't. I have enough money to bring this baby up on my own.'

'It won't be necessary.'

'Listen to me. I don't expect any contribution from you. I only hoped that in time you will grow to love our baby and wish to be a part of his life. We can even become friends. We have already been lovers ...' she added with a smile.

She sounded so reasonable, he thought. If this was a different girl he might have believed her, but Judyta wasn't an average girl. Still pacing a few metres away he watched her from the corner of his eye. Leaning against a thick trunk, with her black hair scattered on the white fur jacket, full lips, shapely figure and a pair of great legs, she looked like a supermodel resting during a photo shoot. She was not only a stunning woman but also exciting company. What was underneath this bewitching exterior?

Judyta grew restless and started walking in Kuba's direction. The snow around her was wet and with each step, her high heels were sinking deeper into the ground. Suddenly, she lurched forward and almost lost her balance. With one jump, Kuba was next to her. He grabbed her by the elbow and put his arm behind her back.

'Judyta, it was stupid of me to bring you here. It's not safe for you to walk in the snow.'

He could see that she was shaken by her near fall and allowed him to escort her to the pavement, firmly grasping his arm. When she found herself on hard ground she relaxed and looked at Kuba in silence for a moment. 'So you do care for me after all,' she said slowly.

At night, Rafal's apartment appeared even more spacious. With only one lamp above the television creating a small pool of light, the uncluttered space with a high ceiling had a cavernous depth. Separated by four floors from the city noise, it was eerily quiet. The total silence was broken only by a ticking alarm clock standing on Rafal's bedside. Kuba found this atmosphere so calm and comforting that he fell asleep the moment he sunk into the folds of Rafal's sofa.

It was half past one when he was woken up by the sound of a key in the lock.

'I expected to find you asleep in front of the television,' said

Rafal, grinning from the door.

'I had a long snooze. The Japanese horror which you recommended instantly sent me to sleep.'

'You could have watched *Sex Mission*. It was on the shelf.'

'It would have been too close for comfort.'

'It is just a comedy.'

'I cannot make up my mind whether my life is a comedy or a tragedy at the moment.'

Rafal looked at Kuba in silence. Then he went to the fridge and took a couple of cans out of it. Raising them in Kuba's direction he asked: '*Żywiec* or *Tyskie*?'

'*Żywiec* would be perfect.'

'What about a bite to eat? Before I tell you what I know, you need to fortify yourself.'

'Is it so bad?'

'You be the judge of that.'

When the smell of sweet and sour chicken was the only reminder of their meal, Rafal slumped down on the sofa next to his friend with an inscrutable expression.

'Rafal, just get straight to the point. I've had enough suspense for today.'

'So she told you that she hasn't been seeing anyone since her visit to London?'

'She did.'

'You believed her?'

'Not exactly.'

'You're right. She not only has another bloke running around her. She moved to a new apartment and this guy has been staying with her.'

'How do you know that?' asked Kuba sharply. He was angry with himself that he could believe even for a moment that Judyta was telling him the truth.

'I have my own mole on the scene.'

'Who is it?'

'One of the girls who works in Judyta's salon. She visits our club so I made sure that she had a good time before I asked her a few questions.'

'She may have reasons to dislike her.'

'She may. But I have checked her story and confirmed some facts.'

'You always liked detective books.'

'Yes, indeed. Most recently Judyta was seen with some bloke who carried her across the street.'

Kuba burst out laughing. 'That was me. Your mole didn't tell you?'

Rafal slammed his can of beer on the coffee table. 'Mama mia. I am trying to help you to defend yourself and you're playing Romeo.'

'She had difficulty walking through the snow in her high heeled boots.'

'And has your chivalrous approach helped you establish any-thing?'

'No,' admitted Kuba.' But she said that she didn't expect any financial support from me.'

'Did she?'

'Yes, she did.'

'I suspect that she already has a sugar daddy supporting her. She is a high maintenance girl, if you hadn't noticed.'

'So what does she want from me?' asked Kuba sitting up.

'Perhaps she's playing games with both of you. It would be a risky one for you, Kuba.'

'Why?'

'Because Judyta's men are not the knights of the Round Table but mafia thugs. You'd be much better off waiting these five months of her confinement at the other end of Europe.'

Chapter 36

Adam, December 1998

It was ten o'clock and Darek was already on his second cup of tea. Karol's men knew better than to waste time on non-essential activities like eating or drinking outside a lunchtime break. However, Darek couldn't focus on his work this morning. He began the various tasks, stopped and moved on to the next job. His mug was a testament to his state of mind. Patterns of brown primer blended into blobs of timber glue, lines of black marker created a collage with smudges of blood from his thumb which he had sliced while cutting a piece of wood for an architrave.

Cholera, he swore. What was Adam playing at? He was lucky that Karol was at a different site this morning. Only last week, he had fired a guy for being half an hour late. Darek had enough of his own problems without having to worry about Adam. Lila, sensible girl that she was, decided that it would be better if he stayed in London for another six months earning as much money as he could. Of course, if he wasn't caught in the meantime and sent home on an express coach, with the door to Britain firmly shut behind him. Her sister would be staying with her during the final weeks of her pregnancy. Their daughter (he wasn't sorry that he was going to have a girl) was due in May. Lila would be the main subject of village gossip as a single and abandoned mother until he came back and made an honest woman of her. He kept promising his prospective parents-in-law that he would make up for the shame all of them were enduring at present and make them proud of him. Only that date kept moving backwards.

It was a chilly morning. A thick dusting of frost gave the world the appearance of deep winter. The air was sharp as a razor and the ground was frozen solid. At ten thirty, there was still no sign of Adam. Perhaps the daft fool had slipped, broken his leg and was now on his way to hospital. He had never been the same after his fall in Dr Patel's kitchen.

Darek decided to borrow Henryk's mobile and went outside to make a call to 26 Cuckoohill Road. At the other end the phone rang and rang. Darek waited until the twentieth ring. Then he pressed the off button and carefully selecting the digits, dialled again. After the third ring, he heard Zofia's voice in the receiver: 'Hello ...' She was breathless.

'*Pani Zofio*, this is Darek. Could you check whether Adam is in his room?'

'Of course. Just wait a minute.'

After a brief moment, she was back.

'His room is locked. I knocked a few times and there was no sound.'

'He didn't come to work. I wondered whether he could have had an accident. He hasn't been feeling well recently ...'

'I know, I know ... I haven't heard him leaving this morning. At about eight, I went shopping.' There was a small pause. 'Darek wait, I can hear Kuba in the kitchen. Maybe he saw him.' Darek heard Zofia's hurried steps disappearing into the distance. When she came back, her tone of voice was distinctly different.

'Kuba said that he hasn't seen or heard from Adam since last night. Usually he prepares his supper about eight and sits in the kitchen for a while. He definitely wasn't there last night. Perhaps he went to visit someone.'

'*Pani Zofio*, he has no family in London. And not many friends. He definitely wouldn't be staying over. In fact, last night he told me he was going shopping because he had run out of food.'

'Let me have a look.' Before Darek could say anything, she was gone again. Jesus Maria, what else was she checking? He noticed that Henryk had also stepped out and was staring impatiently at him. He borrowed his phone only for a quick call.

'Darek, his shelf in the fridge is empty,' Zofia said gravely, suddenly back on the line. 'Perhaps he fell ill last night and couldn't get home?'

'*Pani Zofio*. I will leave work at three. Will you be home then?'

'Yes, of course.'

'In the meantime, I will ask the other guys here about Adam. Maybe he told someone what he was planning to do ...' He hesitated. 'Would you help me to call ... the hospital ... perhaps also the police? Anyone who could have picked him up from the street if he fell ill or had an accident?'

'Of course and I'll make a few calls before you come. I have keys to all the rooms. Perhaps I will be able to find something that will give us some clue as to where he is ... I can enter every room in an emergency. This is an emergency.'

It was a very strange feeling. His mind was waking up from a very deep sleep but his body appeared disconnected from his mind. When he tried to reach for the blanket to pull it up higher, his left arm wasn't responding to his command. The right arm also felt wooden and incapable of any movement. He tried to lift his legs but couldn't get them to move either. The place where he was resting was hard and cold, unlike his bed at 26 Cuckoohill Road which he had nicely padded with blankets. He wondered whether this was Sunday since he didn't remember switching off the alarm clock. Suddenly, he heard a rustling noise close to his head and felt something warm and soft on his face. It felt like a piece of fine sandpaper. Suddenly without opening his eyes he realized what it was. Ginger's tongue felt exactly like this. But the cat had never licked his face. Oh, go away.

When he felt the rough tongue again, he realized that the animal was panting. He opened his eyes. He was staring into the dilated pupils of a dog whose slobbering mouth was suspended directly above his face. The dog was wet and his coat stunk of sweat. Adam raised his hand to chase him off and immediately felt a stab of pain in his arm. He attempted to lift himself up but couldn't. What was going on and where was he? He looked around confused.

He was lying on the ground which was frozen beneath him. Around him, there were tufts of grass which glistened with frost. The dog, which a moment ago had been licking his face now had his muzzle inside a plastic carrier bag which rustled like aluminium foil. After a short struggle, he dragged something out of the bag and started eating it with obvious pleasure.

O Boże, it was a piece of sausage, similar to that he usually bought in Mrs Shah's corner shop. A glance at the bag confirmed that. It was his *Żywiecka* sausage at £4 a kilo!

Unexpectedly, the memories started flooding back. Yesterday he was walking back home, having bought his provisions from Mrs Shah, when a white van pulled up at the crossing. The driver lowered his window and asked him something. He couldn't understand a word. Then all of a sudden the side door of the van slid open and two pairs of hands reached out and dragged him inside. It was so fast and unexpected that he didn't put up any resistance. His hands were twisted behind his back and tied up with a piece of string. His mouth was gagged. He was tossed on the floor and threatened that he would be killed if he didn't cooperate. Only then did he realize that his kidnappers were Polish. He was frightened but even more astonished. Why was he being kidnapped? He didn't have much money on him or anything that could have been of value to anyone. He was an immigrant worker who had no identity and no rights in this country. Surely, this was a mistake.

It was pitch black inside the van and he couldn't see his attackers. But from the grunting and heavy breathing (one of them had a cold), he sensed that there were only two men in the van. For most of the time, they remained silent; perhaps they didn't want to give him any clues as to where they were going.

The van took several sharp turns and the whole of its human cargo was thrown from their places. One of the men swore. Some pipes rolled noisily around the floor. Then they drove over some uneven ground and all the content of the van bounced up and down. Suddenly, they came to a standstill. The side door rattled as if someone was trying to open it from the outside. There was a loud bang, like a kick, and the door finally yielded. A gust of ice-cold wind hit him in the face. The van stopped in a field, completely deserted at this time of evening. He could see a row of houses and a line of street lights in the distance.

He was dragged out by the men who had abducted him, but now they were wearing balaclavas. Obviously they were professionals. This confirmed his belief that the whole affair was a misunderstanding.

As soon as they removed a piece of rag from his mouth, he said: '*Panowie ...*'

They roared with laughter.

'My name is Adam Bugaj. I don't know what I have done to cross you. I have no money ... I have never bought or sold drugs.'

'Adam, do you think we took you for a drug dealer?' Another explosion of laughter.

'It must be a mistake ...'

'There is no mistake,' growled the tall man. He was the only one without balaclava but he pulled his woolly hat low over his eyes and used a scarf to obscure his face.

'What have I done?'

They looked at each other. After a moment of hesitation, the tall man took on the role of communicator. 'You're stealing someone else's business.'

'I work for a Polish builder and have no company of my own,' explained Adam, as calmly as he could.

'Exactly. So you're stealing what's not yours.'

So, this was it. They represented the competition. He crossed someone who was pitching for the same weekend jobs, otherwise they would be after Karol, not him. He started racking his brains, trying to remember how he had got his kitchen jobs.

The headlights of a distant car pierced the darkness of the field.

'*Kurwa*, what's that?' swore one of the men. There was some consternation among them and the tall one spoke again.

'We don't have time for a debate here. We're to teach you a lesson so we will be quick about it. Remember, if you call the police we'll have to caution you again and you won't live to tell the tale.'

Before Adam could take in the meaning of these words the first punch landed on his face. There were several more, with all three men making their contributions. When he fell for the first time, one of the men yanked him off the ground by the collar of his anorak and pulled him up. The other one hit him again in the face and the third in his stomach. Adam buckled and cried in pain. This only enraged the attackers who intensified the beating. When he was lying on the ground they kicked him from all sides. He felt blood running down his face and an excruciating pain in his right shoulder. The last thing he remembered before he passed out was being dragged by his legs across some shrubbery and plastic bags being dumped on top of him. This must have been his shopping.

This was what the dog was now devouring … He couldn't lift himself up so he just stretched his arm out and yanked the bag from the dog to save the remaining contents. This angered the dog and he first started growling and then barking. He wasn't Adam's friend any longer and the barking became louder and fiercer.

'Jasper, come back at once,' came a woman's voice close to him. She paused and listened for a moment, perhaps surprised with the sound of rustling as the dog tried to pull the bag from Adam.

'Jasper, be a good boy. Come back.'

Suddenly Adam saw the reddened face of Jasper's owner framed by a green woolly hat looking down on him. She stared at him for a moment. Her eyes and mouth widened simultaneously and she screamed in horror.

This must have been a dream because it was summer again. He was lying in blazing sunshine on warm grass that felt like a downy mattress. He was pain free and happy. He could walk up any mountain he chose. The only unusual thing was the smell. There were no forest scents around him, no sweetness of the late summer flowers or the pungent smell of dry grass. The smell around him reminded him of an agricultural shop where the odour of fertilizers mixed with the dusty tang of seeds and pest control chemicals.

When Adam opened his eyes, reality appeared even more bizarre than his dream. In the small, cell-like room, everything was white — the walls, furniture and bedding, with the exception of mint-green curtains. The temperature of the room was tropical. Fortunately, he was lying bare chested. Only his lower body was covered by a sheet. This appeared at odds with the season as he remembered it. He glanced in the direction of the window but beyond the green curtain there was total darkness. Only when he tried to raise his head did he realize that he was seeing with only one eye, as half of his head was covered. He looked down and saw that his right arm was bandaged and resting in a sling. It was connected through a plastic tube to a bottle hanging upside down with some liquid. The monitors standing at the head of his bed were humming rhythmically.

His last experience of a hospital was ten years ago when he visited Hanka's mother who had had an operation to remove her kidney stones. He remembered it as a vast place where many people walked hastily along drafty corridors. Being incarcerated in this stuffy little room was a different experience all together. Presumably this was a consequence of being kidnapped and beaten up. What was he meant to do now? How was he going to communicate with the doctors and nurses here? His mind felt foggy and he was drifting off to sleep again when he saw the door open and a nurse with a stop-watch pinned to her chest enter the room. She was followed by Zofia, Dr Patel and Darek.

Matko Boska, what brought them here? He would have turned to the wall if he could. Instead, he was the sole focus of their attention. Four pairs of eyes were looking at him gravely as the nurse continued her explanations. Then she examined the monitors, made some notes on a pad attached to the foot of his bed and left. Darek picked up the solitary chair in the room and moved it next to the bed.

'You're on the mend, man,' he said leaning towards Adam and touching his bare arm. Seeing Adam's questioning gaze, he explained: 'They beat you up badly. Animals. The woman who found you almost fainted when she saw you.'

Adam closed his eyes. The memory of a screaming woman was lodged somewhere in his brain.

'How do you feel?' enquired Darek, patting the bandage on Adam's chest. They looked at each other in silence for a moment. 'What's wrong with me?' asked Adam, trying to hold Darek's gaze.

Darek glanced at Dr Patel and Zofia and leaning closer, whispered: 'You have a broken arm, some bleeding in your stomach and a few stitches on your face. But the doctor said that you're doing well.'

'I can't move.'

'Not yet, but you will. They are looking after you very well.

This is mainly due to Dr Patel's influence. She comes in every day.'

'How long have I been here?'

'Three days.'

'*Matko Boska*. They did a thorough job on me.'

'Do you have any idea who has done this to you?'

Adam shook his head and looked up at Zofia and Nisha Patel whispering at the foot of his bed. The young doctor took it as an invitation to talk to him. She came round to his side. Darek got up and offered her the seat.

'How are you, Adam?' she asked in that reassuring and soft voice of hers. Her eyes were like the eyes of a doe, large and dewy. He could see comfort and surprise in them now.

'Thank you, Dr Patel,' was all he was able to say.

'Don't worry about anything. Just rest and get better.'

Adam looked at Darek. 'What about work?'

'I told Karol what had happened. Dr Patel wrote you a sick note.'

Adam attempted a smile. He imagined Karol reading the sick note from Dr Patel.

'He was very understanding.'

This was a surprise. But he remembered that Karol enjoyed surprising his men.

Dr Patel asked Zofia to translate something to Adam. He saw consternation on Zofia's face. 'Dr Patel says that a police officer will visit you tomorrow. He will bring a translator with him, so don't worry.'

'Police, here?'

'Yes, it will be an investigating officer; a detective.'

Nisha Patel motioned to Zofia that she wished to say more. This time she spoke very slowly making a point.

'Adam, don't worry, he'll be on your side. You have been registered as a victim of violent crime. The police want to find out who has done this to you.' Zofia waved her hand over Adam's body covered by a white sheet.

An expression of sheer horror appeared on Adam's face. He lifted his healthy arm in Derek's direction. When his young assistant leaned over he whispered: 'Please tell her I don't want to see the police. They will take me to prison straight from here.'

Darek smiled. 'Adam they are on your side.'

Resigned, Adam closed his eyes. This was hopeless. Nisha Patel didn't know anything. Even Darek knew only half of the story and the kid had his own problems. He had no intention of dragging him into his troubled life. Shutting his eyes and falling back into the abyss seemed like the best option now.

When he woke up, his room was dark and everyone was gone. It must have been the middle of the night because the lights in the corridor were also dimmed and the whole ward was very quiet. Only the gentle beeping of one of the monitors pierced the silence.

Suddenly, he remembered what Zofia told him. He would have the police visiting him tomorrow. So he would jump out of the frying pan straight into the fire. With his left hand he pulled the covers from his lower body. He had dressings on his knees and his toes were bandaged. Resting his left arm on the metal bedside table, he attempted to lift himself up. He managed to twist his body to the side and gradually leaned forward until he sat up. Now it was only a matter of letting his legs slide off the bed to the floor and he would be ready to walk. Firmly clamping his hand on the metal table he slowly shifted his weight onto his feet. He hissed in pain and fell back. Darek hadn't mentioned what was wrong with his feet. But there must be another way. He let the bed covers fall to the floor and placed his feet on them. It was better this time but a sharp pain shot through his left knee. Inch by inch, he moved his bottom towards the foot of the bed.

When he could reach the metal frame, he pulled himself to his feet. The pain in his feet instantly returned but he remained standing, getting used to it. For the last few months, pain was his constant companion. Only the magnitude of it varied from day to day. It was no different now. Step by step, he shuffled towards the opened door. Holding himself against the door frame, he looked out. There was a pool of light coming from a room at the end of the ward but the corridor was empty.

Chapter 37

'When are we going to meet him?' asked Maja's mother when they had exhausted the usual issues which they discussed in their weekly conversations. 'He seems very nice. You look happy together in that Christmas picture.'

Her mother didn't know how long she had deliberated whether to reveal to her parents that there was someone serious in her life.

'At first, dad was uneasy about it,' continued her mother. 'A bit jealous, perhaps, realizing that it could mean a big change in your life. But he came around eventually and now the photograph is standing on the bookcase for everyone to see.'

'Luke will be happy to hear that mum.'

'And *pani* Hastings looks very … elegant and nice.'

'She is very charming. And has a great personality too. I think she likes me.'

In a long letter sent after Christmas Maja told her family about Luke and enclosed four pictures from her stay in Bath. She did it after a letter from Zosia thanking her for their Christmas presents. Her sister described how beautifully mum looked during *wigilia* in the new top which she wore with her favourite silver necklace. Piotr loved his CDs and dad his new shirt. Yet, between the lines she could read that this Christmas wasn't as carefree as before. Mum started her preparations much later than usual as she took on extra hours in the hospital. Dad was fretting about the size of the Christmas tree and whether they should visit uncle Henryk on Christmas Day as it would involve buying extra presents.

She was now able to make money transfers every month, not that her parents accepted them without protests. On the spur of the moment she wrote to them about Luke, Elizabeth and the reception she received in Bath. She wanted her parents to believe that she was happy and financially secure.

'Have I told you that dad has started working again?' said Maja's mum.

'No.'

'Father Lucjan needed someone competent to reorganize the parish accounts. Hearing that dad was out of a job, he asked me last month whether dad wouldn't mind helping.'

'And ...'

'He is now working for Father Lucjan at the presbytery three mornings a week.'

'That's fantastic, mum.'

'In fact, his mornings stretch into the afternoon as he is also reorganising some other documents. And ... they are paying him.'

'I'm so glad to hear that.'

'Not much ... But it may lead to other things as our parish might take on a new fundraising project. When he is out of the house for a few hours, he is a different man.'

Maja imagined what a relief this was for her mother. Leaving a depressed husband every morning in an empty house was a heavy burden to carry. And this was before they began to feel the full brunt of their reduced circumstances.

'Mum, I thought I might come and see you in late July or early August. It should be a quiet time in my department. Zosia and Piotr will be on holiday. Perhaps we could go somewhere together?'

'That would be wonderful *còreczko*, if you could come. Will you bring Luke?'

'Probably not, mum. He may still be in New York. He was planning to go there for three months but the project is larger than expected and he has been asked to stay longer. He was back in England for a week last month and will probably come over next month.'

'So you're not seeing much of each other now ...'

'Not much. But we make up for it when he visits London. And Elizabeth has invited me to Bath again for next weekend.'

Luke called her at least a couple of times a week. She sensed he was often tired and irritated, complaining that the company expected them to achieve too much in a short period of time. His days were packed with meetings which were followed by long evenings in the office to catch up on paperwork. He lived on take-aways. It was sustainable for a while, but in the longer term, this was wearing him out physically and emotionally. Warned by Elizabeth, she knew that Luke was much more vulnerable than anyone could suspect judging by his happy personality. How ironic it was that she, who had learnt to rely on his emotional support, needed to be strong for him.

Maja thought about her parents' relationship. It was always her father who had the last word. Only when she grew up did she become aware of her mother's role in the family and began to understand her personality. Her strength wasn't apparent in her pronouncements. It was her quiet determination to carry on as usual that made them believe that they could always rely on her. She took on so much without fuss. She was generous with her time, efforts and feelings, never complaining, or asking for appreciation. Was this a woman's role? thought Maja. A stereo-type? Would she be prepared to continue this pattern? How much sacrifice could a modern relationship take?

Sometimes she forgot how Luke made her feel. She had learnt to fight her battles alone and put up her defences when she felt vulnerable. Yet the moment she heard his voice, she was a different person. She longed to feel his arms around her, hear his voice and his laughter, which always lifted her spirits. He called her his girl, his princess, his muse and she loved it. But was it wise to become so dependent on anyone? She should remember that dependence was a dangerous thing.

Half an hour late for her lunch, she was running towards the escalator to go down to the staff canteen. Suddenly, she heard the familiar tune of Mozart's ninth symphony. It took a moment for her mind to register that it was her mobile phone ringing.

'Good afternoon, sweetheart,' came Luke's sleep laden voice. She let her lift go down empty and turned towards the emergen-cy staircase.

'Good morning, Luke. Is everything well?' she asked, trying

not to sound anxious. It was easier to hide things when they lived so far apart.

'Fine, fine. Well, I don't feel like a lark this morning but wanted to hear your voice. Are you going to visit my mother this weekend?'

'Yes, I am. I confirmed that with her yesterday. Your mother is a very generous woman, Luke.'

'She is. But let her spoil you. It will give her pleasure. You deserve it. You've been working so hard.'

'Few people work as hard as you do.'

'I have no choice. But I wish I could get more satisfaction from it. Let's hope that it's only a couple more months. I will make damn sure that this is over by the end of summer.'

'Are you OK, Luke?'

'I am. I just feel overwrought, I work too much and I don't sleep enough. I wish you were next to me ...' Maja could hear a distant ring coming through the transatlantic wire. 'I can't believe this,' Luke cried. 'It's only seven thirty in the morning and someone is already calling me. Damn, damn, damn. I will pull the phone out of the socket tonight. Sorry, darling I will call you in the evening.'

Showered and ready for bed, Maja rolled the quilt out and slid her legs underneath. The coolness of the sheets felt like a caress on her tired feet. She leaned back against the pillows and breathed in the air of early spring coming through the open window. There was no wind and the garden lay in silent still-ness. A bird gave a whiny cry in the distance. She listened for more sounds but none came. She imagined the night sky above Grodek. Remembering it being much darker than in London. The air would be much cooler too; sometimes they had snowfalls at this time of year.

She glanced at the alarm clock on her bedside. It was almost midnight and the house was silent. She reached for her laptop, which sunk deeply into the duvet. With tenderness she ran her fingertips over the black glossy cover. She got so much pleasure from using it. It was a present from Luke. An expensive present. She only found out how expensive it was when she went to an electronics store in Tottenham Court Road to buy a mouse for it. She would never have accepted from Luke a piece of jewellery or clothing as expensive as this. Yet he managed to convince her that a laptop was essential for them to stay in touch. Remembering Elizabeth's words, she relented.

During his last visit to London at the beginning of March Luke asked Maja to find out whether the Kowals were planning to install internet in the house. Zofia told her that Basia had been asking for it. Apparently everyone in her class used the internet for their homework. The line was installed a couple of weeks afterwards, with extra connections for Maja's and Kuba's bedrooms, but no contribution was accepted. Now, in the privacy of her own room she was able to 'talk' to Luke everyday.

Thursday, 20th March
To: lukeboy@aol.com
From: majaz@aol.com

Good evening Luke,
I hope that by the time you'll open this message, yesterday's problems have been resolved and that you had a good night, having unplugged and switched off all the phones.

Has spring finally arrived in New York? I hope that you had time to look around and check, even as you're are rushing from one meeting to another. I heard that Central Park is like Hyde Park, only larger. Do you go there sometimes?

I am very busy as we are now finalizing the JAL Airways Convention which will take place in the Metropole in April. Hundreds of emails ping-pong between London and Tokyo to ensure that we meet their strict requirements. Do you know that we cannot put Japanese guests in the rooms with numbers 4 and 9 as they are associated with bad luck? Also they only wish to occupy rooms with showers; taking a bath means lying in a pool of dirty water.

Tomorrow, straight after work, I will go to Paddington to take the train to Bath. I thought long and hard about a gift for your mum and decided on a box of *Ptasie Mleczko* (Polish marshmallows in chocolate) which is very popular at home and a bottle of cherry liqueur. I will write to you on Sunday night after my return.

Lots of love, hugs and kisses. M

Thursday, 20th March
To: majaz@aol.com
From: lukeboy@aol.com

Dear Girl,
I need all the love and kisses you can send me. Thinking about you makes me smile and gives me more energy than anything, even the spring sunshine.
By the way, I specially walked into Central Park today to check on spring in New York. The snowdrops are already gone but there are plenty of crocuses. The buds on the forsythia bushes are about to burst out with flowers. The grass still looks very last year's, quite different to what you can see in England. Watching a couple strolling and holding hands, I thought that this is what we should be doing instead of wasting the best of spring on different sides of the Atlantic.
I am planning to treat myself to a long lie-in on Sunday, reading and listening to music. Perhaps I will go to Central Park again to do more spying on spring. Marco is cooking Sunday lunch so that is something to look forward to (I may learn something too).
I hope that you will have a good time in Bath, let me know how you get on.
Kissing you from top to toes, with my favourite bits twice.
Yours L xxx

Sunday, 23 March
To: lukeboy@aol.com
From: majaz@aol.com

My very special Boy,
I hope that you had a really lazy Sunday and you have done everything you planned.
Your mum kept spoiling me the whole weekend. First, she let me sleep until eleven (I was embarrassed to wake up so late!). I skipped breakfast as we went for an early lunch to the Pump Room restaurant by the Roman Baths. What a beautiful place!

We had delicious food in exquisite surroundings. The day was very sunny so afterwards we went for a stroll up the high street towards the Circus and the Royal Crescent which is very popular with tourists. Victoria Park is full of daffodils now, and yes, the grass was bright green.

In the evening there was theatre and *An Ideal Husband*. Your mum said she hoped I liked Oscar Wilde and didn't mind the subject. The alternative was the *Lion King* ... The play was wonderful — funny and touching and it was brilliantly acted. We discussed it over a night-cap in your mum's beautiful lounge. Sitting there with her, I thought that when I woke up on Monday morning it would all have been just a dream.

I hope that you had an opportunity to relax and I look forward to trying Italian recipes with you.

Lots of love M

PS

Was the exquisite Japanese dressing gown waiting for me in Bath your idea? Your mum was very secretive about it. Mr Hastings please stop buying me such expensive gifts. They embarrass me. ☹

Sunday, 23 March
To: majaz@aol.com
From: lukeboy@aol.com

Dearest Girl,

I may not be expressing myself very eloquently tonight as we have just finished the second bottle of superb Chianti which Marco discovered in the local Italian store.

I didn't make it to Central Park but I had a long run this morning. Then I sorted out the photos I took since arriving in New York. I am very pleased with some of them. The night shots are particularly interesting. I am hoping to show them to you in May. While I read I was listening to Marco's selection of Neapolitan songs which he sung as he cooked — so I had to indulge him. The rest is a bit of a blur, but pleasantly out of focus.

Re: the dressing gown. Maja, it was designed for you: the cut, the colours, and the delicate patterns — the lot. I knew it the moment I saw it. I imagine you look in it like a willowy geisha, with your hair up. I need to verify that image when I get back. Will you model it for me?

Badly missing you L.

It was the third time she was retyping the programme of the JAL convention. With new instructions coming from Tokyo every day, she prepared a template to which she was adding new information as soon as she discussed it with Mary Williams, the project's coordinator. At this point, there was no point informing everyone involved about the changes. There would be plenty of new ones the next day.

The sudden ring of a phone at her elbow broke her concentration.

'Hello. Yes, it's Maja speaking,' she said with her eyes focused on the screen. 'Yes, of course. What time would you like to meet me? After lunch? Two o'clock. That will be fine. I'll come up to see you.'

Only when she replaced the receiver and took a sip of cold coffee she did realize how unusual this request was. Maureen Johnson, senior HR manager wanted to see her. The assistant who conveyed the message to Maja did not explain the reason for the meeting. Maja's eyes returned to the monitor but a twinge of anxiety settled into her thoughts. What was this about? Had she messed something up and someone complained about it? She quickly dismissed this thought. Her manager, Julia Hodgkins, known for her directness, would have told her if there was a problem.

She lost her appetite for lunch. After forcing herself to have half a bowl of broccoli soup and a few bites of an apple, she took the lift to the fourth floor. The personnel department was located in a large open-plan office which was now unusually quiet. Most of the desks were still empty.

'Can I help?' enquired a young voice. It belonged to a girl with short cropped hair and a boyish body who looked no older than fourteen.

'I have an appointment with Mrs Johnson,' said Maja trying to sound calm.

'She returned from lunch five minutes ago,' said the girl cheerfully. 'Her office is the first on the left,' she waved in the direction of a cluster of rooms located at the far end of the open plan office.

Maja knocked on the door.

'Please come in.'

A middle-aged woman in a dark grey Metropole suit sat behind a large and very tidy desk. Her handsome face was free of makeup apart from a barely visible trace of pearly lipstick. Her hair was neatly swept back showing small pearl studs in her earlobes. A pair of groomed hands rested on a file in front of her.

'Please take a seat,' she said calmly in a voice that command-ed authority. 'You probably wondered why I asked you to come here today.'

'Yes, madam.'

'I thought that it would be best if the subject of our conversa-tion remained confidential. At least for the time being. Please don't discuss the matter with anyone in or outside the hotel.'

Maja breathed in. The small office suddenly felt very stuffy. But she raised her head up and looked at Mrs Johnson to confront whatever was coming next.

'It appears that there was a breach of confidentiality in the hotel. One of our corporate clients reported that the information which he disclosed to us while doing the business here was used by third parties. Since his company has only recently been relocated, the new contact details haven't yet been distributed. This information was held on our customer database to which only staff of Customer Relations, the Reception desk, Events and Accounts have access to. Do you follow me, Maja?'

'Yes, madam.'

'This issue is being investigated at present and I wouldn't be involving you at this stage if not for the fact that in his com-plaint this client mentioned a girl with Eastern European accent who dealt with his conference room reservation.'

Maja felt frightened and angry at the same time. She worked very hard for the company and always conducted herself strictly according to the rule book. But Maureen Johnson's suggestion made her feel guilty, as if she had caught in an act of wrongdo-ing.

'We aren't making any suppositions at this stage,' said Mrs
Johnson in a conciliatory tone. 'Far from it, it's up to the
investigating officer to get to the truth. However, since you have
been indirectly identified I wanted to make you aware of this. I
thought that it would only be fair.'

'Thank you for doing this, Mrs Johnson,' said Maja, not feeling
grateful.

'I also wanted to ask you to look back and tell me if you
remember dealing with Mr Geoff Grant from MasterComp last
November. The company is based in Bristol.'

There was a long silence during which Maja searched her
memory for recollections of Mr Grant and his reservation. She
often remembered minute details of her conversations with
customers but her mind was now blank.

'Mrs Johnson, I am very sorry, I cannot recall my conversation
with Mr Grant. But I recorded all my contacts in the log book
kept by the Customer Relations desk. Perhaps I could look
through it and try to find the record of his reservation.'

'That is a good idea. I will ask Mr Williams to give you access
to the log book. Is there anything else you would like to ask me
now? I realize this conversation may have surprised and dis-
tressed you.'

She sounded so reasonable, thought Maja. She was used to
dealing with unpleasant issues in a very civilized way. But
what was a minor unpleasant incident for Mrs Johnson was a
disaster for her, putting her entire career at stake. Together
with her future in this country and everything else she was
hoping for.

'I will check the logbook and will report everything I find to
you,' said Maja calmly. She will have to defend herself and her
reputation in every way she could. 'Does it mean that someone
is passing customer contact information for commercial gain?'

'Precisely. It may have considerable implications for the hotel
and its reputation. And serious consequences for people involved in this fraud. That's why we are treating this issue with
the utmost seriousness.'

Chapter 38

Kuba, March 1999

At six thirty on Saturday morning, Kuba softly opened the kitchen door. The house was still asleep and he hoped for a quiet breakfast on his own.

'Good morning, Kuba,' said Zofia lifting the boiling kettle from its base. 'You're up early today.'

'Good morning. I'm not the only one down for an early breakfast ...'

'Jan keeps waking up at six. Even at the weekends. So I thought I would treat him to a cup of tea in bed,' she said, drawing her dressing gown around her. Her hairnet was an accessory which Kuba hadn't seen on her before.

Popping a couple of teabags into the pot, she smiled and asked: 'Would you like a cup?'

'Thank you, *pani Zosiu*. I need a coffee to kick my brain into gear this morning.'

'Are you working a lot? You look tired, Kuba.'

'I do feel tired,' he said. He felt emotionally drained. Admitting this would invite questions he wished to avoid.

He watched Zofia arrange two white and blue spotted mugs on a tray. She poured some milk into one of them and dropped a slice of lemon into the other. Then she spooned some sugar and ground it together with the lemon. No doubt, just as Jan liked it, thought Kuba. He almost smiled watching this ritual. This was love. He walked to the sink to fill the kettle again.

'Are you working all weekend?' asked Zofia, leaning against the sideboard as she waited for her tea to brew.

'I'm going to take Sunday off. I need to study, but this isn't what I call work.' He hesitated. 'I may even go to church on Sunday. On Windsor Road. I'm happy to drive you and Jan there if you would like a lift.'

'We'll be fine. Is everything OK at home, Kuba?'

Zofia was a perceptive woman and made it her business to know what was going on in her tenants' lives. Kuba smiled.

'Everything is fine, *pani Zofio*. I just need time to reflect. Prayer and reflection work in the same way.'

'When exercises with the blue band become easy, you will move to the green one. You need to feel your muscles and joints working, every day pushing yourself a bit further.'

'And if I don't?'

Was she flirting with him or just being arrogant? wondered Kuba. Cara Elliot was in her early forties and she had the confidence of a beautiful woman. The passing years must have provided her with countless reassurances of her attractiveness. Sitting on a stool at her feet, Kuba admired her large, clearly defined mouth which was pouting one moment and breaking in a dazzling smile the next.

'You told me that the doctor had given you three months of reprieve. If he is not happy with your knee by July, you will have to have a cartilage operation. It would be good to avoid it.'

'This is the plan.' She flicked back a mop of unruly hair. She was Italian with blonde hair, yet her eyebrows and eyes were dark and this contrast added to her allure. 'I will stick with the exercises but my office colleagues may find it entertaining to watch me perform them.'

'They will admire your commitment.'

'I doubt it but if I am to do them four times a day I have to do them at work.'

After a while, during which Kuba examined her knee, she asked: 'What else do you wish me to do?' Her tone was that of a sulky teenager.

'Walking up and down the stairs is the best exercise of all for this kind of injury. Especially since you had your leg in plaster for over two weeks. It's a very long time and leads to muscle wastage.'

'It's not my fault that the doctors in Interlaken packed me into plaster. I have been skiing since I was five and this is the first time I had an accident. And it wasn't my fault either.'

'The Swiss doctor was very cautious. We can see from the

x-ray that the injury was a serious one,' interrupted Karen, looking through Mrs Elliot's records. 'I could also suggest some massage to regenerate the muscle. It speeds up healing and the disappearance of bruising.'

Cara Elliot's face lit up. 'I like the sound of that. Will I be able to have it done here?'

'Yes, we have sessions during the day but on Monday, Wednesday and Friday we also have massage in the evening. I will ask the receptionist to give you the timetable.'

When the consultation was over, Kuba watched the woman zip up her ankle length boots. Only then did he notice that her clothes, from her socks to her cardigan, were colour coordinated — in various shades of grey. Finally she put on a wool coat, so soft that it instantly wrapped itself around her body, and swung a grey leather bag over her arm. A golden buckle with a Prada label gleamed just below her elbow.

'The post-skiing season has started,' said Karen, closing Cara Elliot's file. 'Next we will have riding injuries, exotic holiday accidents, with the bread and butter of sporting injuries and the usual work-related problems. It makes our work interesting.'

'Women like her keep the clinic in business.'

'With such clothes and handbags she can afford extensive physio treatment.' Catching Kuba's puzzled gaze, she asked: 'Do you know how much a bag like that costs?'

Kuba raised his eyebrows.

'A grand, at least,' said Karen, with badly disguised indignation.

'A thousand pounds?'

'For some people it's a monthly wage. But then the world has never been a fair place. Wealth is often a matter of luck. Some people earn it, others inherit or marry into it.' Karen was unusually philosophical.

'Karen, how many more patients do we have this morning?' asked Kuba hoping that he would have an opportunity to talk to her on his own.

'Three more appointments to go before we break for lunch. Then I need to dash to my old friend Ashley to massage his legs and his ego before an important performance. Why did you ask?'

'I would like to talk to you. But you're obviously busy this afternoon?'

Karen let her glossy hair down for a moment only to scoop it up again and harness into a ponytail. She was thinking aloud: 'I will be finished with Ashley by four thirty. Five at the latest. This is when he leaves for the theatre.'

Kuba looked at her open face, always ready to engage with the world around her, unpretentious hairstyle and practical clothes, and thought how lucky he was to have such a friend.

'I have an idea. Do you fancy an Italian or an Indian tonight? I could pick you up from Ashley's and we could find a place to eat in Ealing. What do you think?' he asked.

'I'm buying!' Karen's face broken in a big smile. But aren't you going to work tonight?'

'I am booked for ten. We'll have plenty of time to eat and … talk.'

'OK. Now let's see how Mrs Jones is doing. I think she's already waiting outside. She'll be pleased to see you, Kuba,' said Karen smirking.

Kuba gave her a levelled look and thought that Karen wasn't only pleased on old Mrs Jones' behalf.

They agreed that Kuba would pick Karen up at five. There was a space directly outside Ashley's house so he pulled up by the brick steps. He vividly remembered transporting Ashley up this staircase with the help of a spotty student from the basement. That was almost two years ago but it seemed like yesterday. So much had happened since then.

The afternoon was surprisingly warm for March. The sun was already half-way down the horizon suffusing the street with orange light. The tall Victorian mansions and the leafless trees acquired a rusty hue. Since he had started driving a cab he had begun to notice not only seasonal patterns but also how the light changed during the day, transforming the urban settings from just picturesque to dramatic. The scene in front of him was like an impressionist painting. The light was still hazy with soft browns and yellows but when the sun went down and the shadows lengthened, the street would appear monochromatic and even sinister.

He heard the thump of the door, and saw Karen waving to him from the landing. He watched her run down the red brick steps, graceful like a dancer. Her extensive professional experience suggested that she was about his age. Yet she had the openness and curiosity of a teenager. She was wearing a patterned skirt that flapped around her knees as she skipped down the stairs.

In a moment Karen's grin appeared in the open passenger window.

'Have you been waiting long?'

'Not at all. Jump in!'

They turned east and soon they joined the slow-moving line of traffic that was crawling in the direction of Ealing High Street. Kuba glanced at Karen who was comfortably stretched on the front passenger seat. She was relaxed and oblivious to the going-ons around them. Her weekend had just begun and she was in the mood to enjoy it.

'Perhaps you would prefer something smarter than an Indian.'

She looked at him and grinned. 'Like one of those places in the West End where a waiter spreads a linen napkin on your lap?'

'If that is what you wish.'

'They wouldn't let me in without an evening outfit and you would need to pop into your three-piece.' Seeing his puzzled look, she said: 'I mean a suit with a waistcoat.'

'I don't have one. I don't remember when I last wore a suit.'

'So an Indian it will be.'

Kuba parked the car in a side road and they walked to the high street. Star of Madras was a popular place on account of its first class Southern Indian cuisine. Its powerful and exotic aromas tempted the punters before they entered the restaurant. The food there was accessibly priced and even at this relatively early hour, many tables were occupied. It was warm inside and immediately their senses were bewildered by exotic spices blended with incense which hung heavily in the air. The restaurant had the shape of a long galley with tables standing on both sides of the central aisle. Along the walls, stood banquettes upholstered in crimson velvet. It was perhaps intended as a reminiscence of the splendours of Indian maharajas whose palaces were featured on the paintings hanging on the walls.

A waiter led them to the corner of the room. He moved the table forward so Karen could sit on the upholstered bench while Kuba was offered a seat with the back to the central aisle.

The waiter was tall and slender and wore a pair of black-rimmed glasses that gave him the appearance of an intellectual.

Karen leaned forward and whispered to Kuba: 'Don't you think he is also a student?'

Kuba nodded and smiled. Then he opened the menu and went straight to the last page. 'What would you like to drink?'

'A cold beer would be nice. Would you be OK with a bottle before starting work tonight?'

'Definitely.' He raised his hand to the waiter who silently appeared at the table. 'Two Cobras. Chilled please.'

Choosing food proved much more of a challenge. The menu of Star of Madras stretched to twelve pages. Each dish had a detailed list of ingredients and a description of the cooking method. By the time Kuba reached page four he didn't remember which dishes featured on the first two pages.

'Do you have any favourites, Karen?' he asked trying to save his face.

'Yes, I do. But I don't like food that's too spicy.'

'I'm happy to follow you,' Kuba said promptly.

'Should we choose two or three dishes and share them?'

When they were wiping the remnants of their curries with the last pieces of chapati, Karen said: 'You wanted to ask me something.'

Relaxed by the food and Karen's company, he almost forgot why he invited her out. She looked lovely in a purple top and a scarf softly knotted around her neckline. A thick chestnut fringe gave her a boyish look. She had the radiance of Audrey Hepburn. It's not going to be easy, he thought.

'Can I help you in any way?' Karen asked again.

'You have been helping me from the moment we met and I am already indebted to you.'

'We all are indebted to someone, somewhere, sometime.'

'OK, I wanted to ask you whether I could work again with you this summer. Also, are there likely to be any openings in your practice once I qualify?

'You're thinking ahead, Kuba,' she said, with some surprise in her voice. 'But that's good. We could start making plans.' She looked at him for a moment and asked: 'Is there any reason why you're so eager to map these things out?'

'I need to earn more money. Cabbing alone will not be enough. I'll have greater financial commitments.' He paused for a moment. He picked up his knife and played with it looking for words. Than he put it down and said: 'It's time I start thinking about the future and ensure that I have a steady income. I want to start planning my professional career. Here in London. To decide about the area I want to specialize in.'

'Whaaa, Kuba. I'm impressed. Two years ago you weren't sure you wanted to train at all.'

'Things have changed,' he said curtly.

Karen said nothing. For a while they sat in silence and neither of them wished to break it. Unexpectedly, Karen stretched her hand across the table and placed it on Kuba's clenched fist.

'It's good that you know what you want to do ...' she said warmly.

'No, Karen. I'm an idiot.' He pulled his hand from underneath hers.

She kept looking at him, waiting for an explanation.

'I am going to be a father in May,' he spat out. 'I need to ensure that I am able to support my child.' He could see that she was shocked.

'I had a fling with a girl last autumn. A very attractive Polish girl. And now she is pregnant.'

'Are you planning to marry her?'

'Oh God no. She doesn't expect that.' He fell silent again. He wondered how to verbalize his feelings about the whole affair without excusing himself. He wanted to be honest with Karen but also wished to keep her respect.

'I have done what I have done and now I have to pick up the pieces.'

'Will she need your financial support when she has the baby?'

'No. She runs a hairdressing and beauty salon in the centre of Opole. She doesn't want any money from me but she wants my emotional support and involvement in bringing up the child.'

'It's reasonable enough.'

'It is Karen.' He swallowed. 'But this was just sex. We weren't even dating. And ... I'm not sure that the baby is mine. She is not ... what you'd you call an ordinary ... girl.'

From a corner of his eye, he could see that the people sitting on the next table had started looking at them, obviously shocked with his outburst. But he didn't care any more. 'This is the gist of the situation.'

Karen's eyes widened and she went still, as if she was preparing herself for an even greater shock. Instantly, he felt guilty; he had no right to burden her with his problems. She sat silent for a moment. Then she reached across the table and took his hands in hers.

'If you're not even sure that the baby is yours, shouldn't you check that first?'

'That is what my friend Rafal told me to do. And I will do this. But deep down ... although I don't trust Judyta ... I think it's my baby. So I need to plan my life to accommodate it. It would be terrible if this poor kid found out one day that he was a mistake.' His voice broke. 'I couldn't forgive myself for this.'

He fell silent. Then he lifted his hands and covered his face.

His distress astonished Karen. She was searching for words that would make things better but nothing came. In front of her eyes, the calm and composed Kuba, who was always able to reassure his patients and inspired such confidence, was crushed by remorse and guilt. She knew nothing about his life in Poland and what he had just told her was a proof that this part of his life had been closed to her.

When she became her usual self again, the rational and compassionate professional, Karen gently touched his arm and said: 'I will help you. As much as I can. We will devise a plan and ensure that you can practise as soon as you finish your course. And the baby? It may turn out OK. You're not the first and you're not going to be the last man who'll have to pay for a mistake. You may not live with the mother but you will do your best by the child. I am sure of that.'

Chapter 39

Adam, March 1999

He never used to nap in the afternoon. It was a habit of lazy people who had too much time on their hands and relied on others to work for them. He slept during the day but that was only when he came back from Ondraszkowa Izba too drunk to do anything else. But even then, it wasn't napping — he just shed his clothes, fell into bed and slept through the day and night until next morning when he felt his own self again.

What he was doing now was very different. Indulgent and time wasting. And he enjoyed it. Dr Patel told him that this kind of rest was as important as any medicine. He, who always prided himself on being strong, recognized that he was in a pitiful state. His arm was no longer in a sling and his wounds were mostly healed, leaving pale scars on his forehead and his left cheek. Despite this he felt like a deflated balloon. He hadn't worked for over three weeks and although this worried him, he knew that he wasn't ready to face a ten-hour day on Karol's building site. A walk to the shop now tired him more than a day-long trek up the Tatras. Going to bed and falling asleep was a welcome escape from thinking and worrying about the future. If only they didn't bother him all the time — Dr Patel, Zofia, the police inspector and even Darek who had plenty of advice on what he should do to start feeling better soon.

He opened one eye and checked the alarm clock standing on a windowsill. It was three in the afternoon. He would have at least a couple hours of peace before everyone else returned home and started interfering again. Since he came back from the hospital, there was always someone who would knock on the door to enquire about his health. He pulled the covers up higher and turned towards the wall. Drifting off to sleep he wondered whether spring had arrived on Bukowski's meadow at the edge

ANNA RYLAND

of the forest.

Every March after a few sunny days, the field, covered with last year's wilted grass, was transformed into a spectacle. Overnight, it became a lilac carpet weaved from thousands of crocuses. They would bow their heads gracefully in the direction of the wind. The ramblers who reached the edge of the forest would stop and stare in amazement. Some would rush to the top of the hill for a better view and to immortalize the sight with their cameras.

This never ceased to amuse him and he was still smiling when he heard a tap on the door. *Cholera*, not again. He closed his eyes tightly and hoped that the caller would go away. But there was another knock.

'Adam, it's me, Kuba. If you're not asleep, I would like to speak to you. Very briefly.'

Adam didn't move but he could sense that Kuba was still standing outside the door. He was getting angry. He wasn't going to be pushed around by anyone.

'I won't be able to come back later. I have an early shift this evening. I ...'

'Wait,' Adam heard himself growl. He sat up and with some difficulty pulled on a pair of old jeans and put on a flannel shirt over a T-shirt in which he slept.'

'Come in.'

The door opened slightly and Kuba's head appeared in the gap.

'Adam, I'll only be a couple of minutes.'

'I hope so.'

Kuba closed the door and hesitantly looked around.

'Can I sit down?'

'If you need to ...' Adam pointed to a chair standing by the bed. It was piled high with his clothes. Without a word Kuba lifted the garments and placed them on the back of the chair. Sitting down he said: 'I can see you're getting better. You've started going out.'

'I cannot let Zofia feed me all the time.'

'I thought that it may help you to get stronger sooner if I showed you a few exercises.

'Exercises?' cried Adam incredulously.

'I worked as a physio. A physiotherapist in Opole. In fact I am retraining now to be able to practise here, one day.'

'Kuba, I have been out of work for three months. I have no money for therapies.'

Kuba lifted the clothes that fell on the floor from the back of the chair. He carefully folded them and placed them on the window sill.

'I am not looking for payment. We have been living in this house for over two years. We are neighbours. Friends, I would say. We should help each other.'

'I mind my own business.'

'I know you do. I have no intention to interfere in your life. I just wanted to help.'

'And how could I help you in return?' Adam snorted.

Kuba had heard the stories of how proud and stubborn the *górals* are. He should have planned this better.

'Actually, I wanted to ask you for a favour. I need a bookcase. I have many books in my room, mostly textbooks for my course, and most of them lie on the floor. Once you get better perhaps you could help me with that.'

The suggestion surprised Adam. He didn't speak for a while. With one hand he was stroking the wool blanket on his knees, smoothing out invisible creases. Then he asked: 'Do you have any wood I could use?'

'No, I don't, but I could drive to Wicks this weekend and get everything we need.'

'I have nothing better to do for another few days, until Dr Patel signs me off, so I may as well use my time.'

'Adam, you'd be doing me a great favour,' exclaimed Kuba. 'I really need somewhere to store my books and papers. I'm struggling to keep them in order.'

He looked at Adam. The man appeared reduced by the illness. His shoulders were more slouched and his movements slower since the accident. His weather beaten face was etched with lines like a shield on which his past battles had left their marks. Kuba wondered whether Adam had always chosen to battle alone.

'Could I look at your arm?' he asked gently.

Ginger licked his mouth again and with a contented purr, jumped up on the window sill. Then he turned around and gave Adam one last glance as if to say 'I will be back' and disappeared into the garden. Adam watched the cat with a smile. He knew that he couldn't wait to be let out every morning.

Forced idleness gave Adam an opportunity to witness the awakening of nature. He loved nothing more than to open the window and breathe in deeply the scent of damp earth and to listen to the dawn chorus every morning. To feel spring with every fibre of his body was better than any medicine. He didn't remember when he was last able to do this. Of course, Greenford wasn't a patch on the hills of Gubałówka and the panorama of the Tatra mountains to which he woke up at home. Yet the piece of garden which he watched through the window was beautiful in its own way.

Breathing the heavily scented air and listening to the sounds of rampant nature, he was able to dream. He leaned his head against the wall and closed his eyes. A sketch of Kuba's bookcase was lying on the bed covers, half-done, now forgotten. He abandoned it when he felt a headache coming. Since he had returned from the hospital, these headaches were almost a daily occurrence.

A knock on the door startled him. Before he had time to say anything, the face of Nisha Patel appeared in the doorway.

'Good afternoon Adam. Apologies for barging in. You must have dozed off because I knocked a few times.' She was wearing a short yellow cardigan with a white T-shirt and a pair of jeans that showed off her trim figure. She appeared relaxed and was looking at Adam with barely disguised curiosity.

'You are looking well. A bit better every time I visit you. I can see you have already taken on a project,' she said, looking at the drawing lying on Adam's cover.

Adam promptly reached for the sketch, folded it and placed under his pillow. 'Just some shelves for a friend,' he said dismissively.

'That's good.' Nisha smiled. 'It shows that you're feeling better. That fall in the hospital lift didn't help your recovery.' It was a mystery to all the medical staff why Adam wondered into another wing of the hospital and was found unconscious in the service lift. Nisha had her own views about it but wasn't prepared to share them with anyone. Perhaps one day, Adam would be ready to tell her what had happened.

'Can I have a look at you?' she asked, pointing to his chest. She indicated that she wished to examine him. Before Adam had time to protest, she took a stethoscope out of her medical bag. She gently tilted his head back and examined his forehead, paying close attention to his left temple. Then she asked him to open his shirt and listened to his lungs. Next, she instructed him to move his arm up and down, backward and forward, complimenting him on the progress he had made since the previous examination.

Adam looked very pleased with himself but had no intention of telling her that only this morning Kuba had spent half an hour with him practising a new set of exercises. Somewhere among the papers on the table were Kuba's sketches of the movements, which he was to practise three times a day.

'OK,' said Nisha putting down her stethoscope. 'I am very pleased with you. In about a week to ten days, you could go back to work. Of course, if you feel up to it. Having said that, going back to a building site may not be the best thing for you, particularly if you are expected to do a lot of heavy lifting. Do you understand what I'm saying, Adam?' she asked.

'Yes,' he said and continued looking at her. She couldn't tell whether this was his way of receiving news or a façade behind which he hid when he couldn't understand the conversation. Although he hadn't become more communicative since the day she met him, he was now more relaxed with her. She could even risk saying that he began trusting her. How could the same pair of eyes have a gaze of a child one moment and that of a shrewd fox the next? she mused.

'Would you mind if I called Zofia and asked her to assist us with translation?'

'Yes,' said Adam, nodding his head.

Nisha took this as consent. She indicated to Adam to button up his shirt and went out looking for Zofia.

When the three of them were sitting down in Adam's room, Zofia perching on the only chair in the room, Nisha spoke again and Zofia translated her words.

'I thought that perhaps instead of going back to Karol you may like to start working with us.'

'With you? We finished your kitchen.' Adam was confused.

'Not for me personally. But for the doctors in our practice. We are going to refurbish our treatment rooms and we need a good carpenter.' She stopped waiting for Zofia to translate. 'We have plans in place. Some stations and cupboards have to have very specific dimensions to accommodate medical equipment and accessories. But we are free to give this work to any contractor we choose.'

Adam held his breath. Was Dr Patel putting him in the same category as other English contractors? He even didn't speak English.

'This is a large project as our practice employs four doctors,' continued Nisha 'You may like to take on an assistant. Someone like Darek. You work well together. Don't you? And his English has improved a good deal.'

Adam's thoughts were racing. Did it mean that both of them could leave Karol for good? Have a proper business of their own? But what about access to trade shops with materials, parts, accessories? There were so many issues to consider. Questions to ask ... Questions that he could not ask Dr Patel.

'What would you say?' she asked. Zofia promptly translated her words adding; 'Wouldn't this be a fantastic opportunity for you Adam?'

'Yes. Thank you, Dr Patel. Very fantastic. If ... if I can do this. I mean manage all parts of the project. We could do a good job on planning and fitting the shelves, cupboards, desks etc. But there are such things as sourcing the materials, accessories ...' he faltered.

Nisha looked at Adam for a moment and smiled. 'Adam I have seen the quality of your work and your work ethic. I mean the way you work. And I liked what I saw. There will be a project manager responsible for the overall refurbishment of the surgery and he will take care of ordering the materials and other peripherals. You'll just let him know what you need. Of course, if you decide to take up my offer.'

Now her whole face was smiling. Her eyes were shining like a pair of black diamonds and her smile revealed a set of dazzling teeth. He didn't realize she was so beautiful. Still in shock, he didn't know what he should say now. Everything was moving too fast for him. He would like to take time to consider things properly but this young doctor, his doctor, was now staring at him, clearly expecting a response. In the past when he wasn't able to face a decision he reached for a drink. It worked wonders — the alcohol relaxed him and eased the pressure bearing on his mind and his nerves. Often, the compulsion to make a decision disappeared all together. But drink wasn't within his reach now and anyway his body was in no shape to handle it.

He knew that if he didn't respond now, Nisha Patel would offer this job to someone else, someone younger and more decisive. So he reached for her hand and kissed it the old fashioned way. This gesture surprised and embarrassed her. She blushed and quickly asked: 'Does it mean that we are in business?'

'Yes, Dr Patel. Thank you. Very much thank you. I want your job and I speak to Darek. He speak to you. After.'

'Detective Inspector Blaine? It's Dr Nisha Patel from Parkway Surgery in Greenford. I have received a message to contact you.'

There was a pause and then a young female voice explained that this wasn't a direct line to the inspector, who had just gone into a briefing and wasn't expected to be free for another hour.

She sighed heavily. She was desperate to wrap up the day and go home. It was six thirty on Wednesday evening, her most busy surgery day, which today had proved particularly difficult.

'Please ask Inspector Blaine to call me on my mobile as I will be leaving the surgery in a moment. Yes, anytime. I will be waiting.'

Before she shut the computer, she checked her electronic diary for the next day. Dealing with surprises was an integral part of her job but she liked to reduce the routine ones to a minimum. Trying to recall what had been decided at the last meeting of the mother and baby care unit, she pulled the cord to close the blinds and checked whether the window was securely shut.

She shivered walking out from the overheated building into the cold evening. The wet tarmac of the car park glistened in the light of the street lamp. Late March felt like November. When she comfortably cosseted herself in the car, protected from the all-penetrating damp and buffeting wind, she thought about Adam. Every day, he and his fellow workers waited at bus stops at dawn while the city was still asleep and late at night when many people had already reached their homes. She saw how hard he worked every weekend — after six days at the building site and yet he never complained or became impatient when things took longer than planned. That's why she wanted to give him good news on Sunday and hoped that there could be more good news in store for him.

She was tossing pieces of sliced tomato into to a bowl of salad that was to accompany a single portion of Waitrose lasagne, when her mobile phone buzzed. Picking it up from the granite top she looked at the display. An unknown number. She glanced at the kitchen clock and relaxed.

'Hello, Nisha Patel.'

'This is Detective Inspector Alan Blaine. I apologise for calling you at such a late hour but I was engaged until now. I need to ask you a few questions. Are you free to talk?'

'Yes, inspector.' Nisha lifted herself up onto the kitchen stool and with one hand caressed the black granite top which she couldn't stop admiring.

'In confidence, I can tell you that in response to the advertisement in *The Greenford Observer* calling for witnesses to the assault on Adam Bugaj we received the registration number of the van in which the kidnappers transported Mr Bugaj to the green. A local resident thought that the owner was dumping rubbish on the green. I trust that you will keep this information to yourself, Dr Patel.'

'Of course, inspector. That is excellent news.' Abandoning the preparations for her dinner, Nisha sat comfortably at the kitchen table and rested her feet on the second chair. 'How can I assist you inspector, Blaine?'

'Dr Patel, in our previous conversation you mentioned that you went to see Karol Kozak, Mr Bugaj's employer to give him the sick note for Mr Bugaj. You wished to observe his place of work and potential dangers to his condition after the accident.'

'Yes that was my intention.'

'You also mentioned that Mr Kozak surprised you with his benevolent attitude towards his employee. It was incongruent with what you have heard about him from Adam Bugaj and his assistant.'

'Yes, inspector. I also got the impression that Mr Kozak had a good knowledge of Adam's accident. I wondered where he could have obtained this information from since I asked Darek Macie-jewski not to discuss Adam's health with their employer.'

'That is interesting. We managed to establish that one of the previous owners of that van was Mr Kozak.'

Nisha got up and walked across the white and black tiled floor of the kitchen towards the fridge. This was Adam's work although the colour scheme was her and Darek's idea. The spot-lights highlighted the simplicity of the design that coordinated so well with the rest of the furniture. She poured herself a glass of white wine and listened to the detective inspector's explanation of how the police received the registration number of the white van. Adam had some luck after all.

'Would you be prepared to come down to our office and make a statement describing your meeting with Mr Kozak?'

'With pleasure, inspector,' said Nisha, savouring the tangy flavour flooding her palate. 'What time would you require my assistance?'

Chapter 40

Maja, May 1999

The door opened with a soft thud and Maja stepped out onto a shining granite platform from a rain soaked train. She shivered. The air was chilly and damp and the temperature in Bristol seemed lower by a few degrees than in London two hours earlier. It felt like March, not the middle of May. Everyone was in a great hurry and soon she was the last passenger off the London train left on the platform. Looking up at the large clock on the wall, she saw that it was only ten o'clock. Even if the journey to Filton took her an hour, she would still be early. She was afraid that if she waited a while, she might lose the resolve to do what she planned.

The terminal's high ceiling, arched doorways and stone walls gave it a resemblance to a church rather than a railway station. The aroma of coffee and fresh pastries that wafted through the open door of a cafeteria felt like an unexpected welcome. Over a cup of coffee she would be able to once again rehearse the arguments she had prepared.

The coffee was hot and surprisingly delicious but it did nothing to calm her nerves. The Danish pastry on the plate in front of her smelt of cinnamon and glistened with melted sugar but she couldn't force herself to eat it. After a moment of hesitation, she went back to the counter and asked for a paper bag. She might get hungry later.

She finished her coffee, reapplied her lipstick and assessed her appearance in her compact mirror. Her face looked very pale, framed by her newly cropped hair. Last night at the salon, her bob appeared shiny and sleek; very professional, as the stylist described it. Now it gave her face a severe expression and her eyes looked sunken and darker than usual. She tightened the belt of her mac, picked up her bag and walked out of the station. Outside there was a large parking area for taxis and beyond it on the approach to the station there were bus stops. It was still raining so she opened her umbrella and hurried out towards the information boards to check which bus headed in the direction of Filton.

Walking from one stand to another, she studied the information but could not see the name of her destination. Suddenly she stumbled and almost lost her balance. Shaken and angry with herself she looked down. A shapeless package half propped against a wall was lying on the wet tarmac. A mop of wiry brown hair stuck out from the other end of the bundle. Beside it stood a cardboard sign: Homeless and Hungry. A pair of dark eyes followed her shocked expression. Unexpectedly, a toothless grin appeared on the tramp's face and he lifted his left hand to point to the rain splashed notice. Reaching for her wallet, Maja saw the bag with the Danish pastry. She dropped a pound coin in the tin and placed the bag with the cake on the quilted cover that shone with dirt and rain. Then without a backward glance, she ran back to the station suddenly remembering that she had seen an information desk in the hall. Will every tramp be a reminder of the night of Nico's death?

Avon House was a two-storey steel and glass building on a purpose-built office estate. Their logos were displayed on a pillar at the entrance. Everything on the estate appeared brand new. Even the shrubs and trees were small and looked defenseless in the open space.

At the ground floor reception, Maja was directed to the first floor. It was almost twelve o'clock when she faced the receptionist of MasterComp. A smartly dressed girl was shielded against the intruders by a glass and wood counter on which there was an unconventional arrangement of fresh and dry flowers and a signing-in book for visitors.

'I don't have an appointment with Mr Grant but we spoke during his visit to London and he suggested I come and see him when in Bristol ...' she began a well rehearsed line.

The receptionist raised her perfectly shaped eyebrows and lifted the receiver.

From the short conversation that followed, she gathered that the man was puzzled with the unexpected visitor but he was prepared to see her before lunch.

'Can you wait until twelve thirty?'

'Yes. That would be perfect,' said Maja, trying to sound like her boss dealing with their corporate clients. 'Can I wait here?' she pointed in the direction of leather sofas. A glass coffee table, with a neatly arranged selection of magazines and newspapers, nestled between the sofas.

'Of course. He said he won't be long. Would you like a coffee?' asked the receptionist in her clipped tone. Maja saw her glancing at the wall clock and wondered whether the girl viewed her as an unexpected nuisance.

'No, thank you. I will have some water,' she said spotting a water dispenser. Trying to steady her shaking hands, she directed a trickle of water into a plastic cup. She took a copy of *The Times* and, putting one leg over the other, sunk into the padded comfort of the leather sofa. From time to time, she felt the receptionist's gaze on her but tried to appear engrossed in the paper. Too nervous to concentrate, she couldn't make sense of any of the articles she forced herself to read. She didn't hear the approaching steps.

'Miss Zalewska?' A large man in a pin-stripe suit was looking down at her with a puzzled expression. Maja was instantly on her feet, offering him her hand.

'Mr Grant, I am so grateful that you have agreed to see me on such short notice. I am on business in Bristol and wished to take this opportunity to speak to you about a matter which we briefly discussed in London. It is of great importance to me,' she prattled.

The introduction confused Geoff Grant and he was now intently looking at Maja, racking his brains for the memory of their previous encounter.

'I won't take much of your time. I imagine you must be very busy at this time of year,' she said.

'Miss Zalewska, let's go to my office,' he pointed in the direction of the corridor that led to glass-walled rooms. 'You need to remind me when we last met.'

Once in his office, they stopped at a round table in the corner which was covered with papers and document files. Geoff Grant scooped a handful and dropped them on one of the chairs. He moved out a chair for her and sat on the other side of the table.

'Mr Grant, I work at the Metropole Hotel in London, currently at the Corporate Events department. Last October, when your company made a conference room reservation I worked in Customer Relations and I took your call. You remembered my accent.'

'Your accent?'

'Yes, when you complained to the Metropole that someone passed your company's details to a third party. You suspected that they were sold for commercial gain.'

'Yes, indeed, I called the hotel about that.'

'You said that a girl with Eastern European accent dealt with your reservation in the first place ...'

Geoff Grant shifted himself uncomfortably in his seat which was too small for his bulky body. 'I don't remember saying that.'

'Are you sure Mr Grant?' She fixed an intense gaze on him.

'I ... I am,' he said while running his fingers through his hair. It was very short and thick and like a brush covered his round head. 'I couldn't have said that as I don't remember you or your accent. Even now as you're sitting in front of me, I cannot recall talking to you before.'

'You see Mr Grant, I also cannot remember talking to you but I dealt with hundreds of customers ... When I was informed about your complaint, it was implied that I could have been involved in passing this information to a third party.' She paused for a moment, weighing her next sentence. 'My whole professional career in the hotel could be undermined as a result of this allegation.'

'But surely it's a mistake. We both know this now,' he exclaimed. He rose suddenly and walked towards his desk. A bottle of water with a single glass stood next to his computer screen. He poured himself a glass and asked whether she would like a drink.

'No, thank you, Mr Grant. You confirmed to me what I believed to be the case — I haven't dealt with you before and you didn't mention me when you lodged your complaint.'

'Certainly not,' he exclaimed gulping the water. 'I hope that the hotel will investigate the issue properly but I am prepared to confirm that I have never dealt with you. Any supposition based on this fact is unfounded.'

He walked back to his desk and sitting down behind it, he asked: 'Ms Zalewska, you're a very brave young woman to come here and confront me about this. I respect this. There is clearly some terrible misunderstanding and I would like to help you extricate yourself from it. Would a written statement from me help you to clear your name?'

Maja held her breath. She hadn't expected this. 'Mr Grant. It would help a great deal,' she stuttered.

Her return journey to Temple Meads was faster and more comfortable. Geoff Grant stopped his black Mercedes directly in front of the main station entrance.

'It would be my pleasure to invite you for lunch Maja, but unfortunately I have a meeting at two at the other end of the town. We will do it when you next come to Bristol.'

'Thank you very much, Mr Grant. For everything.' She held out her hand and he squeezed it firmly. She could not call him Geoff although he asked her to address him by his name. When they completed the business in his office, he gave her his business card, saying: 'When you be looking for the next step in your career, please give me a ring. There are many opportunities in our company. Particularly for young women with your determination and intelligence.'

When she settled herself down in a half-empty carriage she leaned back in her seat and closed her eyes. Suddenly, she felt exhausted. She took a gamble and won but it still didn't feel real. She opened her bag and touched the envelope that contained Geoff Grant's note. She ran her finger along its edge to prove to herself that it existed. Then she took a sip of coffee and wrapped her fingers around the paper cup, comforting herself with its warmth. Giving in to the motion of the speeding train, she felt heavy and sleepy. The emotions which had kept her going since the morning were slowly ebbing away. She thought about her mum and dad, and of Luke, whom she kept ignorant of the problems she faced. This was a battle which she had to conduct alone. She lifted her hand to wipe away a single tear that was running down her cheek but it was too late. It rolled down into the corner of her lips and a second later she felt its salty taste in her mouth.

'Maja, how far are you going to drag me before you'll tell me what's happened?' Amy was gasping for breath trying to catch up with Maja who was marching ahead. It was the end of a busy day and that afternoon in the city felt unusually warm and sticky.

'Just round the corner there is a little café. It's usually quiet at this time of day.'

'Could we just stop here?' Amy pointed to the pub on the opposite side of the street.

'No. We're likely to meet someone from the hotel there.'

'OK, I can see it's a big deal.'

'It is. At least for me.' Maja stopped for a moment and gave Amy a reproachful look. Then she hooked her friend's hand on her arm and continued to stride ahead.

When they placed themselves in a far corner of the café, which was indeed surprisingly quiet, Maja recounted in a lowered voice her meeting with Geoff Grant. Then she told her about her conversation with Maureen Johnson in Personnel.

'So she didn't like that you went to Bristol to clarify things with Geoff Grant?'

'Not at all. She said I went beyond what was expected of me in this case and approached a hotel customer in a private capacity.'

'You're trying to save your skin. You had the right to do this.'

'Exactly. But I interfered in the hotel's relations with a client.'

'Stupid cow,' Amy said loyally. 'But what did she say when you proved to her that you never dealt with MasterComp?'

'This is where things became less clear. Sarah Johnson said that it was Reception who took the call from Mr Grant and reported that he spoke to someone with an Eastern European accent.'

'Reception?'

'Exactly.'

'I smell a rat here.'

I have my own suspicions.'

'Do you think it was Jess who fabricated this story?'

'Possibly.' Maja took a long sip of her drink and looked intently at Amy.

'Well, she was not a fan of yours when you started at the Customer Relations desk.'

'I know. But I did everything to keep out of her way. I don't think I ever upset her.'

'Oh yes, you did.'

'How?' asked Maja with incredulity.

'You progressed too fast. You're pretty and clever and many people like you. How many people like Jess? Apart from the management. The girls in Reception only pretend to be friendly with her because they fear her. She could be mean and vindictive.'

'I guess.'

Having finished her wine spritzer, Amy waved to the waiter. 'I am parched,' she explained to Maja. After ordering a couple more drinks for both of them, she leaned forward and pointing her straw at Maja she asked: 'Have you noticed that she always knows everyone's business?'

'Well ... she is ...'

'I heard that she asks people to tell her things about others. I would be willing to bet that she has her own little spy ring. And yet nobody knows anything about her.'

'It's true,' agreed Maja thinking that Amy was more perceptive then her.

'She comes from Yorkshire and goes back home from time to time. That's it. No one knows how she spends her free time in London. And I have never heard a man's name mentioned in connection with her.'

'Perhaps she is a lesbian?'

'Oh, yes, and I am a rabbi. I have seen how she interacts with male customers, particularly the good looking ones.'

'She was very keen to help Luke when I saw him for the first time in the Metropole.'

'You see ... I wonder whether there is something there and she keeps it very close to her chest. Of course, we have no proof that it was Jess who tried to get you into trouble, but my gut feeling tells me it was her.'

Should she admit that her intuition was telling her the same thing? mused Maja.

'Do you know what, Maja? I'm going to make it my business to start a small investigation into Jessica's past. She has been working in the Metropole for over ten years. There must be people around who knew her a few years back.'

'Amy, for God's sake, don't get me into trouble,' protested Maja. 'They could sack both of us. You said the woman is vindictive.'

'But you cannot let her walk all over you; you have too much at stake,' protested Amy. 'Show her you have guts too. You've managed to impress Geoff Grant, haven't you?' said Amy smiling. 'Leave this with me. I have some friends in the hotel too.' Seeing Maja's alarmed expression, she added: 'We won't get into trouble. I will only make some discreet enquiries.'

Maja looked at Amy. Her porcelain doll-like cheeks, framed by unruly curls, gave her a look of a gypsy. Many times she witnessed her friend's passionate nature, and her quick temper which got her into trouble. But there was no guile in her. People instantly knew whether she loved or loathed them. She was also fiercely loyal and protective of the people she cared about and Maja felt very lucky to be her friend. She leaned over towards Amy and put her arms around her almost knocking a drink out of her hand.

Surprised and embarrassed by this sudden outburst of emotion, Amy said: 'Who's causing trouble now?'

Chapter 41

The text came in the middle of the night. Kuba heard its distinctive ping, but having gone to bed after one, couldn't summon the energy to check who could be bothered to text him so late.

In the morning while showering, he reminded himself about the message. It was half past ten by the time he read it. 'Call me as soon as you get this,' commanded Rafal at 2am. He must have sent it the moment he stepped out of the club. Now he would be sleeping off the long night, having switched off his mobile. Rafal was rarely up before 1pm so Kuba decided to call him just before lunch. It meant that he would have the morning for revising for the end of year exams. He towel-dried his hair rubbing it vigorously until it stood on end. He looked ridiculous and he smiled to himself in the mirror amused with his appearance. Then he walked to the window and pushed it open.

Outside there was a perfect spring day. Feathery clouds were sailing across the blue sky, propelled by a gentle breeze. The cool morning air, heavily scented with spring vegetation, was drifting into the room. He wished he could take a day off and drive to the country or perhaps head southwards to the seaside. The water would still be icy but he would brave it and have a swim. First contact with the cold water would take his breath away, but after a minute or two, the blood rushing in his veins would make him feel warm and truly alive. He missed this sensation. Feeling the fresh air on his face and the naked body, he imagined that the sky was the sea and the clouds were the foaming breakers which he would push away with his arms.

Suddenly, he realised that the noise he was hearing in the background was his mobile phone. As he moved towards his bedside table, the ringing suddenly stopped. The display showed that he had missed four calls — all from Rafal. He snatched the phone with a sudden premonition.

'Kuba, for fuck's sake, where have you been?' Rafal wasn't in the mood for niceties.

'I didn't think you would be up yet.'

'I hardly slept waiting for your call.'

'What's going on?' asked Kuba, trying to keep his voice calm.

'Judyta is in hospital. I thought you should know.'

'Has she delivered the baby?'

'She's had an accident.'

'What's happened?' Kuba heard a hysterical note creeping into his voice.

'No one knows exactly. Lucyna who works with her said that she had an argument with her current boyfriend, the bloke she lives with. Apparently, she ran out of the house and into her car, and as she was pulling out, she collided with a van coming from the opposite direction.'

'Oh, God. Is she badly hurt?'

'She was unconscious.'

'What about the baby?'

'I don't know, Kuba. I thought that you should know what's happened to her. Just in case.'

'Just in case what?' Kuba yelled into the receiver. There was silence. A long silence. Kuba almost heard Rafal collecting his thoughts. 'Sorry, mate. I didn't mean to shout,' he said softly. Then he made an instant decision. 'Could I stay with you if I came to Opole?'

'Of course ...' Rafal sounded surprised. 'When were you thinking of coming?'

'I don't know yet. Soon. I will call you when I book the flight.'

Wearing a green hospital gown and plastic protectors over his shoes, Kuba was pacing up and down the hospital corridor. The intensive care unit was situated in the new part of the hospital. In this ward there were no smells of food which usually lingered in hospital corridors long after meal times. Only a pungent odour of disinfectant and drugs hung in the air and it stuck to all surfaces and clothing. There were no signs of the domesticity that makes hospital life bearable. This ward was strictly about saving lives and no other business had any right to interfere with it.

Having crossed the corridor from one end to the other more than twenty times, Kuba had memorised the colour schemes of the five modern prints hanging on the walls but wasn't able to describe what they depicted. He couldn't think about anything else except Judyta and the baby. He had to see her as soon as possible and find out what had happened. There were long benches standing along the walls on which people sat still, waiting for news about their loved ones. A middle-aged man made room for him, motioning him to sit down. Kuba thanked him but kept walking, unable to remain still even for a moment.

He was exhausted, having got up at 3am to catch an early flight from Luton. After enduring a two and half hour Ryanair flight, he had travelled on a crowded coach from Katowice to Opole. It didn't get easier once he arrived in Opole General Hospital. He had spent the last thirty minutes arguing with the ward receptionist, who refused to accept that he was Judyta's boyfriend and the father of her child. There was already another man who had made the same claims. Now Kuba was at the end of his tether.

He was staring at the receptionist, her plump face, neatly swept hair under a starched bonnet, nylon uniform straining over her large bosom and protruding lips repeating the same firm refusals. He thought that in a moment, he would lift her by her arms and hurl her against the wall decorated with a poster advertising the beauty of Andalusia. He was leaning over her desk, feeling her breath on his face when suddenly he heard a voice behind him.

'Maybe I can help?' The question came from a girl no older than nineteen dressed in a white coat. Her child-like face, framed by dark hair parted in the middle, contrasted with the calm and authoritative manner in which she spoke. The arms of a stethoscope were clasped around her neck and a couple of pens were clipped onto the breast pocket of her white coat. Her name badge suggested that she was Dr Anna Bajor doing the rounds on the ward.

'You wish to visit Ms Judyta Marzec, don't you? And you're her boyfriend?'

Kuba nodded.

'I'll see whether she is well enough to see you. Please take a seat,' she said, pointing to the bench by the wall. This was more of an instruction than a request and Kuba obediently sat down. 'I won't be long.'

True to her word, she was back in a couple of minutes, and now Kuba was following her down the corridor, having promised that he wouldn't stay longer than ten minutes. Looking at the back of the young doctor's shiny hair neatly gathered in a tight knot, he thought about how much he was dreading meeting Judyta. He had to be here to find what'd happened. He was a coward but even cowards have to be able to live with themselves.

The doctor softly opened the door and pointed to the bed directly in front of them. He hardly recognised her. Judyta's face, white like a sheet, was barely distinguishable from the pillow on which she was laying. Even her lips were totally drained of colour. Her raven black hair, scattered on the pillow, looked like it belonged to someone else. She opened her eyes and her gaze met his. He felt a sudden jolt in his stomach — there was so much anguish in her eyes.

'Kuba,' she cried and lifted one arm towards him, but it fell limply back on the covers. He crossed the room in one leap. Sitting gingerly down on the side of her bed he looked at the doctor. He asked whether he could help Judyta sit up. When the doctor nodded, he took her gently in his arms. She clung to him and he held her more tenderly than ever before, even at the zenith of their passion. Now their embrace was full of pain and desperation.

Cradling herself in his arms, she sobbed: 'I screwed everything, Kuba. Everything.' She wiped her streaming eyes with the sleeve of her nightdress and looked up at him. 'I haven't done enough to keep you and now I killed our baby,' she shrieked hysterically.

Only then did he realise that as she clung to him, there was nothing between them. She was no longer pregnant. A shiver ran down his spine. Suddenly, everything around them stopped. His hands continued to caress her back but this was the gesture of a robot. He heard Judyta's desperate sobs and saw that the

front of his hospital gown was soaked with her tears, but all this
was happening in a different reality in which he wasn't present.

'Kuba, you didn't believe he was your son, did you?' he heard
Judyta asking. He looked down and met her reddened eyes. He
wished he could deny her accusation or say something to console her but he couldn't find the words to do this. So he just held
her closer and allowed her to cry out her pain.

'He was yours. Our son. He was the best thing I could wish for.
So perfect. They showed him to me when they took him out and
he was there, as though he was asleep. So beautiful. He had
dark hair but he had your mouth.'

How was he supposed to respond to this? On many occasions
he had seen parents cooing over their babies but what could he
say if he hadn't even seen his son. He didn't want to be the
father of Judyta's baby and didn't share her joy over the pregnancy. He would have to live with his guilt. Caressing her hair,
he asked her: 'What would you like me to do now?'

Still sobbing, she didn't hear his question. Lowering his lips
to her ear, he asked softly: 'Judyta, is there anything I can do
for you?'

She stopped crying for a moment and looked up at him, as if
waking from a dream. 'Could you go to his funeral?' she asked.
'It's on Friday and only my mother will be there.'

'Of course I will ...' he said, trying to steady his voice. He
hadn't expected that. She always managed to surprise him and
yet he was furious with himself for being shocked at her request. It was a perfectly natural thing to ask for.

'I will talk to your mother and I will do everything to make it
special ... for him.'

The chapel was dark and Kuba shivered as he entered it.
Outside there was a glorious spring day. A gentle breeze caressed and swayed the long braids of the weeping willow growing by the entrance. Red tulips were reaching to the sun and
white lilac bushes were spreading their sweetness. This was a
day on which to be born, not buried. A small coffin bearing two
wreaths of white flowers looked very lonely standing on a tall
catafalque. On both sides it was guarded by half used candles,
no doubt, lit many times before to send off other departed souls.

A strong smell of incense hung in the air and Kuba, who always found it nauseating, felt it was particularly oppressive.

Judyta's mother, a thin woman dressed in black, was sitting upright in the second pew. She bore no resemblance to her beautiful daughter. When Kuba took his place next to her, she acknowledged his presence without uttering a word and she remained silent throughout the whole ceremony.

The service was short and impersonal although the priest tried to say all the right things for such an occasion. He reflected on the human mind's inability to understand God's intentions when cutting short young lives. He reminded the congregation about the innocents' role in the redemption of the world's sins. Everyone had a path to follow on earth. From time to time, the organ broke the silence but the sombre tunes did nothing to console the mourners.

Besides Kuba and Judyta's mother, there were only two other people in the chapel. An old couple sat at the back throughout the service and remained in their seats after the coffin was carried away. Kuba concluded that they had come too early for the next funeral.

When the service was over and a solitary pallbearer carried the small coffin out, Judyta's mother accepted Kuba's arm and allowed him to lead her out of the church. They walked together behind the priest as he followed the slowly advancing car with the coffin. Looking at the small white box rocking in the back of a shiny black limousine, Kuba thought how unnatural and wrong the occasion was.

The small procession moved silently through the shady lanes of the old part of the cemetery lined with ancient tombstones. Many of them had an air of neglect and were covered with lichen. Limbless angels and weeping virgins, that had been erected to express the anguish of grieving families, outlived them and their pain. Kuba looked at the medallions with photographs of the deceased, some clouded beyond recognition by the passing years, and contemplated the fragility of human life that rarely went beyond the memory of two generations.

In one of the lanes, there were several gravestones of children, some decorated with photographs: girls with bows in their hair and boys in sailor suits. They had all died around the same time, in 1909 or 1910. They must have been the victims of some contagious disease, he concluded. How many grieving parents were in the town at the same time?

Finally, they reached the new part of the cemetery located in an elevated field where a grave had been prepared for his son. This must have been reclaimed agricultural land which was now overgrown with grass. Above them in the crystal blue sky a lark was singing. All around them, the grass was undulating like a sea, lush and green, specked with wild flowers.

After a short ritual at the graveside and a prayer that they said together, the coffin was lowered into the pit. In no time, it was covered with soil and two wreaths were placed on the little mount. The last thing the diggers did was to attach a metal shield to the wooden cross which they hammered firmly into the ground. The inscription in black lettering said: Wiktor Marzec, born on 19 May 1999, died on 19 May 1999. *May his soul rest in peace.*

So Judyta had called their son Wiktor ... A strong and beautiful name for a special son. He would have been special but he didn't live to see the end of the same day. This thought choked him. He put his hand over his mouth but a sound like a whine tore itself from his chest and he started sobbing.

He cried for his unborn son, for the life he had never had. He wept with bitterness for the mistake he had made in getting involved with Judyta whom he couldn't love and yet they had created a life together. He sobbed because he knew that this guilt would stay with him forever. He had betrayed his child before he was born and would never have an opportunity to redeem himself. He wept for lost innocence — his son's and his own.

Chapter 42

Maja, July 1999

Maja woke up with a start. It was still the middle of the night, and in the stillness around her the only sound she could hear was the thumping of her heart. She was barely able to breathe. Her nightdress was damp from perspiration. Through a gap in the curtain of her room at Cukoohill Road she could see the familiar shape of the old elm in the garden. A night bird gave a piercing cry in the darkness.

She had another nightmare. They were occurring with disconcerting regularity. This time she dreamed that she was running through a series of rooms desperately looking for a way out of an empty house. She was followed by some malevolent presence which she couldn't identify. She reached the last room and she could not escape any further. Standing with her back to the wall, she was waiting for her pursuer to emerge from semi-darkness and advance on her, when she woke up.

These dreams filled her with dread of an impending disaster. She feared that something terrible was about to happen at home and she started calling her mother twice a week, scrupulously interrogating her about every aspect of their lives.

Luke was another source of her worry. He was still working in New York and after the initial spell of irritation with his job he appeared to experience a period of apathy. He clearly didn't care any more about the success of their mission in the Big Apple. He lived for weekends when he could leave the city and for telephone calls to her. She suspected that his depressive moods had returned but was unable to do anything except to urge him to return at the first opportunity.

After a coffee break, she was retouching her make up in the bathroom, trying to disguise the shadows under her eyes, when

she remembered that she had to speak to Amy. She hadn't seen
her at the front desk for a couple of days and assumed that she
must have been working on the afternoon rota. The moment she
sat down at her desk, the phone rang.

'Long time, no see.'

'Amy, you're telepathic. I was about to call you. We must meet
for a chat.'

'Of course. Anytime, but you'll have to come and see me.'

'At the desk?'

'No, silly. Stanmore, my home.'

'Why Amy? I have never been to your house. Surely we could
meet at some place closer to the hotel.'

'Not for a while.'

Maja held her breath.

'I got knocked off my bike at the weekend. My arm is in plaster
and I have a couple of broken ribs.'

'Oh God, Amy. How did it happen?'

'A hit and run accident. He, because it was a he, didn't even
have the decency to stop and check whether I was still breathing. Anyway, will you come and see me?'

'Of course. Can I visit you today?'

The street on which Amy lived was a perfect example of North
London affluent suburbia. All the houses on Grove End Avenue
were double fronted, half-timbered in a mock-Tudor style and
with gabled roofs. Some were covered with wisteria or rambling
roses that were just breaking into bloom. Many had spacious
front gardens partially converted into parking areas for large
family cars.

There was a basket-ball net above the garage door at
number 48. A couple of children were shrieking trying to put a
ball into the net. When Maja opened the metal gate, a girl of
about twelve stopped the game and skipped towards her. A wide
grin lit up her freckled face framed by a thick mane of rich
copper curls.

'Are you Maja?' she asked eagerly.

'Yes, that's me,' Maja smiled back.

'I'll take you to her. I'm Sara, by the way. I love your haircut.
It looks really cool,' she said, scrutinising Maja appreciatively.

'Maja, I'm glad you're here. Amy cannot wait,' exclaimed a well proportioned woman with Sara's hair colour appearing under the entrance porch. 'Amy has told us so much about you.'

'Only good things, I hope, Mrs Cohen.' Before she had time to offer her hand, Amy's mother was already pressing her to her considerable bosom.

Continuously chatting, she led Maja into the house. They crossed a large, wood-panelled hall and climbed a carpeted staircase to the first floor. Entering first Amy's bedroom, she shouted: 'Maja is here. Stay calm.'

Amy was floating in blue and white bed linen on a double bed standing in the middle of a spacious room. She lifted herself up to greet Maja only to fall back on the pillows with a hiss of pain.

'Amy, don't move,' said her mother. 'It's going to hurt more.'

Maja crossed the room and carefully sat on the bed beside Amy. Leaning in to kiss her cheek, she whispered: 'How did you get yourself into such trouble?'

'Trouble is my first name.'

'Amy ...'

'I have plenty of news for you,' she mouthed in Maya's direction. Then, turning to her mother, she said: 'Mum, I am starving. Can we have our dinner now?'

Surprised, Maja glanced from Amy to Mrs Cohen.

'Amy asked to prepare trays for both of you. So if you don't mind, Maja, I will bring your dinner here so you can talk in peace.'

'You won't get hungry in this house,' said Amy when the door closed behind her mother. 'Even on my sickbed, I have no chance of losing weight.'

'You should get better first.'

'The arm is OK, but my ribs hurt every time I move. It's surprising I haven't lost my appetite.'

'Haven't they caught the driver who hit you?' asked Maja, trying to change the subject.

'No, he just sped away but I probably scarred him for life. I catapulted into the bushes and that saved me. He didn't even stop to check whether I was still alive. But it was my fault.'

'Why?' exclaimed Maja with outrage.

'I turned right without indicating.'

'Oh, Amy.' Maja patted her friend on the forearm on which scratches and scabs had created an abstract pattern.

'Never mind, Maja. I'm enjoying being pampered. At last I have time for serious reading. I am also catching up on the old films I've missed at the cinema.'

For the first time, Maja looked around Amy's large bedroom. On the opposite wall to the double bed, there was a TV set surrounded by hi-fi equipment. A modern desk, covered with papers and a variety of trinkets, was positioned by the window. The door in the corner led to an en-suite bathroom. She imagined that in her room Amy was able to lead an independent life from her family.

In the far end of the bedroom by the second window, Maja noticed what Amy often described as 'her corner'. Below a brass lamp with an enormous glass lampshade there was a battered leather armchair partially covered with a shaggy throw. She remembered Amy saying that the chair belonged to her great grandfather who brought it to Britain from some corner of provincial Russia. Next to the chair, there was a round coffee table covered with books, papers and CDs.

'I love your kingdom, Amy. It's so cosy.'

'My mother refuses to dust here. She said there is too much clutter. But if you had four siblings, Maja, you would need a place to escape to. Pull the smaller chair to the bed and make yourself comfortable. I have lots to tell you.' Then looking meaningfully at Maja she said: 'Before I took to the road on my bike that fatal Saturday, I spoke to James about our friend Jess.'

'Amy, I thought about that. I don't want you to get into trouble over this.'

'Too late. I have already gathered the necessary intelligence. Mind you, it cost me three rounds at the Queen's Head. James' memory was getting sharper as he was refreshing his throat.'

'And what did he say?' Maja couldn't resist asking.

'About eight years ago, he was working in Concierge at the time, he thinks that Jess, who was then a junior receptionist, had an affair with Jose, the banqueting manager.'

'An affair?'

'Yes. Jose had a family in Barcelona. A wife and kids whom he visited during the holidays.'

'How does James knows that?'

'Many people knew about the affair. That sort of gossip spreads like a wildfire in the hotel. But there's more ...' Amy paused for a dramatic effect. 'James said that he thinks that she had Jose's child.'

'Why did he say that?'

'She had been transferred for a placement to a hotel in the north, for a year. And Jose returned to Spain to his wife and kids. As you know, even now, relationships between hotel staff are discouraged. Jess must have been about twenty five and desperate to develop her career in the hotel. James said that she did what all unmarried mothers have always done — disappeared to have a baby and either have it adopted or left it with the family.'

'Is there any proof that she has done that?' Maja whispered.

'Not yet. But I'm sure that a bit of digging around will give us some answers. My sixth sense tells me that we are on the right track. Have you noticed she never talks about her family? No one knows anything about her background apart from the fact that she comes from Yorkshire and she goes there to visit her family.'

They heard creaking on the staircase and a moment later, there was a knock on the door. Amy put her finger to her lips and winked at Maja.

'Dinner is being served,' announced Sara opening the door for her mother. Mrs Cohen was carrying a tray with two steaming plates and a couple of glasses containing a golden liquid. She placed the tray on a trolley with wheels, which she gently pushed towards Amy's bed.

'Sara, dear, please clear that coffee table and fetch it over here. Maja will put her tray on it.' Before Amy had time to protest, Sara was sweeping handfuls of books and discs from Amy's reading table and dropping them onto the floor. When she accomplished her task, she lifted the table and placed it in front of Maja. She took a serviette from her mother's shoulder and spread it with a flourish on the table.

The lamb casserole with young vegetables was delicious. Wiping the remains of the sauce with the last piece of potato, Maja thought that it would indeed be difficult to diet in Mrs Cohen's home.

When they satisfied their appetites and Maja returned from the kitchen with more juice, she found Amy regally supported on several pillows. She patted the covers and invited Maja to sit next to her. Lowering her voice, she said: 'I have a feeling that we are onto something and I cannot wait to find out more.'

'How are we going to do that?' asked Maja anxiously, forgetting that she planned to persuade her friend to abandon the idea.

'I thought that the simplest approach would be to follow her.'

'Follow her? You're mad Amy? I have no intention of spying on her.'

'I don't suggest that either of us do it. She could recognize us.'

'And get us sacked.'

'I know some people who would find such an assignment fun and a challenge,' continued Amy, unperturbed. 'With an overnight in Yorkshire thrown in ... it's a better deal than a day selling burgers in McDonalds.'

'Amy, we will be breaking the law doing this. And if anyone finds out ...'

'We won't be so amateurish as to risk being found out. Anyway, this is done on a daily basis in every corner of the world. How do you think the press gets their exclusives?'

Chapter 43

Adam, July 1999

They marched side by side like soldiers. Shoulder to shoulder they walked through the glass door and along the corridor towards the high counter of the surgery's reception. They were to meet Dr Nisha Patel at twelve thirty. It was only quarter past twelve but the waiting room was already empty. The surgery was closed to the general public on Saturday apart from emergency cases and Dr Patel asked them to come to make an initial assessment of what work needed to be done. She expected them to tell her how they wished to proceed.

A black girl was sitting at the reception desk. Her highly piled hairdo was bobbing backward and forward as she moved her arms to reach for documents spread out on the desk. For a moment, her large eyes rested on Adam. 'Please sit down. Dr Patel is still with her patient. She won't be long.'

They turned around simultaneously and crossed the empty waiting room towards a row of plastic chairs standing by the wall. Old magazines were piled high on a coffee table that had clearly seen better days. In the corner, there was a children's play area with a couple of fatigued tables and half a dozen chairs battered by the energetic hands of young patients.

Adam saw Darek looking around and knew what he was thinking. There was much scope for improvement in this place.

'Tea or coffee?' The receptionist was standing in the middle of the waiting room, observing them with curiosity. They looked at each other surprised and then they returned their gaze to the girl. Her long ebony legs were barely covered by a miniskirt that tightly hugged her hips. A green lacy top stretched over her pert breasts. Adam noticed that her appearance wasn't wasted on Darek who grinned widely.

'Perhaps you would prefer a cold drink?' asked the girl, puzzled by their lack of response.

'Coffee with milk would be nice.' Darek soon found his voice.

'Of course. Sugar?'

'Three spoons,' said Darek, looking for confirmation at Adam, who just nodded.

'OK, three spoons it will be,' said the girl, raising her eyebrows. She spun on her heels and was gone, leaving a whiff of sweet scent in the air.

'I saw the way you looked at her when she turned around,' said Adam reproachfully, 'You're almost a married man.'

'True. But I'm not a monk either.'

At this moment Dr Patel walked into the reception area. She glanced at the papers on the desk and picked up a file.

'Dr Patel, would you care for a cup of coffee?' asked the receptionist. I am boiling the kettle.'

'I would love a cup. Milk no sugar.'

Seeing three mugs lined up on the counter, she said. 'Thank you very much, Serena, for taking care of my guests. They will be working here so I'd better introduce everyone.'

They drank their coffees sitting companionably in the waiting area while Dr Patel gave them what she described as a background briefing — about the surgery, its patients and their needs. Darek appeared to understand almost everything she said and translated Nisha's words to Adam. Serena added amusing observations about the work of the surgery. Adam wondered whether this was for Darek's benefit as the boy laughed appreciatively, eager to hear more. He took a notebook from his pocket and scribbled down some ideas which suddenly came to his head. When he lifted his eyes, he saw that the rest of the party was laughing at some remark of Serena's. He had no idea what this was all about but he smiled. Clearly they were welcome here.

Karol flung his mug down with such force that half of his coffee slopped out. Darek watched a milky brown stain appear on the freshly erected conservatory wall they were constructing for a famous TV presenter.

'So you want to leave me?!' Karol roared, his face turning crimson. Adam thought he could smell alcohol on his boss' breath.

'Not now, Karol. In two weeks. That will give you time to find replacements for us,' said Adam calmly.

'You think I will find a good carpenter just like that?' he flicked his fingers, waving his arm expansively.

'That's the first time you told me I'm a good carpenter,' remarked Adam, suppressing a smile.

'Don't push your luck. If not for me, you wouldn't be working in London. Even after you injured yourself, I kept a place for you on my team. For a whole month.'

I injured myself? A sudden rush of anger flashed through Adam's mind. What was he playing at? Everyone knows what happened to me. Instead he said: 'I was and am still grateful that you took me on. I've worked very hard for you. So did Darek. We often worked well after six. Now we wanted to play fair with you and tell you in advance that we wish to leave.' Adam looked at Darek who stood beside him and let him do the talking, as they agreed.

'Now you'll be using the skills you learnt here working for the competition. That's how you're paying me back?' Karol sneered.

Adam shot Darek a warning glance. It would be foolish to let Karol know their plans.

'We aren't going to work on a building site any more. We will be installing kitchens, for private clients. We could stay a few days longer, if you needed us.'

'Don't flatter yourselves. You're not indispensable.'

Adam sensed that Darek was about to open his mouth and say something to Karol that they would both regret. So, stepping forward, he said: 'We know our place, Karol. We want to help if we can. Would you like us to continue for another two weeks?'

'Do I have a choice? With two weeks left to finish this project,' he said resentfully. 'Go back to your work and I'll let you know by the end of the week how long I need you. And if I find out that you're encouraging others to follow you ...'

'Yes, Karol? Then what?' hissed Darek. Adam jerked the sleeve of Darek's shirt. 'We wouldn't do that. Also, there are no more openings where we're going.' Prodding Darek's back with his thumb, he said: 'Let's go. There is plenty to do here.'

That was the last week they spent in Karol's employment. On Friday morning he told Adam and Darek that he wouldn't need them on Monday.

Karol, in a remarkably good mood, met Adam and Darek early on Friday to tell them that they should collect their wages at the end of the day. He didn't need them anymore. He had found a man to replace Adam and there were plenty of all-rounders like Darek. He picked up a couple of guys and was planning to give them a chance to prove themselves.

'I already feel sorry for them. I won't miss him,' whispered Darek when they were packing up their tools.

'He made it clear that he won't miss us,' said Adam, shutting his tool box. So this was the end of a chapter in his life. A turbulent one, full of unexpected twists and turns which he wouldn't forget. Despite this, it brought him closer to his goal. Deep down, he knew that it was a price worth paying. Now they were embarking on a path that would be straighter and hopefully easier. He hadn't left Kościelisko in vain.

They planned to sleep in next Saturday morning. After weeks of a punishing routine, their aching bodies demanded some rest. At two in the afternoon, they were to have their first meeting with the project manager at Parkway Surgery but until then, the day was theirs. Adam thought that he might go shopping and perhaps buy something nice for dinner. He would invite Darek so they could celebrate a new stage in their lives. This thought came to him unexpectedly and he surprised himself with the idea. He had never cooked for anyone in London. The range of dishes he could rustle up wasn't wide, but he could prepare a hearty *bigos* and an acceptable *golonka*. A spicy sausage stew could be just the thing to enjoy together at the end of the day. They would wash it down with a beer or two.

However, on Saturday Adam woke up before six, as usual. He tossed and turned and pulled the cover right over his head to block out the light. But the lack of oxygen only made him feel dizzy. He reached for his jacket and pulled out a notebook and pencil. He had plenty of ideas for the Parkway Surgery. He wanted to impress both the project manager and Dr Patel who had put her trust in him and Darek.

In addition to storage solutions, they would suggest a few decorative changes to make the treatment rooms look smarter and to give each of them a unique identity reflecting their function. In his mind's eye, he could already see these transformations. Dr Patel gave them the freedom to develop the best solutions for the surgery's needs and to be creative with their executions. This pleased Adam more than anything else. On very few occasions in his working life did he have an opportunity to use his creativity. Usually, he followed someone else's ideas and orders. So he was now covering page after page with drawings, comments and reminders to himself to check one thing or another. Darek had a keen eye for design so he would discuss the colour schemes with him. They would need to spend some time in kitchen and bathroom showrooms to see how various finishes worked together. They would also have to discuss how they would divide the work. For a moment, he reflected on the nature of their relationship — that of a foreman and his assistant. Darek had proved his loyalty to him and showed how hard he could work. Perhaps now was the time to change his status — to that of a partner in this venture. A junior partner, perhaps?

A distinctive buzz came from the pocket of his jacket. Adam looked at his alarm clock. It was only seven thirty. He glanced at the display of his mobile and raised his eyebrows. 'Darek?'

'Sorry for waking you up.'

'What's going on?' Adam asked with irritation. He was enjoying this rare moment of peace and reflection in bed.

'I am a father, Adam,' Darek yelled into the receiver. 'I have been awake since three. It feels so strange.'

'I bet it does. It's hard to take. Congratulations, Darek.'

'If I was in Poland with Lila, I could get a better grasp of the situation. Jesus Christ, I feel like at the time when I got totally sloshed and didn't know what was happening to me.'

'It's a big change, I know ... You will get used to it.' Unexpectedly, old memories started flooding in. It wasn't easy for him too, although his situation was different. The Bukowski family welcomed Hanka's baby son but not his father. She could have done so much better than marrying the penniless jack of all trades whose drunken father was found frozen to his sledge outside the local inn. This resentment didn't lessen even when Bukowski's granddaughter made her entrance to the world and soon secured herself a large place in the old man's heart.

For Darek's sake, Adam hoped that the boy's new family would appreciate the sacrifices he had been making.

'Darek, you must come over. Let's have breakfast together and in the evening we will celebrate. Properly.'

Walking into the kitchen of 26 Cuckoohill Road, Darek inhaled deeply. There was nothing in the world like the aroma of *jajecznica* cooked on butter and with Polish country sausage. The familiar smell instantly brought to mind the images of Sunday mornings at home. This was the only day his overworked mother had the time and inclination to indulge her men with their favourite breakfast. She used at least a dozen eggs and a loop of sausage which she finely chopped and gently fried using a large knob of butter before adding the eggs. Sometimes she sprinkled some chopped chives on the creamy mass after spooning it out on the plates waiting in front of her husband and three sons. Oh God, it smelled and tasted like heaven brought on earth. If Eve knew the taste of *jajecznica,* she wouldn't have been tempted by an apple. Every speck of egg was mopped up with the moist rye bread bought that morning from the local bakery.

What Adam was cooking in the large frying pan looked very appetizing too. Woken up at three in the morning by Lila's sister breaking the news about the arrival of his daughter, Darek not only felt excited and confused but also ravenously hungry. He would have been easily satisfied with a bowl of cornflakes but the smell of *jajecznica* made him realize how hungry he was. Seeing Adam with a tea towel slung over his shoulder, surrounded by plates, knives and a pile of egg shells, Darek could not suppress a smile.

Glancing in his direction, Adam said: 'Put the kettle on. Mugs are in the cupboard above the sink and my coffee jar is on the table.' Turning his attention back to the frying pan he added: '*Jajecznica* is almost ready. You will need good sustenance on a day like today.'

'That's exactly what I feel. Thank you Adam. I didn't know you have talents in the kitchen.'

'I don't test them very often. But even Hanka is partial to my *jajecznica*.'

Neither of them expected that this first shared meal would be a watershed in their relationship. For the first time, they talked about their families and their responsibilities. Telling Darek about his children, Adam realized that he didn't really know them — beyond their superficial likes and dislikes. What was worse, he had never attempted to get to know them. He was busy on the farm and the children were Hanka's responsibility. Would he be able to change that when he returned home? Would they be willing to get to know their father? He wanted to believe that the reason why he came to London was to improve their life, to give them a better future. Soon he realized that what propelled him to venture to London was above all the desire to free himself from Bukowski, his money, his influence and his interference in every aspect of his life. Was this in the best interest of his children? What about Hanka? Did she still love him? Would she be willing to free herself from the presence of her father?

'Won't Lila resent me for not being with them during the first weeks of Kasia's life?' asked Darek, cleaning the last specs of *jajecznica* with a piece of bread and washing it down with coffee.

'I don't know, Darek. That depends on the kind of woman she is. And whether she believes that you're working here for her and your daughter. Only you will be able to answer that.'

Adam's words perplexed Darek. He leaned back in his chair and rested his head on the wall. Adam could guess that the boy's thoughts were now in Poland, in Lesko, at the foot of the Bieszczady mountains where his baby daughter was starting her life without his assistance and presence.

'Were you ever truly happy, Adam?' Darek asked suddenly.

Startled, Adam looked at him. 'What do you mean?' What a strange question, he thought. 'Was I happy with my Hanka? At work? Where I lived?'

'All that. Did you ever feel that you were in the right place at the right time? Did you feel that you were making the people you loved happy?'

What could he say? Usually he felt that it was safer not to dwell on such issues. Was he happy years back when he was still at technical college? There were many things that interested him and he was dating Hanka at the time. She was such a beauty with her long shiny hair and bold sexy laugh that went straight to men's hearts and loins. Many wished they could put their arm around her slender waist just above her pert ass. He was a looker too. He could pull almost any girl he wished to in Kościelisko. Hanka was the prettiest though and the daughter of the richest farmer and she flattered him with her attention. Life appeared so full of promise then.

'I was happy once but it was a long time ago and I almost forgot how it feels. It's different for you. Your life is like the first chapter of a book. There is so much to come yet. You're clever, good looking and not afraid of hard work — you will go far.'

Darek looked at Adam for a moment and then turned his eyes to the window. 'I know that this job is a great opportunity for us, and I am very grateful to you for taking me on. Now that Kasia is born, your offer means a lot to me. To us. I am happy with Lila, truly I am. She is a great girl, lovely in many ways. She isn't just a pretty face. But I think sometimes that if I had another chance of starting my life over, I would work harder at school, learn languages and claw my way up to a really good job in Poland or abroad. Some place where the Karols of this world wouldn't be bossing me around.' Darek took the last gulp of his coffee and got up. 'I will wash up.'

Adam looked at Darek, his open face, intelligent eyes and fair hair that boyishly curled on top, and thought how easy it was to like him.

'You still have time to make something of yourself. When you return to Lesko you may have to hit the books but you're clever enough to figure that out for yourself. You've learnt a thing or two here and your English is not bad at all. This is a good base to start from at home. Just don't let anyone tell you that you're not good enough for something. Never,' snorted Adam, pushing his chair back to the table.

Darek heard a distant buzzing but his still unconscious mind could not identify its source. He turned around and pulled up his blanket. For a moment, the noise ceased. Yet after a couple of minutes it was again seeping into his mind. It wasn't his mobile phone — it had a different ring. Instinctively, he reached under Adam's bed to check whether his mobile was still there. It was silently lying on the carpet. Yet the distant buzzing was getting more irritating by the minute. Suddenly he knew. It was the sound of the bell at the front door. He sat up, hitting his head against the underbelly of the only chair in Adam's room. He swore and started massaging his aching forehead. He was no stranger to sleeping on the floor in the narrow passage alongside Adam's bed but this time it wasn't bad luck that put him there.

They had had a good meeting with Patrick O'Connor, Dr Patel's project manager. He liked their plans for the treatment rooms and recommendations for updating the furnishings and décor. They agreed that on Monday they would go together shopping for materials and fittings. They understood each other well and got to like the personable Irishman almost straight away. At the end of the day, he invited them for a pint to the Irish pub that happened to be just around the corner. A pint of Guinness became two and soon Darek, who had many reasons to celebrate, was downing his third pint. A plate of steaming Irish stew went well with the drink and Patrick insisted that it had to be washed down with another drink. By eleven thirty, it was too late for Darek to go home and wake Mrs Patel, so Adam suggested to his business partner that he spend the night on the floor in his room.

The doorbell blared impatiently. Darek sprang to his feet, cursing someone who was obviously bent on waking up the whole household on Sunday morning. Trying not to trip over his scattered shoes and clothes, he walked towards the door. His throat felt dry and his head was very heavy. Bare footed, he crossed the hallway towards the front door. A glance in the hall mirror reminded him that he had a large brown stain on the front of his best polo shirt. He also smelled revolting and should avoid human contact until he cleaned himself up. But this person obviously had urgent business at 26 Cuckoohill Road. He opened the door and was instantly blinded with morning light streaming into the house. All he could see was the dark silhouette of a large man standing outside. For a second he thought it appeared familiar when the man bellowed: 'Where is Adam? That *sukinsyn*.'

Without a second thought, Darek blurted: 'He is still asleep,' gesturing to the door behind him.

'I will personally teach him a lesson this time,' roared Karol. He shoved Darek aside with one movement of his arm and barged into the house. In three strides, he crossed the hall and threw open the door to Adam's room. By the time Darek caught up with him, Karol was kneeling astride the prostrate Adam, with both hands clasped around Adam's neck.

'So the previous accident has not taught you anything. You … son of a bitch. You reported me to the police who ransacked my house and frightened my family. You fucking little shit. I was magnanimous and welcomed you back to work …' he hissed, lifting Adam by his neck. Adam's face was scarlet red as he struggled to push Karol away. His mouth opened and closed without a sound.

'Karol, stop!' screamed Darek from behind. 'I will call the police.'

'Do this, *sukinsynu*.' His grip on Adam's throat eased up for a moment. 'I will teach you a lesson too. One you won't forget.'

None of them heard the footsteps behind them. Only when, with a loud clunk, a metal object hit Karol's head, did Darek turn around. Kuba, in only his underpants, was wielding an iron and with his arm still in the air, judging whether he needed to strike again. Karol, who for a moment lost his balance, leaned forward easing up the grip on Adam's neck. It was enough for Kuba to grab him by his arm, pull him up and push him out of the room. In the hallway, Karol came to his senses and started to struggle but Kuba shoved him out through the open door.

'I have already called the police,' he yelled. 'If you don't clear off fast enough, they will arrest you here.' He slammed the door and bolted it.

When Kuba turned around, he saw that the hallway had suddenly become crowded. Zofia and Jan were standing in the doorway of Adam's room listening to Darek's account of what had happened. Maja and Basia, in their nightdresses and with frightened expressions, were hovering half way down the staircase.

'Apologies for waking everyone up so early,' announced Kuba. 'We had an intruder in the house and he received the welcome he deserved. The police will do the rest. There is no need to worry. I believe they are following him and he was paying his last visit to Adam. *Pani* Zofio,' Kuba turned to Zofia, who was now leaning over Adam. 'I'm afraid I have broken your iron. The thug had a hard head. That was the first thing I saw in the kitchen.'

Zofia waved her hand dismissively. 'What a beast!' she exclaimed looking at Adam's neck. 'He could have killed you, Adam.'

'That was exactly what he intended, *pani* Zofio,' whispered Adam, touching his throat tentatively.

'But why?'

'He was trying to finish the job which his henchmen attempted a few weeks ago,' explained Darek.

'So that was him …' said Zofia incredulously. 'We must report him to the police.'

'The police are now looking for him, *pani* Zofio,' said Darek, flattening his hair with one hand and trying to keep his stale breath out of Zofia's reach. 'He dropped all pretence this time. He thought that Adam had reported him to the police and he came to get revenge.'

'So the police know enough to arrest him.'

'They must have had their own sources.'

'They must have,' agreed Zofia.

Chapter 44

'Maja let's go to the end of the garden. I don't want the rest of the Cohen clan to eavesdrop on us.'

It was the end of an unusually hot day in the middle of August and the air in central London was heavy from pollution. Walking to the station from her air conditioned office, Maja felt as though she was wading through treacle. Her blouse became stuck to her back within a few minutes of leaving the hotel and her nylon tights were burning her legs. An hour later in Stanmore at the back of the Cohen garden she was strolling barefoot on the cool grass among the flower beds and scented shrubbery and felt like she was in a different world.

'Can you grab a couple of those folding chairs?' asked Amy carefully lifting herself from behind the garden table. 'We can use them over here.' She pointed to a place under a willow tree that shaded the end of the garden like a huge parasol. She winced as she walked. 'When I bend, the pain still comes back,' she said.

'Don't be silly. They're not heavy. You'd better listen to your doctor and ... your mum,' smiled Maja.

'Stop sucking up to my mother. She is already thinking about adopting you. You're the most sensible of my friends in her opinion. And you love her food.'

'She is an exceptional cook. I've never eaten so well.'

'That's why I will never be able to drop below size fourteen, even on my sickbed. But why doesn't her food go into your hips?'

'It obviously agrees with me.'

'You can tell her that later. Now I have something more important to tell you,' said Amy, lowering her voice.

This sounded ominous and Maja stopped unfolding the canvas chairs. 'Amy, I have very mixed feelings about the whole thing.

I fear that this could backfire on us.'

'Snow White, sometimes you have to fight back and you need firepower to do it. Anyway, it's too late for any regrets. We have a lot to fall back on. Good or bad news first?'

'Is there any good news?'

'Of course. Maja, for God's sake, just plonk down those chairs here and let's get down to business.'

'Amy, I ...'

'We have plenty of ammunition. A hand grenade, I would say,' said Amy, carefully lowering herself into her canvas seat. 'The bad news is that we have to pay the messenger. More than we've budgeted for. He needed an extra night at a B&B to complete his mission.'

'This is the least of our problems. I wonder what we'll do with these explosives.' Maja sighed heavily. She knew she couldn't leave things as they were. She had to act but feared that the next step could bring changes she wouldn't be able to cope with. She looked down at her bare feet resting on the grass and around the riot of colours and scents that was Mrs Cohen's garden. Every time she visited Amy's home, she fell under its spell — its domesticity, warmth, security and the cheerful nature of Mrs Cohen. She wished she could stay here for ever.

'So what did your sleuth manage to find out?' she asked with a note of resignation.

'As we suspected, Jess has a secret, a pretty huge one. It's a six year old daughter, a very cute dark haired girl called Paloma.' Amy looked at Maja, gauging the effect of this revelation. 'Well, the name itself is a give away of her parentage. She lives with Jess' mother in Skipton and attends the local Catholic school.'

Maja sat silently, absorbing Amy's revelations. There were plenty of single mothers around, looking after their children the best they could. And they definitely didn't make a secret out of it. Many of them were proud of their independence and their achievements as single parents. She suddenly felt sorry for Jessica. Hiding the existence of her daughter, she denied herself the joy of being able to talk to her friends about her. To share her little accomplishments.

A chilling thought passed through her mind. Jessica may not

feel that way at all. Obviously very ambitious, she put her career first and she was prepared to pay any price to avoid jeopardizing it. Any price ... How determined was she to get where she wanted? And how ruthless about eliminating obstacles in her way.

'... do you think?' She suddenly heard Amy's voice. 'Maja, have you got your head in the clouds again?'

'I suddenly felt as if I knew Jessica better than I thought. I have no idea what she has against me but I can see now how much her career means to her.'

'You didn't know what a conniving bitch she was?' Amy laughed with incredulity.

'I had no reason to fear her.'

'Maja, you'd better prepare yourself to fight if you don't want her to push you out of the Metropole. I am sure that Jess isn't wasting her time. She is probably looking for another opportunity to undermine you.'

With a sinking heart, Maja knocked on the door of Maureen Johnson's office. The memories of their previous conversation felt raw in her mind. What was it going to be this time? Mrs Johnson didn't call staff to her office for a chat.

'Please come in, Maja.' The warm tone of the invitation surprised her. As before, she took a seat on the other side of the polished desk. This was the place where many people received the news that their services were no longer required.

'I wanted to update you on the progress of the investigation into the theft of our customer's personal data.' Had Jess prepared another surprise for her? the thought flashed across Maja's mind.

'Since your actions were under consideration in this case, I wanted to let you know the findings of the investigation. This information is strictly confidential at this stage,' stressed Maureen holding Maja's gaze for a moment.

'Of course.' Maja's throat was so tight that her words were barely audible.

'Inspector Morrison found that the theft was committed by an employee of an IT company managing the Metropole's database. He copied the information while carrying out a routine maintenance and sold it to an online marketing company. None of our employees had a part in these rogue operations.'

Maja felt her heart pounding.

'It was very unfortunate that following the initial complaints we directed our attention to the front of house operations where you worked. I realize this must have been very distressing for you. That's why I have called you today to tell you the news in person.'

She should have been feeling relieved and happy. She should thank Mrs Johnson, leave her office with a smile and run to the locker room to call Amy. Instead she felt a surge of anger. She would not be able to forgive and forget Maureen Johnson and the management she represented that they suspected her of dishonesty. After she had shown so much loyalty to the company and dedication to her work.

'You're all in the clear now, Maja.'

'I ... I am very grateful for you telling me this Mrs Johnson. Truly I am. But could you let me know how it happened that I was under suspicion in the first place? What have I done to lose the hotel's trust in me?' Having uttered these words, she was surprised how harsh they sounded.

Mrs Johnson cleared her throat. 'It's not my place to divulge the details of internal processes to employees but I can reiterate what I said before that the information about the complaint came to us from the Reception desk. This is where many customers are directed by the switchboard. But of, course, it was a mistake. Just try to forget it now.'

The interview was over. Maureen Johnson shuffled the files on her desk, impatient to terminate the conversation. She had important business to get on with and her role wasn't that of an agony aunt to hotel staff. With her fingertips, she touched her hair, checking that no loose strands escaped from the clip at the back of her head. Then she placed her groomed hands on the papers in front of her. Her face was calm and her eyes were impenetrable.

Maja stood up. Looking straight at Mrs Johnson, she said: 'Thank you very much. I greatly appreciate that you let me know the outcome of the investigation. And for your ... help.'

Travelling down in the staff escalator, Maja saw that in the bluish lights of the lift her face appeared tired and taut like a mask. She wondered whether Maureen Johnson ever lost any sleep over the employees' problems she handled.

When Maja returned to her desk, the first thing she saw was a yellow sticky note with Sophie's familiar handwriting. 'The boss wants to see you. Please pop into her office.'

Maja's first reaction was that of alarm. Did news of the investigation spread further than she hoped? Would she now be explaining herself to her boss? Under the message, there was a smiley. Would Sophie have drawn it if she thought that Helen Peters was about to impart some grave news to her?

'I know that you have a lot on your plate at the moment, Maja,' said Helen Peters, indicating for Maja to sit down. She walked around her desk and propped herself against it, facing Maja. 'I hesitated before calling you here because I know that you need a break. Not a course.'

A course? Perhaps it isn't bad news after all, thought Maja.

'It would be a break from the office and you may enjoy it. It's only two days. The course has been designed for the hotel sector and HQ is keen for staff, particularly in the corporate customer-facing roles, to familiarize themselves with the subject. Internet marketing is the future. A number of people from the Metropole will be attending, so you can compare notes, if necessary. Maja? What do you think?'

'Of course, Helen. I will go.' Oh God, I need to sound more enthusiastic, she thought. 'I'd love to go. I will catch up on my work after the course.'

'No need. Enjoy the course. I will distribute your work in your absence. But please prepare a report from the course. The main points, I mean. So the other girls could learn a thing or two.'

When Maja walked into the conference room, there were already several people there looking through the information folders and chatting to neighbours.

She pinned her badge to her blouse and sat down at the end of one of the rows. The air conditioning was ferocious and in a couple of minutes she was putting her jacket on. Outside it was a glorious August day, the perfect occasion to air summer clothes. Not everyone compromised style for comfort. A dark girl sitting in the front row in a stunningly simple red dress appeared unaffected by the arctic conditions around her.

Curious about the course content, Maja began to leaf through the manual. The logo of the training company was embossed on the front of the folder. A branded pen and a coaster were inserted into the pocket of the manual. She smiled thinking how effective such a promotion was. These small items would stay on her desk for months.

When she looked around again, the room was already full. At nine thirty on the dot the presenter began his introduction. He warned the audience that they had a very full programme.

'Isn't he keen?' commented her neighbour to the right. A mop of red hair gleamed in the semi-darkness. Underneath, there was a pair of blue eyes and a wide mouth that was now grinning at Maja.

Smirking at him, Maja tapped her folder with a pen and whispered: 'There is a lot of stuff here.'

Encouraged, the man offered his hand: 'Steve McKenzie.'

'Maja Zalewska,' she whispered.

'Are you Czech?'

She shook her head.

'Lithuanian?'

'Close.'

'You look Eastern European.'

'I am Polish.'

The presenter shot them a warning glance. 'The coffee break is at eleven.'

Embarrassed, Maja lowered her head and turned her manual to the course outline. She noticed that several people in front of them had turned around. From the corner of her eye, she noticed that the girl in the red dress was also looking at her. She froze. Jessica Dryer was staring at her across the crowded room.

The feeling of pleasant excitement about the day ahead disappeared. Why did this woman always make her feel threatened and defensive?

Barely able to control her irritation, Maja started furiously taking notes, ignoring Steve who was muttering his apologies. The course was conducted at a very fast pace. The presenter raced through concepts using numerous slides and film clips to illustrate successful marketing initiatives. Remembering that she had to prepare a report from the course, Maja was taking voluminous notes.

Soon there was a coffee break. Most of the people left the room. Steve, undeterred by her unfriendly manner, asked whether she would be having coffee. Maja shot a glance towards the front of the auditorium. Jessica was gone. She had no intention of meeting her in the lobby.

'I would love a cup. Would I be allowed to have it here?'

'I don't see why not,' said Steve glancing around.

'I'll have to make an urgent call.'

'Then I will bring our coffees in.'

'That would be wonderful,' she said enthusiastically. 'Milk, no sugar.'

Some ten minutes later, Steve came back carrying two cups of coffee. Maja greeted him with a radiant smile.

'You wouldn't believe the queue. And they had run out of milk by the time I got to the table. But they also replenished the biscuits, so I snatched the best,' he said proudly, pointing to the large peanut cookies wedged at the side of their saucers. 'I hope that you're not allergic to nuts.'

'Not at all. I love nuts.' Seeing Steve's smirk, she corrected herself. 'Not the human variety.'

As they drunk their coffee, dipping the biscuits that proved to be as hard as roof tiles, Maja felt compelled to satisfy Steve's curiosity about her life in London. In return, Steve told her that he came from Elgin, a pretty little town on the northern coast of Scotland. During the summer he worked in a local hotel, doing almost every job possible.

'If this didn't put me off working in hotels for life, nothing ever will. It was a good school.' Seeing Maja's questioning gaze, he explained: 'The job has taught me to treat customers the way I would like to be treated myself, regardless of whether they were paying two hundred or twenty quid for the night.'

Before the lights were dimmed again for the next session, Steve asked: 'Are any of your work colleagues on this course?'

'Yes, a head receptionist from the Metropole is here too. But I would rather spend my lunch break talking to you.'

Carrying her lunch tray, Maja walked across the cafeteria looking for an empty table. She spotted one at the far end of the room and moved briskly to take it before someone else had the same idea. As she approached it, she noticed that there was already a cutlery set and a glass of juice standing on it. She thought about the towels on the beach strategy and smiled. Fortunately, a couple at the next table were about to leave. She waited for a moment and then placed her lunch things down, making room for Steve. Seeing him wading through the crowd she waved energetically. Then her arm fell down limply. Just behind Steve, she saw a figure in red moving towards her.

'Have you seen the puddings? What a selection!' Steve exclaimed enthusiastically.

Maja greeted him with a pale smile. Then her eyes met with Jessica's who was about to sit down at the next table. It was too late to move. With as much enthusiasm as she could muster, she asked: 'Enjoying the course, Jessica?'

'It will be very relevant to me.'

'I hope so too.'

'In your work?'

'Yes ... at least my boss thinks so.'

Jessica laughed scornfully. 'Protection again. That's why you're here.'

Maja gasped. She couldn't believe that Jessica was capable of such open hostility. Any doubts she may have had about who got her into trouble disappeared instantly.

'Would you like to move to another table?' asked Steve, looking from one woman to another. 'The air is very pungent here.'

At that moment Maja made a decision. No, she wasn't going to back down and give Jessica more satisfaction. 'No, Steve. This table is fine. Only my perspective is wrong.' She got up, walked around the table and sat down with her back to Jessica. As they were rearranging their plates on the table, she asked: 'Steve, you promised to tell me how you came to work at the Four Seasons.'

Their eyes met once again, this time in the mirror. Maja left the cubicle and walked across the brightly lit bathroom towards the row of wash basins. As she opened the tap, a stream of water gushed out, bouncing off her hands and splashing her skirt and blouse. Looking at herself in the mirror to assess the damage, she met Jessica's eyes. She was standing a couple of wash basins away carefully lathering her hands. Her crimson nails peeped from the foam like drops of blood. Seeing Maja's soaked clothes, she smirked.

Maja pressed her lips and walked towards the paper towel dispenser. She pulled out several sheets and started drying her clothes. She managed to blot most of the moisture but a large dark patch remained on the front of her blouse. There was nothing else she could do. She buttoned her jacket and instantly felt the wet fabric sticking to her stomach. She winced and caught Jessica's glance in the mirror.

'Covering up doesn't always work,' she sneered.

'Says who? An expert in deception?'

Jessica's eyes narrowed. 'Do not try to pick a fight with me. You'll regret it,' she hissed.

Maja looked at her. Now or never. She remembered Amy's words. Another recollection, now a distant memory, flicked into her mind. She hadn't fought then.

Maja glanced around the bathroom — it was silent and empty. She walked towards the exit door, opened it and flicked over the notice that hung outside so it now said: 'Cleaning in progress. Do not enter'. She closed it and leaned against it. Looking defiantly at Jessica, she said: 'I made a mistake not standing up to you. You've bullied me like you bully your staff. But no more.'

'Mind your words. I can get you fired.'

'You tried it once already. It didn't take me very long to figure it out.' There was a moment of silence during which the temperature in the bathroom rose by 50 degrees.

'You're fantasizing.' Jessica reached into her handbag, took out a tube of moisturizer and started applying it to her hands. 'You have no proof.'

'Yes, I do. I spoke to the client,' said Maja, crossing her arms and raising her chin.

'You did?' Jessica stopped applying cream to her hands.

'Yes, I did. Although, I have to admit, you're very good at hiding evidence. You have many years of practice.'

'I'm warning you.'

'Frankly Jess, when I learnt that you have been hiding the existence of your daughter for six years, I felt sorry for you.'

Jessica froze. If her eyes could kill, I would be dead, thought Maja.

'You've been spying on me ...' she hissed. Her eyes were now like black narrow slits.

'Your secret is out, Jessica. I didn't have to look very far.' Maja held Jessica's gaze. It was a foul game but the one Jessica had been playing all along.

'You have no right to violate someone's privacy. My private and professional life don't mix.'

'I noticed. You're prepared to pay any price for professional success. You'll climb to the top.'

'It's none of your business. You're new to the hotel.'

'I've been working in the Metropole for two and half years. And I've worked too hard to allow anyone to destroy my reputation.'

'Two years isn't much.'

'With a university degree in my pocket, I waited at tables and cleaned toilets to get where I am now. So I am not going to let you take it away from me. I will fight back, remember that,' she said slowly.

Jessica stood frozen.

Maja put her bag over her shoulder and looked again in the mirror. The damp patch was still visible on her blouse so she buttoned her jacket higher. She looked at Jessica. 'You gave me one hell of a ride but I am prepared to keep silent provided that you don't step on my toes again.'

She took a lipstick out of her handbag and applied a shiny layer to her mouth, once and then again. Then she dropped it into her bag. Turning again towards Jessica, she gave her a level look and said: 'I should add, for your benefit, I'm good at keeping secrets,' and she walked out of the bathroom. Outside, she flipped over the sign hanging on the door.

Chapter 45

Kuba, October 1999

The softly peaked clouds sailing past Kuba's window were turning slate grey. Gradually their underbellies became darker and they floated like giant fish across the horizon. The sky was growing inky blue, as if someone was pulling a blanket over it. Soon a single orange strip at the edge of the horizon was all that remained of the day. Then, without a warning, the dusk turned into night.

People rarely noticed that fleeting moment, unless they were free to gaze into the sky the way he was doing just now. With his chin in his hands, Kuba was sitting at the desk looking out through an open window. He had stopped reading some time ago but only when the lights went up in the houses on the other side of the road, did he notice that he was sitting in total darkness. The books and papers on his desk dissolved into shapeless objects and only the smoothness of the textbook cover under his fingertips reminded him that he had decided to study tonight.

Unexpectedly, a rustling sound came from the sky above him. A gaggle of geese was flying directly over their house towards the dark hills of Northwood. Over twenty birds were flapping their wings and honking loudly. They were flying low and he could feel a rush of air trailing behind them. Soon, they would be flying south for the winter.

For him, autumn was the season of change. In autumn, he had started new schools, received new shoes and new clothes in preparation for winter which was always considered more important than the other seasons. His mother had died in autumn and his world had turned upside down. Nothing had ever felt the same since. Several years later he had taken a coach to London in November for the journey which was to change his life. Now, he was ready to take another big step.

Their last morning patient had just left the surgery and they were breaking up for lunch. It was a cold and clear day. The vivid blue of the cloudless sky created a stunning backdrop to the trees that had just changed into their autumn colours.

'Let's go to Franco's for lunch,' suggested Kuba, impatient to get out of the building. Such Saturday afternoons were made for country rambles, or at least dog walking.

Karen needed no persuading and soon they were out in the street, walking towards Franco's. From a hundred metres away, they smelled the aroma of Italian coffee, melted cheese and grilled vegetables.

'Oh God, I'm starving,' admitted Karen. 'All Franco needs to do is open the door to his café and the crowds will flood in.'

Every seat in the small eatery was taken but they were able to grab a table outside, just as a young mother hurried her brood out.

At Franco's, the service was always prompt and soon a young waitress, probably one of his nieces, was taking their order. She recommended they try roasted pumpkin soup with homemade olive bread.

When a green bottle of San Pellegrino was placed in front of them, Karen asked: 'Have you made up your mind about what you want to specialise in once you qualify?'

'Yes.' Karen's intuition always surprised and impressed him. 'Working in the practice has made a great difference. I learned a lot trying my hand in all the main areas of therapy.'

'You have been a great help. I'm sure the boss will give you a good report. But remember, the practice is not very large and you may like to look beyond the areas we treat here.'

Their soup and bread, warm and smelling of olives, was served and the food temporarily absorbed their attention.

'I didn't know that pumpkin soup could taste so good,' exclaimed Karen, pausing after a few hasty spoonfuls. A line of orange liquid settled on her upper lip.

Kuba looked at her and smiled. There was nothing pretentious about Karen. She approached everything with the same enthusiasm, generously giving her time, attention and talents

to everyone who needed her. Her beauty was equally radiant.
She wore very little make up but her face didn't need embellishments. Her thick brown hair, always pulled back, shone like
fresh chestnuts. When she smiled, her smile spread from her
mouth to her eyes.

'Why are you grinning at me? she asked.

Kuba took a serviette and dabbed Karen's upper lip with it.

'Have I made a mess of myself?'

'No, Karen. You never make a mess out of things. Your mission is to bring order. I am the best example of that.'

'Oh, Kuba.'

'Back to your question.' He refilled their glasses. 'I have a
fairly good idea of what I'd like to do next. I would like to
specialize in geriatric physiotherapy.'

'I would never ...' Karen was looking at him wide-eyed. 'It's a
very interesting and ... challenging area. But if I may ask, why?

'I very much enjoyed working with your elderly patients.
Much more than with the Cara Elliots of this world.'

'I don't blame you.' Karen laughed. 'I've got used to them.'

'I felt that older patients needed me more. This may sound
very selfish, but they appreciated what I did for them. I have
learnt a lot from them. They gave me the desire to keep learning, to be able to help them more.'

Karen stopped eating and was looking at him intently. 'You
keep surprising me, Kuba. I am impressed with the clarity of
your plans.'

'It took me a long time to get there Karen. I'll be thirty one in
two weeks' time.'

'Ancient indeed.' She giggled and vigorously stirred her latte.

'I also enquired ...' he said tentatively, 'about the possibility
of working with the elderly in a residential home in Watford. I
saw the job ad in one of the journals in the college.'

Karen stopped drinking her coffee. 'I'm sure that you could get
more hours in our practice.'

'I hoped that you might say that.'

'But ...'

'If I stayed in your practice I would always be considered your
protégée. I enjoy working with you Karen, but ...'

'No buts.' She raised her hand. 'I understand Kuba. This is

your future. Make sure that you choose what's best for you. But don't look over your shoulder. What others think and say won't matter in the long term.'

'It takes a few years and many mistakes to gain such confidence,' said Kuba suddenly changing the tone of his voice. 'The brighter students of life don't need to make so many blunders to learn what's best for them.'

Placing her hand on his, Karen said: 'Don't torture yourself over Judyta … and the baby. She didn't give you a choice.'

'It wasn't the first time I let other people make decisions on my behalf,' he exclaimed. 'Even …' he hesitated. 'Even you did — but you acted like a friend.'

Karen said nothing. There was a long pause during which she could see that Kuba was battling with the desire to tell her something. He looked over her head and then into his coffee. His voice was barely audible. 'I thought I would never have to come back to this. I tried hard to forget it.'

'Kuba, you don't need to tell me anything. I will never judge you on some past mistake.'

'It's like a scab that has never dropped off a wound. I think about it every day. You … you may be able to understand.'

'So don't scratch it. Not yet.'

'If I don't tell you this, I'll never tell anyone. Seven years ago in Poland, a couple of years after I started my placement in the hospital, I was asked to treat a woman. She was young, pretty and full of herself. Having broken her leg skiing she wanted to get back on her feet as soon as possible. She had ambitions to become a pop singer. So she insisted that I give her more intensive therapy and exercises than were advisable at her stage of recovery. I am not sure what happened next — whether she overdid them or injured herself coming home drunk from a party. Anyway, her knee and leg stared swelling and it led to all sorts of complications that required an operation. She lied to the consultant in charge of her case that she was doing everything I had recommended. Later in the hearing, she insinuated that I wasn't experienced enough to handle cases like her and it was all my fault.'

Karen took a deep breath and stared intently at Kuba while he kept his gaze fixed on the content of his mug.

'I left the hospital without attempting to clear my name. Like a coward. I justified it to myself because I hated confrontations. I also felt I wasn't experienced enough to defend myself if I was challenged by the medical authorities. You see, Karen, I found it easier to run away ...'

'That's why you were so reluctant to go back to the profession?'

'Yeah ... I lost respect for myself.'

'Kuba!' Karen exclaimed. 'I never met a man who inspired more respect than you. Stop talking nonsense. I watched you working with old people and with primadonnas and I believe that you have a natural talent for the profession. The way you relate to patients cannot be learnt. You could teach a lesson or two to even the most experienced physios. And ... you're a great guy. Someone a woman can trust.'

Kuba lifted his head and held her gaze for a moment. 'Karen, you should expect more. Don't get involved with men like me. You deserve much more.'

She tried to protest but he took her hand in his and held it gently as if it was a precious object. 'I'm getting my professional life straightened but emotionally I am still ... fucked up. Sorry, those are crude words. Mixed up. That best reflects how I feel. At least at the moment.'

'It may change.'

'Perhaps one day. When I prove to myself that I am in control of my life and I can achieve what I want. What I need to do ... But you should not compromise your expectations. You have so much to offer to a man. You're generous, clever, beautiful. You will make someone very happy.'

And you don't want to be that lucky guy, Karen thought bitterly. I'm not able to make you happy after all.

He read her thoughts. 'Karen, it's not you. I am not happy with myself. At least for now. But I am a very lucky sod.'

She looked at him, confused. She saw a flicker of a smile returning to his face.

'If you haven't lost all respect for me after what I've just told you.'

'Stop talking nonsense ...'

'Then I'm very lucky. Very lucky to enjoy a friendship with a woman like you.'

Chapter 46

Kuba, November 1999

Kuba finished his breakfast and made a fresh pot of coffee when Maja came into to the kitchen. Her blue dressing gown enveloped her like a soft cloud. She had just woken up and her eyes had a dreamy look. On her left cheek there was still an imprint from the pillow. Her hair, that had again grown longer, was scattered on her shoulders. Leaning against the counter, she stifled a yawn.

'You're up early, Kuba.' She deeply inhaled the aroma wafting around them. 'The coffee smells so good.'

Without a word, he filled another mug and handed it to her. Maja gave him a sleepy smile and wrapped her fingers around the mug. Her hands, with long and slender fingers, appeared even more delicate than usual.

'Thank you.' She lifted the coffee to her lips and closed her eyes as she took her first sip. Her lashes made shadows on her cheeks and her top lip curled up as she brought the drink to her mouth. He was watching her mesmerized. Was this dreamy fairy the same woman who every morning marched out for her daily battles armed in her navy suit?

The experience with Judyta would stay with him for ever. At times, he wondered whether he would ever be able to look at a woman without suspicion or resentment. So why did the girl standing in front of him touch him so deeply? She always did, he remembered.

Maja finished her coffee and went to the sink to wash her cup up. 'That was exactly what I needed.' She smiled at him but by this time, her smile had lost its dreamy quality. 'I'd better get on with my day,' she stated in a matter-of-fact tone. 'Are you going to be busy today?'

'Yeah ... I expect so. Studying, tidying, shopping. I cannot live on pizzas and toast alone.'

'I ought to buy some food too. The canteen makes my life so much simpler but I forget that I need to eat at weekends.'

'What time are you planning to shop for food?' he asked with sudden interest.

'Sometime early afternoon.'

'Are you calling on John Sainsbury?'

'I guess so.'

'We could go together. I will take the car. It will save you carrying your bags.'

'Would you?'

'Of course. It would be more fun shopping together. I need some sensible advice on what to buy. To avoid junk, I mean.'

She looked at him and smiled. The glance was long and direct.

'OK. And thank you for the lift. I will probably buy twice as many things if I don't need to carry them.'

It was half past seven when they staggered back to the kitchen with their bags. 'I never enjoyed shopping before,' said Kuba, dumping two handfuls of carrier bags on the kitchen floor.'

'Let's hope we'll be able to fit everything in,' said Maja, opening the fridge. 'We will have to eat a lot tonight or throw a party.'

'The house seems very quiet. We will probably have to rely on ourselves to clear the surplus.'

'Or ... I will cook supper for both of us.'

'Do you always treat your aiders so well?' Kuba was now grinning.

'Only when they prove particularly loyal.' She slung her jacket on the back of the chair and started unpacking the shopping. 'What do we have here ... Kuba, do you fancy pasta? With ham, tomatoes and peppers. Or ... I have two packets of baking potatoes. What about *placki zieminaczane*?'

'*Placki*! Any time,' he exclaimed. 'Last time I ate a plate of *placki* I was in Poland six months ago. I love them. They are the best kind of comfort food! Thinking about them, I already feel ravenous.'

'I love them too.' Maja put the bulbous spuds on the counter. One, two ... six ... that will be plenty. I also have an onion somewhere. She went to search her cupboard. 'But I am not sure I can make them as crispy and golden as my mum does,' she warned.

'Since I have never tasted your mum's *placki*, I won't be making any comparisons.'

'I am so full I cannot move,' said Kuba, wiping his lips with a piece of kitchen towel and pushing his chair away from the table.

There was a dark starless night outside and the house was very quiet but the kitchen had the atmosphere of a village fete. Maja waited until everyone had finished their evening meal before embarking on the big fry up. She grated raw potatoes and onions and fried pan after pan of golden discs that smelled of childhood and home comfort. Kuba started helping himself to *placki* as soon as Maja lifted them sizzling out of the oil. He was trying to combine eating with making a salad, so shreds of cabbage, carrots and onion lay scattered on the kitchen counter, while oil glistened on the cabinet handles.

'You're a fantastic cook, Maja,' he said appreciatively, popping a few golden crumbs that lay around the plate into his mouth.

'I learnt a few things at home but don't practise enough. I am growing lazy eating in the hotel every day.'

'I could help you practise every weekend,' he said with a mischievous smile. 'I will do the driving and ... appreciating. I may even learn a thing or two. Then he added: 'Before your boyfriend comes back and your weekends become busy again.'

Maja stood up, collected the dirty dishes from the table and carried them to the sink. Without a word, she started washing up.

'Maja, we could put them into a dishwasher.'

'I have almost done it,' she said and continued washing up in silence. Then she suddenly turned around. 'I may not be in London for much longer.'

'Why?' Kuba asked startled. 'I thought you're settled in your job.'

'They seem to be pleased with me. At least my boss is,' she said, peeling off the washing up gloves. Then she took a kitchen towel and started drying the dishes.

'Maja, stop doing that,' Kuba said impatiently. 'What's worrying you?'

'I have been asked to consider a placement in the Metropole New York. For three months over the winter period.'

'So that's good news, isn't it? On the job front, at least.' He was now regarding her intently.

'It will give me an opportunity to learn new things. The Metropole's American operations are run differently. And I will see New York.'

'You don't seem to be excited about the prospect.'

'It complicates things. A lot. I was planning on visiting my family this Christmas.'

'Isn't your boyfriend in New York?'

'Yes, but he will be coming back soon. He cannot wait to come back home.'

Not surprising, if he has you waiting for him on this side of the Atlantic, Kuba thought. He nodded thoughtfully and said: 'I see. You will be swapping places.' He walked over to Maja and put his hands on her shoulders.

'Maja, you need to do what's best for you. You've had a rough ride to get where you are. None of us get the same chances as people born here. So don't throw it away.'

He saw anxiety in her eyes. Then her top and bottom lips come together and tightened.

With his thumb, he touched her cheek tenderly. 'Don't be too hard on yourself. People who love you and care for you will understand, and wait. You're entitled to make yourself a priority and have some fun as well. You have been working so hard. Take this opportunity to see a bit of the world. Be a little selfish for a change,' he teased her.

She smiled, with a weak little smile, to show him she knew that he cared.

The doorbell rang but they didn't hear it. There was a sound of steps running down the stairs and then crossing the hallway. Basia was talking to someone at the door. A moment later, the door to the kitchen swung open.

'Hi.' Karen's face flushed by the cold air appeared in the doorway. A smile froze on her lips. She was looking from Kuba to Maja.

'I ... I dropped in to ask for the ... book ... The one I lent you. Mary is writing a paper for Physiotherapy Journal ... There were some references.'

'Hello, Karen. Please come in.' Kuba knew that he had to take control of the situation.

'Karen, Maja, let me do the introductions. Karen, this is Maja my housemate and Polish friend. She has just treated me to my favourite Polish dish.' Kuba waved in the direction of the table. 'Maja, Karen is the best physio in North West London, my mentor and my boss at Alan & Taylor. She persuaded me to go back to physiotherapy.'

For a short moment both women looked at each other. Then Maja spoke. 'Why don't you sit down with us. We're about to have a cup of tea. Perhaps you would like to taste one of these.' She pointed to the large plate of *placki*. They are not very healthy, I'm afraid, but we both had a craving for them.' She tucked loose strands of hair behind her ears and pulled down her blouse. With her face red and shiny from standing over a frying pan, she must had been a real sight, she thought.

Kuba reached into the cupboard and placed a plate on the table. Then out of the cutlery drawer, he produced a knife and fork.

'What do you think, Karen? Would you risk one of them? They are good.'

Karen took her jacket off and, without meeting his eyes, said, 'I am not risk averse, as you know. And they do look delicious.' Transferring one onto her plate she asked: 'How do you make them?'

'I grate raw potatoes, chop onions, add some plain flour, an egg, salt and pepper and fry them quickly so they become crispy without absorbing too much fat. That is the idea anyway,' Maja smiled.

'They look similar to Jewish *latkas* ... And they are delicious.' Karen said appreciatively, slowly chewing the first mouthful.

'*Latkas*? Patches?' asked Maja amused. 'What a fitting name?! They look like patches and will do for dinner if you don't have anything better.'

Patching? Isn't that what I am trying to do now, thought Kuba. He filled the kettle and switched it on.

'Three teas. Two white and one ...?'

'With lemon,' prompted Maja. She turned away and walked to the fridge to hide a smile. Kuba knew very well how she liked her tea.

Putting a tub of yogurt and a sugar bowl on the table she said: 'With a sprinkling of sugar and a spoonful of natural yogurt *placki* taste even better.'

When Karen finished her fourth *placek* and wiped her mouth with a piece of kitchen towel, Maja asked: Would you like the recipe?'

'Definitely. I can see why you like them so much.'

'You could practise them together with Kuba when I am gone.'

Karen looked at her surprised. 'Are you going back to Poland?'

'No, in the opposite direction. I have been offered a placement in a hotel in New York.'

'What a fantastic place to work and visit!' exclaimed Karen, her expression relaxed. 'Are you looking forward to it?'

Maja smiled warmly. 'Very much so. I'll be joining my boyfriend who is working there.'

Instantly, the atmosphere lightened. Without looking at Kuba, Maja took a slice of lemon which he placed on a saucer in front of her and dropped it into her tea. As she pressed it against the walls of the cup, the brown liquid turned amber gold, releasing a deliciously zesty scent.

Kuba caught a shadow of a smile passing her lips and knew that the understanding between them was as strong as ever. He thought how much he would have liked to give her a hug — just as a thank you.

Chapter 47

'Mummy, mummy. A fish. A blue fish. It's making bubbles.'

'Yes, Tommy. A very pretty fish.'

'Another fish! Big yellow fish,' a child's voice squealed in delight.

'This one is like the fish in your bath. Look, there is a crab.'

Adam smiled. There was also an octopus lurking in the sea-weeds, a red starfish and shells scattered among the rocks. It was Darek's idea to install this colourful mosaic at the level of the table on which mothers undressed their children for weighing and examination.

Through a half-open door, Adam could hear more joyous exclamations and giggles. Then a nurse explained something to the boy's mother. Even with his pigeon English, he was able to understand that she was happy with the changes made to her work station.

There were a few final touches to add to some rooms and lights fittings to adjust, and their biggest project would be completed. The payment for it was already in the bank, topped up with a generous bonus, a gesture of approval from the Parkway Surgery doctors who were delighted with the outcome.

Now that the leaves had fallen off the trees and every morning the ground was covered with a shimmering veil of frost, there was time for them to go back. Darek has already booked their tickets home and now they had a few more weekends to finish things off, buy gifts for their families and a few items for themselves, which were easier to find in London than in Zako-pane or Lesko. Adam was planning to purchase new tools which he might need straight away. How ironic it was, he thought, that no customs officer was likely to object to him taking tools out of Britain. Yet bringing them into the country from Poland would guarantee him a seat on a coach destined for Poland.

During the last month, he had visited more home improvement
stores and specialist independent outlets than during his entire
stay in London. Never parting from his notebook and red pencil,
he made notes on what merchandise they carried, and how it
was displayed and promoted. In well-run shops, products and
related accessories were always located together, often with
advice on how they could be used.

He noticed how important the position of the products which
the retailer wanted to sell was — at an eye level — while others
were on the bottom or top shelves where they were less visible
and accessible. He wondered why he had never noticed that
before. Or was the art of merchandising practised more skilfully
in London? As well as the shelf layout and aisle width, lighting
was designed to guide the customer as the retailer intended. If
he was to make his store successful, he would have to apply the
same principles. And his staff, when he would be able to afford
them, would greet their customers in smart uniforms and with
a smile. He remembered the sour-faced owner of the hardware
store in Kościelisko and how he treated those who came with
small orders.

He had paid the last instalment on his loan in the summer
and now his account had a healthy balance. That was the
capital he needed to fit the shop and buy stock. He might even
take an additional loan, but he would keep it to a minimum,
until he assessed the potential of his business in Kościelisko.
His business. He whispered these two words like a magical
spell. The idea of being in charge of an enterprise, which he
would shape and develop the way he wanted still didn't seem
real to him. At other times, the responsibility frightened him.
He wasn't a natural risk taker. But the idea was so intoxicating,
like reaching for a bottle of vodka that could send him into orbit
by the time he saw the bottom. The only difference was that he
could lose himself in this enterprise without losing his head.

'What are you going to call your business?' asked Darek pushing
a plate with thickly cut bread, that accompanied their minestrone, across the table. Minestrone soup and spaghetti were per-

manent fixtures on the menu of the Irish pub which was just around the corner from the Parkway Surgery. Adam had got used to its fare rather than acquired a taste for it. But to his surprise he had grown to like the dark grainy bread which the pub served.

'I haven't thought about that yet.'

'You should. A shop's name should be distinctive … and easy to remember. It'll become your second name.'

Adam dipped a piece of crust into the thick soup. He looked up at Darek. Of course, he was right. It was essential that he had a good name for his store. How could this young lad could be so business savvy? He had grown to trust him and respect his judgment. This trip had changed him in so many ways he would not have imagined possible before. He could even speak a few words of English now.

'You're right, Darek. Adam's Supplies wouldn't do.'

'It sounds flat. Boring. You want your business to have a modern image,' Darek's brown eyes were challenging him across the table.

'Hmm, dependable … yes. I would like to think that my shop would be the first port of call. That people will be popping in to ask for advice. I will stock basic tools for every need.'

Darek stopped eating for a moment. Then, waving his spoon, he exclaimed: 'What about: "For your every need".'

Adam hesitated. 'That sounds like a book title. You said the name should be easy to remember.'

'Perhaps: "Your every need". There is already promise in that name.'

'Your every need,' repeated Adam, testing the strength of the words. 'Every need.' It sounded a bit arrogant. It contained an assumption that he would be able to help everyone.

'Adam, you need to think big. If the market proves tough then you'll adjust your plans to suit your means. All entrepreneurs do this.'

Adam was staring at Darek with an open mouth. So this is what he was going to become — an entrepreneur. A local man returning home with capital to do bigger things than the town was used to. Then he thought about Bukowski and the contempt with which he had always treated him. What would please him more: to see his father-in-law's face when he found out about Adam's plans or the satisfaction of telling him that he wouldn't be working for him anymore.

'Darek, will you come to Kościelisko to help me design the fascia of the shop and open it with me?'

'Of course, Adam. It would be my pleasure. Perhaps I will also bring my girls to show them real mountains.'

With a pair of silver headphones on her head, mug in hand and a magazine under her arm, Basia was trying to open the kitchen door, pressing the handle with her elbow.

'I can help you,' offered Adam, dropping the potato and a peeling knife onto a chopping board. He crossed the kitchen and opened the door. Basia smiled and nodded in gratitude without taking off her headphones.

A thought flashed in Adam's mind and he decided it was now or never. Touching his head, he indicated to the girl that he wished to talk to her. Basia's eyes opened in surprise — they had never spoken to each other before — but she obliged and took her headphones off. Their contact was limited to greetings in the morning and at the end of the day when they passed each other in the hall.

It was a very long time since Adam had conversed with a young woman of Basia's age. On a few occasions he had witnessed Basia's mood swings and they frightened him. She was not only from a different generation but she seemed to inhabit a totally different universe. One that was filled with loud music and populated with electronic gadgetry.

'I would like to speak to you briefly,' muttered Adam.

'Yes ... about ...?' she tilted her head to one side puzzled by the suggestion.

'Could you come back in, just for a moment?'

'Of course,' she said. She turned around and placed her mug and magazine on the kitchen table. She looked at Adam expectantly.

'I noticed that you like the cat.'

'The ginger puss that comes to our garden? I love him,' she cried enthusiastically. 'It's a shame we can't adopt him. He is such a sweetie.'

'You see ...'

'Yes ...'

'He got used to me. I have been feeding him.' He admitted shamefully. 'I ... I felt sorry for him.'

'Of course, I understand, I adore him too.'

'Your mum may have told you that I will soon be returning to Poland. For good.'

'Yes, mum mentioned that dad will be looking for another tenant after the New Year. Would you like me to take over feeding the cat when you're gone?'

Adam nodded, feeling uncomfortable with the explanation he had given her.

'I would be delighted to take over,' she exclaimed. Her eyes shone and the distant expression totally left her face.

'But you see ...' Adam hesitated. He took a deep breath: 'Your mum wouldn't be very pleased to learn that on cold nights I allowed Ginger to sleep in my room.'

Basia's eyes opened wider. 'So this is where he was. You know, one evening I was calling him in the garden and he suddenly disappeared. Vanished. I knew he hadn't jumped over the neighbours' fence. I would have seen him do that.'

'He may have jumped into my room through the window. He is a very independent cat.'

'Adam.' By now, Basia was sitting on the kitchen counter, excitedly swinging her long legs sideways — like pendulums. She was weighing something in her mind. 'It's great that Ginger, as you call him, is used to staying here. I always wanted to have a cat but apparently Mrs Patel is not keen on pets. But since Ginger is already used to this place and he never causes a problem ... we will continue as before.'

'If your mum won't object.'

'Adam, she didn't object to Ginger wandering in and out of our garden and our kitchen because she didn't know he was a permanent resident here. That's what she needed to believe ... to observe Mrs Patel's rules.'

'I guess so.'

'Do you think that Ginger will still come to your room when you're gone?'

'Most likely.'

'So there is no problem.' Basia jumped down from the counter. 'I will move into your room and I will look after him.'

'Will your parents agree to that?'

'To me moving down?' she laughed. 'They'll be delighted. They won't have to listen to my music. So everyone will be a winner, including Ginger.'

Chapter 48

Maja, November 1999

Maja folded her drenched umbrella and entered the dark interior of a Mexican bistro. Shaking the rain off her coat, she looked around. Almost instantly, a young man dressed in a black shirt and trousers appeared in the doorway. He offered to take care of her umbrella, suggesting that she also leave her coat. Dark and slim, he fitted well with the décor of the place.

'A table for one, madam?'

Stamping her wet shoes, Maja scanned the cavernous room. Its rounded ceiling and walls were decorated with spindly metal shapes and backlit by diffused lights. Small tables with lit candles appeared to float in the darkness.

'I am looking for Mr Maretti ...' said Maja, attempting to control the trembling in her voice. Straining her eyes to focus on the faces of the few people already occupying the tables, she was trying to anticipate the shape of the threat awaiting her.

'Mr Maretti is waiting for you downstairs,' the waiter cut into her thoughts. Pointing to the staircase on the right, he offered to take her to him. She followed him down the dimly lit curve of the staircase, which snaked down to the basement. Downstairs, there was a similar room to the one above, with an identical decorative scheme.

At the far end of the room, at the table tucked next to the bar, a man sat with his back to the wall. At first, Maja couldn't see his face. The stout figure sat motionless. Against his dark suit, Maja could see his surprisingly delicate hands holding a small cup of espresso. A glass of water was standing beside it.

'Miss Zalewska?'

Maja nodded.

With a wave of his hand, he invited her to sit down. 'Maretti. Gianni Maretti.'

As the waiter helped Maja to move the chair out, Maretti asked with a strong Italian accent: 'Café, tea or some other drink, Miss?'

'Just a glass of water, please.'

Although his face was in semi-shadow, Maja was now able to distinguish his features. The dark colouring was clear evidence of his Mediterranean origins. From under greying eyebrows shone a pair of deep-set eyes divided by a nose that was as big and strong as the beak of a bird of prey. His thick hair, once probably black, was combed back.

Was he the man whose shadow had hung over her during the last two years? In dark corners and empty streets? Was he the man whose presence she felt at the other end of telephone lines which went dead? These piercing eyes were not unlike the ones that haunted her dreams. She imagined that these small hands were skilled instruments of crime.

The game was over now. By coming here, she had decided to confront her fate. She was paralysed with fear but she wasn't going to show him how successful his attempts at intimidating her had been. She had lost Nico but her hurt now had a different dimension. She owed it to Nico to find out why he died and this was the only way to do it. This thought made her reckless. It made her strong.

Looking straight into his eyes, Maja asked: 'So why, Mr Maretti do I finally have the pleasure of meeting you?' Her voice sounded more steely that she intended.

He looked at her in silence for a moment, took a sip of his water and said: 'Miss, you're a brave girl.' His voice was softer than she expected. 'I wasn't sure you'd come. You came and you came alone, as I asked, which only confirms that I was right about you. All along.'

He spoke slowly in a low and measured voice. 'You deserve an explanation. For these two years of our acquaintance.'

'A strange acquaintance, Mr Maretti. With only one side knowing what's going on and controlling all the moves.'

The waiter brought a bottle of water and placed a glass in front of Maja. She looked up to him, indicating she wanted it poured.

'So what game have you been playing with me?' She took a sip and placed the glass back on the table, controlling her shaking hand with a great effort.

His eyes appeared to narrow. He expected to do the talking. 'You're the only witness of Nico's death. You were with him during the last moments of his life. My bosses wanted you out.'

'Out?' Maja cried. 'Simply because I agreed to go to the theatre with Nico?' A sudden realisation took her breath away. The assassins thought that she saw Nico's murder. All these months, she had no idea of the danger that was hanging over her.

'You got mixed up in the larger scheme of things, *signorina*. You never knew this and could not appreciate your situation. You were a silent witness. A deadly one, as far as they were concerned.' He took a sip from his cup and with great precision, placed it down on the tiny saucer. 'You don't know how lucky you were that they left it to me.'

'Was I lucky, indeed? What are you planning to do with me now?'

Ignoring the last question, he continued his explanation. 'Old Mazzini tried to protect you. He removed your details from the restaurant files. One by one, he let go of the girls who worked with you so there weren't any links leading to you. But it wasn't very difficult to find you. In fact, I got your description from the Spanish guy who helped with the washing up at Bella Italia. Although Lorenzo, who really liked you *bella*, tried to brainwash the stupid dunce about the pronunciation of your name, suspecting that there would be people asking about you.'

Maja imagined Lorenzo's efforts to mislead poor Pedro as he was bullied by the mafia henchmen. She hadn't realised she was putting other people in danger. It was a relief to think that Lorenzo was now back in Umbria. She would go there one day and thank him.

'You could have gone back home. But you didn't. You stayed on the course, building your life here the way you intended. To make something of yourself. You changed job and got promoted twice. You didn't take the crumbs that life threw at you, as many of us who came to this country have done. People with no family, no connections, no past here.'

Maja was astounded. This man knew so much about her. Was

he her guardian angel? An angel of death to be precise.

'I cannot believe that you know all this.'

'If you were a man, I would say you have balls. Any man would have respected this. Your *mamma* and *papà* should be proud of you ...' His voice seemed to wander off.

'They asked me to deal with you. No pressure about how and how soon. They knew it would have been a clean job, with no clues. Such as a mugging gone wrong. From time to time, papers write about such cases. Young women that wonder the streets late at night pay a high price for not being prudent.'

Maja felt the hair on the back of her neck rising and her throat tightening. She imagined her parents receiving news of her unexpected death in London.

Maretti continued in a low voice. 'But you were prudent ... with your choices. And smart. I liked this. So I decided to watch you for a while. The longer I watched you, the more I liked what I saw. When I saw you close for the first time, in the bistro with your girlfriend and then in the park with your young man, I thought, *Com'è bella*! I could see why Nico became fond of you so quickly. He could have had any girl he wanted.'

'You're the man who sat beside us at the bar in Kensington High Street,' Maja cried in disbelief.

'*Si, signorina*, it was me.'

'Even then you were plotting how to murder me!' She looked around. They were alone in the restaurant basement.

'No, I wasn't there to get you. I wanted to have a close look at you. At times, I hoped that you would make a mistake and get the police involved. Then you wouldn't have left me a choice and things may have turned out differently.'

'Why are you so sure that I won't call the police the moment I leave this place?'

'You're too smart. And you have big plans for your life and your young man. You wouldn't risk that for someone who is already dead. However dear he might have been ... in the past.'

'So you're not going to tell me why Nico died?'

'It was a mistake. I can tell you this. The stakes were high and he got entangled in the grand scheme of things.'

How could she leave it at this? Maja thought bitterly. Nico's death now appeared even more pointless than before.

As if reading her thoughts, Maretti said: 'Miss, forget all about that. Now you know that you wouldn't be safe if you warred with us. Your young life will be spent on better things.'

'So this meeting is a warning?'

'A friendly warning ... I wish you happiness Maja. I really do.'

Emerging from the cavernous darkness of the restaurant, Maja was greeted by a blue sky and blinding sunshine as if the heavens had opened after a storm. She shaded her eyes and as she started crossing the road, she stepped straight into an enormous puddle. Exactly at the same moment, a woman pushing a pram rode into the water that rose like a tide and flooded their feet up to their ankles. The women looked at their sodden shoes, then at each other and burst into laughter.

As they scrambled up on the pavement, the young mother offered Maja a terry nappy: 'This may help ...' With the second nappy she proceeded to dry her own feet.

'I didn't know they have so many uses,' said Maja, smiling gratefully at the young woman.

'Oh, they do. Many more than disposable ones.'

By the time their shoes were back on their feet, the women were chatting happily and decided to walk together to Notting Hill Gate underground station. The baby in the pram didn't stir once during the commotion.

When they reached the station, they waved good-bye to each other. Walking down the steps of the underground station and thinking about the happy disposition of the young mother, Maja realised that she almost forgot why she had come to Notting Hill. The meeting with Maretti was like a bad dream that happened a long time ago to someone else who was mad enough to face the evil man.

Chapter 49

The departure lounge of London's Terminal 3 was pulsating with the restless energy of waiting passengers. Flight announcements, security messages and the hubbub of conversations hung in the air like smoke. To isolate themselves from the activity around them, some people immersed themselves in books and newspapers. A group of students wearing matching sweatshirts with the University of Yale logo monopolised the whole aisle. The young people were snoozing, having stretched their lean bodies across the seats. A few metres away, a woman swathed in Muslim dress was trying to control a couple of small children who made repeated attempts to escape. Simultaneously, she was keeping an eye on numerous pieces of luggage scattered on the seats around them.

At the end of the aisle sat Maja in a short duffel coat. Around her neck was coiled a voluminous red scarf that reached down to her boots. Every couple of minutes, she looked up at the monitor updating the details of departing flights. It was still very early so she took a book out of her bag to kill time. A lavishly illustrated Fodor's New York was to give her the essentials of the city in which she was to work and live. She was distracted for a moment but as soon as she sensed movement around her, she looked up at the flickering screen. Screwing up her eyes, she was trying to locate the departure gate of her flight. She followed the long list from top to bottom. Once, and then again. The entry disappeared. A moment later, information came up showing that the 9.30am American Airlines flight to New York was delayed by two hours.

'Oh, no, came the groan of male voices from the next aisle. Deflated Maja took her coat off and sunk into her seat. She looked impassively at the group of students who were now preparing themselves for a prolonged hibernation. An old couple next to her decided to do the same. Soon, she was surrounded by snoozing people that created a strange oasis of calm around her. It reminded her of the journey she had taken over two and half years ago from Lublin to London. As the crowded coach had sped through the night across Central Europe, she had sat among sleeping people, feeling lonely and assailed by doubts about the wisdom of the step she had taken. That journey proved to be a turning point in her life. She instinctively felt that she was about to take another momentous step.

Unexpectedly she had been offered a week's leave to go home. Helen Peters told her that this was the least the hotel could do to compensate her for sending her across the ocean just before Christmas.

The whole Zalewski family drove to Warsaw to meet her at the airport. Her mother took holiday leave and her dad told Father Lucjan he would work double time before and after Maja's visit so he could spend six days with his eldest daughter who was being posted to New York.

As the plane came down to land, she saw a familiar patchwork of fields outside Warsaw. She felt a mixture of joy and anxiety. So much had happened in the lives of her family of which she was no longer a part. She only shared her good news with them and suspected that they did the same. She doubted that even Zosia was now totally open with her. In her absence, their lives had moved on and Zosia and Piotr were no longer the children she remembered. Walking out onto the concourse of Warsaw airport, she started scanning the waiting crowd for familiar faces. Suddenly, she heard the cries: 'There she is,' and 'Maja!' A dark haired boy, almost as tall as her, was frantically waving an enormous bouquet of flowers in her direction. Next to him, stood a willowy young woman. A floppy red beret was perched at a rakish angle on her hair, which cascaded down her shoulders. Maja could not take her eyes off Zosia. She was just a girl when Maja had left Grodek. Now, she was a young woman ... a younger version of herself.

Her father stepped forward. He looked as she had always remembered him, tall and serious. Perhaps his shoulders were now slightly stooping and his face appeared more angular. He crossed the distance between them in a few steps and enveloped her in his arms. Feeling the familiar scratchy wool of his winter coat on her cheek and smelling the scent of Old Spice cologne, she knew she was home again.

Later that evening, when they had cleared up after a dinner which had consisted of all her favourite dishes, her mum came to her room.

'Perhaps you're tired and want to sleep now?'

'Not at all. I am too excited. I'm so happy to be with you.' She shifted to one side, making room for her mother on the bed. 'Please sit down with me. It seems such a long time since we sat like this.'

Her mother now looked relaxed in her favourite yellow dressing gown. Her freshly styled hair didn't appear as perfect as at the airport and her skin smelled of her familiar wild strawberry night cream. She was more her old self than the woman dressed in her best Sunday coat and hat who had come to greet her daughter at the airport. They sat in silence for a while just enjoying each other's closeness. Maja placed her head on her mother's shoulder. 'I have been worrying about you,' she said.

'Oh *córeczko*. No need for that. You have your own problems there.' She put her arms around her daughter like she used to when Maja came to her with school dilemmas.

'Tell me honestly, how are you coping with dad not earning much and Zosia and Piotr constantly needing new clothes, books ...'

'I am all right. I took on a few extra hours in the rheumatology clinic. They always need help at the weekend. And we are fine.'

'You must be working so hard.'

'No different than usual. Dad often prepares dinner and Zosia and Piotr are a great help around house. We have all adjusted.'

Maja thought about the theatre evenings and restaurants to which Luke took her. An image of the exquisite Christmas dinner which Elizabeth had prepared for them last December flashed before her eyes and the feeling of guilt choked her.

'Mum, in a few months I'll have a pay review. If I do well in New York, my salary will increase.'

'No, Maja,' her mother said firmly. 'You have done enough for us. More than enough. In your job, you need smart clothes, good shoes and a decent haircut. You cannot look like the poor relative of these English girls ... or the American ones,' she smiled. 'My smart little girl.' She patted her hair.

Maja felt tears welling in her eyes and lowered her head so her mother wouldn't see them.

'You need to start saving ... for the future.' Her mother was caressing her cheek. 'Wherever you decide to stay, I will support you. But don't blame your father for wanting you back. His world is changing fast. Too fast for the men of his generation. But he is so proud of you and everything you have achieved. We all are. Zosia has been telling all her friends about your work in London. She looks at your pictures and examines every detail of your clothing. She loved your luggage. She said that it looked so sophisticated.'

'Silly little sis.'

'You have changed, Maja. You have matured ... You're confident and independent. We'll always be here for you but you already have a life of your own. One day, you'll have your own home and family. I don't mind if that's at the other end of Europe, as long as I can see you sometimes.'

Remembering these words, Maja felt a lump in her throat. She brushed away a tear that rolled down her cheek. Then she reached into her handbag and out of her wallet, she took a photograph she had taken during her last evening in Grodek. There they were, mum and dad sitting at the table with Zosia and Piotr standing behind them with their arms around their parents. Everyone was smiling at the camera. They knew that this moment was being captured for them all to remember. Only an hour before, both Zosia and Piotr had asked her whether she was planning to come back home. Her father said that New York seemed like a different world and he hoped that she wouldn't forget her roots.

She was too sentimental about the whole thing, as Amy had pointed out. But she couldn't help it, that was how she was. She should be delighted that a chance to work in New York had fallen into her lap (Amy's words) and take every opportunity to see the Big Apple and everything it had to offer. The placement in New York was a promotion, Helen Peters recommended her for it because she saw 'her potential'. Deep down Maja always knew that this trip to New York was a distinction, a reward and she would have to prove that she deserved it.

"Think about all those clothes you will be able to buy,' exclaimed Amy. For a bargain price. I will definitely come to visit you when the January sales begin. People travel to New York just for a couple of pairs of designer jeans.'

'I imagine I will be working long hours.'

'Oh, Maja, of course the company will want to get their pound of flesh from you. But you will have the weekends to enjoy yourself.'

'I hope so. I would love to see a Broadway show. I also promised my brother I would send him photos of the most famous skyscrapers in New York.'

They were sitting in the corner of the bistro at the back of Kensington High Street, where eighteen months earlier, Maja had trampled on Luke's jacket. Its deep booths with padded leather seats and lamps that hung low, casting a soft light, created an atmosphere of intimacy. Unsurprisingly, the bistro was popular with couples.

'Aren't you dying to see Luke again?' asked Amy, with a knowing smile.

'It has been almost five months since we saw each other in London,' said Maja, giving Amy a level look. She was not going to comment on the existence of an exquisite lace basque that was lying at the bottom of her suitcase. 'Of course, I miss him and I look forward to spending time together. But it may not be as much as I wish and he hopes for.'

'Maja, tell me.' Suddenly Amy's tone was challenging. 'Instead of squealing with excitement, as every normal woman would have done, you're wearing a long face and searching for a reason why the whole trip might be a flop.'

'You exaggerate. But things are never as simple as they seem.'

'We make our lives as simple or as complicated as we wish,' said Amy sagely. 'People can choose to be happy or they can decide that they would rather be miserable.'

'Are you telling me that I am self-indulgent?'

'Well, you don't always see things from a wider perspective.'

'Perhaps I am afraid that my good luck won't last.'

'You're afraid to be happy ... To open yourself to good things in life,' said Amy holding Maja's gaze. 'Good stuff rarely comes on its own. We all get some shit too. But in the end it's worth it because the crap makes us realise how lucky we are when good things come our way.' With a loud slurp, Amy drank the dregs of her cocktail.

'Look at those two,' Amy nodded in the direction of a couple sitting in a corner booth. An olive skinned man with ebony curls framing his perfect jaw was leaning over a plump, bottle blond girl whose eyes were following him adoringly.

'How do you think that is going to end?' asked Amy truculently. 'As soon as he gets well acquainted with her curves, he'll dump her for another adoring fan who may have a better figure, a cuter smile and a larger bank balance. Do you think that she would listen to me if I came over to her and told her that she is wasting her time? Of course not. She wants him more than he wants her and she counts herself lucky to be with him, even for a short while. And why not? He could be charming company and a fantastic lover. Much better than her cousin Derek with whom her family has been pairing her since they were children. Always playing it safe? You're going to miss a lot.'

'Are you suggesting that I should forget myself and ... do something wild?'

'You don't know what you're missing until you try the dish. Surprise me Maja.' Amy smiled mischievously. She waved to the passing waitress pointing to her drink.

Maja remained silent for a moment. Then she asked, in a hoarse voice that seemed to come from the bottom of her throat: 'What makes you think, I have never been like that girl in the corner?'

'You're too cautious for that. Secondly, you're far too pretty. Usually, it's the guys who compete for your attention not the other way round. They are attracted to you like flies but as soon as they come close to you, you freeze them off.'

'Same for me,' said Maja to the waitress, who had finally appeared at their table to take Amy's order. 'You're wrong, Amy. Totally wrong.' Amy stared at Maja surprised. 'Once, I was like that silly girl. I was besotted with the best looking boy in my year. I was blown away with his attention, and the way he was able to express it. With words, gifts and kisses. I couldn't believe how lucky I was. The guy with whom half the girls from my academic group were ready to jump into bed had chosen me. And do you know what? It was a bet,' cried Maja, her eyes blazing. 'He made a bet with his mates that he would get me, the ice queen, into bed before the end of the first term.'

Amy leaned forward, looking straight into Maja's eyes 'So what Maja? He was an asshole. And you learnt to recognise them.'

'At my own expense. Humiliation and loss of face. I went to the same course and shared a hall of residence with people who laughed behind my back ... Do you know what it feels like?'

'If they could see you now, they would be jealous.' Amy put an arm around her friend and said softly: 'Think about everything you have achieved since you came to London and be proud of yourself. You did it all by yourself. No rich parents, benevolent uncles or patrons supported you. If someone gave you a helping hand, it was because you impressed them. You're tougher than you realise, Miss Zalewska. Even Jess will now think twice before she starts scheming against you again.'

Amy looked at her friend who was staring ahead, her lips set in a straight line and her fingers wrapped tightly around her glass of wine. 'Maja, I have made a fool of myself more times than I can remember. Some of those mistakes hurt like hell but I stopped tormenting myself with them a long time ago. I tried to remember the lesson but made myself forget the pain they caused. You must do the same. Don't shut yourself out from good things that may come your way.'

Maja looked around. The elderly couple, with their paperbacks now closed, were dozing. The students snored away, reconciled with the long wait. Even the young Muslim mother had managed to placate her children with food and drink. Maja was the only person still looking around and fretting about that two hour delay. She glanced at the little girl sitting opposite her. Swinging her chubby legs, she was devouring a sandwich, unconcerned that half of its filling had already fallen on her lap.

She took a gulp of juice from a plastic bottle and wiped a dribble running down her chin with her sleeve. After a couple more bites, she pushed the sandwich away. Then she lowered her head and looked at her mother. Before anyone could stop her, she sprinted towards the litter bin and stuffed the rest of her food into it. Maja smiled, witnessing a display of such confidence from someone so young. Here was someone who knew what she wanted and who would be taking life by the scruff of the neck.

The girl caught her glance and smiled back. As with everything else in this small person, her smile was huge. Her mouth stretched wide across her face, between the black ringlets that danced around her cheeks. Her eyes narrowed mischievously and sparkled like two onyx stones. Maja and the girl held each other's gaze for a moment and then the girl slipped down from the seat and approached her. Stretching her hand towards Maja, she touched the coils of her red scarf. Feeling its softness, she pressed the scarf to her cheek, closing her eyes. Maja gasped. It was a gesture she had made when Luke had presented her the scarf in Bath. Then came another recollection from a year earlier when she had run down the stairs of Her Majesty's Theatre hugging Nico's scarf to her cheek. She would never forget that beautiful evening and the horrific events that followed it. So much had happened since then.

'Leila, leave the lady alone and come back,' ordered the mother. The girl didn't move. Gazing into Maja's eyes, she was caressing the cashmere scarf. Obviously accustomed to being ignored by her daughter, the woman just picked the girl up and, making apologies to Maja, carried her to their seats. Maja sat smiling.

Then she reached for her mobile phone and tapped a message to Luke. She smiled to herself as she pressed the send button, remembering that she was his special girl. Perhaps she was special after all. She must be doing something right if they were sending her across the ocean to the company's flagship hotel. When she arrived on the ferry at Dover, she didn't feel special. On the contrary, everybody around her appeared smarter and more sophisticated.

She couldn't remember the moment when she stopped seeing

herself as a provincial Cinderella who felt inferior to the people around her. Did Luke's presence in her life have anything to do with that? Perhaps she had outgrown her old perceptions.

She heard the ping of the arriving message on her phone and raised her eyebrows. Surely, it couldn't be Luke, it was the middle of the night in New York. She pressed the envelope symbol and her face lit up.

My Winter Fairy,

I'm considering suing AA (a common reaction here to any disappointment) for depriving me of two additional hours of your company, love and affection. I am starved of them all. Come, come soon and rescue me, my Love.

Your abandoned ...

It was her Luke — affectionate, generous and funny. He may not be as strong as she thought but how could she doubt his love?

She typed a response, smiling to herself as her finger worked up and down the keypad.

Chapter 50

Adam, March 2000

Finally they reached the front of the queue. With mixed feelings Adam handed their tickets to the attendant. The man glanced at him and returned the tickets with a smile.

'Have a good flight.'

'What did he say?' Adam asked Darek.

'He wished us a nice flight.'

'A flight?'

'I think it's British Airways who founded this attraction. Let's fly.'

They stepped into a slowly moving glass capsule as other thrill seekers walked in.

Adam had many doubts about Darek's idea to explore the newest London attraction before they went back to Poland. During his three years in London, he had never had time to be a tourist. The only sights in the city he knew were those caught from the top deck of a London bus when he travelled to work or on an errand. But most of the capital remained unknown territory for him. Darek must have guessed this because he suggested that they had to see something of London before they waved good-bye to the city.

'What are you going to tell your kids when they ask you what London is like? That you have no idea?'

This argument convinced him that his authority as a father, husband and a man of the world would be compromised unless he could answer such questions.

Now they were standing with a dozen other people in this fish tank and, as it was slowly moving up, unrestricted views of the capital were unfolding before them. They had been lucky with the weather. It was early morning and the air was crisp, signalling a clear day ahead. The sun rising from behind the horizon was casting long shafts of yellow light, like a theatre reflector, on the buildings beneath them. Slowly, the city was emerging from the mists and shadows.

Then he saw it — the famous Big Ben. The old clock tower of the English Parliament with its iron spire, glass circle and gilded frame that now glimmered as the rays of the morning sun were licking its face. He had seen it many times on television, on post cards and even in the old guidebook which he had brought with him to London and never used. But the real thing looked so much more magnificent. 'Darek, take a picture of it,' he commanded. He felt his voice tremble. 'And Parliament.' After all, he would have something to show to his family. He would be proud to share this moment with them. The camera was their joint investment. Darek was to take the pictures and once they were developed, send them to Zakopane. Suddenly, Adam heard a voice behind him. He turned around and saw an oriental looking man smiling at him.

'He is asking whether we would like to have a picture with Parliament. Me and you. He'll take it,' explained Darek.

Adam regarded the man. The capsule was sealed so he could not run away with their camera. He nodded to him in agreement. Darek put his arm around Adam's shoulder and they looked into the lenses. They were real tourists now.

'Cheese,' shouted the man.

'What?' exclaimed Adam. 'He wants food for this?'

'Adam, smile,' urged Darek. They grinned at the same time. As the shutter clicked, Adam couldn't help thinking that he was recording a special moment of his own history for posterity.

As the pod of the giant ferris wheel slowly moved up, they were able to see further and further afield. Beyond the ancient buildings of the city, there were large patches of greenery and a labyrinth of streets with increasingly smaller houses. From east to west, the city was threaded through with the winding ribbon of the slowly flowing river which reflected the morning sun like a piece of steel.

For the first time, Adam was able to appreciate the magnitude of the city where he had been living for three years. He looked down on the streets below, on which people were barely visible. These ant-like creatures moved this living and breathing machine towards its prominence in the world although their individual contribution was rarely remembered. History will take even less notice of the immigrant underclass that will remain nameless and their part unrecorded, like a shameful deed that no one acknowledged in public.

'You're very quiet,' remarked Darek.

'Only now do I see the bigger picture ...'

'I know, Adam, I thought the same. People at home will think us more important, experienced ... more worldly ... But we know that the opposite is true.' He stopped to take more pictures.

'I guess this place has changed us,' said Darek. I don't mean that I only learnt useful skills working with you and even with Karol. I look around and begin to believe that I can be my own boss, have my own house, do business the way I think is right. Being here gave me the courage to think beyond what I thought possible.'

'So what are you planning to do when go back home?' A couple got up from the metal bench in the middle of the capsule and Adam, who suddenly felt very weary, slumped down on an empty seat and motioned Darek to do the same.

'The Lesko council is renovating the local castle which is going to house a museum and a gallery. Some rooms will be converted into a hotel. They need carpenters, decorators and electricians. Lila's brother is already on the team and she went to enquire about the job for me telling them what we have done for Nisha Patel. She promised that I will bring references from London.'

'I think that Dr Patel will be only too pleased to help you with this.'

'I hope so. But as soon as I can, I also want to get on a course in the local college to study engineering or the foundations of architecture. I do see things in my head and I would like to bring them to life. I enjoyed working in the Parkway Surgery so much.'

'That was a great opportunity for us,' admitted Adam. 'Dr Patel put so much trust in us ... I still find it difficult to believe.'

'She saw your skills, Adam.'

'And your imagination, Darek. I think she really liked you. Such a lovely woman,' Adam said wistfully. 'And still single. It's hard to believe.'

'She is a very busy doctor. And probably fussy. And why not. Perhaps she has bigger plans.'

For a moment, they were both looking ahead at the distant horizon. As they were now descending, the buildings around them were growing larger.

Suddenly Adam turned to Darek. 'I haven't told you this. In fact, I hardly thought about this myself. I have a piece of land which my mother left me when she divided the farm. For years, my brother has been growing potatoes on it. I have been so busy working for my father-in-law that I never thought about a better use for it. It's on a hill away from the main road. There are marvellous views of the Tatras from there.'

Darek was looking at him astonished. Adam wasn't one for making confessions. He had never said more than a couple of sentences at a time.

'I want to build a house on that field. My own house. It would be for me and Hanka, for our old age. I would like you to design it for me. One day ... but not in the too distant future. I will make that store of mine the best hardware store in Zakopane and with the money from it I will build us a house.'

'Adam, I would love to do that.' Darek was looking at Adam amused. 'You have really changed.'

'You're right, I have. Three years ago I would not believe any of this could be possible. And now look at me. I think like you. Almost.'

'So when you get back to Kościelisko you'd better tell your brother to find another place for his potatoes.'

They laughed so loudly that the other tourists turned to them, hoping to share the joke.

Glossary

p19 *Żywiec* – A popular brand of Polish lager

p26 *Jak się masz?* – How are you?

p26, 154 & 164 *Złoty* – Polish currency

p37 *Szarlotka* – Apple tart

p53 & p340 *Bigos* – 'Hunter's stew' of meat and cabbage

p54 & p340 *Golonka* – Stewed pork knuckle

p54 *Pierogi* – Dumplings

p63 *Cześć* – Hi

P65 & p228 *Kurwa* – Fuck; *Kurwa mać* – Fuck you

p257 *Kurwa* (in relation to a woman) – A slut

p68 *Flaki* – Spicy tripe soup

p88 *Cholera* – Damn

p95 *Babka* – Medicine-woman

p99 *Wójt* – Major

p120 *Dzień dobry* – Good morning

p154 *Rosół* – Chicken broth

p157 *Babciu* – Granny

p192 *Polana* – A clearing

p198 *Fucha* – Moonlighting

p198 & p304 *Góral* – Originating from the mountains

p275 *O Boże!* – Oh God!

p276 *Panowie* – Gentlemen

P260, 261 & 278 *Matko Boska* – Holy Mother

p282 *Pani* – Mrs

p282 *Wigilia* – Christmas Eve supper

p283 & p386 *Córeczko* (a diminutive) – My little daughter

p342 *Jajecznica* – Scrambled eggs

p345 *Sukinsyn* – Bastard

p366 *Placki ziemniaczane* – Potato pancakes